Come the Wind

BOOKS BY ALEXANDER EDLUND

THE BOOK OF BANEA

Vol. 1 — A Woman Warrior Born
Vol. 2 — Come the Wind
*Vol. 3 — Fire Borne *

THE KEELIC TRAVERS NOVELS

Keelic and the Space Pirates
Keelic and the Pathfinders of Midgarth
*Keelic and the Perdition Quest**

* Forthcoming

Come the Wind

THE BOOK OF BANEA

VOL. II

ALEXANDER EDLUND

LANDSTRIDER PRESS

Come the Wind

Published United States 2018 by Landstrider Press

v3

www.alexanderedlund.com

ISBN: 978-0-9969936-6-1

Table of Contents

CHAPTER 1

Her Ladyship of the Green Blades

BREEA WOKE TO FIND HER CHEEK STUCK TO THE ground by cold, congealed blood. The blood was her own, dripping down her sides from cracks in the frozen flesh of her back. She lay where she had fallen in battle, sixty paces from the top of the massive wooden ramp that led from the open city square below to what had been the doors of the Temple behind her, now a towering pile of dark rubble. Her mouth was dry with the taste of rock dust.

Beside her, the servant girl Dori was on her knees, head bowed, weeping as she held Breea's cold right hand in both of hers. Tears cut tracks through the rock dust on her face and her blue-and-white servant livery was dull beneath the gray. The Batusha guild master Scaukra Tafitamar and the girl Simarn were near though Breea could not see them.

Stone grit crunched, and the hem of a cream-colored dress came into view.

"Back!" said Simarn.

Breea turned her head to look up and saw the young woman limp forward holding a heavy crossbow aimed at Scaukra's mailed chest. The bow trembled in her grip. Scaukra ignored the girl—his eyes unfocused and bleary with perplexed loss.

Breea tried to say *I am yet living, Scaukra,* but the pain of her wounds left no breath for speech. As though he heard her, his eyes dropped down. She gave him a weak smile. After a stunned moment, his face lightened. He turned to Simarn—and went still.

"Back!" repeated Simarn. Her fingers tightened on the release lever of her crossbow.

At the threat Scaukra's face closed, and his hands drifted toward his weapons. He did not know who Simarn was, nor she him—they had never met. After Simarn had pierced the Oregule through the skull with a bolt from her crossbow, Scaukra had arrived in the piazza below leading an army of cityfolk in battle against the last of the Temple guard. The people's battle cry had been "Breea!" and their banner her bear-fur cloak. In victory Scaukra had climbed the ramp to declare the city hers and laid the heavy fur over her wounded body. Simarn had witnessed this, but she trusted no one.

Breea tried to tell them to stop, to explain to Simarn that Scaukra was not an enemy, but her dry throat managed only a cracked whisper.

At the sound Dori looked up and shrieked in surprised joy. Simarn flinched and her bow kicked. The bolt punched Scaukra in the chest. He stumbled back and tripped over stone, legs flailing.

Breea cried out and pulled her right hand from Dori's grip. Her left hand still held one of her twin daggers from the battle with the Oregule. Pushing with both arms, Breea levered her shoulders up. Sight dimmed as pain flared across her back. With a cry of desperate effort, she dragged her right leg up under her, and planted it. Putting her right hand on her knee, she pressed her body upright until her back was straight. Turning her attention within, she reached for the essence-core that made her an Alach weaver. A deep spark answered, then waxed hot. Pure green light flared in her left fist from the emerald-hilted dagger.

Breea stood and the bear-fur cloak fell away. Using what remained of her inner fire to keep the worst of the agony at bay, she walked forward.

Scaukra lay on his back among broken pieces of the temple, blood splattering from his mouth. The bolt had passed through chainmail, leather, and bone, lodging in his left lung. A mortal wound.

The greater part of Breea's power was spent—used in her fight with the temple Oregule. All that remained she was using to keep herself upright. Scaukra was moments from death. Looking at the only man in the city who had helped her, she swayed. Dori rushed to her side to steady her.

Forlorn, Breea looked about. South, a thousand townsfolk with bloody weapons stood near the base of the ramp and watched in awed silence. The streets and buildings of the ancient capital beyond were cloaked in brown and gray smoke with columns boiling into the winter sky where fires raged. To her left and right, the black edifice of the long, curved wall that separated the Temple city from the rest of the capital stretched into smoky haze; and behind, where the once towering face of the Temple and its twin spires had soared, there lay a steep-sided pile of broken stone that spilled over the wall and covered the upper section of the ramp. Dust still hung in the cold morning air. She turned back to Skaukra.

"Are you going to save him?" asked Dori.

The question surprised Breea. Dori was not asking if Breea could save him, but would she. In the light of Dori's faith, Breea's resolve returned.

"I will."

Yet how? For essence-strength she had only her twin blades. Worse, she could feel the carrion-chill of the Spider Oregule medallion among the stones behind her—all that remained of the Legend Time creature which had ruled Yash from the depths of the Temple. There was no telling what would happen if she tried to weave with its medallion so near. The Oregule wolf-beast that had destroyed her home had returned from death from such a medallion. Yet, for Scaukra, she must weave.

Looking for her second dagger, she found it, but the cold-broken flesh of her back made bending for the weapon impossible.

Dori followed Breea's gaze. The girl went to the dagger, and defying the edict forbidding women to touch weapons, picked it up. She returned and offered it with both hands.

Marveling at the servant girl's continual bravery, Breea nodded her thanks, then wrapped her fingers around the handle. The curved blade and its emerald hilt-stone flashed into shimmering life. Dori snatched her hands away with a little gasp, but she didn't retreat.

Breea said, "Help me down beside him."

With Dori's aid, Breea knelt. She put one of her weapons on Scaukra's mailed chest and guided his hand to the hilt, then gripped her other dagger in both of hers. His eyes closed on her gaze. In his face she read his readiness for death. Breea had never seen a man at once so brave and terrified, yet content in fellowship with her beside him at the end of his battle.

Breea tore her eyes from his face and looked instead into the emerald hilt-stones of her daggers. She *listened*. The essence-power of the stones was bound to the blades in ways she did not understand, and could not weave.

Frustration warped into rage, and with a cry she poured her heat into the gems, forcing a path to their power. Emerald essence flashed into the air, whirling like a thing alive as it sought a return to its source within the emeralds.

Dori cowered and crawled out of the way.

Breea held the path into the stones open, letting the emerald essence flow, then began to weave—binding the essence of the stones to the weft of the only healing pattern she knew. Slashing green turned to healing blue.

To Scaukra she said, "Wake, warrior."

His eyes opened in confusion.

Breea shifted her gaze to Dori, and said, "Take out the bolt."

Dori's face was white with fear, yet she stood, hiked her skirts with tight fists, and stepped into the azure light. Kneeling by Scaukra's side, she took hold of the bolt with one trembling hand.

"Swift and smooth," said Breea. "Straight out."

Dori leaned over Scaukra and braced her other hand on

his mailed chest. Blood rose between her fingers through the chainmail. He turned to her, and she hauled on the shaft. Scaukra spasmed with a splattering scream, flinging Dori aside.

Breea wove, half wild with the strain of keeping her own pain sufficiently at bay to feel the patterns of Scaukra's body. Her healing was too simple, but where it failed she willed the gaps closed with pure power, binding the essence of the blades with her inner flame over and over into the warrior's body. Blue radiance filled the air and Breea felt her own wounds knitting. With a final effort, the light faded and Breea collapsed over Scaukra. Agony rippled out from the still broken flesh of her back, but she gritted her teeth against crying out.

With her head on Scaukra's chest, she could see Dori was struggling to rise from where Scaukra's spasm had shoved her. Somehow the girl still held the bloody crossbow bolt. Dori straightened, then gasped and clutched at her side with the other hand. Drawing a tender breath, she held the gory bolt out to Simarn.

Simarn took it without hesitation and put it in her bag, then walked a few steps away. She bent and put the foot brace of her crossbow to the ground. With a grunt she straightened her legs and heaved on the cocking lever, pulling the string back until it clicked. Breea was impressed. She had never known a woman other than herself who knew how to cock such a bow. There was more history to Simarn's tale than what she had shared last night. When Breea had rescued the young woman from the Rose tavern, it had been Simarn's willingness to act and fight that had enabled Breea to save her without slaughtering an entire tavern of men. It burned Breea's heart to know that the women who had refused to escape with her were still in that tavern.

Simarn pulled a bolt from her bag and armed the bow, hefting it to guard the approach from below. Breea turned her head to see if a new threat approached, but the sloped ramp held only scattered stones and the bodies of three Temple guard felled by Simarn during the battle. The girl was lethal…to more than enemies. Breea *listened*— Scaukra's heart beat slow but sure.

Dori approached Simarn from behind and touched Simarn's shoulder. The young woman spun, ferocity flaring.

Dori held her ground and said, "Help me with her."

Simarn glanced down the ramp then nodded.

The girls moved to kneel beside Breea, but before they touched her, she said, "Bring Batusha. Armorers District. They will come."

Simarn, who had yet to put down her bow, clenched her jaw. The young woman did not want to leave, and Breea was grateful for her guardianship.

Dori looked at Simarn's weapon, then up at Simarn's face. "I'll go, milady."

Before her ladyship could object, Dori rushed down the long ramp. The vast piazza beyond the Temple wall was silent and still—the cityfolk there kneeling among the dead, heads bowed toward Breea, their weapons forgotten. Some rose at Dori's approach. She kept her eyes neutral, looking at no one, maintaining the bearing of an important servant on a mission for her lady. The crowd made a path. She held her breath against the stench of bodies gutted and broken by the battle. Dark blood filled the cracks between the cobbles, and the soles of her slippers made wet, sticky sounds as she passed.

Down the street beyond, she hiked her skirts and ran as

fast as she ever had. More bodies lay scattered and fires raged unchecked, filling the air with acrid smoke. After hiding from a band of men with gory weapons, she decided that the Armorers District was too far. There was another way. The Batusha Weapons Guild protected the Lute and Swan where she served. She looked around, saw no one, and ran.

Cries and the clash of fighting echoed down the smoky streets, urging her to greater speed. Twice she took another route to avoid horrible things happening among the fine houses and walled gardens of the upper city. When she arrived, never had the white stone of the Lute and Swan looked so beautiful.

Before going in the servants' entrance at the back, she beat the dust from her skirts, wiped her face with an underskirt, then retied her hair, catching her breath. No one would listen to a slovenly servant. To calm and steel herself, she thought of her ladyship bleeding at the foot of the destroyed Temple.

Inside she walked with purpose, ignoring the stares of the other servants, and tried to imagine what she would say to the Batusha guildsmen.

When she strode into the marble entry hall, the doorman scowled at her, but did nothing as she walked across, right up to the alcove where a tall, armored figure watched her approach. She curtsied, but still had no words.

The warrior beckoned, and she stepped into the unlit alcove. There were two other men there as well, at the back. In the close space they smelled like workingmen she knew, sweat and toil, but here also was leather and steel and—a little shudder quivered through her—blood and entrails. These men had been in battle.

"What word, little bird?" said the foremost.

She curtsied again to cover her speechless pause and said with lowered eyes, "She needs you."

Chainmail slithered and leather creaked as the men stepped close. A red gauntlet lifted her chin, and she found herself staring far up into the fiercest eyes she'd ever seen.

"Where?"

"At the Temple."

Before she could say more, the men brushed past her and were gone.

The doorman was staring at the wide-open door, then turned on Dori. Before he could muster comment, Dori fled after the warriors. The three were running north toward the Temple. Were none of them going to the guild hall? She huffed, then bunched her skirts and set out the other way.

The streets of the Armorers District were quiet in a way that made Dori stop and look around. She heard voices ahead and peered around a corner. What she saw she could not fathom. Something filled the street in dark heaps. Armed boys in red jerkins over chainmail clambered over the piles. One sat on the highest pile with a crossbow on his knees, watching the street in both directions. He noticed her, and called to his fellows. They looked up, commented on her, and went back to their work of collecting arrows.

Dori wound her way past scattered bodies, trying not to be sick. The stench was a hundred times more foul than the battle at the foot of the Temple. She stopped when there was no path through. The bodies of black-robed Temple guards covered the paving stones like a rumpled blanket.

Trying to look above the carnage, she called, "Where is Batusha Guild Hall?"

They stopped and one drew a short sword. After a

shocked moment, Dori understood that they weren't going to attack—the boys were scared. Their jerkins bore the emblem of a starburst of weapons. The sigil of Batusha.

"Take me to your guild master," she said.

The boy on watch slid down the pile of bodies. "This way."

There was nowhere to step that was not a man. Looking down she found that the hems of her skirts were soaking red, and cold blood was seeping into her slippers. She covered her mouth to stifle a cry and hold her gut down.

Motion made her flinch, but it was only the boy tossing his unloaded crossbow to another. He clambered across the bodies and offered his hand with a gallant gesture.

By the time they arrived at the guild hall, tears streamed down her face and her whole body shook. Batusha warriors were clearing bodies from the entry and lifting out a battering ram.

"She seeks the guild master," said the boy.

All of the men within earshot paused in their work.

Dori curtsied with a wobble, and said, "Her ladyship needs your help."

"Who?" said a warrior with a saber at his hip.

"Her ladyship of the green blades," said Dori.

"The Master," was a whisper that rippled out among the men.

Dori's world spun and she gripped the boy with one hand. Her ladyship was the Master of the Batusha Weapons Guild? The warrior on the Temple ramp had called her master. And Simarn had put a bolt in his chest.

To Dori's guide, the saber warrior said, "Get Master Bay-ope."

Dori refused to let him go. The boy blushed, and then

stood firm.

Another ran into the interior of the guild hall. The men returned to work until another warrior strode out of the building, a Ranan by his massive build, holding two battle-axes in one hand by their hafts. The wool of his clothing might once have been green, but it was so soaked with blood that it was impossible to tell. Something told Dori that none of that blood was his, and his bearing said that he was a nobleman.

Of the saber warrior he asked in a drum-deep voice, "Breea?"

The Batusha man nodded toward Dori.

The Ranan looked at her with surprisingly gentle eyes.

Dori curtsied low and said, "My lord, her ladyship is hurt at the Temple. A guild man is hurt as well. Three guildsmen run to her from the Lute and Swan."

"Your doing?" asked the big man.

"Yes, my lord. Her ladyship asked me to find Batusha. She rooms at the Lute."

Without another word the Ranan went out the door. A minor host swept after. Dori followed, holding back revulsion as bodies slid and squelched in her passing. Once past the slaughter, she leaned against a building and heaved up her breakfast.

Spitting and wiping tears from her face, she straightened—then recoiled. There were six figures standing close. Boys. Batusha boys. Relieved, she sagged back against the wall, then glared at them. The tallest was the boy who had helped her before.

He had his crossbow back, the butt resting on his hip.

"Tam Beddig," he said. "Batusha aspirant, my Service to

you." He offered his arm.

Wordless, Dori hooked her arm in his and let herself be guided north toward the Temple.

————✦————

At the sound of running, Breea raised her head. Three Batusha warriors pounded up the ramp. One wore red leather armor painted in a gold filigree and a cloak of red wool lined in black fur. She knew him as Neprawn the Tall, a master warrior and one of the first to acknowledge her as Master of Batusha Guild after her battle with the prior guild master.

Simarn aimed her bow, and the men slowed to spread out.

"Simarn," admonished Breea. "They are…" She wasn't sure what they were. Not friends, and not enemies. They were survival in this corrupt city, and something else that she had yet to fathom.

"Allies," she said.

Simarn dropped her aim and Neprawn strode forward, falling to his knees beside Breea. In front of his chest he saluted her by slapping the back of his fist into his palm in the guild salute known as chak'ood. Breea blinked at the earnest worry in his bearded face.

"Anule," she said, and he dropped the salute.

His eyes went to the emerald throb of her daggers, then to the blood soaking her back. Neprawn reached toward her, then turned to his fellows who were exchanging glares with Simarn.

"Spears and cloaks."

The men turned and ran back down the ramp.

Breea felt awkward, sprawled over Scaukra. She

gathered power. Her daggers flared with light, then went dark. Panting with the failed effort, she watched Neprawn study the ground, reading the signs of the past hours in dust and blood. His brow clenched and his eyes swung from Scaukra to Simarn's crossbow. The young woman looked away.

Morning sun broke through the clouds and bathed the city in a pale winter glow. Across Breea's back its warmth felt like a comforting hand and she raised her head to feel its caress on her face.

She *listened*, and memory opened.

It had been the first clear day of spring after her eighth winter. Before dawn her mother had taken her up into the alpine meadows above the library. Sitting among the heather in her mother's lap, wrapped in a blanket, she remembered the scent of melting snow and the heady green of plants preparing to flower. When the sun broke over the distant mountains, Breea felt as though its warmth was flowing through her whole body. When she turned to share her discovery, she gasped. Her mother's face was glowing as though lit from within, her eyes shining with care as she gazed down at her daughter.

Grit crunched under boots and Breea jerked out of the memory. The two Batusha warriors were back with four spears and armloads of Temple guard cloaks. They began to clear a space of stone to spread out the cloaks. At home, the Limtir Tomeguard used the same technique to make litters.

It was not the way she wanted to travel.

Her voice was weak. "Neprawn."

He bent close.

"Help me stand."

Neprawn's face went solemn. Before touching Breea, he

looked at Simarn to see if the girl had heard the order. Simarn looked worried, but the bow remained lowered. Neprawn slid his hands under Breea's shoulders. He lifted, rising.

Gasping as her wounds stretched, Breea's free hand gripped the edge of his leather breastplate. After the wave of pain subsided, she nodded for him to let her stand. He let go, then steadied her when she wavered. The weight of exhaustion and the searing agony of cold burns reminded her of the aftermath of her battle with the wolf Lupazg in the mountains north of Limtir.

I survived you, she thought. *I shall survive this.*

Soaking up sunlight, Breea brought her dagger to her chest and gripped it with both hands. The hilt stone sparkled as she gathered the light. Using its warmth to sustain her, she began to weave it into her body.

As the air about her began to glow, Neprawn went down on one knee, head lowered. The other warriors followed suit. Simarn looked at the men on their knees in reverence, then knelt, though with difficulty for tumbling stones had struck her legs in the Temple's collapse.

Breea was about to tell them to stop this foolish obeisance when someone called to her from behind. She took an unsteady step back and turned. There was only the massive pile of black rock. Was the Oregule medallion calling to her? She limped to where the circle of white metal lay among stone fragments. Frost obscured the symbols etched on its face, and all she felt from it was putrid cold. The tip of her right ring finger prickled where the medallion had touched her, and she raised her hand to see a pattern of eight dots in blood on the tip that were almost a match for the wolf-print in red scar tissue on her index finger.

Realizing what the pattern of eight was, she covered the wounds with her thumb, then walked past. She *listened*, and the call clarified. She began to climb.

Behind her, Simarn heard shifting stone and looked up to see Breea's glowing form struggling to ascend the giant pile of rock. Simarn ran to the base of the pile, but had to dance back from a small cascade of stone and dust. As it settled she moved again to follow Breea.

"No, lass," rumbled a voice behind her.

Simarn ignored it, but a huge gauntleted hand clamped on her shoulder, holding her back. Simarn jerked away and whirled, then found her crossbow plucked from her hand by the warrior her ladyship had called Neprawn. She stepped in and reached for the dagger at his waist, but her hand was caught and her wrist held.

Simarn trembled with anger. When she raised her head in defiance, the towering warrior said, "You honor her. But to climb that is death. Only the Master." He looked up.

Simarn yanked her arm and Neprawn let go. She grabbed her crossbow and he let her have it as well. She stalked away, right to the base of the pile, and turned to face the men, crossbow cradled in her arms, ready. The big warrior looked at her, but seemed to decide not to object.

One of the other Batusha warriors came up the ramp. He scratched his scalp, and while looking at Simarn said, "Ye gave her back the bow. Why'd ye do that? That's a bolt hole in Scaukra. Ye see any other crossbows up here? Why'd ye give her back the bow?"

"Put Scaukra on cloaks," Neprawn replied.

The smaller warrior shook his head in disgust, gave Breea's struggling form an awe-filled glance, then walked back to Scaukra and the third Batusha warrior, and said, "He gave her back the bow."

"Kill it, Levan," said the third man, and tossed cloaks at him.

Simarn checked her bow, settled her shoulders, and ignored the occasional looks of the men. The path of her life had narrowed to a single track—protect the lady who had saved her. Nothing else mattered, for to lose the lady…she could not face the idea, and tightened her grip on the bow.

Above, Breea felt a need bound by cold—felt it wanting the sun. At the apex of the pile she sat, groaning at what the climb had done to her shattered back. The healing she'd done for Scaukra had aided her, but the climb seemed to have undone that, and blood trickled down.

The city lay under a haze of foul air that obscured the view of its concentric walls that spread down the long slope to the great Yasharn River. Looking north she could see into the whole of the Temple city. People wandered among the black stone buildings as though in a dream, without purpose. One stood out, standing amid rubble in a side street. An old man—the one she had traveled half the world to find. Watching her, he was weeping. It was Duyazen Kedalmtel, the old high priest who had Called at her naming, "A warrior is born!"

Breea gasped. She was living the first vision of the Calling he had reluctantly shared the day before: I see you standing atop a pile of stone that was once the blessed Temple.

But the call that had driven her to the top of the rubble came not from him, but from below. Breea stood abruptly. The Temple itself was calling—begging for her help. What had she destroyed? Was the Temple alive? A weight of aloneness and fear settled over her. There was no one in all the world to help her. No one who had the knowledge or power to aid her in this. She was the only Alach.

With trembling fingers, she reached out and touched the black rock and felt there the cold echo of Oregule weaves. Baring her teeth, she threw her warmth against them. The rubble shifted. Breea drew a dagger, and raised it to the sky.

—ꝏꝏ—

On the ramp below, Neprawn stood with his back to the Temple and watched Levan and Alman lift Scaukra onto a bed of overlapping cloaks. They rolled the cloaks tightly to spear hafts on either side. Scaukra's eyes snapped open and his hand tightened on the blade he held against his chest.

"Come the wind!" he cried.

The two men stopped to look at him, then turned as one, looking up past Neprawn, their eyes going wide. Neprawn whirled, drawing his saber. Breea had climbed out of sight, but beyond where she had vanished a trembling spear of purest green stabbed the heavens. The rubble groaned and blocks of stone crunched as they shifted.

Neprawn leapt forward, bellowing at Simarn, "Come away!"

The girl ran, bow clutched to her chest. She passed Neprawn, and he reversed direction, skipping backward, covering her retreat. Levan and Alman grabbed the spear ends and ran with Scaukra between them, heading for the bottom of the ramp. Simarn halted midway. Neprawn stopped near her and scanned the crowd filling the vast open square below to judge their mood. People were crying out, pointing, some fleeing. The air trembled and Neprawn turned and cried out himself, but not at the star of green burning at the apex of the destroyed Temple, but at Simarn, who was running back up the ramp.

—*ɷɷ*—

Breea went inward to the deepest core of herself, reaching for all that was left of her. It burned. Reaching without she called to the wind for strength, then stabbed the rock. Her blade sank to the hilt and light the color of spring leaves ignited in the blade's pommel. Hateful weaves evaporated down through the stones until she met the source of the call beneath the Temple. Her power flowed over it like oil. It was an orb—the giant one that the Oregule had used to fight her—and it wanted the sun. Cold wrapped it, was within it. But it wanted the sun.

"Come," said Breea, and wrapping herself around its loathsome chill, she pulled.

The earth groaned. Massive strands of essence-power that tied the orb to the city flexed and tore as the orb began to ascend. It pushed up through blocks of stone, through rubble and beam. Breea's dagger came free as the block was shoved aside. The orb was five hands across and cloudy within—the color of old pus. The great round crystal settled against her outstretched hand.

Memory rushed through her, the whole history of the Temple. There was the heady accomplishment of the Alach who had forged this crystal stone and set it in eternal guardianship of the city. What followed summoned tears of loss—the coming of war with the Oregule, the failure of faith, and the corruption of the priesthood—visions of hatred, torture, and war. Overwhelmed, Breea tried to pull away, but the orb followed, nestling against her, seeking her warmth. Her hand was numb, an ache of cold spreading up her wrist, reminding her of the horror of her victory over Lupazg. However, this cold was dead, a remnant. There was yet an uncorrupted heart within the stone, a warmth long suppressed, crystal memories of a golden age of sunlight before the coming of the Oregule.

To fight the cold history of despair, Breea brought to bear memories of her mother and father, her friend Taumea, her lover Ambard, and Bay-ope of the Tomeguard, wrapping them with the strength of Limtir Mountain, the purity of its air, the clarity of its streams, and the feeling of summer sun on cool stone. With these visions she burned through the hatred woven into the crystal and found in its heart a pure intent, releasing it for the first time in two thousand summers. Breea fell back as the orb burned bright. She felt its power reach into the sky, summoning a roaring blast of purifying cold air.

———*o/o/o*———

Below, Neprawn caught up with Simarn as the girl dodged tumbling rocks to snatch Breea's bear-fur cloak from the debris to save it from being buried.

Looking up, Neprawn said, "Gods!"

Simarn backed away from the rubble mountain, staring up at the glow of gold light streaming into the sky. The ramp swayed as the ground heaved. She bumped into Neprawn. For once she didn't recoil, and he laid a protective arm across her upper chest. Protect her he would, but it also served to keep her close. He wasn't going to follow her up there if she was that daft, so the closer to this wild friend of the Master, the better.

When the wind came roaring down from above, he twisted away, cradling her to him to shield her from the blast of icy air. He stumbled forward in the force of the gale and she gripped his arm, dropping her crossbow to hold on.

—⁓⁓—

Dori's blood-soaked slippers chilled her feet, and her legs ached from her run through the city. Leaning on Tam's arm, she kept pace with the young warriors. Her ladyship was in need.

They rounded a corner to a street that stretched away to the Temple. The Batusha boys stopped. There was a gap in the sky where the mighty Temple had stood. Dori looked at Tam's face and watched it go from shock to a pleased awe. The boys looked at one another, grinning in disbelief.

"As he foresaw," said one.

"Aye," said Tam. "The Temple has fallen." He turned to them and together they intoned, "Our blades in Service. Our blood in thanks."

They set out once more, three ahead and two behind, passing people who had begun emerging from their homes. When the crowd began to block their path, Dori's escort closed ranks and one of the boys cried, "Way!"

Dori marveled at the command in the boy's voice.

People turned. When they saw weapons, armor, and the Batusha sigil on the boys' tunics, they stepped aside. Ahead, a needle of green light pierced the sky from the remains of the Temple. The city grew quiet.

"Her ladyship," said Dori.

A tremor passed through the cobbles.

In doubt, one of the young warriors asked, "The

Master?" He did not look so brave any longer.

"It is," said Dori with conviction.

They rushed up the street only to come to a disorganized halt as green light flashed to gold, waxing like a second sun then spearing skyward. Some townsfolk fled, but most knelt in reverence. The sky seemed to descend over the Temple, and a cloud of dust erupted down the rubble pile.

When the screams began ahead, Tam shouted, "Aside!"

The boys swept Dori off the street and through an open gate. In the courtyard beyond they whirled and formed a ring around her. The ground shifted and they all stumbled. In the street outside, wind caught the kneeling people, knocking them over and drowning their cries with its roar.

The wind sang into the courtyard, bowling over Tam and the boys. Dori alone remained standing. Sudden cold sucked the breath from her and she was back at the Lute and Swan, singing to Simarn as the young woman sobbed for all that had been taken from her.

The vision vanished and Dori found herself standing in winter sunlight. The wind was gone. Around her the Batusha boys lay where they had fallen. Tam, on his back, stared at the sky with eyes filled with horror and guilt. Another boy lay on his side and reached out. "Da!"

Dori turned to the street and saw more of the same—dozens of people in the throes of visions. One man stood among them as she did. They looked at each other for a moment, then the fellow bent to another writhing at his feet, offering words of comfort. Dori sucked in a breath.

She knelt beside the boy who was calling to his father, and laid a hand on the side of his face. His skin was ice cold. He seemed to relax, and she turned to others, saying soft things, touching faces. One flinched from her, and she let him be. She turned to Tam—and found him watching her with haunted eyes.

He opened his mouth to tell her—but one of the boys behind her surged to his feet, sniffing and wiping his eyes. Tam blinked and the strength of a young leader returned to his face, blocking off whatever he'd wanted to share with Dori. She looked down to hide a sudden sense of disappointment.

Tam stood, and they all rose with him. In silent accord, Dori and the boys walked into the sunlit street and turned to the Temple.

—◦◦◦—

Breea lay wedged in a hollow among the rocks where the wind had blown her. Her emerald dagger was lost and her sun-weaves had unraveled. Without their aid the pain from her wounded back was like a thousand burning coals pressed into her flesh.

Gold light spread down the rocks and the Temple orb came into view. As the light bathed her in warmth, she cried out in relief as pain left her. The orb summoned her.

Frowning, Breea looked at it. Too tired to reason, she tried to obey, but found herself too weak to move. The summons was repeated.

Frustrated and indignant, Breea cried to the thing, "Help me!"

Essence-power slammed into her and she cringed. The power faded and the summons came once more, but with a sense of fearful need.

The orb needed her help? She had nothing to give. The stone tried to descend toward her, but the crack was too narrow. She managed to sit upright, but knew she would be unable to stand, much less climb. She stared up into the pale brightness of the crystal. It was beautiful now, beaming the warm glow of early morning sunlight.

Opening her essence-self, Breea said, "Again."

The feeling was incandescent. For the space of a hundred heartbeats, she let the heat pour into her. Then she stood. The orb moved aside to allow her to climb back to the peak of the rubble, then sidled up to her. The summons it gave was so powerful it was nearly a compulsion. Breea faced the orb, then touched it with fingertips only.

The sky whirled dark with storm cloud. Bolts of lightning lashed out, striking the towers of a massive, walled city—a Legend Time city. She knew its shape from the books of her youth—Carsythe, capital of Mericsland. Fires burned and tiny figures thronged the walls. Stone and balls of fire sailed through the air. On the plain beyond, row upon row of siege engines launched hundreds of missiles. A great siege tower nearly the height of a Gamanthea-Dur tree was approaching the city's outer wall. A sally port opened on the city's southern flank and a band of armored horsemen broke forth, charging the tower against a storm of arrows. Despite armor, half their number died in moments.

"No," said Breea.

The view whirled to the high hills northeast of Carsythe where long haired Urdjra ringed an immense round tent with a fine view of the siege. The animals looked like a cross between a hoar-cat and bear, but twenty times larger. A massive man stepped from the tent. He wore a long white cloak of shaggy fur over chainmail that appeared to be made of translucent stone. He surveyed the battlefield, searching, then up at her. The man snarled, and Breea tasted carrion.

She jerked back her hands, holding them against her chest to ease the piercing cold that nipped them. After a moment she realized that she was holding her fingers to the skin within the twin arcs of scar that Lupazg's medallion had frozen into her chest in their final battle. The warmth of her inner flame answered the cold with heat that eased the pain, but did nothing for the memory of what she'd seen.

The man's eyes had radiated a twisted, piercing essence. An Oregule.

Chapter 2

Where the Azsark Grows

Among the leafless apple trees, Anila and Spe stood with their heads bowed before their father. Winter chill nipped their ears through the thin cloth of their headscarves as they endured the scolding.

Da bellowed, "Worthless twaets!"

Spe flinched, and Anila hoped her little sister didn't break. Anila explained each time why the public disgrace was necessary to give them a reason to run away to the Azsark, but Spe was still too young to know the difference between Da's real fury and this ruse. If Spe broke and got sent back to the village, it meant double work for Anila, and worse, an apple-switch whipping after dark for both of them.

Da kicked an apple from the basket they'd dropped off the cart, and said, "Why must I be cursed with chancre-blossom bitches? I've a mind to sell the pair of ye at market."

At the mention of the slavers' market, the extended family helping to prune the trees averted their gazes. Spe's jaw trembled, and Anila prayed her strength.

Da bent over Spe with a malicious sneer. "They'll strip ye bare on the block. Disobey them, and they'll whip ye bloody they will, and worse." He poked her belly, making her whimper.

Anila could sense the crest of Spe's despair about break. Gritting her teeth, Anila breathed in, making the air her own, then pursed her lips and blew out the Breath. She sent the little wind whirling behind Da's legs, where it lifted a pair of leaves and set them to whirling on end.

Spe gasped, then caught herself as she turned to look at her sister, whipping her head back to stare at the ground.

Da took her apparent denial ill, and cuffed Spe with an open hand, sending her sprawling. Hot anger surged in Anila, and she sent the whirl of air to ruffle Da's back and hair. He turned, and Anila stepped to Spe, lifting her into her arms. Anila sprinted away.

"Git!" shouted Da. "If I see ye 'fore dark, I'll whip ye bloody!"

Anila set Spe down, and though they knew Da wouldn't chase them, they ran as if he was, dashing in and out among the rows, fast as they could. Spe was faster now, her little legs whipping her skirts in a frenzy as she dodged like a hare. In the rush of the pretend chase, they forgot Da and took turns chasing each other. Anila had to use her longer legs more than once to keep out of reach of Spe's lightening turns. At the edge of the orchard, they collapsed onto the brown grass under the last row of trees.

As they caught their breath, Spe stared at her sister with a big question. Anila ignored the look and stood, brushing bits of grass and dried leaf from her skirts. She didn't speak to the question because she was afraid of what she'd done. She looked to the sky to ask forgiveness, and thanked Het that Ma hadn't seen. Da was getting meaner each time he gave them an excuse to run way, but it would have killed Ma to see her using the Breath where anyone could see, even to protect Spe.

Spe saw the look skyward. It looked like Anila was asking for patience with her, just like Ma always did.

In spite, Spe quoted Ma. "You'll get us flayed, girl."

Anila felt the words strike. Spe was right. Anila had risked a fate worse than slavery to keep Spe from a simple beating. Flustered and angry with herself, Anila walked away along a wash of sandy soil leading out of the orchard. Moments later the patter of Spe's winter sandals came up beside her. Feeling Spe's worried gaze, Anila held out a hand, and Spe gripped it firmly with warm fingers.

A stone cairn and old cart ruts marked the start of the next orchard. The girls crossed the cart track and entered a gulley cutting into the land, following it until they were twenty feet down in a narrow cleft. From the back of a shallow cave they pulled out two big baskets filled with hay and folded wool cloth. Both set the forehead straps onto themselves. The air was sharp away from the sun, and they walked fast to stay warm. At the sound of voices, Anila thrust Spe under an overhang and froze. They'd never heard of anyone walking the wash before. The voices grew louder, but she couldn't make out their direction.

A patter of sound made them both start. Anila stared at the water that splattered down into the sand. Laughter above. Anila relaxed. She knew what it was. She'd seen boys relieving themselves in the orchards. They made a competition of seeing who could spray their water the farthest. Spe was looking at her in fear, and Anila gave her a comforting squeeze.

"Only boys," she whispered in Spe's ear.

Spe didn't understand, and Anila said, "Lord Isa's men must be pruning today, like us. The wash cuts through his orchard."

Spe still didn't understand, but trusted that Anila wasn't afraid. They waited until the wash grew quiet, then emerged with caution, continuing on their way. They walked for an hour, the canyon growing deep and dark. Ice crunched underfoot in the damp places. They stopped to make improvised shawls of the cloth from the baskets, and Anila was surprised to find Ma's best warmest wool in the larger basket. Anila wrapped Spe with the cloth, making a layered shawl of it.

Spe sniffed at the cloth and said, "Smells like Ma."

Anila smiled and lifted Spe's basket, placing its loop across her forehead. They set out down the deepening canyon.

A few bells later, as Anila lifted Spe down a steep step in the wash, Spe asked, "How far?"

"Soon," said Anila. This was Spe's fifth visit to the Azsark canyon, and she always asked at the step, "How far?" Anila and Ma used to make the trip until Ma's illness got worse and Da sent Spe with Anila instead. Even though she had to carry Ma's larger basket, Anila liked the trip better with Spe. Spe was far too small for the basket Anila once used, but they were free together, and best of all they could play Breath of the Gods because no one ever came here. Ma said the land beyond the orchards was a piece of the Haunted Lands that crossed over the mountains from the west. Regular folk saw spirits and worse, but Anila and Spe loved the place. Ma did too, Anila could tell. It was safe—from Da, from everything.

A breeze caught them from behind, passing with a bitter chill. They stopped and turned back up the wash.

Spe wrinkled her nose, and said, "Sommat died."

Anila raised her nose to scent the air, looking up at the rims of the wash. The stench had to be coming from above. They hadn't passed anything like this on the way down. When nothing more happened, they continued down the wash.

In another hour, fitted stones began to show through the sand, and they hurried, glad to be getting close. Ahead, a warm glow bounced from wall to wall, lighting the way. The girls surged into a run. Sandals scraping on sandy stones, they burst from the dark gulch into a canyon alight with afternoon sun.

Spe's basket flipped off her head and went rolling away, spilling hay. They both froze. Anila rushed over and picked it up, looking for any visible damage. Spe stayed were she was, watching with big eyes. They both knew what it meant if they returned home with a damaged basket. Anila started picking up hay, stuffing it back into the basket. Spe suffered the basket to be put back on, and they set out down the wide thoroughfare of an ancient, buried city.

Every year summer rains revealed more of the buildings embedded in the hundred-foot-high sandstone walls of the canyon. Doors and windows were a thousand caves, some quite deep, leading back under the earth. In the spring thousands of birds came to nest in the higher openings, and Anila knew of two pairs of scrub-wolves who used certain caves every year to raise their pups. Carved statues in grotesque and sometimes beautiful forms stuck out from the corners of broken eaves. Other washes coming down were side streets coming to meet the great way. In places they had to clamber over piles of stone, or sweeping arms of sand which spread onto the road from the side ways.

The wide canyon-road opened in a flow of sand and gravel onto a vast open space—flagstone paved and encircled by the petrified city emerging from sandstone cliffs. The girls stopped and looked out at the big tree growing upon a walled hill in its center—the Azsark apple. Its gnarled branches were bare, the limbs and twigs dark in winter sunlight. They crossed the square to the wall at the base of the hill, walking through a broken arch in its span then up stone steps so big Anila had to help Spe on each one. Near the top, the stones were so heaved about by centuries of root growth that the girls went up the hillside instead. At the top they set their baskets down and knelt in the winter grasses beside the massive bole of the tree.

Anila recited the secret prayer of Ma's family. "May all I say and all I think be in harmony with thee, Breath within, Breath beyond, mighty of the trees."

Da thought the Azsark was his own discovery; every male head of the orchard-tending Hox clan had thought it so down the generations, but it was the women—the line of Ma's people—who were the true stewards of the Azsark.

Spe stood and said, "Can we go now? Please? The winds are singing!" She took a deep breath through her nose.

Anila could smell the wind as well, and blinked at the

notes of sea air mixed with the memory of apple blossom and ancient stone. They shrugged off their improvised shawls and laid hands on the black bark. Warmth bloomed in their chests and Spe giggled. A breeze whirled about the tree, lifting last summer's leaves. Spe squealed and ran around the tree with the swirl.

———⸭∾∾⸭———

High in the eastern wall of the square, a woman peered out from a window-cave.

"Taumea," she breathed. "Taumea!"

Her husband ran to her from a back room, bow in hand, setting an arrow to string. He put his back to the wall on the opposite side of the window from his wife, then leaned around, squinting into the sunlight. What he saw made him squint harder.

"Blood and martyrs," he said.

Valiena tore her eyes from the whirling girls to look at her man. Over the months of their flight from the Temple's hunters, he had changed—the ways of the Library of Limtir eroding like the land over this city, revealing what lay beneath. She hadn't heard him say "blood and martyrs" since he was a boy newly arrived at the library.

"Look," he said.

The girls had dashed down the southern slope of the hill and were running across the square to a gap in the cliff walls, leaving a trail of leaves drifting down in their wake. Taumea shielded his eyes and peered ahead of them. The entire city drained through the gap there, down a thirty-foot fall to a deep plunge-pool. He'd scouted the gap weeks before, noting that it was no good as an escape route.

The girls weren't stopping. It was hard to tell, but they seemed to be going faster than should be possible.

———⟋⟍⟋⟍———

Spe called to the air, and the wind pushed them along. As the gap approached, Anila let Spe go ahead. Ten strides from the edge, Anila swooped forward, wrapped her arms around Spe under her arms, and lifted her.

Anila sprinted for the brink, clutching Spe to her chest. Her little sister's arms were outstretched, her knees tucked up tight to keep her legs out of Anila's.

At the edge, she leapt. Spe heaved a breath and voiced a piercing scream. Anila felt heat ignite in her sister, and it felt like she was suddenly hugging a bonfire. They fell as a roar of wind rose, smacking into them. Anila sang, shaping her sister's power, folding and doubling the wind to control their descent.

———⟋⟍⟋⟍———

From the window, Valiena watched the bigger girl leap off the cliff with the little one, and reached out as if to catch them. Taumea turned his head away. When the scream hit their ears, both winced, and Valiena doubled over in empathic pain. The scream went on. And on. They turned to each other in horror and dawning confusion until the cry cut off.

Valiena looked a question at Taumea.

"Thirty feet down," he said. "Not a span farther."

As one, they ran for the tunnel that would take them to the top of the plateau above.

—◈—

For Anila, landing was the hardest part. Gathering a pillow of air without peppering them with sucked-up sand took all her control. She rotated back at the last moment, trying to land on her feet, but the air slipped out from under them, and she went back too far, hitting the sands by the plunge pool on her rump. Spe went tumbling, her wild call cut off abruptly. Anila rolled and scrambled to her sister. Spe was on her back, staring upward with a gleeful and slightly stunned expression.

"Best ever," she said.

Anila looked back up the thirty-foot drop. It had been better. Calling the wind from still air was the hardest, and she felt proud of their descent this time. Last time they'd ended up in the plunge pool, breaking its ice, but with the Breath upon them they were impervious to cold. They'd laughed themselves silly.

Rocks rattled and Anila turned to see Spe hopping boulder to boulder down the wash. With each little leap Spe made a squeak and a gust of wind buoyed her across the gap to the next rock. Anila ran after, singing the whorls of Spe's bursts into thicknesses of air that she used like stepping stones between boulders.

Down the steep gorge they hopped and passed like feathers until they came to the mouth of the canyon. At the lip of the final drop, they paused to catch their breath and take in the view. Cold sea air flapped their layered skirts and tugged at wisps of hair that had escaped their headscarves. Below, waves crashed among broken fingers of rock that reached far out into a sea flecked with white. Near to them, birds cried and whirled in agitation. Spe pointed, and Anila nodded. A great sea eagle hovered, stationary on the wind—the inspiration for their first attempts at using the Breath to fly.

—◦◦◦—

Taumea pounded up the ancient stair that led to the surface, rapidly outpacing Valiena. She held the urge to call to him to wait. Light spilled into the tunnel as he smashed through the brush they had placed to hide the tunnel mouth. Turning south, he vanished from her sight. Valiena ran into sunlight and saw Taumea powering up the near dune, his boots gouging deep in sand. He vanish over the peak. Valiena sprinted after him, cursing him for not waiting while admiring his power, and in the same breath blessing his speed to reach the girls—or whatever lay ahead.

—◦◦◦—

Taumea crested each rise and leapt off the top, running down the far side through sagebrush in fast, long strides. The top of the plateau was a rough country of striated sandstone and dunes grown over with gnarled sagebrush. In the valleys he dodged boulders and scrub pine before scrambling the next ascent.

Where sand gave way to stone, the land fell away in a rough slope to the canyon that drained the city. He ran and leapt a reckless path down to the gap and hunted along the edge until he found a rock shelf that would give him a clear view to the bottom. On his belly he scooted forward until he could gaze right down into the canyon—and saw nothing.

No bodies, no girls. Eighty feet below, the boulder-choked canyon floor was empty.

Perhaps the stories of spirits in this place were true. People never visited the Haunted Lands because visions and night terrors drove them mad, thus it was the best place to hide. Yet other than nightly dreams of Breea in peril, neither he nor Valiena had felt anything amiss in this ancient place. A breeze smelling of the sea went sighing along the stones. He caught a sound on the air but couldn't get a bearing. He scooted forward for a better view until his shoulders were off the shelf, and heard Valiena call softly for him to come away from the edge. He looked downstream, but a bend in the canyon gave little view there. Upstream at the base of the dry fall he saw what he'd missed before. He scooted back and Valiena joined him, though she kept well back from the edge. He motioned upstream. They climbed through brush and fractured stone until they were directly above the falls.

He edged to another precipice and confirmed what he'd seen. Standing back, he climbed to the highest vantage near. Southward, less than half a league away, the plateau ended in cliffs above an inlet of the Leuvat Sea. Rock and brush blocked most of the view, but what he could see of the water shone pale and wind-tossed in the late afternoon light.

He rock-hopped back down to Valiena, and said, "Footprints in the sand. At the base of the falls."

"Opalah bless us," said Valiena, and rested her head on his chest. "I was afraid…" She didn't finish, and leaned back.

He gave a nod. Why were there footprints and not bodies?

"Nothing else," he said. "They vanished."

Valiena said, "Where could they go?"

"The canyon is no path for girls," he said. "I heard a cry to seaward. Could have been a bird. Came on the wind."

"The wind?" said Valiena, and looked into the city square at the trail of leaves leading from the tree.

Taumea read her face, and said, "They were no vision. Visions leave no footprints, and the leaves remain."

Turning back in the direction of the sea, he said, "Let us look down canyon."

Valiena stiffened, looking past his shoulder into the square. Between them she raised her hands and made the sign for *Soot*.

Tendons stood out in Taumea's neck, but he remained immobile. Movement caught the eye, and if Valiena could see an enemy, then that enemy could see them. He figured their background from the enemy's vantage, grateful to see that they were low enough on the rim to not be silhouetted against the sky. He and Valiena had fled to the haunted city to avoid the Temple Soot assassins hunting them. It had worked until now.

In front of Taumea's chest, Valiena pointed to give him a bearing on the enemy, then seemed to struggle with the signs for distance that he'd taught to her.

Giving up, she whispered, "Other side of the square. Making for the tree." She frowned, watching, then said, "Tracking. He's tracking."

Not us, signed Taumea. They hadn't come to the ruins via that route.

Valiena's eyes smoldered.

Taumea studied the rugged canyon rim before him. It was a steep maze of brush and shelving rocks. Plenty of cover if they could get low without being seen.

Valiena held her breath and made the sign *wait*. When

she ducked down, Taumea moved with her.

"He's behind the hill," she said.

"Which means he'll have some elevation in seconds," said Taumea, and slid down the back side of the boulder.

They made a difficult traverse among branches and through narrow cracks, and were both breathing hard and bleeding from scratches when they got to the flat stone Taumea had used before. Handing his bow and quiver to Valiena, he crept out on the stone until he could see the top edge of the falls upstream. A cloaked man stood there, dressed all in black, looking down the canyon. The man bent and put his face near the stone, swinging back and forth.

Taumea couldn't fathom what the man was doing, but he was armed with sword and dagger, and was clearly following the girls. Nothing good could come of a lone warrior tracking little girls in the Haunted Lands, and there was something off about his movement. Too fluid. For no reason Taumea could name, it made his gut twist to look at the man.

Taumea motioned behind his leg without looking back, and Valiena passed him his bow with an arrow nocked. The man below stood and shrugged off his cloak. Raising a foot, he pulled off a boot, tossing it aside. As the other leg came up for its boot, Taumea drew, still prone, and let fly. The man's pale face snapped to look right at Taumea, and he knew what they faced.

The man whirled aside, letting the arrow flash past. Taumea opened his hand for another arrow. It was there, perfectly placed in his fingers by Valiena to enable him to nock, draw, and release with a single motion.

Six arrows in as many seconds, and the thing was untouched. Neither did it hide, remaining in plain view.

Taumea no longer considered the thing a man. Taumea stood, showing himself, and the creature bared teeth in a growling hiss. Taumea reached for another arrow.

The fletched shaft Valiena held trembled in the air. He took it and she pulled another from her quiver. Six arrows from Taumea at this range from high ground should have killed anything, even a Yasharn Soot assassin. Taumea's face held that deep and deadly calm which marked him in battle. His feet slid farther out on the ledge, and Valiena felt like her heart would shatter seeing him so close to the edge, but she shifted after him, keeping the next arrow ready.

The creature leapt from the rim, aiming at the far gorge wall. Taumea swiveled and released—the arrow was barely off the string before his hand was back for the next. Beast and arrow met in midair. It yowled and landed on a sloped shelf, nearly losing its grip, talons gouging the stone. Taumea leaned out, bow drawn to his ear, angled down, waiting to see where it would go next. It jumped, and he rotated down, leaning out, one boot slipping as he released.

Valiena leapt for her husband as the beast below sailed into the arrow's path. Another yowl heralded a hit as Valiena yanked Taumea back.

Without a word, he grabbed the next shaft and ran, taking a flying leap to the next rock on the edge of the chasm.

—◦◦◦—

Anila's gaze turned from the eagle on the wind and fixed on the broken lines of rock that stretched out into the sea below them. Today they were going to go farther than ever before, a daring adventure they'd whispered about all summer long, waiting for the east winds of winter.

Anila took Spe's hand and said, "Ready?"

Spe nodded. They walked left, out of the mouth of the gorge and onto the dry tuft grasses of the steep slope. Hand in hand they leaned into the wind and took easy steps down, being sure to avoid stepping on last year's bird nests. In a short while they arrived at the first segment of the stone finger that reached out into the sea. The top of the first segment was flat, bare rock, white around its rim with bird droppings. They didn't pause, walking out until they came to the first gap. They could feel the wind rushing up out of the narrow chasm, and hear the thunder of waves. Anila leaned over the edge, putting her face in the breeze. Not to be outdone, Spe leaned out too, reaching her free hand into the wind, letting it rush through her little fingers. Waves roared and churned through the gap fifty feet below, and sea spray rose on the air, moist and fresh.

Anila squatted beside Spe, wrapped one arm around her middle, and said, "Together!"

They leaned forward and called to the wind. It roared upward so powerful that they both sat back on their haunches. Careful, they moved back into place with their hearts hammering. The wind here was like a thing alive and willing to answer to them.

"Softly," said Anila.

They sang and the wind surged. Anila leaned into the stream with Spe and pushed off. They hovered above the gap. Spe looked down and tensed. Before Anila could caution her, heat bloomed from Spe and a roar of wind tore spray from the waves below. Anila raised her voice, shaping a gust to blow them across the gap before Spe's torrent could hit. They landed in a heap on the other side, bruising knees and hands.

Spe said with tears in her eyes, "You didn't make a pillow!"

Nursing her knee, Anila didn't answer, and wondered if they were being foolish. This wind was frightening in its eagerness. She looked back up the cliff.

Spe saw Anila considering going back, and set out across the next rock top before Anila could stop her. Anila rose and limped after. Standing at the next break in the rock, she looked at Spe's determined face, and then back up at the gorge mouth.

A pillar of ice cold stabbed down her spine. A black-clad figure stood there, looking back at her. A man. She reached for Spe, but her sister was already gone, riding a poof of air across the wide gap. Panicked, Anila whirled to watch Spe land, then spun back to the cliff. The man was coming down the slope. He had seen them using the Breath! Anila leapt with a cry and sailed the air to Spe, who was hopping in a circle singing, "I can fly. I can fly!"

Anila screamed, "Spe! Look!"

Spe froze, her joy slapped away by mortal fear. They had been seen.

CHAPTER 3

Dauthaz

THERE WAS A HALO OF LIGHT AROUND THE periphery of Breea's vision. She tried to blink it away. Raising a hand to rub her eyes, she stopped and held up both hands. They glowed with a warm radiance the same color as the Temple orb.

Breea groaned and said to the orb, "I should crack you in half. You know what they will do." She looked down at the crowds below. "They shouldn't worship me."

The orb seemed unrepentant, rotating slowly, giving off a gentle shimmer of refracted sunlight—like Breea did now.

"If this doesn't go away by nightfall, I'm coming back for you," she said.

Breea began the climb down, thinking about what the orb had shown her of Carsythe. Even leaving this day she could not see reaching the city in time. How could it stand before an Oregule? How had they resisted this long? The city had been invested long before she left Limtir.

At the bottom of the rubble pile, she stood over the spider Oregule's medallion. Her finger tingled where the medallion had torn the pattern of eight spider eyes into the tip. She looked down the ramp where Neprawn and Simarn stood staring in wonder. They knelt, heads bowed.

Breea shook her head in negation, and shouted, "Neprawn!"

He leapt up and ran to her, but before he could salute or kneel again, she said, "Find something to wrap this."

"I Serve," he said, turning to run back down the ramp.

Simarn had risen from her knees. The girl held Breea's bear-fur cloak, but seemed afraid to approach. Breea beckoned for her. Simarn walked up, pausing to pick up her crossbow. Breea walked down to her. When they met, Breea took the bow and cloak, set them aside atop a block of rubble, then embraced the girl.

"You killed an Oregule," said Breea. "You saved me. Thank you."

Simarn gripped Breea so tightly that pain flared in Breea's orb-healed back. Moved, Breea held her for a long while, then stepped away. Simarn seemed calmer, though tears wet her cheeks beneath downcast eyes. Breea retrieved her bear-fur cloak, shook some of the rock dust out of it, then draped it around Simarn's shoulders. Breea lifted the crossbow and examined the weapon. It was large and well made, as heavy as it looked. Breea was impressed that Simarn had the strength to arm it, even with the cocking lever. Though Breea had not seen the moment of Simarn's attack on the Oregule, she remembered the sound of the bow's release and the sight of the Oregule's head jerking back as the bolt passed through its skull.

Breea handed the weapon to Simarn, and said, "Don't leave it cocked. Too simple to fire when you don't intend, and with constant tension the string and bow will fail."

Simarn nodded, accepting the crossbow and instruction with humble deference.

Breea added, "Take care not to touch the release until you are committed to kill."

Simarn tensed, but Breea couldn't tell if it was guilt for almost killing Scaukra, or that Breea was displeased by the act. For herself Breea was unsure what to make of this girl who had one day been a tavern slave, and the next capable of facing a seven-foot-tall warrior-beast with the eyes of a spider—face it, and then kill the thing, saving Breea's life.

Neprawn strode up with a piece of Temple guard cloak and a leather thong. Breea took them and walked back to the medallion. Using a dagger she flipped the thing onto the cloth, then lifted the edges and tied them.

"Master, I will carry it," said Neprawn, indicating the bag.

Impressed by his bravery, she handed it to him. "Do not touch it, even through the cloth."

"I will not, Master," he said.

Breea nodded to him, then turned to face the city. The square below was filling with people walking in from the streets that fanned out through the upper city from the Temple. A disturbance rippled through the crowd as a lance of warriors advanced from a street and people scrambled to make way. Breea could see why. No one stood in the way of Bay-ope Gardasim. Behind him were fifty guild warriors along with a few Limtirians. Relief and gladness brought tears to her eyes. She walked down as Bay-ope pounded up the ramp, his strides making the wood structure quiver and shake. He halted in front of her, breathing hard. Behind him the Batusha warriors spread out on either side, then chak'ood, coming to attention. Sabar and Ootha were there with a few other masters.

"The girl said you were wounded," said Bay-ope, staring at her glowing skin and blood-stiff clothing.

"I am," she said. "I stand by essence alone."

He nodded with worried eyes, then looked past her at the ruin of the Temple.

"He's dead," she said. It was what she had said of Lupazg in the forests of Limtir Mountain when Bay-ope and Taumea had come to rescue her.

Bay-ope remembered and grinned through his beard, but it was a grim smile. They had all believed the Oregule dead. Bay-ope swept his gaze over the entire scene, then stood aside, his eyes lingering on the sack held by Neprawn. She could see questions in Bay-ope but walked past him, unwilling to talk of the battle or the golden glow atop the rubble pile.

"Anule," she said to the Batusha warriors. They dropped their salutes and formed lines to either side of her. The Limtirians bowed to her, then took positions behind Bay-ope as he followed Breea.

Near the base of the ramp, she stopped at the improvised stretcher where Scaukra lay unconscious. Kneeling beside him she set her hand on his where he still held her dagger.

Her weaving was all that kept him alive. The dagger was no longer helping, for its power had returned to the hilt gem. Gentle, she removed it from his grip and remembered his look of loss when he thought her dead. At the same time she recalled his betrayal of the Batusha Guild, giving the Temple word of her coming through his woman, a healer named Pareetha who had been bound to the spider Oregule. Yet his dedication to Breea felt unquestionable. There was a complicated story in the man—and with her leaving the city, it was one she would likely never know.

Below, beyond the edge of the crowd, a strong young voice called, "Way!"

Breea stood and sheathed the dagger. A moving opening in the crowd approached, though she could see no one within. The crowd parted and five Batusha boys with crossbows and drawn swords gaped at her glowing form. One of the Batusha men gave an order and the boys sheathed swords, then saluted Breea, back-fist to palm.

"Anule," she said.

At another order they sidled to the side, leaving Dori standing alone in the middle of the ramp. Dori looked exhausted, the hem of her dress dark with blood and dirt. She started to curtsy, but Breea stepped forward, holding out a glowing hand.

Dori dared not take it, so Breea embraced her. "Thank you, Dori," said Breea. Standing back she said, "Take me to the Lute and Swan? I do not recall the way."

"Yes, milady," said Dori, at once honored and mortified to be so familiar with a goddess.

Breea turned back and called around the bulk of Bay-ope. "Simarn?"

The girl came at a run, and though her face showed her

relief at being called—to be wanted and of use—she was also strangely closed, as though all that existed for her was duty to Breea. Addressing that would be a discussion for another time. Breea turned back to the wall of awed townsfolk at the bottom of the ramp. She had the girls flank her and took a hand of each.

"Bay-ope, call a path for us."

The Limtir captain bellowed, "Way!"

The crowd melted back like a skein of ice before boiling water.

As a blood and dust-covered Breea walked the streets—openly wearing blades—at one hand a servant, and at the other a woman carrying a crossbow, a reverential, baffled, and sometimes hostile silence fell upon the crowds of people who saw her pass. For her own part, Breea knew exactly what kind of message she intended.

At the Lute and Swan she found her strength waning. Dori and Simarn offered their arms and aided her up the long stair to the top floor. Alone with the girls in her rooms, she allowed them to undress her. Both gasped at the red mess of her back, then helped her into the bed.

—◊◊◊—

Someone was on the bed. They shifted and Breea hissed in pain as the covers pulled on the tender flesh of her barely healed wounds. Groggy, she relaxed back into sleep—the sound of battle like a dream.

Her eyes opened on a dark room.

Beyond the walls men cried out in pain. Rising in the dark, she struck someone off the bed and drew a blade from the belt at the headboard. The dagger's emerald burst to light as a body hit the floor beside the bed and a crossbow snapped, sending the bolt into the ceiling. A woman's voice whimpered in pain. Simarn. Feeling a stab of guilt, Breea oriented to the sounds of fighting, strapped on her dagger belt, and sprinted naked from the room, both blades in hand.

The double door to the hall was shut but she could hear the clash and grunts of a vicious fight beyond. Breea slid to a stop and closed her eyes. She felt eight people beyond, fighting one on one. A confused mass of others lay prone or writhed upon the floor. She decided to make an entrance and tried a weave she'd never before dared to attempt. Reversing her blades to Adder Posture, she channeled all her rage and fear through the weapons and struck the door with their points. The effect was more than she hoped—the doors detonated outward in a blast. Men tumbled from the shock wave. Lamps snuffed out in the wind.

Naked, Breea stepped into the dark hall, her skin alight, daggers like sickles of emerald in her fists. The floor was littered with living and dead Batusha warriors, Limtir warriors, and Temple assassins so soot-blackened that only their eyes reflected her light.

"Batusha, slay!" she said.

The fight was over in seconds as stunned Temple assassins—more deeply affected by her presence—were killed with little resistance.

Ootha stood and kicked his dead opponent in the face, then spat on it. He shook his saber free of blood, sheathed it, and turned to Breea. His face went slack with shock and sudden appreciation as he realized she was bare. And glowing.

Breea hardly noticed, for there was a man at her feet quivering as his mouth foamed. Poison. Others as well.

Anyone cut by Soot blades. She sheathed hers and knelt by the man. Calming her racing heart, she struggled to listen for the patterns of his body. Her healing weave was a simple mending of flesh, but this was something different. She needed the tome of healing, but his body was dying, losing all its rhythms. As quickly as she could, she wove a net of blue over the man.

A Batusha warrior came running and tripped over a body as he stared at Breea.

"Limtir holds the kitchen and rear," he reported, retrieving the snuffed lantern. "We hold the foyer, stairs, stable, and carriage house. Runners make for the guild hall."

"What of the other floors?" asked Ootha.

"No word," said the man. "I heard little as I came up."

"That means nothing with Soot abroad," said Ootha. "Seek word floor by floor. Take Lanthem."

The two men ran as everyone but Breea looked down the hall in the opposite direction, where heavy footfalls announced Bay-ope's arrival. Breea moved to the next man, creating a weave that she hoped would hold his life until she could do something for the poison. As his shaking eased, the heart of the Limtirian beside him failed. Breea cried out in frustration. She could feel men dying all around her.

On her knees in the blood of men who had died to protect her, Breea drew both daggers and drove them into the floor.

"Help me!" she called to the Temple orb.

The building trembled and gold mist rose from the polished floorboards.

Eyes alight, Breea ran back into her rooms. She went to the wardrobe where Dori had stacked her books and found Simarn sitting on the floor behind the bed, crossbow in her lap, tears on her face.

Breea said, "Forgive me. I awoke in fear. Where's Dori? I need water to wash wounds."

Simarn struggled up. "The blame is mine, milady."

Breea tugged the heavy book from the shelf, sad to hear Simarn call her by a title, but thrust the concern from her mind.

"Please find Dori," she said.

"Yes, milady."

Bay-ope ducked under the door frame with a gown which he placed around Breea's shoulders. Breea handed him the book and slipped her arms into its sleeves, then ran back to the hall where nothing had changed. Men appeared afraid to move in the mist.

"Light the lamps," said Breea. She knelt and touched a dagger. Its gem shone, and she opened the tome, propping it open on the body of a Soot assassin.

"Bring the wounded, and the poisoned," said Breea.

Bay-ope strode past her and added, "Remove the dead."

Men jumped to action—except Ootha. Breea glanced at him. He had acquired a small black crossbow and a matching box of bolts which hung from his belt. The Batusha warrior took a position in the doorway, where he could command a view into Breea's rooms and both ways down the corridor. He cocked the bow and armed it. With Ootha and Bay-ope to guard her back, she threw herself into the weaving.

Guided by the orb's memories, Breea found herself using the orb's own cache of sunlight to heal. The weave was half memory and half her own. When she faltered it showed her men and women in yellow robes healing the sick in a room filled with sunlight. The warp and weft of their weaves were subtle beyond her understanding, but the greater patterns were enough to fill in most of her missing threads.

After a while she realized that there was another weaver near, helping her, and looked up to find Limtir's healer, Yavay'adil picking up the warp of her intent and power, weaving it with care into new arrivals. With each new wounded, she reached farther into herself to sustain the great weft of restoration. When there was no more within, she reached for her daggers embedded in the floor.

Yavay'adil caught her hands, and said, "Enough."

She struggled against him, weak. Angry, she looked up at him. His blue eyes enveloped her with calm, and she relaxed. Exhausted, she rested her forehead upon his chest. Her skin no longer glowed. Sleep beckoned, and her eyes closed.

A faint voice said, "Master, the Army of the Blessed comes."

Breea surfaced in a haze of fatigue and stood away from Yavay'adil.

Sabar had arrived with a crowd of Batusha warriors behind him. Their expressions were grim.

"We must get you to the hall," he said. "We cannot defend this place."

"The army?" she asked.

"They have taken all the eastern gates and prepare to march on the Temple, the guild hall, and this inn. They slay all in their path. The city is lost. We must retreat to the hall, and thence to the docks. Ships await."

Breea looked into the rooms where Dori, Simarn, and a dozen other servants were tending rows of wounded laid out upon the floor of the round foyer. The wounded who were awake were staring at her. The scene reminded Breea of the overflowing infirmary of Limtir during the battle with

Lupazg. On that day she had run, and never known how many lives it had cost.

"We will stand," she said.

Angry, Sabar said, "Master. Even you cannot—"

Breea stepped forward and slapped her open hand on his red leather breastplate. From some hidden well of power she summoned enough essence to blast a stream of warmth into him.

Sabar choked and collapsed to his knees. Those around took a collective step back.

"Do not tell me what I cannot," said Breea.

Chest heaving, Sabar looked up into her eyes. He wasn't in pain. She had not hurt him. Completely the opposite. She knew he felt a power coursing through him he could never have imagined.

"Master," he said between breaths. "You bless me." He dropped his head, overcome.

Breea struggled against the weakness that threatened to sweep her into darkness. "This inn will stand," she said. "Go."

He sprang up, slapped back-fist to palm, and said, "I Serve."

He turned to his fellows and swept them down the hall.

Ootha, still at his post in the doorway, would not meet her gaze, which was fine with Breea. She didn't have the energy to deal with resistance from Sabar's brother. Stumbling only slightly, she retrieved her daggers from the floor.

Bay-ope, Yavay'adil, and Ootha followed her into her chambers. She stopped by a table covered with food and picked up a pitcher of some kind of fermented juice. Tilting it to her mouth, she drank and drank. She set it down with a clank, then walked on to her bedroom, too tired to care about the crowd of men shadowing her. The bed was soft and she ached with the need to lie down, but instead she tossed her dagger belt onto the quilts and went to the wardrobe.

There was nothing to wear. All her clothing was gone—ruined in battle or at the guild hall. Only her boots remained, freshly cleaned and oiled.

"Breea," said Bay-ope.

She ignored him, riffling through the endless dresses, blouses, and skirts in the wardrobe. There were no pants of course.

"Breea."

She heaved a breath, then turned to her old friend and mentor.

He said, "This inn will fall—"

"No!" It made her a little dizzy saying it so, but she caught herself before falling.

"Lass…" said Bay-ope, his eyes pleading.

"I wish to dress," she said.

Bay-ope's gaze hardened, and he stalked from the room. Yavay'adil and Ootha followed. Dori closed the door on their backs.

Breea said, "Dori, there are no pants."

"Milady, there are none to wear, for a lady." She tried to mime that all had closures at the front for men.

Breea sighed. "Help me find something?"

"Yes, milady. These at this end might suit your ladyship best. Lord Dupalo had them made for you this day."

There were a dozen dresses of the finest cloth Breea had ever seen, but she could not wear a dress into battle.

"Bring me my pants," she said. "I don't care how dirty they are."

Dori looked pained.

"Cursed city," said Breea. "What did they do, burn them?"

"Milady, a priest of the Batusha Guild took them. Very respectful, he was."

There was a knock at the door. Breea growled in frustration. Simarn bent and cocked her crossbow, then looked at Breea for permission. Breea was too tired to *listen* to see who was beyond the door. She gave Simarn a nod, then motioned for Dori to open the door. Simarn armed her bow and Dori rushed over and swung the door open.

Ajalay, the Tetr-Sanis of the Library of Limtir, blanched at the crossbow aimed at her face. The sounds of moving furniture and brisk orders came from the rooms beyond. Breea motioned Ajalay in, and Dori shut the door. Simarn lowered the crossbow without apology, despite Ajalay's disapproving look. That was impressive to Breea who had seen nobles bend to obedience under Ajalay's unyielding gray eyes. Breea herself had obeyed the leader of Limtir as a mother and mentor after the vanishing of her mother and her father's death.

Ajalay said to Breea, "Bay-ope tells me you intend to defend this inn against the entire armed might of Yash."

Breea pushed aside the chagrin she felt at Ajalay's stern words, and replied, "What of it?"

Ajalay raised her chin, taking Breea's measure. "Then you had best look the part," she said.

"Part?" asked Breea, feeling in spite of her defiance almost like a little girl again—not quite understanding.

"A queen," said Ajalay, "does not lead barefoot and half naked." She turned to Dori and said, "Brushes, combs, oils—all that you have."

Dori didn't bother to answer, sprinting for the servants' exit. Ajalay looked to Simarn. The Tetr seemed to expect the girl to help Dori. The girl stood firm, shifting the crossbow to her other arm.

Ajalay's eyes narrowed. She turned to the wardrobe and said, "Which do you hate the least?"

"Aja," said Breea, disbelieving.

The Tetr ignored her and pulled out a white dress. She held it under Breea's chin. Breea backed up, sitting on the bed with a thump, anger making its way through her exhaustion to flush her cheeks.

Ajalay said, "I should have taught you more statecraft. If you fight here, the capital of Yash will burn. Tens upon tens of thousands will perish and your name will become a curse to frighten Yasharn children for the next thousand years. You brought down the Temple, yet the people are willing to forgive you that crime for they feel their hearts free of cold web and piercing claws. It is known that this is your doing—however, if you burn this city, there is no hope for Yash."

"Aja, what can I do?"

"You lead," said the Tetr. "You lead as a queen as this world has never seen, not in two thousand years."

Feeling Ajalay's belief in her, Breea straightened.

"Like your mother," said Ajalay.

The breath left Breea. Her mother was a queen? An Alach queen. Like her mother.

Dori ran in with a crowd of serving women burdened with every hair manipulation device, cream, powder, oil, and perfume known. They sat a stunned Breea in a chair before an immense silver mirror and set to work.

"Do not be gentle," said Aja. "We have no time. Move."

They cleaned Breea's face and neck and hands and dug

the dried blood from beneath her fingernails. They brushed and creamed her black hair into flowing submission, then put her in a white gown with long sleeves. Breea refused the dainty white shoes, pulling on her boots instead. The dress brushed the ground so they wouldn't be visible.

Aja stepped back to admire her, though Breea could see deep concern in her gray eyes.

"I have a gift for you." Ajalay reached around her neck and lifted woven-gold chains to reveal the Tetr-Sanis medallion, an emerald the size of an egg carved with the likeness of an open book.

"Aja, no, I am not the Tetr—"

Ajalay stepped close and laid fingers on Breea's lips.

"This is the secret to my power. Language. Memory. Weaving." She lifted the gold chain over Breea's head. "By right it is yours. Alach made, and by Alach to be wielded."

The stone settled on the white cloth between Breea's breasts, centered within the twin arcs of scar made by the fangs of Lupazg's medallion. Warmth and memory flooded her body and she gasped.

Aja nodded. Stepping back, she bowed to Breea. Too stunned to respond, Breea watched Ajalay gather the dagger belt and buckle it around her waist, arranging the folds where it gathered the dress, accentuating Breea's shape.

Dori said, "Men will swoon."

Simarn chuffed, and said darkly, "In fear."

A pounding on the door made them all start.

"Master Banea!"

Dazed by the whisper of knowledge from the emerald, Breea opened the door herself. The bearded Batusha priest beyond gaped and forgot his message.

Ajalay's voice cut through his wonder. "What

knowledge, Arin?"

He closed his eyes to remember, then intoned, "High Priest Duyazen, Lord of the Temple, Primad of Yash, Voice of the One in Wisdom, seeks Het's Champion, Chosen of the One."

Breea couldn't believe that the bitter old man she'd met the day before was the high priest again. She turned to Ajalay. Aja's eyes were steady, looking into hers. The message was clear: You are queen.

Breea turned back to Arin and indicated that he should lead the way. Two Batusha master warriors who had been to either side of her door fell into step in rear-flanking positions. Simarn followed directly after.

There were Batusha warriors throughout the chambers— ripping down curtains, moving furniture away from windows, and breaking out the glass. Siege preparations. They froze in motion as she came into view.

Someone said in profound appreciation, "Bless me!"

Breea blushed and said "Anule" to those who had come to attention at her entrance. The dress felt strange around her legs, at once giving her a feeling of freedom and restricting the length of her stride. Down the lamplit stairs she had to remember to lift the skirt to keep from tripping. Armsboys came running up the stairs with bundles of arrows. They scooted to the side and watched her pass with impressed grins.

The beautiful marble foyer was a whirl of men and boys running, stacking supplies, and arranging weapons. The double doors to the carriage stop were open wide. Cold, smoke-scented air chilled the room. Batusha stopped work and struck back-fists to palms.

"Anule," said Breea, and activity resumed. "Arin, where

is the high priest?"

"Master, we hold him at the street. He comes in procession with a pa-hoc of the Temple guard."

Breea considered. She needed to think as a queen. Look the part, Aja had said. An Alach queen. She went to one knee and pressed her fingertips to the floor.

"Are you there?" she asked. "I need your light."

The marble floor warmed under her fingers and a sense of the city emerged in her mind. A three-headed snake would soon strike from the east, a cold pestilence at each tip. Three army columns, and leading each—Dauthaz. The orb's need was intense.

"What do you need of me?" said Breea.

Breea saw her dagger piercing Lupazg's eye.

"What of the army?"

A High Temple priest in full regalia lifted a baby into a shaft of sunlight. His arms trembled as he cried, "A warrior is born!"

Breea jerked back her hand. Her own Calling! Duyazen giving her Calling. Did the orb mean that Duyazen would handle the rest of the army? Or that she should fight as a warrior? She stood and found that she was glowing once more, her exhaustion gone. The room was silent, men and boys staring. Arin was on both knees, hands and head bowed to the floor. Everyone except Simarn and the two guards began to follow Arin's example and lowered themselves to the floor. It was a peculiar sight, all these warriors, some of the best she'd ever seen, putting their heads to the stone for her, but it also meant that she looked the part of an Alach queen.

To finish the look, she touched the hilt stones of her daggers, and let a breath of warm power flow into them. The gems waxed bright.

"Anule," she said and walked outside. Simarn and the two Batusha masters followed after. Arin realized she had walked off and jumped up to follow in their wake.

Following an open walk from the carriage stop around to the front of the inn, Breea emerged on the top landing of the fan of curved steps leading down to the street from the main doors of the Lute and Swan. Arrayed down the steps were three ranks of spear-wielding Batusha warriors backed by a rank of bowmen. In the street a strange kind of open carriage draped in yellow cloth held a black stone throne with one occupant. Circling it were fifty priests holding tall, brightly burning tapers so that Duyazen was ringed by fire and lit by its light. Behind the carriage stood ranks of Temple guard leading back up the street. Duyazen's robes were bloodred with a broad sash of sparking gold across the chest. Upon his head was a red-and-gold hat of intricate folds with a single peak at the front. At Breea's appearance, he stood.

Behind her Arin called, "Make way for Breea Banea. Chosen of the One, Master of Batusha, Dauthaz Bane." Simarn whispered in his ear, and he added, "Queen of Limtir!"

The Batusha warriors parted and Breea descended at what she hoped was a stately pace, lifting the hem of her dress to keep from tripping as she had seen Aja do countless times on the stairs of Limtir.

Duyazen's gaze was so rapt upon her that Breea could not tell his intent. She readied herself, studying the faces of the priests before her. The priests stood with eyes fixed ahead. Only the tremble of the tapers betrayed the emotion beneath. They were frightened. Four stepped aside, allowing Breea to mount steps covered with gold brocade.

Faces filled the windows of the inn. People leaned out every door and window up and down the street.

Duyazen hadn't bathed since she last saw him. The man's eyes were a whirl of fervor and mixed emotion. Breea sensed his heart racing, but his expression was one of stone. He raised his robe-covered right hand to his chin, and with his other hand drew back the sleeve, revealing a hand with only thumb and forefinger. On the forefinger was a gold ring set with an amber-colored stone. He brought the ring to his lips, then stretched the arm to Breea.

Breea did not understand what the motion demanded, then she wove a boundary to keep her anger under control. Duyazen's face went a shade paler at what he saw in her eyes. Seeing his fear was like drinking from a chalice of confidence, and the worst of her rage faded. Breea bent forward and touched her lips to the now trembling ring. He dropped the hand with a subtle look of vindication and victory, resparking her irritation. She straightened and with her right hand drew the dagger on that side. The blade channeled her anger and the air shimmered green around her hand.

A tremor rocked Duyazen, and she felt him resist the desire to step away. Breea brought the hilt to her lips and kissed the sparkling emerald. Holding his gaze, she extended the weapon gem first, blade back. Duyazen's eyes went a little crossed as he watched it approach. Despair crept into his face and Breea realized he was terrified of the weapon. Breea granted him mercy and damped the fire within so the gem's glow dwindled. She gave Duyazen a little nod of encouragement.

The high priest leaned forward and touched the stone with his lips. His eyes went wide and he straightened quickly, smothering the little smile of pleasure at the strength that had surged through him like a cascade of warm water. To give him a moment to compose himself after her peace offering, Breea sheathed the weapon and looked beyond the carriage, taking measure of the force he brought. Barely a hundred men. She wondered how much control he truly had, or was this all that remained of the Temple garrison?

A table and chair were brought. Breea sat and the priests around the carriage stepped out five paces, clearing a wide space around the carriage.

Duyazen said, "Though you slew the white Dauthaz, his servants remain."

Breea wondered how he knew of the Oregule. Very few had seen her battle with the creature.

"It was an Oregule," she said. "The white one. They are an ancient enemy."

The old priest said, "In the Army of the Blessed there are Dauthaz who command with the appearance of men. Your champions shall strike them down and feed the gutters with their pale unclean blood."

Seeing Breea's amazement at his words, he leaned in and said, "I have seen it. The One has spoken. You are the Chosen. Blessed by the One to cleanse the Dauthaz filth from holy Yash."

Breea wondered if his god had spoken to him, or the Temple orb.

Duyazen sat back and called in a strong voice, "Champions!"

Breea glanced at the Batusha masters standing just beyond the taper-holding priests, but they were not who Duyazen had called. A rumble of boots came from the dark street to the north. Men in scale and thick leather armor flowed past the Temple guard and lined the front of the inn. The first three wore armor of blue, opalescent scales. Their skin was tawny, hair short and black, and even by firelight their eyes showed a remarkable azure hue. They stepped between the priests and knelt, bowing heads to Breea.

"The brothers Nassa of the Aska-Wuthos," said Duyazen. "Commanders of the 8th regiment of the Army of the Blessed. Five hundred shall be saviors of the Holy Temple. The One in Wisdom grants five pa-hoc to his Chosen to act as her champions." The lines of his face relaxed into a an expression of deep pride.

A closer look at Duyazen's features revealed the source of his pride. His hair was white and his skin paler, but the eyes were the same. These were his kinsmen. How had he gotten them into the city? The man was far more cunning than she had thought. Had Duyazen been planning to act against the Oregule before her arrival?

As his kinsmen they surely held orders from the old priest, but she needed soldiers. Duyazen held them in high regard even to being a match for Dauthaz. If true, five hundred dedicated men was true power to wield. Breea leapt to the ground in front of them. They looked up, saw her fierce approval, and the eldest rose. The younger men followed his example.

Duyazen said, "Chosen."

She turned her head to him.

"The Dauthaz are many," he said.

"The gutters shall run white, High Priest."

His eyes flashed, and he gave a command she didn't recognize. The priests went up to the carriage, and set their tapers into brackets around the rim. They hauled thick rope harnesses from beneath the front of the carriage and set them across their chests. Breea watched, appalled and fascinated, as they turned the carriage around, then leaned ahead as one. The carriage rumbled away northward with a Temple guard quadrant before and behind.

In the quiet after their departure, screams wafted over the buildings from the dark east sky. The Dauthaz were killing everyone in their path.

Rage carved dark paths across her soul, and essence-fire followed them. Her body flashed to light. She set her hand upon the eldest brother and poured her heat into him. His legs gave way.

Bracing himself on the cobbles with one hand, he said, "Bloody Serpent, that's good!"

The next brother refused to show fear, standing with head high. His legs gave way as well. The last, younger than the others, blinked at his fellows, then clenched his jaw, inflated his chest, hooked his thumbs in his belt, and braced his legs wide. When he fell with a sob, his brothers caught him, grinning.

"Armor for the Oregule Slayer," said Breea to Arin.

Arin stood shoulder to shoulder beside Simarn. Both looked awed.

"Yes, Chosen." He touched a knee to the ground with head bowed, then spun and ran up the stair.

Breea bent her knees and touched her fingers to the cobbles. The bulk of the army column was six streets away, falling behind a knot of ice and rot only two streets away. She could feel the orb weaving beneath the streets, sowing doubt in the minds of the regular army. In contrast, the Dauthaz were a knot of malice. By their footfalls there were at least fifty.

She rose and took quick stock of the crowd of warriors available to her.

"Five masters to me!" she said.

Ootha and Sabar leapt down the steps with Neprawn and two others.

Arin came running back with Batusha aspirants and armsboys in his wake. The boys stripped off their armor and Arin tried various pieces against Simarn. He did not know what to do about her legs in the dress.

"My lady?" said Simarn.

Breea walked up to her and drew a dagger. A swift circle of the girl, and the dress was sheared midthigh.

"Forgive me," said Arin as he reached up around her leg to strap a leather bracer to her thigh. Simarn looked away, her fingers white on the crossbow. Arin had her kneel and lifted a mail shirt over her head. Simarn stood, running a hand over the mail in wonder. At Arin's word the Batusha aspirants helped Simarn don leather greaves and pauldrons.

Ootha walked up to Simarn. He was massive in comparison—twice her shoulders would not have spanned his. Her head came up, defiant, and he gazed down into her eyes for a long moment. He unhooked the black Soot crossbow from his belt and offered the weapon. Simarn seemed unwilling to relinquish her big bow, but when he offered her the box of poisoned bolts as well, she traded weapons quickly.

Ootha turned away with a wicked grin. "She'll do," he said. The men near them chuckled.

Simarn glowered at them. Politely, and wisely, they averted their eyes. Breea would have to tell her later that Batusha had just accepted her as one of their own and their amusement was approval of the highest order.

"Three columns," said Breea, squatting and carving lines into the cobbles with a dagger tip. "One at us, one the Temple, and one for the guild hall. Each is led by Dauthaz. We masters will hide in the buildings across and strike their flank when they assault the inn. You," she said to one Aska-Wuthos brother, "take two hundred of your men south two streets. Wait for the main body of the army, then draw them south. Don't get caught between them and the column heading for Batusha. Go west at need, but draw as many as you can. You," she said to another, "north, the same. Split and delay the column. Kill as few as you may. They are not our enemy. The high priest will take care of the army. Your parts are to hold and distract the main body until we slay the Dauthaz. You will know a Dauthaz by its strength and speed. In open combat, champions and masters only to face them." To the last Aska-Wuthos brother she said, "You with fifty will support Limtir at the rear of the inn."

Breea stood.

Arin walked among them with formal bearing, and blessed each, "The One to your blade."

Men dispersed in all directions, leaving Breea standing with five Batusha masters, Arin, and Simarn. Breea lookup up at the inn. Ajalay and Yavay'adil gazed down from its highest windows. They and Dori were as safe as could be, and she chewed on a problem with her plan. She needed all the Dauthaz here where she could meet them together.

Sheathing her dagger she said to Simarn and the masters, "Into the building behind."

She hiked her dress and ran up the steps though the spearmen. On the landing she used a dagger to shorten her dress, then raised both daggers and called upon the Temple orb. From her blades, green-gold light leapt into the night sky.

Weaving her will into the orb's threads flowing beneath the city, Breea thought, *Come, Dauthaz! I hunt you.*

A hundred cold snarls rippled against the essence of her thought.

To the men inside the inn and on the steps, she shouted, "Strike death! Do not fail, and do not stop, for what comes are not men."

She ran back across the street and through a shop door that Ootha drew closed behind her. In the soft light of her body, she walked among the masters and gifted her essence to each in turn. They swore and laughed and pounded the back of each in turn as he exclaimed in shock. Simarn stood by, and as Breea considered whether to grant the girl essence-power, a chill rose in her heart.

She whispered, "They come."

Blades sighed from scabbards.

They heard the order for bows to attack. Breea faced the door and drew her daggers. Green firelight filled the room. Cries and clash began outside.

Her voice resonant with hatred and singing with essence-power, Breea cried, "Kill!"

Ootha threw open the door and led the masters out, striking into the backs of Dauthaz wearing officer uniforms of the Yasharn military who were hacking through the thrusting spears of the Batusha warriors holding the stair. Breea faltered as the Temple orb whispered strategy and weaves to her. Dauthaz spun and attacked with fluid speed. The Batusha masters met them blow for blow, shattering and bending the inferior weapons of the Dauthaz, yet the beasts came on with fang and claw, and there were too many.

A Dauthaz spied Breea and charged her, then staggered

from a bolt through the throat. White blood sprouted from the wound. It came on as Simarn's bow clicked in reload. The beast sagged to the cobbles in front of Breea as the poison took hold and it lost control of its limbs. Breea cocked her head, listening.

Batusha wavered in the press. Breea crossed her daggers and wove her power with that of the orb. The weave tightened and her blades swept an arc—down, out, and up.

Golden mist rose from the ground at the feet of the Batusha men. Dauthaz recoiled.

At Breea's back, Simarn's bow snapped, but she fumbled her reload as a dozen Dauthaz charged around to flank the masters, seeking Breea. Breea exhaled and extended her blades. The Dauthaz on each side slammed into walls of air.

Before her the sabers of the Batusha masters were reaping a white blood harvest. Glamours fell from the Dauthaz as they died, revealing fangs and claws and spider eyes where a man's should be. Bodies piled and white blood flowed away over the cobbles. Bay-ope leapt from the stairs of the inn and roared like a hundred angry oxen. He crushed two Dauthaz to the stones with his axes, and dozens of the creatures turned to face him. Arrows and bolts were taking their toll as archers in the windows and atop the stair found their marks. The Batusha masters advanced.

Two of Simarn's bolts were embedded in the air walls to either side and her bow was silent as she sought a target.

The Dauthaz had fallen by half—down or twitching in agony. More sprinted in from the north and south. Trembling in the flow of essence-power, Breea waited for the moment they had all come. The beasts piled against her walls, frantic to get to her. Some were climbing the buildings.

"Inside!" she cried over her shoulder. Simarn ran, then stood ready in the doorway.

With a cry of effort, Breea wove her will deep into the earth. Singing out, she raised her arms. Heat billowed her dress, and the air walls to either side collapsed. The Dauthaz charged.

The Batusha masters leapt back to protect her. Breea stood her ground, coiling burning essence about herself, feeding it into the hilt gems of her blades.

The white pupils of the first Dauthaz to reach Breea showed huge in its eyes the instant before Breea struck it with a blade like a shaft of green sunlight. There was a flash of green-gold, and every foul weave that drove the beast shredded at the same time.

The scream it made clawed at Breea's ears, echoing up the street. The next one met the same fate. They came on, streaming past the masters, heedless of the blows they took doing so. Breea flipped her blades to Adder Posture and let the charge slam into her weaving.

The night exploded with light, and the first rank fell thrashing at her feet. The rest came on, and she stepped in to meet them. There were too many to meet blade to blade, yet no weapon or claw reached her; rather, the shimmering air about her rippled and bent, catching their blows. Her strikes fell like rain, and the night flickered like a green lightning storm. Slashed Dauthaz toppled one upon another, piling before her, the sound of their death cries rising to a horrific chorus.

The last Dauthaz to live had to climb a mound of its brethren to approach her. Bay-ope's ax cut the creature in half from behind. It gurgled hatred and slid back down the bodies of its brethren in two pieces.

Smoke rose from where Breea stood, and she staggered back, realizing that the soles of her boots were smoking. Heat shimmered from cracked cobbles where she had stood. Gasping hot air, she executed boundaries to halt the essence-power flowing up from below, only to have her intent ripped away by the column of heat.

Bay-ope peered over the body pile at the shimmering ground, then grunted. He winked at Breea, then turned to the inn, bellowing orders.

The power from below faded as deep weaving from the Temple orb bound the deep source. Breea stepped back to lean against the building.

"Tomes," she said, breathless.

That had been more dangerous than she'd thought. The Temple orb had shown her how to draw upon something far greater and more dangerous than the orb itself—the deep essence of the world.

In the doorway beside Breea, Simarn's eyes were wide and fevered as they roved for a target. Breea put a comforting hand on the girl's shoulder, then went to see how her masters had fared.

None of them had fallen, but all were bleeding from multiple wounds—their armor slashed and torn. When she reached for the strength to weave them whole, a wisp of cold essence brushed her. Breea hurried to a section of street free of blood. She dropped to her knees and placed her hands upon the stones. The cobbles hummed with the rhythms of combat—one man wielding her power was facing a single foe of vile, potent cold. The Dauthaz had a champion of their own.

CHAPTER 4

Breath Within

TAUMEA SCOUTED FOR THE BEAST AT EACH vantage into the canyon. Despite an arrow in the hip and another in its right shoulder, the thing was making better time than he. At the next overlook, he caught sight of it a hundred feet farther along the rocks of the canyon floor. This time it paused to look back at him. Taumea felt a chill. He brought up his bow, but the creature leapt from sight. With a curse, Taumea charged along the rim, leaping the next gap, and the next, struggling to make up the ground he was losing. Where were the girls? Cold desperation drove him ahead.

The scent of water grew strong, and he slid to a halt at the cliff edge overlooking the Leuvat Sea. A hundred feet below, the beast was descending the steep talus and grass leading down from the base of the cliff face. Taumea set his one arrow to string and drew all the way to his right ear.

—⁓⁓—

Anila and Spe stood immobile, staring at the man coming for them. Another figure appeared on the cliff above with a longbow. The bow bent, aiming down. Anila felt the ice gripping her heart shatter. Lifting Spe, she ran for the next break in the rocks. Anila shouted to the wind, and a rippling bridge spanned the chasm to the next rock. She ran across, tottering under Spe's weight. On solid rock once more, she sang a note to release her hold on the air, then ran across the stone to the next gap. It was too far to bridge. Breathing hard, she forced herself to turn around and look up at what came for them.

—⁓⁓—

Wind buffeted Taumea. The creature was limping down the slope, all its attention on the girls. Taumea studied the grass whipping in the wind around the beast and adjusted his aim. He would get only one strike. After that the thing could simply move out of range. In truth, in this wind, it was already out of range. Taumea held, then exhaled.

Battle calm settled him and he released. The arrow soared down, wavering in the wind. The creature paused as the girls ran an invisible bridge to the next rock and the arrow sliced down inches in front of its chest. The beast leapt aside, spinning in the air to see where its attacker was. It landed and looked up at Taumea then turned and leapt down the slope in long bounds. Taumea glanced behind for Valiena and the arrows, but she wasn't there. Desperate, he leaned out and looked both ways along the rim. It was a sheer wall—no way down. All he could do was watch.

—◈◈◈—

Spe wriggled to be free of Anila's grip, and Anila let her sister slide down beside her. Spe looked at the next gap, more than fifty feet across, then hid her face in the folds of Anila's woolen coat.

Limping slightly, the man came off the steep slope onto the first section of flat stone.

He wore no boots, and there was something wrong with his toes. At the first gap, he paused, and hope surged in Anila. The gap was fifteen feet to the next rock. He stepped up, putting his toes over the edge. Anila groaned in horror. From each toe, a curved white claw extended to grip the stone. Bending his legs, the man leapt, clearing the distance easily. Walking across, he drew his sword.

Anila bent to Spe, and said, "Breathe, Spe. Call your wind."

Spe whimpered and pressed her face into Anila, gripping tighter.

The man was at the next gap. He surveyed it, then looked at the girls. He smiled, exposing white fangs.

Tasting carrion on the wind, Anila screamed, "Spe!" But her little sister merely flinched and held on to Anila's clothes so tight that her small fists where white. Anila knew the gap behind was too far for her to bridge alone, but she had to try.

Anila whispered, "May all I say and all I think—"

The wind calmed behind her, and the beast stopped as though sensing her call upon the essence.

"Be in harmony with thee."

The man snarled and stepped to the edge, extending his claws.

"Breath within," said Anila, and stepped back onto air.

The man-thing drew his dagger.

"Breath beyond!" cried Anila as the man bent his knees.

She sang out, "Mighty of the trees!" and dragged Spe out to the middle of the gap.

The creature leapt.

Spe turned to look at the beast soaring across the far chasm. He landed, stepping into stride without pause. Spe sucked in a deep breath and uttered a sharp cry.

Wind like a fist of stone slammed into the man, flinging him back across the gap. There was a crack like thunder and a backwash of wind struck the girls, blowing them off Anila's half-made bridge.

———

Up on the cliff, Taumea sank to his knees. They were gone. The beast was as well, blown back across the rock face to tumble down the chasm behind. Taumea did not know how he knew, but he felt something immeasurably important had been lost with those girls. Thunder rolled on the wind.

Valiena came limping, her skirts torn, arrows swinging at her hip. She saw the sag of Taumea's shoulders and knew they'd failed.

"Taumea?" she asked, coming up behind him.

He didn't answer, staring out to sea.

"Opalah!" said Valiena, and gripped his shoulders.

Where the girls had fallen a spume of spay was rising, two little forms within. It bent and dumped them in a wet heap upon the stone.

Taumea rose and Valiena slid her hand into his. His return grip was painful.

"How do we get to them?" asked Valiena. The girls weren't moving.

Taumea said, "We have no rope. It could take a fortnight to find a route. The night's cold may kill them. If they are like Breea, it will not. On either path their fate is beyond us."

Valiena faced the half-moon in the east, a knowing rising within her.

"Finding them is why we are here," she said.

Taumea took a deep breath then let it out in a gust. "Let's go steal some rope."

Valiena hugged him fiercely.

—◈—

On the rock Spe was the first to move, sitting up to look around. The Breath burned in her chest and she whimpered. She pushed on Anila. "Wake up. It hurts, Ani."

Anila's eyes opened and she lifted her head, cringing at pain where her head had hit the stone. She pushed herself up, looking for the beast, but it was gone, as was the figure on the cliff. She untied her scarf and felt for the pain on her head. She found a lump and blood turning sticky in her wet hair. Spe whimpered and pushed against the middle of her chest with her fingers as though to push down the fire. Anila could feel Spe's heat growing.

"Pray," said Anila.

Spe cried out, tears overflowing, looking to Anila in pain and fear.

"Say it with me," urged Anila. "May all I say and all I think—"

Spe cried out, beating at her chest. Anila gathered her up, holding her arms down with a hug. Spe writhed and thrashed and her Breath became something molten. Holding her was like gripping the sun. Spe screamed. Anila hung on, her own fire answering in kind, burning in her breast.

Spe's skin glowed and steam flowed out of her clothing, whipped away by a whirl of wind that Anila hardly noticed. Spe's back arched, and her cries cut out like a snuffed candle. The fire vanished, and Spe's body sagged.

Overwhelmed and exhausted, Anila curled over her sister. Sobs rose up, racking her whole body. After they passed she sat curled over Spe, feeling her little sister breathe.

Straightening, she found herself sitting in a pocket of calm. The sun had vanished behind the mountains to the west. She could sense the sea wind hissing around her a few feet away. The sound of the crashing waves was muted. She reached out and found a denseness of air surrounding her. At a sung note it unraveled, and the cold sea breeze whirled about her.

Anila shifted Spe around so that Spe's head was on her shoulder and Spe's legs were over her hips. Anila shifted her own weight until she was kneeling painfully on the rock. Singing a soft call, she held Spe's thighs and urged the wind to help her stand. Rising with little effort she almost smiled at her cleverness, but Spe's cold skin against her cheek took away her pleasure. The warmth in Spe was out. Anila knew she had to get her out of the wind, and quickly.

Walking took some practice as the air lifting Spe needed constant adjustment. When she saw the sword, she stumbled and almost fell. The weapon lay on the rock like a sliver of pain. She gave it a wide berth, then contemplated the distance of air to the next pillar of rock. The memory of being blown off her bridge was sharp, making her heart race. Thinking about what she could do to make crossing possible without Spe's strength, it dawned on her that the distance to cross didn't matter. She didn't have to bridge the whole thing. All that mattered was where she stood.

Before starting, she recited the prayer to the Azsark, imagining the whole sequence she would need to reach the other side. Sing, step, release behind, sing, step, release.

Anila called the wind, wrapping it into a tight, dense pillar, and stepped onto the piece of air. Another call and she stepped forward, releasing the pillar behind. To her dismay, the pillar where she stood began to drift in the sea wind. Bending her knees to keep her balance, she called a breeze to push. The pillar of air surged across the gap and she stumbled onto the rock.

Trembling, Anila hitched Spe higher, then walked to the final gap. This time she made a full bridge and walked across the smaller chasm. On the far side she walked a short way up the hill and sat on a tuft of grass with profound relief. Holding Spe to her with one arm, she wiped tears of relief from her eyes with her other hand.

"Wake up Spe. I need you."

There was no response.

She looked up at the last few birds soaring along the cliffs, jealous—then thoughtful. Did birds fly by calling the Breath of the Gods? It didn't seem likely. They flew by the strength of the wind. She didn't need Spe's Breath. The wind was the strength. Gritting her teeth, Anila heaved Spe up and stood. She closed her eyes and listened to the sea wind. Its Breath was wilder than Spe's, but when she sang, it bent to her call.

With a gale at her back, she went up the slope to the canyon mouth. The warmth of the Breath was upon her so she laid Spe on a flat rock, took off her woolen coat, and wrapped Spe within. Hefting her sister once more, she used what she'd learned on the rocks below and made steps of air up the faces of the boulders that choked the canyon.

Full dark had come by the time she made it to the upper fall. Shivering, she sat on the sand staring up at the stars in the black sky above the lip of the fall. Her fire was spent. Despair forced her head down.

—◊◊◊—

When the voice came, there was daylight all around, but raising her pounding head seemed too great a task.

"What's your name?" asked an accented voice.

"Spe."

The voice tried it out.

"Like tree," said Spe.

Gentle hands lifted Anila. The rope around her chest hurt, but she was too tired to object.

CHAPTER 5

You May Regret the Choice

HANDS PRESSED TO THE COBBLES, BREEA
listened to the clash of battle rippling through the essence-
fabric that the Temple orb had woven throughout the city. A
powerful Dauthaz was locked in combat with a brother of
the Aska-Wuthos. Breea stood to find Simarn at her right
shoulder and Neprawn at her left. Breea ran for the inn's
stable. Her two protectors kept pace.

Batusha warriors rushed after, but she called over her
shoulder, "Hold the inn!"

At the threshold of the stable, Breea paused to calm

herself. Her power felt wild, slipping free of boundaries and ready to lash out in hot violence. She released her dress and rested both hands over the Tetr medallion. Breathing deep, she thought of the giant forests of home and calmed, though she chose not to bind her power fully.

When she opened the first stall, the mare inside stepped back from her glowing form. Breea reached for the horse with her essence-self and called. The horse blew out a breath and stepped up to her, dipping its head into her hands.

Neprawn stepped in and offered his linked hands as a step. Breea mounted and urged the mare from the stall.

Simarn stood aside with a forlorn look.

Breea considered the girl who had slain the Oregule and saved her life, then said, "Follow me to the Temple. Neprawn, can you?"

"Aye, Master."

Breea set her legs and gripped the horse's mane with one hand. With her other she stroked the animal's neck and said, "Fly, *r'hame!*"

Her power flowed into the horse and it staggered to one side, hooves striking sparks from the stable stones. The mare caught her balance and leapt from the stable, each hoof beating a shower of sparks from the stones.

Neprawn blinked at the sight, then looked at the girl beside him. Simarn's chainmail fell to midthigh, the shorn end of her dress peeking out beneath. Linen pantaloons covered her to the knees, but unlike the master she had no boots, only simple, blood-stained women's shoes. She was shivering. Before she noticed his gaze, he strode to a stall and opened the gate. He knew the stallion within, for it belonged to a powerful noble who had more than once hired Neprawn to guard his person on journeys upcountry. The horse's name was Balor. It eyed him.

"Ho, Balor," said Neprawn.

Balor stepped forward and sniffed Neprawn's offered hands. He reached up to scratch Balor behind the ears where he knew the stallion liked it most. Balor ducked his head and pushed into the scratch, knocking Neprawn off-balance.

Grinning, Neprawn stepped back and whistled for the stable hands he knew were hiding in the back.

When there was no response, he bellowed, "Saddle!"

Four young men and one elder scuttled from the rear. They brought tack and a fine saddle with felted flaps. As they worked, Neprawn stroked the stallion's head, watching Simarn from the corner of his gaze, wondering at the haunted strength of her eyes. The stable hands finished and stepped away with nervous bows. Neprawn mounted.

To Simarn he said, "Fore or rear, lass?"

For the first time he saw indecision in her.

"If you sit before me, you may use the bow at need."

As he'd expected, she approved of that. He reached down for her on the right side of Balor. She stepped forward, still unsure, raising one hand. Neprawn gripped her wrist. She pulled back.

He said, "Take my wrist and hold fast."

When her fingers closed on his massive wrist, he lifted her into the air, then caught her left leg with his free hand and sat her astride in front of him, facing away.

"Oh!" she said.

"I'm going to adjust your seat," said Neprawn. "Don't kill me."

Before she could react, he scooted back in the saddle then pulled her tight against him.

"Grip his mane," he said, guiding her free hand.

Balor tossed his head, not liking the weight and strange balance, but Neprawn held the reins with a firm hand, then urged the horse into a trot.

—⁓—

Close to the battle, Breea found the street packed with army soldiers straining for a look at the duel. Blade-crash echoed from the stone faces of the buildings and the soldiers murmured. Breea slowed her mount to a walk, urging her into the throng. Men turned and gaped at her glowing form. They made a path.

Breea rode into the wide square before the Temple wall. The packed bodies of Yasharn soldiers and hundreds of Aska-Wuthos shaped an open ring fifty strides across. A few priests holding burning tapers ringed the ground, lighting the battle within. More were coming out the gates in the Temple city wall. Up on the wall, gold glinted from Duyazen's sash as he turned from watching Breea's arrival back to the battle.

The eldest Aska-Wuthos brother circled a Dauthaz dressed in black with red trim—a Yasharn general who wielded a long, curved two-handed blade. The Dauthaz looked like a man, but Breea could feel its cold power. The pair closed and Breea's breath caught. The clash of steel on steel sounded like a rock fall of metal stones. Their weapons moved with a speed she'd seen only from Taumea.

The Aska-Wuthos brother saw Breea on the periphery of the ring and broke away. Before the Dauthaz could close, the Aska-Wuthos saluted her with his blade and cried with cheerful deference, "My queen!"

The general whirled to her and cried, "Dauthaz!"

"You are," replied Breea in a woven voice which carried

her words for hundreds of strides in all directions.

She needed a way to reveal the thing's true face. The Temple orb spoke to her through the Tetr emerald, and she reached a hand toward the orb high above. A shaft of golden light lit the plaza, and the Dauthaz's features were unmasked. The crowd of warriors gasped and yelled in disgust and fear. Where a man's eyes should have been there were eight round spider eyes. It looked around.

Breea said, "There are none left to help you, Dauthaz."

To the Aska-Wuthos, Breea said, "Champion. Slay the beast."

The brother leveled his scimitar at the Dauthaz and grinned savagely. The creature hefted its blade and looked at Breea.

She wove a thought to it, mind to mind: *Face me, if you prefer.* Green light sparkled about her hips.

It ran instead, charging the crowd to the left.

Breea's champion drew back his blade and flung it with a grunt. The weapon flipped once and took the Dauthaz in the back, the tip piercing the beast's spine. It screamed as it fell, the cry echoing from the Temple wall. The brother strode up to the struggling creature and ripped the blade free. He swung for the neck, but the battle-dulled edge failed to cut through. The brother raised it twice more, splattering white blood in long arcs as he hacked. He gripped the thing's head by its pale hair and raised it, dripping.

There were no cheers. The crowd seemed stunned. Breea dismounted and walked over. The Aska-Wuthos brother knelt, offering the severed head. She acknowledged the offer, then motioned for him to drop it with the body. He tossed it beside the corpse.

There was a gesture to be made, the same as Ajalay with

the daggers of SaKlu the betrayer. Breea now knew how Aja had burned leather, metal, and gem on the flagstones of Limtir. Releasing all boundaries, Breea sent her will deep into the earth and with care, wove a channel for its essence-heat. Moments later the headless thing burst alight with flame.

The Aska-Wuthos brother stood back. The fire waxed hot, roaring into the night sky. The entire crowd backed away.

The beast's sword remained longest, burning whitely. When it was done, Breea struggled to bind the power, gasping as the essence of the deep earth resisted. By strength of will she slammed the channel closed. The light of the Temple orb faded. Where the Dauthaz had lain, the cobbles glowed orange. Every soldier in sight was on both knees, and some were prostrated on their bellies, hands held out to her. Irritated by such signs of worship, she glanced up at Duyazen. He lifted a hand to touch his forehead and raised the palm to the sky. Breea clenched her jaw and turned away.

In the east a hint of dawn light had begun to fade the stars above the peaked roofs of the city. The battle was done. Breea sighed. She was ravenous, parched, and her back ached and itched. The mare she'd ridden was gone. She resigned herself to a long walk back to the inn and set out.

The host rose before her and parted in a slow rustle of armor and shuffle of feet. Orders were given behind her in a language she had never heard. The Tetr medallion translated—it was an Aska-Wuthos order to form up and march. Boots thundered then fell into step behind her. Did they know where she was headed? Were they prepared to cross the world?

Ahead through the Yasharn throng, Neprawn and

Simarn came riding double on a magnificent stallion. Simarn leveled her assassin's crossbow at any soldier who failed to give way fast enough. Neprawn dismounted and handed the reins to the young woman. He put back-fist to hand with a crack.

The simple salute pleased Breea and she smiled up at him as she walked past.

"Master," he murmured.

Breea started to ask Neprawn to help her mount, but the approaching slap of sandal leather on cobbles stopped her. Simarn raised her bow.

Arin appeared, running up the dark street.

He seemed about to prostrate himself, but Breea stepped close and hooked her arm in his.

"No more," she said. "No one grovels to me."

"Chosen—"

Breea grew stern and whispered into his ear, "Bow to me again, and you won't see the dawn."

Speechless, he offered his arm for her, and they strode down the street arm in arm. The tramp of boots followed them all the way to the Lute and Swan.

Ignoring the essence-rot stench of Dauthaz bodies, Breea ascended the steps to the inn with Arin. The followers in the street behind her could no longer be ignored. At the top of the stairs, she dropped her hand from Arin's arm and turned to face the men who trailed her. It was no shock to see two Aska-Wuthos brothers leading a few hundred of their soldiers in good order. What stopped her heart was the solid mass of black-clad Yasharn soldiers following them. The Aska-Wuthos drew up in perfect array at her feet. A quiet flood of Yasharn rolled in after, and soon soldiers filled every piece of open street. This demanded a response, but she was unsure of the kind. She looked at Arin. His eyes were shining with a fierce and vindicated joy. He saw her gaze and stepped to the edge of the landing. He raised his hands skyward and intoned a rhythmic call. The Yasharn soldiery knelt as one. The Aska-Wuthos remained standing but bowed their heads.

Bay-ope stepped up beside Breea as Arin began to chant.

"My queen," said her friend Bay-ope with a quirk of grin behind his beard.

Breea almost slugged him in the ribs, then sighed and grew serious. She looked north toward the Temple. If she answered the orb's request to save Carsythe, she would have need of any and all who would follow her. Follow, and likely die, in her name. Sadness and desire for home dragged down her shoulders. Home that was no more—taken and corrupted by the Oregule wolf, Lupazg. All her paths led to fury and strife. Duyazen had seen it: *A blade always in your hand, all blood, all ruin, all death.* She closed her eyes against such a fate.

When she opened them, Arin was standing aside, and all eyes were upon her—Batusha, Limtir, Aska-Wuthos, and men of Yash. The belief in their thousand faces rushed through her—a sensation of collective will so strong she realized it could be woven. In their admiration she felt...calm. Her path was set.

Breea stepped forward and wove her voice to carry.

"This day I will march to save a kingdom that fights the same scourge that once corrupted the High Temple. It is an ancient enemy. My ancestors fought them, as did yours. My people know them as the Oregule. I will march the world to hunt their cold evil. All who wish to raise blades against the Oregule and their Dauthaz servants are welcome to draw blades at my side."

The Aska-Wuthos brothers drew their swords, raising them to the sky. Their men followed, and in a great sighing of drawn weapons the Yasharn soldiers made a forest of blades as they whispered her words to their fellows up the street.

"Know this," said Breea, and turned her gaze upon the Yasharn. "The new edicts are no more. I lead by the justice of Limtir. People may worship in what way they wish, and any woman may carry blade or bow and use them at need."

A few of the Yasharn swords wavered.

Rage blew the heat within to white-hot violence. Breea drew a dagger and thrust its point high. Men flinched as a shimmering lance of emerald stabbed the dawn sky.

In a voice that echoed she said, "This is my edict."

The men of the Aska-Wuthos took a knee and brought the guards of their swords to their foreheads. The Yasharn soldiers took this as the way to salute Breea, and imitated them.

Breea cut the essence to the dagger and slammed it back into its sheath. She turned and walked into the inn.

Inside the vaulted and lamplit entry hall, immense wood dining tables had been flipped on their sides to make a maze for attackers. Behind the barriers Batusha bow and ax men stood to attention at her entrance. A nobleman in rich finery with ten liveried attendants stepped into Breea's way and bowed low.

The path between barricades was narrow, and Breea was forced to halt. The hilts of her daggers flashed her irritation.

A servant called, "Lord Dupalo, Baronet of—"

Breea faced the servant and his voice cut off as though he'd taken a dagger in the throat.

The nobleman rose with a flourish, met Breea's gaze, and withered on the spot, sliding from her path with a moaning whimper. Breea swept past him as Batusha warriors looked at one another with impressed grins.

The dining hall was much the same, barricades and waiting warriors. A stage for music and plays was packed with bowmen and armsboys with ready arrows. Murder holes had been hacked through the ceiling. The hall had been transformed into a killing chamber. Breea turned to the right and went up a stair to the colored-glass doors which gave onto the carriage entry hall. On the far side of the room, Dori stood at the base of the stairs to the upper floors. As Breea approached she curtsied low, but would not meet Breea's gaze.

"My lady," said Dori.

"I'm hungry, Dori. And I need a bath."

"Yes, milady," said the servant. She looked past Breea and her eyes widened. Breea turned to see Simarn with her black crossbow and chainmail.

Breea went up the stair. Dori seemed worried, but afraid to speak. Breea was focused on food, a hot soak, and sleep. If it didn't threaten to destroy the city, she didn't care at the moment. At the top floor she halted. Wounded men were arrayed neatly on pads. The air carried the scent of blood and a low murmur from half a dozen Temple priests who stood over the wounded in prayer. Here and there a mote of gold light would appear and fade like summer fireflies.

Dori was waiting to see Breea's reaction. This was what had worried the girl. Breea walked through the pallets and looked into her chambers. Faces turned to her and hands raised in supplication. She walked to them and touched their fingers. Scaukra was there as well, asleep. The floor of the front hall was covered with wounded men. She could feel the weft and warp of curative essence rising from the floor, and some of the pain in her back faded. Through open doors she could see that other rooms were empty of wounded, though Batusha bowmen stood at the windows facing the street. The weaving was only here, where she had summoned the aid of the orb. The door to her sleeping and bath chambers was closed, guarded by two master Batusha warriors.

"Milady," said Dori. "If these rooms no longer meet your desire, Lord Dupalo has prepared all the suites on this floor for your ladyship—"

Breea interrupted her. "Is the bath hot?"

"Yes, milady."

The masters opened the doors for Breea. Simarn and Dori followed her in, but Neprawn and the others remained outside when Dori shook her head at them and closed the doors. Breea sat at a table of food and bit off a hunk of bread, washing it down with wine. Dori pulled a tapestry rope. Moments later servants brought hot dishes and drinks, and Breea gratefully sank her teeth into aromatic meats and gulped hot tea.

Waving Simarn over, Breea said with a full mouth, "Eat."

Together they finished everything on the hot food platter, but before Dori could have another brought, Breea stood and walked into the bath chamber. Steam rose from the water. She unhooked her dagger belt and handed it to Dori, who held it like a holy object, looking for a place suitably noble to place the weapons. Getting out of the dress was more complicated. Dori began to help, but Breea drew a dagger and with a ferocious grin cut the dress off her body.

Breea stepped into the deep pool, hissing at its sting on her tender back.

Dori quietly gathered the dress remains, frowning in thought.

To Simarn Breea said, "Join me?"

The young woman looked unsure, but she set her weapon on a table.

Breea said, "Disarm it."

Simarn removed the bolt and carefully released the string. She started to shrug off the chainmail, bending forward, but Breea said, "Wait. Chainmail eats hair. Kneel."

Breea stepped out of the water and dried her hands on a robe. She tucked Simarn's hair into her blouse. Gripping the mail at the shoulders, Breea hefted it up. Simarn ducked out of it, and Breea draped the armor across the seat of a chair. Simarn sighed and gripped her aching shoulders. She looked exhausted. Dori helped her out of blouses, pantaloons and shoes, then Breea helped her into the bath, worried by how cold the girl's skin felt. Simarn hissed like Breea at the heat of the water, then they both settled in like cats in sunshine.

They soaked in silence for a while. When Simarn sniffed, Breea raised her head and saw tears running down the girl's face. Simarn's dismay seemed laced with fear.

Breea said, "What frightens you?"

Simarn blinked and two more tears rolled down her face. Breea moved closer to her, waiting, but Simarn stared into the water and would not speak.

Disappointed, Breea wet her hair, then asked Dori for soap. When her hair was lathered, she offered the bar to Simarn. When they were done with the bath, they sat in soft robes before a roaring fire, staring into the flames. Breea nodded off.

When she woke, Dori was placing more wood on the fire.

"Where is Simarn?" said Breea.

"Asleep," said Dori.

"Did she speak?"

"No, milady."

Breea sat up and watched the flames spread to the new wood.

"She has traveled from slavery to war in a day. Is there a cure for a soul's hardship?"

After a pause, Dori said, "Peace, milady."

Breea said, "You speak well."

Dori blushed at the praise, then said, "Milady?"

Breea waited.

"War is not her fear. She is like you in war."

Like me in war, thought Breea. What in truth did that mean? She held her hands to the warmth of the fire and looked at them. Her fingers were long and lean, and possibly a little delicate in appearance. By prophecy they were fingers that would hold a weapon until the end of her days. The thought did not frighten her. Oregule frightened her. Losing friends frightened her. She thought back to the battle at the High Temple and the moment that Simarn's crossbow bolt had taken the Oregule through one spider-eye. Breea marveled at the self-possession it must have taken for a farm girl to stand before the terror of the white beast and strike it down. There had been elite Tomeguard in Limtir with less strength of will.

Breea said, "What then? What does she fear?"

"It is not my place, milady."

"Of course it is," said Breea. "You are my friend. One of few in this city. The world is either trying to put a blade through my heart or is kneeling before me. I don't know which I trust less. So please talk to me."

Dori put the last sticks of wood on the fire, then said in a rush, "Milady, Simarn fears you will leave her behind."

It fit. Breea had declared that she was leaving to journey back across the world. What must that mean for Simarn?

"If she wishes to come with me, she may."

Dori nodded, and Breea saw tears building in her eyes.

Touched, Breea added, "You may also."

A sob burst from Dori and she fled.

Breea held the impulse to call after her. Instead she lay back on the couch and drew out the Tetr emerald. She held it to the firelight and watched the dance of color through the gem.

To herself she said, "Though you may regret the choice."

CHAPTER 6

Apples for Da

ANILA WAS WARM BENEATH HEAVY BLANKETS, AND the air smelled of sage and onions. Spe giggled somewhere near, and Anila sighed in peace. Then she remembered. She thrashed free of the blankets. She was in some kind of stone chamber with doors leading to light on one side and dark on the other. A woman in traditional Yasharn dress squatted in front of a glowing hearth with Spe hanging on her back, arms around her neck, legs kicking. They both turned to look at Anila. The woman's hair was the color of ripe wheat grass, and though her eyes were soft, her face was drawn in the lines of a woman who had seen much. Spe let go and slid to the sandy floor, then dashed to Anila, smacking into her with a hug.

A man walked in with a bow. Anila dropped protective hands over Spe and called the biggest gust she could muster from nothing. The man sailed back through the doorway in a cloud of dust and sand.

"Wait!" cried the woman in accented Yasharn.

Spe was beating at her, shouting for her to stop, but Anila knew the man. Spe didn't understand. He was the one from the cliff. He and the woman had to be from the Temple, come to take them to the scaffold and the flayer's knife for being Dauthaz. Sand lifted from the floor as she whispered the Azsark Prayer.

The woman stepped back, and called, "Taumea?"

"Never felt a girl hit so hard," came the reply in that strange accent. "Excepting Breea."

Anila looked for escape, but there was only the dark doorway away from where the man had vanished.

The woman said, "Spe tells me your name is Anila. We wish to help you."

Spe tried to pull away, but Anila held on to her, saying, "Da is waiting for the Azsark's bounty, Spe."

Spe froze—then thrashed free of Anila's grip and dashed outside Anila's whirl of air.

Betrayed, Anila stared at her little sister.

Spe shook her head.

Anila begged, "Spe, come away. Da is waiting."

Spe's face was serious. "Some things are worse than Da."

"Them!" said Anila, flinging a hand at the woman and the hidden man.

Spe didn't answer. Anila let the circling wind calm. The sand around her fell to the ground.

"Ma wants us home," she said. "We have to go back. We must."

Spe looked torn.

The woman said, "You may go as you wish. May Opalah bless your path."

Anila blinked. Had the woman invoked the blessing of a Dauthaz god? None from the Temple would give such a blessing.

The woman turned to the fire and bent to stir the pot there.

Spe looked at the lady, then walked up to Anila. Anila opened her hand and Spe gripped it.

"If you're hungry," said the woman, "you might want something for the journey home."

Anila felt close to tears. They were so late Da was going to take the switch to them like never before, and what could she say—that a man with claws in his feet had come for them? And how did they escape? To Da the Breath of the Gods was Dauthaz. And what of the Azsark's bounty? How could they fill the baskets with these strangers near? Atop all, hunger was an ache so strong that it made her weak inside.

"It's really good," said Spe. "Better than Ma's."

"Here," said the woman. She tipped the pot into a clay dish she held with a cloth. "Spe, will you bring this to your sister?"

Spe dashed over, then carefully took the bowl with the cloth. The woman dropped a hunk of biscuit and a wooden spoon into it, and Spe brought it to Anila. The luscious smell sent quivers through Anila's body, and she gave up, sitting in defeat.

As she ate, the woman filled another bowl and walked it through the door to the light.

Spe leaned over to look where she'd gone, and said with importance, "He's on watch."

The stew was full of meat, onion, and desert yams. It was the best thing Anila had ever tasted other than Azsark apple. She licked the bowl and stood. A thanks was required now. She took Spe's hand and walked into the next room, where the man and woman stood on either side of a square opening in the wall that looked out over the Azsark square from a high vantage. Sight of the tree filled her with longing and dread—longing for the safety and warmth it gave, and dread for every future she had so far imagined.

The woman said, "I'm Valiena."

Anila bowed her head. "Anila Hox. Thank you for the bounty gift."

Valiena smiled at her and said, "There's more."

Anila glanced at the man, but he was staring out the window as he ate.

"We must—" Anila choked as the smell of carrion filled her senses. She stared in horror as both man and woman swept up bows with set arrows, and drew them right at her. The strings snapped and arrows whipped past, making solid impacts in the room behind.

Blade out, the lord charged past Anila. She turned as he passed, watching him throw a dagger at the man-thing striding in from the shadowed corridors beyond. The blade struck something in the center of the beast's chest with a sharp clink. It staggered from the blow in a way the arrows protruding from its chest had failed to elicit.

The lord's sword swept around in both hands in a

crosswise slash that made the air sing. The man-beast parried the blow with its sword with such force that the lord's blade bounced back, quivering. Unbalanced, the lord leapt back, but the man-beast followed with a slash that tore at the lord's armor, scattering scales. An arrow whipped past and took the beast in the knee. Its return stroke missed as its leg gave way.

Anila pulled Spe back and out of the way, called a wind, then leaned around the doorway to see the fight.

In the hearth room, the lord Taumea stood blocking a door leading back into the cliff, and she knew the depth of her mistake. He was protecting them! She whispered a prayer to the Azsark to keep him safe.

Taumea heard her voice as he wove his blade in a graceful pattern. The creature snarled and imitated Taumea's pattern. Taumea shifted his weight and grip, and the beast responded with the correct counterstance, a stance known only to the Tomeguard of Limtir. It attacked with a Tomeguard lunge, which Taumea parried and counterslashed, opening the flesh of its forearm. It roared and hacked at him.

Taumea's blade caught the sword and directed it aside. The beast attacked again, a mighty overhead blow that cut a gash in the stone of the ceiling. Again Taumea's blade was there, tapping it aside, putting the weapon where he wanted. The thing bared fangs and took its own sword in two hands and struck. Taumea's blade met every stroke, sending the enemy's weapon off target each time—a singing whirl of steel that the beast could not beat down. Its power was terrible, but Taumea had trained with its match for strength, the strongest man Taumea had ever known, Bay-ope Gardasim. Taumea's defense was a style honed to meet any physical power, known only to himself, Bay-ope, and Breea.

Every few strikes Taumea riposted, wounding the creature again and again. Pale blood drooled and splattered from its every move, and the scent of cooked flesh filled the chamber. It came on without pause, but Taumea knew its every move. He'd trained this man. Somehow this had been a man of the Tomeguard.

The thing came on, slashing wildly. Smoke began to curl up out of its clothing around the neck, and a pink glow shone through the clothing on its chest. It never seemed to tire, though half its blood slicked the floor. Taumea's breathing was smooth and deep. Having taken measure of the thing's skill, his blade flashed in patterns the creature could not anticipate, leading it to mistakes and further wounds. From behind, Valiena put the rest of their arrows into its legs, yet it remained standing. The stench of cooking carrion grew, burning Taumea's eyes. The beast lost all form and its attacks doubled in power. Taumea's face darkened to a deep red with the effort it took to stand before the frenzy. Strike by strike he was forced back through the doorway and into the next room.

Valiena cried, "Help him!"

A breeze puffed past him, and the beast found its legs swept back by a blast of air. It fell, arms out. As they hit the floor, Taumea's sword swept down and split the beast's skull from the back. Taumea yanked his blade free, and with a single side-swing beheaded the thing. The body went still, pink light streamed out from its chest as smoke curled up around. With a sizzling sound, the body sagged to the ground and lay still, though its limbs twitched as though to continue the fight.

Taumea was breathing like an overworked bellows, and he swayed. He planted the tip of his sword on the floor, and leaned on the hilt with both hands. Valiena rushed to him and wrapped his left arm around her shoulders. He used the sword like a crutch as she helped him to the wall by the window where he sagged to the sandy floor.

Valiena brought him a wineskin from the room beyond. Taumea took it and dropped it in his lap, then reached out and hooked a finger in the neck of her blouse and drew her down into a kiss. She took his head in her hands and kissed him hard. After, she rose with a flushed face and sparkling eyes. He drained the wineskin and heaved a great sigh, staring at the skull of the creature that had once been a man he knew. What its presence said of Limtir he pushed from his mind.

Looking over at the girls where they remained cowering beneath the window, he said, "Well struck."

Anila and Spe uncurled, but remained where they were.

Valiena brought him the entire pot of stew, setting it on a blanket in his lap, then vanished into the next room.

When he was done he set the bowl aside and rose. In the light of the window he examined his blunted blade with a grimace, then went to inspect the beast's weapon. Valiena approached from the other side, wary of the body.

"Its blade is Limtir forged of Rana steel," he said.

"Limtir?" asked Valiena.

Taumea used the tip of his sword to turn the beast's face upward. The features were distorted and slashed, but he could see the man it had been.

"Ead," he said. "Fourth rank. Kerri's son."

Anila sat straight. Now she understood. Some at least.

"What is it?" whispered Spe.

Anila bent to her, and said, "That's a Dauthaz from Limtir."

Taumea turned on them. Both shrank under the dire calm of his gaze.

"No, child," he said. "We are of Limtir. This is not."

Anila didn't understand. The village priest said Limtirians studied dark magic, traveling the world to spread their poison. The creature certainly seemed a match to that.

Taumea went to a knee beside the body, and said, "We fought and killed one like it last summer."

He picked up the beast's blade and slid it under the headless thing's chest and lifted, rolling it over. The cloth of its shirt was burned away around the center of its rib cage. Embedded in the charred breastbone was a small ruby orb.

Taumea drew a dagger to dig it out, but Valiena said, "Don't."

Taumea tapped the orb with the blade tip. It made a musical clink. "Not like the white wolf," he said. "Crystal. The white one had a medallion. Cold, not hot. Breea should see this." He turned to Valiena and said, "Are we ready to move?"

Valiena glared at him and he watched her decide not to argue. To the girls she said, "Come away," and motioned for them to walk around Taumea and the corpse. He waited until they were out of sight before digging out the orb.

Valiena guided them to a side room, where blocks from the ceiling lay amid piles of drifted sand. She lifted Spe onto a stone then sat facing her. Anila settled next to Spe.

"Have you seen anything like that ever before?" asked Valiena.

They both shook their heads.

"I have," said Valiena. "Much worse, and the only person who could kill it is like you."

The girls didn't answer, but Spe touched her chest with

a frown of remembered pain.

Valiena asked, "Are there more like you?"

"No," said Anila.

"Ma can Breathe," said Spe.

"Spe!" said Anila, sharp.

Valiena nodded to herself. The girls' power was a secret. She asked them, "Why are you in these ruins?"

They didn't answer.

She asked, "Is it for the Azsark?"

They both looked up with frightened eyes. Another secret. She had heard Anila mention it before but wasn't sure what it was. She suspected it had something to do with the big baskets they had brought and the giant apple tree in the square.

"You are expected at home?"

Their fear was different this time—personal, and dreaded.

Valiena said, "Can we help?"

Anila didn't know what to do. These people were scary and powerful, like priests or lords, but they seemed kind too, yet claimed to be from Limtir. It didn't make sense, but protecting the Azsark was the duty of the female line. Ma had said it over and over.

Taking a chance, Anila asked, "Why are you here?"

"We are hiding," said Valiena. "Waiting for the friend I told you about."

Spe asked, "The Haunted Lands don't make you scared?"

Valiena smiled. "No. All I dream about here is my friend. Other than that, I find it peaceful. The yams in the dunes are so sweet. Three kinds of sage too."

Anila and Spe shared a look. Ma always said that only

the people of her line could stay in the Haunted Lands.

"Why are you hiding?" asked Anila.

"From the Temple most of all," said Valiena. Her eyes were stern and the look reminded Anila of Ma.

"Can you Breathe?" asked Spe.

Valiena worked out what was being asked, and said, "No, but my friend can. She calls it weaving. I think she would like you both very much."

Spe grinned shyly and swung her legs.

Anila said, "We're here to collect the Azsark's bounty for Da. He sells them."

"Bounty?" said Valiena.

"Apples," said Anila.

"Best ever," said Spe.

Valiena frowned. The tree was bare. That implied stored apples.

Valiena asked, "Will you stay here for a moment?"

Anila nodded.

Valiena walked in the next room and shook her head in disbelief. Apples for Da. Two girls like Breea picking apples in a Legend Time ruin. Hunted as Breea had been. It felt prophetic. Taumea stood over the corpse and was using a rag to clean blood from an arrow pulled from the body.

"They're here to gather apples."

Taumea didn't comment.

Staring at the tree in the courtyard, Valiena said, "What if another like this comes for them?"

Taumea dropped the arrow into his quiver and pulled another from the thing's slack leg. He shook the arrow tip to dislodge a clot of pale blood, then began wiping it down.

"Their family is waiting for them to return," she said.

Taumea glanced at her, put the arrow in his quiver, and

pulled another.

Valiena walked to the window, and said, "Who would send two girls into the Haunted Lands for apples?"

Taumea joined her at the window, still rubbing an arrow. "Will their family come for them?"

"No," said Valiena. "That I do not think they will do. Something in the family is without light." She looked back toward the room with the girls, and said, "They're frightened to go home, but feel they must. I don't think they'll tell anyone about us. Their weaving is a secret."

"Would get them flayed," said Taumea.

Valiena nodded and felt a quiver of unease ripple through her.

Taumea slid the arrow into his quiver and looked at his wife. "We do not know when Breea will return. You and I can survive here for as long as necessary, but those girls cannot. There's a mother and father in the village looking to their arrival with these apples. If they fail to return, an outcry will be made. This city will not protect us if the Temple catches our trail here."

Valiena folded her arms. He was being kind not to speak directly of the Temple assassins that had been hunting them since the summer with Breea.

"Let them go," he said. "They have ways of protecting themselves."

Valiena said, "What of a return to Limtir?"

"With them?"

She shrugged.

Taumea looked at the body of Ead. "Limtir is no longer our path."

Valiena unfolded her arms and laid her hand on his armor. "Our path is to help them, Taumea. I feel it."

He gazed out at the Azsark, then said, "Breea would approve."

Valiena looked at him. He was serious. She hugged him.

In the back room, Anila let the listening tube dissipate. She wondered what Ma would say about these people. Who was their friend who had the Breath of the Gods?

Spe said, "Are we going home now?"

"Yes," said Anila. "We gather the Azsark's bounty and go home by night."

Spe looked as though she wasn't sure if she liked the idea. Anila felt the same, but the Limtirians spoke true. Someone would come looking for them. Yet would Da even tell? And if he did, would anyone come? They were in the Haunted Lands. There were stories…

She wondered what it would be like not to be found, then quickly discarded the idea as guilt washed over her. The whole family was relying on them. Ma. Da mostly. He kept all the coin earned by selling the apples.

"We need a story for Da," she said. "A good one."

"I could get hurt," offered Spe.

"I did," said Anila, touching the dried blood matting her hair beneath her blood-stiff scarf. "It made me swoon. You stayed with me through the cold night."

"I kept you warm!" said Spe. "And scared away the desert wolves."

"Good. But simple stories are best. I wouldn't say anything about wolves."

Spe blushed, then asked, "Can we tell Ma about…" She didn't have words to express all that had happened.

"We'll see."

"The lady and the lord know," said Spe. "He killed the smelly man. We helped."

Anila knew what Spe was saying. The Limtirians were not like anyone Anila had ever met. They had no fear of the Breath. No fear of anything. She felt drawn to them, but the memory of the woman being flayed at Iplock that Ma had made them watch was a terror worse than the dead thing in the other room. Ma's words were like her grip—iron. *Tell no one who you are. The knife is what awaits a child who shows the Breath.*

"Are we going to show them the larder?" said Spe.

Anila considered, then nodded.

Spe grinned and scooted off the stone block. She bounced on her toes a few times, ready to go.

Envious of her little sister's perpetual happiness, Anila took her hand and walked into the room with Valiena and Taumea.

They didn't look much like the villagers whose clothing they wore. She'd never met a lord or lady, but she was sure that's what they were. Both had bows in hand. Two big bundles with rope straps lay on the floor.

"We need our baskets," said Anila.

To avoid the dark tunnels that the beast had used, Taumea led everyone up to the plateau and down another way to the square. It made Anila nervous to see how watchful the Limtirians were.

After crossing the square, she rushed up the steps toward the Azsark, then back down to impatiently help Spe. At the top they went to their knees by the trunk and laid their hands on its rough bark. Warmth flowed up their arms and into their chests, easing all fears. Both girls relaxed, bowing their heads.

At the base of the hill, Taumea and Valiena exchanged a look, then followed the girls up the hill.

The girls' baskets lay where they had been dropped. Taumea and Valiena put their bundles down and sat on a root of the Azsark. The midday sun held little heat and the air was still and cold. Valiena shifted so that her side was touching Taumea.

Anila and Spe sat back on their heels together. Anila rose and gathered her basket and the cloth she'd used as a shawl. Her face was haunted.

Valiena rose. "All is well?"

Anila set her basket strap over her forehead and walked down the slope without answering. Valiena went to Spe, laying a hand on her headscarf.

Spe looked up with tears brimming. "It said good-bye."

A sense of providence rushed over Valiena. She picked up Spe and set the child on her hip, lifting Spe's basket with the other hand. Taumea hefted both their bundles, picked up their bows, and walked with Valiena down the hill.

They followed Anila to the western side of the square, up wide steps and through the empty door of a once grand building. Inside they walked a maze of rooms until they found a sand-filled courtyard open to the sky. Anila climbed the soft sand to a second-story window.

Valiena and Taumea followed her up, then down a dark hall beyond to where Anila waited at the top of a spiral stair of pale stone. Anila knelt on the first step and lifted an oil lantern onto the landing. She used flint and steel to light a bit of tinder which she used to catch the wick of a lamp. Spe was getting heavy, but with her arms clamped around Valiena's neck, showed no desire to walk on her own. With care, Valiena followed Anila down the steps.

At the bottom a metal door stood ajar. The room beyond was thirty strides across. Rows of barrels and orderly piles of grain sacks covered more than half the floor. Shelves lined the walls, filled with a few hundred glass bottles and at least a thousand crockery jars. From the ceiling hung clusters of desert yams, row upon row. The air smelled of earth, grain, spice, and vinegar. In the center of the room was a round wellhead, covered. Above it hung a geared crank with bucket. Anila went to the right, where a wooden door stood shut. She pulled, and it swung open on oiled hinges. In the room beyond, shelves were lined with apples the size of her head. Spe wiggled to be let down, then took her basket from Valiena's other hand.

Valiena watched as the girls dumped out the hay and cloth, then began making nests of hay lined with the cloth, setting apples within with careful reverence. The scent of the room drew her in and she stood breathing, almost dizzy with the smell of apple. One thing on the shelves that wasn't an apple was a rectangle of folded wax paper. Around it in an arc were bunches of wildflowers, their stems braided together. Valiena stepped closer and could smell their scent, still fresh.

Taumea stepped in, and paused to look around. In his hand was a wax-sealed jar. Symbols were cut into the wax. He tilted it to the lantern light. Valiena looked, and covered her mouth with a hand. The symbols were written in Abitalen, the language of the Abital Prophecies that named Breea a warrior and heralded the end of all. They backed out, moving away from the apple room.

"Are they all marked so?" whispered Valiena.

"All that I checked. How old do you reckon the food in this larder?"

"A few seasons at most. The yams haven't shriveled. The grain smells good. No mold, no vermin. Are you saying someone is alive who knows Abitalen other than Breea and Ajalay?"

Taumea checked that the girls were still occupied, and said, "They were Alach weavers, the Abital."

"Yes, some of the last and most powerful, to hear Breea speak of them."

Taumea said, "Either they live yet, or their works remain."

"Opalah bless," breathed Valiena. "An Abital city. Breea will be so excited."

Taumea was looking at her. She didn't understand. His eyes flickered to the girls. Valiena gasped a cry and slapped a hand over her mouth.

Anila looked up, saw the jar in Taumea's hand, and ran out of the apple room.

"No, you mustn't. It is sacred. Please, I beg you, place it back. Please?"

"Forgive me," said Taumea, and returned the jar to the shelf.

"May the tree bless," said Anila to the room. She glanced at the Limtirians and went back to packing her basket.

Valiena felt the blood draining from her face like a cool wave pouring down her head. Taumea's hands steadied her as the room began to sway, though her eyes stayed fixed on the two girls. Two Abital weavers.

CHAPTER 7

A Warrior Arms Herself

THE TETR MEDALLION WHISPERED TO BREEA OF things that could be done with fire. She sat up and checked that she was alone. Simarn was asleep and Dori out of the chamber. With the emerald in one hand, she calmed her mind, weaving boundaries of stillness. Thus protected, she reached out with woven senses and connected her inner heat to that of the burning wood. Warmth flowed in both directions and flames roared in the hearth. She jumped at the searing sensation of the flame's heat rushing through her. Clenching her fist around the medallion, she tightened the weave to reduce the flow. Making a warp of her intent into a bridge, she called to the hearth fire. A whirl of flame flowed out to her and spun about her arm. A door latch clicked. Breea slammed down on her power. A twisting wreath of smoke rose from where the flames had been.

Dori entered and frowned at the scent of smoke. She walked up to the hearth and poked at the fire with an iron tong, arranging what remained of the logs, clearly puzzled by how low the fire had burned. Breea unclenched her hand from the medallion, grinning at what she'd accomplished. She longed to share it with Dori, but restrained herself.

Dori curtsied to Breea, and said, "Milady, there are many who seek your counsel. In the parlor."

Breea grew grim. She stood and looked at the white dress.

Dori hesitated, then said, "Milady, there are new things in the wardrobe. Pants even, for milady. Near to a skirt in shape, fine wool with shimmer-cloth lining."

After a moment of reflection Breea said, "Bring the pants." A dress was what the Yasharn expected, but she was not Yasharn.

Pleased, Dori said, "Yes, milady."

The pant-skirts were beautiful and ingenious. Breea gave Dori a quick hug of thanks and chose one of finely brocaded wool that fell to the ankles of her boots. Over two layers of soft white undershirts, she donned a white blouse of generous cut that gave her freedom of motion.

Once dressed, Breea stretched and squatted to test the range of motion for combat. Pleased with the result, she allowed Dori to brush her hair. The sensation reminded her of Valiena. Worry for her friends hit hard. Breea stood abruptly, then stepped toward her daggers on a side table.

Dori ran ahead, saying, "Permit me, milady."

Breea allowed Dori to retrieve the weapons belt, but took it from Dori's hands and belted it on herself.

Dori looked disappointed.

Breea said, "Thank you, Dori."

Dori mumbled, "Milady."

"Dori," said Breea. She waited for the girl to look up. "If I must kill, then it will be with blades that I take up with my own hand. A warrior arms herself." It was what Bay-ope had taught her many years ago.

A side door opened and Simarn appeared. She had not been sleeping, but dressing. Her hair was braided and bound into a knot at the nape of her neck. Over her chainmail shirt was belted a long-sleeved tunic of thick rusty wool that had marks upon it made by armor. On the belt was sheathed a dagger with unadorned hilt. Breea wondered who was arming her. A new dress showed a few inches below the tunic and mail, shorn below the knee. Below this she had wrapped furs around her legs. On top of the fur she had strapped on Batusha leg armor. She held the assassin's crossbow with both hands, and at her hip was hooked the black leather box of poison bolts.

The young woman was dressed to travel the warrior's road. Despite being Alach, Breea knew enough from Bay-ope and Taumea to understand that she herself had only begun on that path. If this was Simarn's choice, then she deserved to know what that decision would mean. Breea released boundaries on her power and, more deeply, she let loose her emotion, letting them flow together within—letting Simarn see unspoken the cost in heart's-blood that Simarn would have to bear if she took up arms on Breea's journey. Simarn tried to hold the gaze, but the intensity of

Breea's eyes was too much.

Before Breea could turn, Simarn hooked her bow to her belt and gave reply by slapping the back of her fist into her to palm in the Batusha style. Holding the guild salute, Simarn looked up and met Breea's eyes with a wild fervor all her own.

Breea's dagger's sparked as pleased warmth spread through her, for in that gaze she saw herself—Simarn was indeed like her, not in a love of war, but in the reasons one went to war. She gave Simarn a nod, acknowledging the pledge. Grateful tears welled in Simarn's eyes and she looked down.

Without binding her power, Breea walked to the door to the parlor and waited for Dori to rush over to open the double portal. Breea strode out to meet the assembled crowd.

Below the hearing of all but Breea, Dori whispered to Simarn, "She is become queen."

The soft click of Simarn arming her crossbow made Breea grin. Daylight from tall windows illuminated lords, barons, warriors, priests, and army generals. They fell silent at her entry and tried to interpret what her expression meant. Breea found that it did not matter to her what conclusions they drew. The truth was that she no longer cared what these men did. They could follow or hang themselves. She had a path and friends to walk it with her. She felt reckless and free, like standing on the cliff edge above Jewel Lake before leaping.

She swept her gaze across their faces—a panoply of cold, curious, worried, worshipful, and incensed men. Where her gaze lingered, men blanched or stepped back. Having made sufficient entrance, Breea bound her power.

A man stepped out. He was a tall priest-general of the

Temple, imposing in a uniform of black edged in gold. Contempt twitched his lips, and Breea restrained the urge to cut him down. His first words were cut off as a leader of the Aska-Wuthos shouldered past in gore-splattered armor. The brother took a knee before Breea. His siblings strode up and knelt in turn. The Yasharn general held his tongue, for in Yash it was a sacrilege to interrupt another man's obeisance.

Affection for the Aska-Wuthos softened Breea's heart. The brothers were making sure that the first act of this meet was a gesture of fealty.

The medallion whispered to her, and she said in their native tongue, "Brothers, rise."

As they stood, their blue-scaled armor shifted with a soft hiss. She would need such men to free Carsythe, yet Breea found herself with no words. How do you ask men if they will die for you? Their beautiful armor was splattered with blood, both pale and red. Perhaps like Simarn, these men had already answered that question.

Taking a chance, she said in their language, "Make ready to travel."

"Yea!" they said in unison.

Breea wanted to hug them. They reminded her of the finest of the Tomeguard back home. Suppressing the surge of sadness at the thought of lost Limtir, she gestured for them to stand aside. The brothers stepped back into deep bows, and the eldest said in Yasharn, "My queen." Holding the bow, the younger two checked each other from the corners of their eyes. Neither found objection and they imitated their brother. "My queen."

Did Duyazen know what strength he had given to her through these men? If he did, then the high priest was a true ally. While the Aska-Wuthos took positions flanking the

Batusha masters at the doors behind Breea, she struggled to hold the boundaries on her power, for the Yasharn general was staring at Simarn with unguarded loathing. The injustice to so brave a girl was too much, and essence-heat expanded in a blast, shredding Breea's boundaries. Piercing light ignited in her daggers and her skin shimmered into pale radiance. The Yasharn general turned to her in shock.

His face worked.

The Batusha priest Arin stepped up, taking a breath, but Breea silenced him with a hand.

The general mastered himself and stood straight before her, staring past the top of her head.

"I request a private audience with your...self," he said.

After a moment Breea gave a curt nod. Here was not the time to crush this man. Arin directed the general away. Breea closed her eyes and executed a boundary, cooling the fire. When she opened them, the glow was gone from her skin.

No one in the room dared to move.

"This day," she said, "I march for Carsythe."

Confusion and relief were the main reactions of the crowd. A few looked at her with reverence.

For those who might aid her, she said, "All who wish to cross blades with true Dauthaz and who can travel at speed will be welcome."

There was a murmur of assent from some and general talk she couldn't sort. She turned to another Batusha priest whose name she did not know, and said, "Take down the names and complement strength of all who will join." She thought a bit more, and turned to the Aska-Wuthos. "We will need a place of muster."

"It shall be done, my queen," said the eldest.

A sudden desire to be rid of the city swept Breea, but

instead of walking away, she turned back to the assembled leaders. Ajalay would never forgive her if she abandoned this opportunity to wield her sudden influence.

"What do you seek?" she asked.

They shoved forward, speaking at once. Batusha warriors behind Breea took a step forward and the crowd shrank back. This strength of desire to talk to her made her curious. What could these men want of a girl of Limtir who had destroyed their Temple? She nodded to the closest, a wealthy man by his dress and ornament, yet without noble hauteur. *A grain merchant*, whispered the medallion, though how it could tell she could not see.

He bowed with a nervous flourish. "Chosen One. Should your holy army require any volume of grain, I humbly beg you take mine."

Breea frowned. It seemed beyond reason that in two days that she could go from a hunted woman to a queen receiving gifts. Yes, her skin did glow when she was angry, and the high priest had declared her Chosen of the One, but there was something more here. The merchant seemed sincere, but kept his eyes low, looking at the rug in front of her dress.

"Why?" asked Breea.

The man's shoulders tightened beneath his finery. Breea knew the power of a long stare—having endured many from Ajalay—and said nothing, waiting.

The merchant twisted in discomfort, started to look up, but when his eyes reached the level of her gently sparkling daggers, he jerked his gaze back down.

Finally he said, "The wind. I saw it in the wind."

"Saw what?"

"Your holy journey. The soldiers. Eating porridge of my grain."

Breea asked in a softer tone, "In a vision?"

"Yes, Chosen One."

Breea looked at the assembled crowd. Very few of the faces now held disdain or disbelief. One young nobleman was staring right through her with haunted eyes.

Breea said to him, "And you?"

He blinked when another nudged him, and he stuttered, "T-take them!"

Breea said, "They would be?"

"Arms. Arrow and spear, finest in the city. I serve the Temple, Chosen One. I supply the guard, the Holy Temple's finest, I mean to say. Take all that I have. Chosen." His face was red with shame.

Others had similar feelings or were trying to hide them. Breea stepped forward and put a hand on the shoulder of the grain merchant. She felt no weaving within him. They were not compelled by warp of essence. What had the Temple orb done to these men? Perhaps it did not matter. She needed all they would give.

"I accept," said, Breea. "How many wish to make offering to save Carsythe?"

More than half the men in the room bowed. Breea turned to find Arin ready with his brethren. Priests in flowing red robes gathered those making offerings into another room.

To the remaining, Breea said, "What of you?"

Their needs varied. Those seeking compensation for burned homes and similar judgments she sent to High Priest Duyazen. Others simply asked her blessing, which she gave in words only. As the room cleared, she noticed a gray-bearded fellow hanging back. He was dressed in dark, layered clothing of fine weave and elegant cut. He watched her with sad, intelligent eyes.

After the others were gone, he stepped up with noble deference and bowed in the Limtir style.

In cultured tones he said, "Tetr-Sanis, my honor in Service."

Breea didn't like him calling her Tetr, but it was a reasonable mistake given the emerald Tetr's medallion shining on the front of her white dress.

She asked him, "Are you a scholar?"

"Not of Limtir, though I had the honor to study at the great library for a time in my youth."

"What need have you?" asked Breea.

The old man said with calm conviction, "You are a woman of honor."

Breea stood straighter under his regard.

He said, "I seek your counsel."

"My knowledge is yours," said Breea. "Though Ajalay's may better serve you. She is here. We will find her."

"By your grace," said the man, "it is you whom I seek."

His eyes held hers for just long enough to communicate that he wished to speak in private.

"Dori?" said Breea.

The servant came at a brisk, dignified pace—expression flat, eyes held slightly downward. Breea was impressed by the girl's "noble servant" demeanor and spoke to her with formal kindness. "We require a room for discussion."

"Milady," said Dori with a perfect curtsy.

As Breea and the noble followed the girl, Breea gave small nods to Neprawn and Simarn. The pair fell into step a few paces behind. Dori led them to a small sitting room with only one door and a single tall window.

Before Dori closed the door, Breea nodded to them.

Dori curtsied, and Neprawn struck back-fist to palm.

The noble scholar waited for Breea to sit before taking a seat. He looked out the window before speaking, and Breea followed his gaze. She imagined that the window would have once had a view of the spires of the Temple set against the sky.

"I am Lord Iltish Keharna," said the noble. "The lineage of my family in this city reaches to the Legend Time." He looked at Breea, gauging her reaction.

Breea's heart began to pound. She sensed no essence-power in him, but she perceived a new depth behind his sad eyes. The term Legend Time was a word of Limtir. What did he know of the Legend Time that he wished to speak of in private? She leaned forward.

Her reaction seemed to please Iltish and the sadness receded in his gaze.

"Tetr, I must admit to an act of thievery."

Breea was unsure how to respond.

He continued. "My time at great Limtir was one of duplicitous purpose."

"How so?" said Breea.

"I stole knowledge of Limtir."

Breea sat back. "Reading and study are not theft," she said.

Iltish tilted his head to one side, half nod and half denial. "It is when you read as I do."

"A copyist?" said Breea.

He nodded. "What I see I can write as the man who penned it."

"Why?" said Breea. "What did you copy?"

"Things my family thought significant. Knowledge of shipbuilding and navigation, some of warfare, others of rulership, and much of history. We prosper through all times because we know all times. In trade our ships are the fastest, our navigation beyond understanding of even the best captains of our rivals. In war we advise the victor, and he is victor because we advise him. Thus it has been for centuries."

Breea knew she was sitting with the head of one of the ruling families of the capital, but something he'd said seemed strange. "Why do you say your family thought Limtir knowledge was significant? You don't agree?"

Iltish looked out the window again as though missing what was no longer there.

"Our family pride," he said, "our distinction, is our sight into the changing cycles of history before they manifest." He paused.

Breea waited.

His eyes were bitter. "Yet we did not foresee the new edicts. We did not foresee the Oregule and their power."

"They are newly come to the world," said Breea impressed that he knew their true name.

"No," said Iltish. "They are old. Older than anything known, and their cycle returns. We should have seen it. I should have seen."

Breea sensed that Iltish was getting to what he truly wanted to say.

"We keep a library of our own," he said. "I think you may wish to see it."

"What did you not see, Lord Keharna?"

His nostrils flared and he clenched his jaw on sadness and rage.

"Prophecy," he said. "I did not foresee you."

Now Breea looked out at the vanished Temple.

"When a girl child is born," she quoted, "and the

Yasharn priest is asked in his High Temple for a Calling for the child, and he gives the cry, 'A warrior is born!' men will know that the first Bane has entered the world."

Iltish finished, "All known will end."

When Breea turned from the window, her power was upon her—dagger hilts sparkling, and her eyes windows on an essence-fire no man could meet. Lord Keharna slid out of his seat to kneel before her, head bowed.

He said in Abitalen, "My Service to you, Alach."

Breea felt stunned, but as the Tetr medallion whispered, Breea began to study the noble. Here was a cunning man. He offered secret knowledge to a scholar, and, more, secret knowledge of Breea herself. He called her Alach. That was clever, yet Iltish's rage and sorrow were pieces that didn't fit a man simply seeking alliance with rising power. Breea silently thanked Ajalay for the gift of the medallion.

Remembering how the Batusha warriors spoke of Service, she said, "You wish to give your service to me?"

"I do," he said. "If it be your will."

"Why?"

"The Time of Legends returns, Tetr. You are its herald."

Breea shook her head to clear the roaring that rose within her at his words. It was the sound of the river of blood from her dreams. Her hands went to her daggers, and she focused on the words of the Tetr medallion explaining the potential manipulations latent in Keharna's offer of service. The roar faded, and she understood that Keharna was hiding something. He was thrusting for a target and she needed to parry.

She asked him, "From where comes your sorrow?"

His face fell and she knew her parry had also been riposte, apparently to the heart.

Breea gestured to a seat. "Sit."

Iltish rose stiffly, and sat rubbing his knee.

"Not used to kneeling?" asked Breea.

His noble demeanor returned, a mask over deep pain, and he favored her with an ironic grin.

"I find it hard to reason," said Breea. "People kneeling to me. Two days ago I was hunted and reviled."

Iltish said, "You still are, Tetr."

Threat, or a warning for her safety? She wished Ajalay were here. She felt out of her ken with his man. If not for the Tetr medallion, she would be allied to him for unknown ends. He had knowledge she wanted, though.

"What do you know of me?" said Breea, and her voice showed more of her need than she had intended.

"Have you found them yet?" he asked in turn.

A question for a question, and, more, a question she did not understand. Irritation sparked and she said nothing. The medallion spoke, and she came to understand that knowledge was coin to this man. The problem was that he also held the bank, and she felt like a pauper. She decided on a different approach, more like Ajalay.

She stood and said, "Be ready to ride in three bells. We will muster outside the city."

He adapted quickly, and said, "Tetr, forgive me, but I fear that I am too frail for such a journey."

"Then I cannot accept your service. I bid you well, Lord Keharna."

Breea stepped toward the door.

"Tetr."

Breea imagined herself Ajalay, and turned around slowly.

Lord Keharna was standing, and looked at ease. Breea

realized that she was playing his game. Both he and the medallion were speaking, but she wasn't listening. Essence-fire was burning anger and frustration for fuel. Breea let her inner fire bloom and the air about her began to shimmer.

Lord Keharna gaped.

"You will speak true and plain," said Breea, approaching him. "Dissemble again and I will cut you down."

He backed away and bumped into the table, sending ornaments crashing to the floor.

The door behind Breea swung open and Neprawn stepped in with sword drawn, followed by Simarn, her black crossbow centering at Keharna's chest.

The lord gave a shaky nod.

Neprawn sheathed his blade, then tapped Simarn's shoulder. The young woman backed out with him, bow aimed until Neprawn shut the door.

"Sit," ordered Breea.

Lord Keharna sat. Breea remained standing.

"What do you know of me?"

Keharna gathered composure—hands clutched in his lap. She could feel his heart racing still.

"You are the first of the Alach reborn," he said. "First and greatest. Your birth was ordained. Your children will—"

Breea interrupted. "Children?"

"The six you must find to meet the Life Bane."

"Find?" said Breea.

He nodded. "A child to a Bane. Six Alach-born children who are destined each to destroy an Oregule. A child each of earth, wind, life, light, fire, and sound, or song. My translations—"

"Translations of what?" said Breea, stepping toward

him.

He lowered his chin in careful deference, and said, "Tetr, I have translated The Prophecies of Lutna, Chosen of the One."

"In Limtir?"

"No, Tetr."

"In your library?"

"Yes, Tetr."

Breea sighed in frustration. Alach children? Why did her father's journal say nothing of this? Had he known? Did Ajalay? How could she leave with such knowledge so near at hand?

"Where are they?"

"Tetr, Lutna did not write of their births, nor of their homeland. This was by design, for the Life Bane will hunt them."

"As I was," said Breea. "I will visit your library. But tell me first, what is it you wish of me?"

She could see Keharna considering his reply, and wondered how much he would risk to keep his secrets. She dropped a hand to a dagger.

Its emerald sparkle was reflected in his eyes as he said, "Tetr, I wish a man flayed."

The statement sounded like truth; the Tetr emerald concurred.

"By me?" said Breea, growing angry at the idea.

"No. I hoped you would enable the death."

"Whose death do you seek?"

The color was returning to Keharna's face. He straightened in the chair and said, "May I elaborate, Tetr? Temple edicts have held no power for my family for a thousand years. We ignored the new as much as the old, as did many others. My wife's family is of noble Meric lineage. She and my daughter practiced with Sacha blades as my wife and her mother had. It was a family secret as secure as our library. They came for my wife and child in the night. Soot first, slaying the house guard, then Temple guards broke the doors. At dawn they flayed my wife and daughter in the Temple square as an example to the city. The Keharna family brought to heel. Until you, it never dawned to me that the Temple might have true magic to wield to look into a man's locked house—into secret chambers."

Sad and sickened, Breea nodded. "It was an Oregule," she said. "In the Temple. A spider."

He frowned, his eyes reflecting an inner pool of bottomless sorrow and guilt. He said, "Had I believed the prophecies and made watch for the sign of your Calling…" He didn't finish.

Breea got up and went to the window. The day was half gone. The street below was busy with men and gear.

"Whose death do you seek?"

"High Priest Duyazen Kedalmtel."

Dismayed, Breea said, "Why Duyazen?"

"They came in his name."

"The Oregule had Duyazen's fingers eaten."

Keharna didn't reply, but she could feel his lack of care. She said to him, "Do you know why?"

He frowned. Breea took that to be as close as he would get to admitting he didn't know something.

"They fed his fingers to an isl lizard a joint at a time because he refused to accept the new edicts."

Lord Keharna replied, "Thousands died in his name before he was replaced."

Breea crossed her arms. "Ask him in my name if he

ordered the death of your family. He will not lie upon my name. Will you do so?"

"I will, Tetr-Sanis."

"Lord Keharna," said Breea, gathering her thoughts. "You can be of service to me."

He smiled, but warily.

"Duyazen may be the salvation of this city, perhaps the whole Yasharn realm. Be his adviser?"

"Forgive me if I cannot swear bond to that, Tetr," he said.

"But you will see him. Talk to him. In my name."

"I will."

Breea considered whether to threaten him with her return should she learn of Duyazen's death, but decided that she had pushed him enough. That the Temple orb communicated with Duyazen spoke well of the priest, for the orb wanted nothing so much as the well-being of its city, but who knew what Duyazen had done in the past? In any event, she had little time.

"Let us go to your library," she said.

Breea and Lord Keharna strode through the inn and down the main stair, Simarn and Neprawn following. Batusha warriors saluted her and Limtir guard bowed as she passed. Siege materials were being hauled back to the guild house, but Breea had no thoughts beyond the answers that she might learn in Keharna's library. Who were these children that were hunted by the Oregule? Who was her mother, and, more important to Breea, where was she now?

As they went down the front steps of the inn, Lord Keharna's retinue of liveried and armed servants brought a small carriage from the stable.

A disturbance behind made Breea turn. A Batusha

armsboy was dashing toward her from the foyer, a ripple of chaos and curses rising behind him. Seeing that he had Breea's attention, he put on a last burst of speed. Simarn began to raise her bow, but Neprawn put a hand on her arm. The boy planted his feet and skidded off the top stone of the stairs. He landed in a crouch a few steps above Breea, then stood to attention, back-fist to palm.

Breea grinned at the display.

"Master," he said. "Priest Arin requests your presence."

Breea frowned, then her shoulders sagged. The Yasharn general. The man was waiting for an audience with her. Heaving a tight sigh, Breea looked up at the windows of the inn, unsurprised to find Arin looking down at her from the top floor. Anger sparked her blades alight. Torn, she weighed certain knowledge of her fate against the worth of meeting a hostile man she reviled. Her duty was clear, and it was an agony. Personal need was nothing against the fate of a city—or a nation—under siege by an Oregule. The people of Mericsland needed warriors, not words of her own fate.

Turning on Keharna, she opened her mouth to speak, then turned back to the armsboy. "Find Ajalay. Bring her here."

"Aye, Master," said the boy. He ran.

To Keharna she said, "Will you wait, Lord Keharna?"

One corner of his mouth quirked. What did he find amusing? He bowed his head in acceptance.

Breea whirled, cursing obtuse men under her breath, and strode up the steps two at a time. Men got out of her way, giving muted salutes to avoid catching her enraged attention. Arin met her at the top stair, saw her mood, and lowered his eyes. He led her to another set of rooms on the floor. Flanking the closed door were two Batusha warriors.

Breea said to them, "You are relieved, warriors."

They saluted and walked away. She did not want anyone overhearing this conversation, or whatever was to follow. That she might have to kill this man felt likely.

Breea turned to Simarn and Neprawn and held up a hand to tell them to wait. Neprawn took station beside the door. Simarn watched him, then stood to the other side. Breea took a breath, squared her shoulders, and motioned for Arin to open the doors.

The general stood in the center of the opulent room, arms folded, facing the door. Light from the window behind gave him a dark silhouette accented around the edges by sparkles of gold where the light caught the embroidered edges of his uniform. Breea stepped in, then waited for the doors behind to close. The medallion whispered the general's name, Ashar Ohan. He was the firstborn of a noble family that traced its line to the chiefs of one of the three Yasharn peoples who founded the nation after the Legend Time. Against his family's wishes he'd joined the Army of the Blessed, rising through the ranks on a wave of victories against every foe of Yasharn religious aggression, and was now second in command of the Yasharn army. Despite her dislike of the man, Breea marveled that he had come to her alone when he could have invaded the city instead. It meant that he wanted something from her. Regaining her focus on the room, she found him studying her. She had no idea where to begin.

With a twist of mouth, the general said, "The Chosen."

Breea bristled at his distain, and said, "Why are you here?"

He acted as though she hadn't spoken and said, "The specter to cry the death of Yash."

"A false prophecy," said Breea.

"And a spreader of heresy," he replied.

Fierce, Breea said, "Had I wanted the death of Yash, nothing would remain of this city but cinders and bone."

His eyes narrowed at the threat, but was there a hint of astonishment as well? Had he provoked her, only to be amazed by the result? She controlled herself and said, "General Ohan, did you know that new edicts were writ to find me? Slay me? What the Oregule who ruled your Temple failed to see was that while my Calling was made here in the High Temple, I was born in Limtir. Chosen or not, I can touch the essence of things, and I have been given a vision."

Ohan didn't move, his face dismissive.

"General, Carsythe is under siege by a beast like the one which corrupted your Temple. I intend to break the siege and save the city."

Ohan's eyes held the glint of steel as he crossed his arms, and said, "The Army of the Blessed will remain. You will take nothing from Yash." His intent was clear. He stood between her and the army, by force if necessary.

Breea was almost amused, for the general did not know his danger—alone here with her. She decided to show him, and locked her gaze to his. It was a relief to relax her boundaries and let the molten power billow up within. The general's face went pained, but instead of looking away, he stepped forward and gripped the haft of his sword.

Connected to him by the thread of his gaze, Breea saw in him a ferocious and unyielding will backed by a faith that would meet any challenge, even hers—especially hers. This man had taken the edicts against women bearing arms as god-spoken writ. Yet here he was, on his own, to judge her himself. Why was he here? Not merely to keep her from taking his army. His world had collapsed in a day—the

Temple destroyed, Dauthaz revealed to have corrupted his forces. Could he be here looking for answers? Crushing Lord General Ohan was not the way. Breea bound her power.

Released, he sagged and caught himself before falling. So as not to embarrass him as he recovered, Breea walked to a table set with food and drink. She poured herself a goblet of wine, and after a moment of thought, poured a second. Picking up both, she turned to the general and extended one, hoping that Ohan would accept it. There was a space of three paces between them.

The general stared at the goblet for a long while. He seemed to know what it represented, an offer of peace, even of alliance. Not meeting her gaze, he crossed the distance, took the goblet, and drained it.

"What were they?" he asked.

"Which?"

"They whom you slew in the street."

"Dauthaz," she said. "True Dauthaz—men changed…warped in form and rotted in heart by the Oregule that ruled the Temple."

The general didn't respond. He poured himself more wine, his face angry and eyes hollow with an echo of loss. Had the general cared about the men the Dauthaz had once been?

"Is that why you are here?" she said. "To discover how this happened to your men?"

He set down the wine, and said, "I am here to keep you from stealing the hope of Yash."

Breea didn't bother to conceal her sigh.

Ohan said, "Isswarn has crossed the River Arve."

"Invading?" asked Breea, thinking of the maps she'd studied back home. The River Arve was the southern border between Yash and Isswarn.

He seemed pleased to have her at a disadvantage of knowledge. "Their vanguard rides the deep-forest isl."

Breea wasn't sure if she believed it. Deep-forest isl were immense reptiles, rare, and rightfully feared. It sounded to Breea like a Legend Time story, and in that thought a wash of inner heat rushed through her. *All known will end.*

The general watched her face and said, "I have seen it."

Breea nodded. "As I saw Carsythe. The Kaul ride Urdjra."

The Lord General looked grim. "Not since the time of elders have the Isswarn tamed the isl for mounts."

Fascinated, Breea asked, "How do you fight isl?" She imagined herself fighting a giant lizard.

Startled by her change in tone, Ohan studied her.

"With spears," he said. "And the blood of legions."

It seemed General Ohan was learned in Legend Time warfare.

"Could you use nets?" she asked.

His eyes narrowed, looking at the idea. "Perhaps."

Pleased that he liked her idea, Breea took a sip of wine, but she could sense that he was thinking again how to stop her from taking any of his men.

"I came to Yash to find the priest who gave my Calling."

"The high priest," he said.

Clearly he'd already spoken with Duyazen. The priest was the only one who knew of her Calling.

Breea said, "I found an Oregule instead. The second I have fought. I am called to Carsythe to face another. General, I need an army. Not a great one, but swift."

The muscles of General Ohan's jaw flexed and his lips twisted as though tasting something sour. The general squared his body to hers and folded his arms.

Breea pressed on. "I need believers, General. Men who will endure forced marches and face the white eyes of Dauthaz."

He said, "Duyazen has gifted you the Aska-Wuthos."

"I will take any more you can spare," said Breea.

Ohan seemed unmoved.

"Lord General, Carsythe will fail without my aid, and eventually all of Mericsland in its wake. If Mericsland falls, the Kaul Kaul will sweep across the isthmus at Twinport and you will have another invasion at your back. I have seen it." She hadn't exactly, but she knew it to be true.

The general grimaced and reached for his wine cup, then restrained himself. A tremor shook him.

"I would stop you," he said, but didn't finish the sentence. They both knew he could not, and perhaps should not.

"Very well. Bladed-woman. Arm yourself with the blood of Yash. Those that will follow you."

Elated, she bowed her thanks. The realization that she was about to attempt to lead an army rushed up inside and tempered the joy. She found her hands had strayed to the Tetr medallion for comfort.

Embarrassed, she dropped them and asked, "What supply is available?"

The general reached into the folds of his uniform and retrieved a small leather case. He opened its clasp and pulled out a square of parchment and a stick of black wax. Laying the parchment on the wine table, he used a lamp to melt three spots of wax onto the parchment. With the hilt of his dagger he pressed a seal into the largest, then licked his thumbs and pressed them into the wax of the other two. He offered the writ to Breea.

"Take that and the final number of your cohort to the stores master. The Aska-Wuthos will know where."

"Thank you, Lord General," said Breea, taking the parchment. "I will have need of horses."

His jaw clenched, but he nodded at the parchment with his seal. Breea was stunned. What power had he granted to her with this writ? He must know that she would need at least a thousand ready mounts, which meant three or four times that in spares. Why would he do this?

His enmity was mixed now with respect. It seemed that Lord General Ohan believed her to be the Chosen, and he wanted her gone. If he considered the writ payment for her absence, she would gladly accept.

In a formal tone she said, "Lord General, I shall wield the blood of Yash as it were my own."

"Spend it well," he said, "And may Het bless their blades."

She opened the door for him and nodded to Dori. The servant led the man away. Arin stood aside, watching her for instructions. She beckoned him over.

"Take this to the Aska-Wuthos," she said. "It is a writ of supply from Lord General Ohan."

Arin took the piece of parchment with an air of profound respect.

"I Serve," he said, and bowed to her, backing away a few steps before turning to hurry off.

Breea looked at Simarn and Neprawn to ask them to follow, then walked down the hall to the great stair, pacing herself so as to avoid catching the general.

On the front steps of the inn she found Keharna and Ajalay in full discourse, talking almost at once. It took Breea a moment to realize that they were naming books, one after the other without pause. Bay-ope stood near and raised a hand in the sign for *scholars*. His mustache moved slightly, which was his tolerant grin. Breea took a step toward him, but found a Batusha priest bowing low.

"Master Banea," he said rising. "Your wisdom will grant us a path to service."

Was he asking for assistance? Advice? He'd never spoken to her directly before. A crowd of men was waiting nearby, watching.

"What do you need?" she said.

The priest was older than Arin, though of lower rank.

"Master Banea. Are we to abandon the hall?"

"I had not thought of that," said Breea. She studied the men who were awaiting her decision. Some were old warriors upon whom the red leather and polished chain armor seemed to weigh heavily. Others looked to be servants. There were even a few women. Wives?

She asked the priest, "Where is Planner Longat?"

"Upon the field of muster, Chosen."

Ajalay and Lord Keharna had stopped their naming contest and were watching her. Breea looked to Bay-ope for help, but he gave no indication of an opinion and seemed to be waiting for her decision as well. It felt like the Sanis testing of high summer all over again, but worse. This was no academic test. Her decision in this moment would forge the fate of these men.

"Step near," she said, waving for all of them to approach.

The old warriors obeyed and the rest followed their example. There was a lesson Taumea had taught her years before: See the leader, slay the leader. It applied in many ways to many situations. Breea looked for a leader among them. She chose the one old man who met her gaze without apology. His shoulders were broad under his armor, and though it hung somewhat loose upon his aged frame, his bearing held that air of experience and power Breea remembered from elder Tomeguard.

"What is your name, warrior?"

"Master, I am Deckin Longsword, and I Serve."

"Deckin Longsword," said Breea, glancing at the huge broadsword at his hip. "What do you advise? Should the guild hall be abandoned?"

"Master," said Deckin, rising up to his full height. "It should not." He said no more. Apparently if she could not figure out why, then it was not worth explaining.

Breea studied him while she thought what to do. He withstood the gaze and only the raised pace of his heart betrayed to her that he felt anything more than a girl's stare.

"I concur," said Breea. She turned to the priest. "We shall leave as many as are necessary to maintain the hall and train new aspirants. Any man with a family may remain if by staying he will better serve the guild in these tasks."

Others had come closer to hear what she was saying.

"I am going to war against a nation. There will be Dauthaz, and worse. But war may come to Yash as well. There is no surety, except that the world tomorrow will not be the one we leave today. Do as you see fit in Service."

Deckin cracked a *chak'ood* salute, and all the warriors of Batusha within earshot of Breea's voice responded in kind. She acknowledged them, then stepped forward. They parted and she walked up to Ajalay and Keharna, grateful that the men had accepted her judgment. Being worthy of these warriors was one of her true wishes, but each test of her leadership felt like the first. A part of her longed for the instant need of battle, where there was no time to ponder the ways in which she might fail in the eyes of such men. With a pang she realized that in her heart she felt that Batusha were her Tomeguard.

Lord Keharna was staring at her with a cryptic expression somewhere between respect, calculation, and fear. Ajalay's head was elevated with a proud, proprietary air. Bay-ope winked.

Breea felt herself blush under their gazes.

Behind her was a whisper of voices as people discussed her statement and passed it on to others. One young voice louder than the rest cried, "Didja see Deckin stand full in the sweep of the Chosen's eyes? Like a rock he wa—" The voice cut off with a little *whoof.*

Breea almost turned to see what that was about, but she saw Bay-ope watching them, and he was grinning through his beard. She relaxed. If men were playing like that, then all was well, or as well as could be with war roaring down upon the world. Of course, war was what Batusha had been forged to meet.

As I am, she thought.

Returning to the moment, she said to Lord Keharna in Limtiric, "Where is your library?"

He gave her a short bow and led them down the steps. A Batusha boy came dashing down the stair. He halted and saluted a few strides away. Breea sighed and wondered how the boys always seemed to know exactly where to find her. They never looked around for her, but ran an arrow's path to where she stood. She waved him near.

"Master," said the boy, "Priest Arin requests your presence."

"Did he say why?"

"He's arguin' with one of them black robes from Temple, Master, and Lord Dupalo. Somethin' about this inn, I reckon."

Lord Dupalo was the inn-keep, but what happened here after she left was not an issue that concerned her.

"Tell Arin he will decide in my stead."

The boy slapped back-fist to palm and dashed up the steps.

Breea scanned the work of Batusha and Limtir Tomeguard clearing the inn of their siege preparations, and found her watchers. A trio of boys stood still amid the activity, their eyes on her. Others as well, more subtle, were watching her. Many looked uncertain. Insight struck—in their view, where could the Master be going at this moment? Breea clenched her fists.

This was no time for quiet rooms and stories read in soft lamplight—no matter their import, and no matter how deeply she longed for the peace it might bring. Now was the time for arming.

Keharna's carriage rolled up, and a liveried servant opened its door for her. At the top of the steps, one of the boys turned and ran back into the building. The other two were talking, gesturing as though debating how they might follow Breea. Knowing what she must do, she got into the carriage. Ajalay stepped in, followed by Bay-ope. The carriage leaned like a ship and sank down as he entered. He had to lean forward with his elbows on his knees to keep his head from cracking the ceiling.

Breea felt Keharna climb aboard on the outside, and frowned. She unlatched the door on the far side and swung her head up and out. He turned to her in surprise.

"Come sit with us," said Breea. "We will pause here."

Breea swung back inside. Bay-ope shifted to make as much room as he could. Keharna entered with dignity.

"Tell me of these Alach children," said Breea.

CHAPTER 8

This Path is Forged in Blood

THE MOON SHED LITTLE LIGHT INTO THE NARROW canyon as Taumea scouted ahead of the girls—all three of them. A small grin relaxed his face as he thought how Valiena would flip her hair with dismissal if she knew he thought of her as one of the girls. In truth, trusting them as a unit gave him the confidence to range out. Together the three were a potent fighting force.

He halted and listened to the wind whispering through the orchard trees above the canyon, then examined a patch of moonlit sand. The only tracks were the day-old footprints of the sisters. Wondering how the creature from Limtir had tracked the girls, he made a random-looking mark in the sand to let Valiena know to continue past this point. Did weaving leave a scent? Spe's eyes would follow him from time to time, her gaze not on his face, but at his belt where he kept the beast's gem in a pouch.

Touching the round gem through the leather, he set out. Soon the canyon shallowed. He crouched to keep his head below ground level, and paused to listen and check the night breeze. The cold air smelled faintly of rotten apple. Bow in hand, he stood in slow increments. Nothing moved except stiff branches in the wind. He could see the cairn Anila had described, gray in moonlight, and beyond it the black trunks of the orchard tended by the Hox clan.

Still thinking about the sisters, he considered the worth of their skills upon the battlefield. If they could be convinced to hone their weaving with an eye to combat, their fighting power would eclipse his own. They might eclipse an entire regiment.

In the long days of hiding since Breea's departure for the city, he often thought back to what she had done to Ajalay's study and the men who had attacked her there—the living flames and blasted pieces of men. Breea did not seem to realize that she was the same as those she read about in her book of Alach history. He wondered what she would do when she did.

After scouting the area in three concentric circles, he took off his pack and settled down at the mouth of the gully to await the girls, bow across his lap. He did not like what he had found, or not found. The girls were a day late returning home, and there was no sign that anyone was waiting for their return. The quiet of the orchards felt desolate. It reminded Taumea of the last day of his childhood—the night visit to the scholar in his dank riverbank cave after the invasion. The blood soaking into the river sand had been black, like a hole in the ground. The cold of that night had felt like this. Muttering a curse, Taumea stood and shouldered his pack, then jogged back down the wash to meet the girls.

———◦◦◦———

Valiena's neck ached under the weight of the apple basket strap. She leaned forward, gripping the straps with both hands to take some of the strain. The pain was getting worse, but it could not keep pace with the rapid advance of her anger at parents who would force a girl of Anila's size to carry such weight. Beside Valiena, Anila walked with resolute steps, breathing in little drafts and bent forward against the weight of what had been Spe's pack. Spe walked ahead of them, her hands pulled into her sleeves and tucked under her arms.

Valiena saw another of Taumea's all-is-well signs in the sand and said, "Rest."

She leaned her bow against the canyon wall, then gripped the rim of Anila's pack, lifting. Anila pushed off the strap and they let the basket slide to the ground. Anila walked behind Valiena and took some of the weight to allow Valiena to remove her strap. Her neck spasmed with the release of weight. Valiena shrugged off the pack of camp gear she wore on her chest. She stretched her back and rubbed her neck, then sat on her pack. Spe came over and settled on one leg and Valiena wrapped her cloak around the girl. Anila sat in the sand with a thump.

"Are you cold?" asked Valiena.

"Work is warmth," said Anila in a morose tone.

The girl looked half broken. Valiena knew the look from her years at Petrall Temple—it was the face of a girl walking through fear toward inescapable pain. A tremor of anger in Valiena made Spe look up at her. Valiena patted the girl, and she laid her head on Valiena's shoulder. Valiena thought of Taumea's certainty that they had to help the girls return to avoid an outcry. Valiena hated the idea, but saw no other path. She wanted there to be an outcry. She wanted someone to pay for the fear these children endured.

On the far canyon wall, a little patch of moonlight danced with apple-branch shadows, and Valiena asked Opalah for strength and a clear path for the girls, these two little moonbeams. She felt Spe's breathing settle into sleep.

The wind above sighed to a pause and the branches relaxed, shaping the moonlight on the wall into a pair of fangs. Valiena blinked. The vision vanished. She opened her cloak and reached for her bow, then paused. Twin fangs were the pattern cold-burned into Breea's chest by Lupazg's medallion.

"Lr'icuna," she whispered. It was what she had named Breea at the start of this journey—*she who shapes destiny*.

Valiena woke Spe, then stood the child to the side. Valiena walked to the far wall, touched the pattern of moonlight, then turned her face to the bright crescent above. Purpose flowed through her like hot wine.

"Bright are the ways of the illuminated path," said Valiena, quoting her mother.

Spe had gone to help Anila lift her basket. They froze at the sound of sand-muffled footfalls. Valiena leapt back to her bow and drew its arrow to her ear. Anila clutched Spe protectively as she sang a soft, urgent note. Sand leapt into the air around them.

Taumea came loping out of the shadows. He slowed to a stop, and Valiena could see him taking in their readiness with an approving eye. Valiena eased off the string, but she knew something was wrong.

He walked up to her, and signed, *Are well?*

Valiena nodded. With one hand she signed, *What word?*

In the shadows his face was hard to read, but she could see his eyes checking the canyon rims. He adjusted his pack and looked at the sisters. The sand had settled, but they hadn't moved, perhaps sensing his dark mood.

To Valiena he said, "No threat."

Valiena didn't believe him. He was ready to slay.

"I have been given a sign," she said. "Our path is illuminated."

He looked into her eyes for a moment, then said, "There is death nearby."

"Whose?"

Taumea didn't answer.

"Coming or done?" asked Valiena.

The girls were watching them, clearly hearing everything.

"I do not know," said Taumea.

Valiena said, "We must get to Breea. I saw her sign. We cannot protect them alone. We need her."

When Taumea did not respond, Valiena took a breath to argue for her path.

Before she spoke, Taumea said, "I concur."

Valiena sighed in relief, but watched him. It was what a Limtirian would say.

He said, "I will scout the village and bring the parents.

Ahead there is a ledge you could defend at need. With them."

Valiena understood his tactical thinking. He wanted them in a defensible spot so that he could move unhindered. And kill unhindered. There was something out there that he wasn't willing to name and he wanted to hunt it alone.

They picked up packs and apples, following Taumea to the place he had identified. He took off his pack, then lifted Valiena up so that she could climb atop the ledge. He handed both packs to her, then the girls.

Anila wanted the apples to go up as well, but Taumea said, "Unless you intend to throw them at an enemy, they will not aid you."

Anila went sullen.

Taumea signed *my love* to Valiena.

She cupped her hands toward him in Opalah's blessing.

"Wait," said Anila. "Do not bring Da."

Taumea waited for an explanation.

"He is not of the Azsark. He does not know the Breath. He cannot know."

"Your mother, then," said Taumea.

Anila looked scared, but did not object.

"Where will she be?" said Taumea.

Anila's voice sounded crushed. "House of the headman."

Taumea left them at a run. Valiena watched him vanish into the shadows and wondered if their enemies sensed their death in his coming.

—————

At the mouth of the canyon, the wind had died and the

trees stood still in moonlight. Taumea left the gully at a lope and turned north, running a long row between trees until the outskirt buildings of the village showed dark ahead. He went to one knee in the dead grass and looked from building to building. Stepping quietly, he moved up to the first hovel. From within came the sound of muffled weeping. Over the scents of piss, horse dung, and applewood smoke, he smelled blood. Moving through the buildings, he came to what passed for a town square where the main road bisected the town.

In moonlight, eight poles lined the far side. Atop each a villager was impaled.

At the sight, a deep, hot calm settled over Taumea. He stood from his hidden stance, then set his bow and quiver before him. Taumea drew one of his long fighting daggers. Methodically he cut away the peasant clothing that hid his Limtir armor. Standing free of disguise, he raised the blade to the dead.

With dark and formal intonation, he spoke in a language now gone from the world, "Your names upon my blades do sing."

Bootfall announced a patrol. They came strolling down the moonlit street at a relaxed pace. Taumea watched as the men paused before the impaled people.

A soldier took hold of a man's foot and gave it a tug. A whine of unbearable agony spilled from the man. The soldiers chuckled and went to the next in line.

Taumea stepped into the moonlight and scraped the hilt of his dagger across his scale-mail. The soldiers whirled. Taumea advanced as the men scrabbled for their swords.

The first died silent from a dagger through the eye. Before the second could clear his weapon, Taumea's blade was embedded to the hilt in the man's temple, the tip jabbing dark and wet out the other side of his skull. Taumea yanked his blade free as the man fell.

Up the street was a house that looked to be the finest in the village. If the girls' mother was not one of the women impaled, she would be there. He turned to look the other way. At the end of town, the village Temple was an unimpressive building despite its stone facade. A single lamp lit the wood door. Along its side Taumea counted twenty horses tied to a makeshift hitch rope strung along the side of the building.

Taumea crossed the street and retrieved his bow and quiver, then walked down to the Temple. Beyond the door he could hear snores. He leaned his bow and quiver against the stone wall and tested the latch. The door swung open with a creak. Taumea unhooked the lantern and threw it in. Oil spilled and languid flames lit the worship hall with quaking yellow light. Pews were stacked at the far end and men slept in two rows upon the floor. Drawing both of his daggers, Taumea walked in.

An officer at the other end of the hall sat up, drew his sword, and bellowed, "Arm! Up! Shit-eating whoresons! Arms! Arms!"

Taumea strode the hall, every strike of his blades a death blow. By the time he reached the other end, the few remaining soldiers weren't even trying to arm themselves. Their only thought was escape. It was a chaos of bare feet and panicked breathing, but no screams. No one that Taumea struck lived long enough to scream.

Taumea cut down one that tried to flee to his right, and the last four sprinted along the other wall. He let them go but blocked the officer from retreat.

The man held his sword at low guard, a dagger in his other fist.

"What are ye?" he asked, his eyes darting from the bodies scattered on the floor and back to Taumea. "I seen knife work like that afore, Soot. We're here by pontiff decree. What temple are ye? Pioc? Antren?"

"Limtir," said Taumea.

The Temple officer froze. Taumea attacked, catching the man's halfhearted counter with crossed daggers. Guiding the sword out of the way with one blade, Taumea sliced a blow that opened the man's neck from throat to spine.

Outside, a horse's hooves pounded away. Flicking blood from his blades, Taumea jogged to the door. He sheathed the daggers and took up his bow. He drew on the fleeing soldier and released. He had another arrow ready before the fleeing man screeched and tumbled from his mount. Taumea belted on the quiver and stepped around the side of the building where he could hear men trying to saddle their horses. Two arrows in swift succession quieted them. That left one more. A dog was barking furiously up the street. When the animal paused for breath, Taumea caught the sound of panicked running. Taumea walked through the houses and looked down rows of apple trees. A figure flickered dark and pale as it sped away, catching moonlight and shadow among the trees. Taumea bent his bow and let fly. The man fell. Taumea was already on his way. The young man was trying to crawl with an arrow through his back, sobbing and groaning. Taumea took a dagger and opened the man's throat, then retrieved the arrow. After checking the tip, he cleaned it with the man's shirt and dropped it into his quiver.

Back in the village, smoke had begun to billow from the door of the Temple. He looked around, but no one dared to leave their homes. Taumea jogged down the street, retrieved his arrow from the dead soldier there, then returned to the Temple and pulled the remaining two arrows from the bodies of men at the horses' feet. He walked the line of nervous animals, taking note of which looked best. He saddled five, then unhooked the hitch rope and guided all twenty away, up the street toward the headman's house.

The house was roofed with clay tiles, one of only a few buildings in the village not thatched with reeds. Its gut-paned windows were dark, and no smoke rose from its clay-and-branch chimney. Taumea led the horse string around the back and found a dry stone wall surrounding a broad garden space. Taumea opened the gate and led the horses into the garden space, talking to them softly, then tied both ends of the lead to a fruit tree.

He walked to the rear door of the house and pushed it open. A breath of wind puffed out at him, and he skipped back into the moonlit garden. The horses shifted uneasily.

"Tiyha?" called Taumea, holding out empty hands. "Anila and Spe are safe and long for their mother."

There was a long silence, then he caught the sound of a sob. Cautious, Taumea approached the door and said, "May I enter?"

There was no reply. He made his way into the dark house. The plank floor creaked under his weight. To his left moonlight glowed through the skin of a window. The room held a broad bed and a large man prone on the floor at the foot. He wasn't dead, for his head turned at Taumea's entrance. In a shadowed corner of the room, a small woman succumbed to a ragged, chest-deep cough.

Taumea considered the scene. He walked up to the man. He was fat in the middle, wore a thick wool tunic woven of artistic design, and stank of fear and piss—his own, for his breeches were stained dark.

"You must be Da," said Taumea.

The man opened his mouth to speak, but there was a whirl in the air and his eyes bulged. His chest heaved, but drew no air. His face went purple and arms flopped in distress until he fainted. Air whirled back and his chest stuttered into breath.

Taumea looked into the dark corner and said, "They are waiting for you."

Rough, the woman's voice said, "What are you?"

"I am Taumea," he said. "An ally of your daughters." When there was no response, he added, "And the tree."

The shadows shifted and the woman emerged, steadying herself against the wall with one hand. In the other she held a darkly stained rag. Her eyes glinted in moonlight, and Taumea felt shifts of air moving about him like sniffing hounds. He held perfectly still as she judged him. Her eyes dropped to the gem pouch on his belt.

"A token of something that wished to harm your children," he said.

The woman retreated a step. "What are you?" she asked again.

"I am he who has slain twenty Temple men this night so that you may be with your children. You are Tiyha? Mother to Anila and Spe?"

She moved closer to him and sniffed the air, eyes on the pouch.

"What token?" she asked, flipping the bloodstained rag toward his belt.

"A gem," said Taumea, "cut from the dead flesh of the creature that hunted your girls."

Tiyha stared hard at him, then said, "Show me."

Taumea untied the pouch and rolled the gem into his palm. Tiyha sang a few notes, watching Taumea's reaction as a whirl of air lifted the stone from his hand and delivered it to her. When it settled into her hands, light flickered within and she jerked away, dropping the stone. A coughing fit took her and she fell to her knees. Hacking, she scrambled for the gem, and gripped it. The coughing eased.

Da groaned and his eyes fluttered. Taumea kicked him in the temple, hard, knocking him silent. Tiyha blinked at this, then wiped blood from her mouth.

Taumea was done waiting. He stepped over to her, and helped her rise.

"Come," he said.

Tiyha looked at Da upon the floor. Her gaze was not kind.

Taumea said, "He has no power now."

"He will tell of…" She didn't name the tree.

"The Azsark can protect itself," said Taumea.

At the name the woman gasped and clenched her fist around the gem, but her eyes glinted hope.

She whispered, "He told the Dauthaz where it was. Where they were…"

"And I killed it," replied Taumea. "We will not return to the Azsark."

Tiyha pulled away from him, and Taumea suppressed a sigh. He kept his voice low and calm and said, "It spoke to your girls, Tiyha. It said good-bye. There is another path for your children, with an ally like them, and greater than both."

"What do you say?" said Tiyha.

"Breea Banea," said Taumea. "An Alach like those of the Legend Time."

"Alach?"

"A woman of prophecy. Warrior-born," said Taumea.

"Warrior-born," breathed Tiyha. She held the gem to her breast and fainted.

Taumea tore blankets from the bed and rolled her gently into them. The woman's husband groaned. The kick had not killed him. Taumea thought of the damage the man could cause if he spoke of his wife wielding the Breath. If Anila and Spe were correct, he was the only other person to know of the Azsark, which meant that Tiyha spoke true—he was the only one who could have so accurately directed the Dauthaz to his daughters. Without further consideration, Taumea drew a dagger and slid the blade into the man's heart. Taumea cleaned the weapon on the man's tunic then sheathed the blade.

He lifted Tiyha, finding that she weighed no more than a bird. Taumea checked that she still held the gem and hoped that she would survive the journey ahead. At the very least she would see her children again. Outside, Taumea untied the horses, and with Tiyha across his arms like a child, he walked back into town. The Temple down the street was burning well. The extra light let him identify a blacksmith's hut. He walked to the hut, laid Tiyha under the front eve, then tied the horse lead to a ring set in the wall.

Taumea pushed open the door. The air within was warm. In the darkness beyond, a breath caught.

"I need whetstones," said Taumea. "One coarse, and your finest."

He took a coin and flicked it into the room. It bounced off a piece of iron with the clink of silver. There was no movement in response. Taumea peered in, looking for the hearth so he could light something and search for the stones himself.

A bare whisper came to his ear.

"Soot."

After a breath Taumea understood that it was not a curse, but a warning. He stepped in and aside. A crossbow bolt from the other side of the street whisked past and lodged in the wall. Taumea lifted his bow from his shoulder with one hand while drawing an arrow from his quiver with the other. Arrow nocked, he checked the moonlit street. It was empty, and there was no movement from the buildings across. He went to a knee and looked through the horses' legs. A dark shape was running up behind them. Taumea released, aiming under the bellies, but the horses were shifting and one screamed as the arrow took it in the leg.

Taumea charged out of the hut and bellowed at the horses. They yanked the ring out of the wall and tried to scatter, but were tied together. The figure beyond danced back, then grunted as Taumea's next arrow took him through the neck.

Taumea jogged after the horses, using them for cover. Soot rarely worked alone. He released an arrow at a sense of movement across the road. In reply, a crossbow bolt whisked past his head. He released another arrow at the far shadows, then dodged down an alley between houses. He sprinted back around toward the blacksmith's hut. Sliding into a shadow with a view of both his back trail along the houses and out the street, he waited. Down the main road, the burning Temple whooshed as its roof collapsed and orange light made dancing shadows across the town.

When nothing else happened, Taumea stalked up to the edge of the main street. The body of the assassin was gone. The horses were up near the headman's house, confused and slowed by their lame companion. Nothing else stirred. If there was a full ril of assassins in the village, Taumea reckoned he would already be dead. He stood and walked to the blacksmith. The door was closed. After a careful check in all directions, Taumea swept up Tiyha. Something clinked in the blankets, and he nearly spilled the pair of stones tucked into the blanket folds. Taumea nodded, for it was further proof that the Soot had retreated. Little chance that the smith would risk placing the whetstones if he hadn't seen the other assassin leave with the body.

With Tiyha in his arms, Taumea walked up the street to retrieve the horses. He set her in shadow, then caught the dragging end of the lead rope. He released the wounded animal from the string, then tied one end of the lead to the saddle of the best horse. He tucked the whetstones into a saddlebag and went to retrieve Tiyha. With the woman cradled like a child on one shoulder, he mounted. Leading eighteen horses, he rode back into the orchards.

———◦∕∕∕◦———

A woodcock called, and Valiena jerked awake. Predawn light was paling the strip of sky above the canyon. Her back was to the rock wall, cloak spread like a blanket. Under her arms the girls stirred. Anila's head snapped up, and a breath of wind lifted Valiena's hair.

"Ma?" said Anila.

Sand and grit cascaded down, preceding a rope. With the rope in both hands, Taumea leaned out over the canyon and walked down the stone wall to them. At the ledge he had to be careful of Spe, who was staring up at him with wide eyes. Valiena moved the child out of the way and Taumea hopped from the wall to stand with them. He touched warm fingers to Valiena's cheek and neck, and she tilted her head, pressing into his hand.

Spe tugged on Anila's sleeve. The sisters shared a secret look, and Spe took Anila's hand. They took a breath and sang.

Valiena and Taumea turned in surprise, then braced as wind whistled past. The girls rose on a shimmering plank of woven wind and vanished over the rim of the canyon. Taumea shook sand from his hair.

Distraught, Valiena said, "What are they doing?"

Taumea looked at her with a hint of grin.

Valiena put hands to hips and glowered at him.

He said, "They want to see their mother."

"She's up there?"

"She is. And like them. Like Breea."

"A weaver?" said Valiena.

He nodded. "That. Though I meant impulsive in the use of their gifts. We may hope they are as dangerous as Breea."

"Dangerous?" asked Valiena.

Taumea didn't answer her and looked down off the ledge. Leaning out with the rope, he walked back off the edge to the canyon floor. He reached up and helped Valiena down, then began tying the apple baskets to the end of the rope. When he turned to face her, he had that fierce, grave expression he got when he needed her to understand something of deep import. Back in Limtir she'd thought the look was endearing. Now it gave her a dark chill.

Taumea said, "We're going to need everything those girls can do, Val. This path is forged in blood."

CHAPTER 9

The One to Your Blades

OVER THE FIELD OF MUSTER, LAYERS OF SMOKE from hundreds of evening cook fires clung to the earth, shrouding the men gathering to Breea's banner. Where the muster blazes burned, the smoke flickered orange, like summer storms on a far horizon. The smoke did little to muffle sound—the tramp of boot and hoof mingled with a dog's bark, the creak and rattle of carts, and orders bellowed by officers striving to bring order in the gathering dark. On the edge of hearing, a flute played. Breea leaned forward trying to catch the melody, for the song reminded her of the library—a girl's life among scholars and warriors, and also of the battle with Lupazg that had set the halls awash with the blood of all those she knew. Under her cloak she traced the fang-shaped scars where the Oregule's medallion had marked her. The Tetr emerald lay hard and warm against her fingers. It whispered of cavalry column arrays, flanking outriders, and the hazards of a night march. Breea clenched her fist and told it to be silent.

The emerald on its gold rope was a bitter weight now, a physical reminder of what felt like betrayal from the two people she needed most. When Ajalay and Bay-ope had appeared in the city, their presence had been a gift beyond what she could imagine, a balm to all her fears. That they would remain in this stinking pit of a city was not a thing her heart could fathom. Her mind knew their reasons were sound. Ajalay was too weak for a forced march, and Bay-ope had to remain to keep her safe. With invasion coming, the city needed them, but so did Breea. She blinked back tears. There were six Alach children out in the world who needed her. Children hunted by the Oregule as she had been.

She walked to the tower stair and went down the narrow, dark spiral. At the base of the stair, she walked out of the tower and onto the dirt foundation of the unfinished wall. In the last light of the dusk sky, she recognized a brother of the Aska-Wuthos waiting with Simarn and her Batusha honor guard. The brother knelt and the Batusha warriors *chak'ood*, back-fist to palm.

"*Anule*," said Breea.

Batusha stood at ease. The Aska-Wuthos brother remained kneeling, head bent. Breea was unsure what to do. She knew the importance of rank and respect, Ajalay had taught her that, and Breea accepted the salutes of Batusha in that regard, but why was this man kneeling?

To the brother she said, "Stand."

"My queen," he said, and stood with fluid ease. Breea recognized the inherent grace of a man trained as a warrior from birth. He rested his left hand on the hilt of his sword in a relaxed but dignified pose, and gazed out past her shoulder. Breea waited, taking a moment to admire the patterns of evening skylight reflected in the blue iridescence of his scale armor. He didn't move. She glanced at the Batusha warriors and caught Sabar smothering a grin.

Breea asked the brother in his own language, "Have you new word?"

He froze for a moment. "My queen, I have…no new word."

A number of the Batusha warriors grinned and looked sideways at one another. What was this young man doing? This brother was the youngest of the three, his armor and garments newer and less worn, and perhaps a bit more colorful and dashing than his elder brothers. She guessed he was about her age…she stopped and felt herself blush. She hoped the night was far enough advanced that no one saw.

"Very well," she said. "Thank you. Please assist your brothers in the muster."

"My queen." The young warrior bowed, then strode off.

Ootha stuck out one foot, bent the knee, and with a dainty flourish laid a hand upon his saber hilt, tilted his head to the sky, and gazed into the distance with great interest. Warriors chuckled.

Breea favored him with a tolerant grin and said, "Masters, if you will assist him."

They grew serious. Their sworn duty was to protect her.

Breea said, "I am sure he will need your experience. I

wish to walk with Simarn before I join the muster."

"Master," said Sabar and Ootha in unison, striking back-fists to palm. The pair of masters led the rest away back along the wall toward the road. Neprawn lingered, but Breea gave him no sign that the order excluded him. With a glance at Simarn, he strode after the rest.

With no eyes upon her, Breea felt her body relax. She beckoned to Simarn. The young woman approached, black crossbow held across her chest, unarmed but ready. The girl's eyes flicked side to side, checking shadows along the unfinished wall. *Where did she learn to do that? Neprawn?* Warmth for the girl made Breea smile at her. Simarn, the fresh-born warrior. Breea took the crossbow from Simarn's hands and hung it on the girl's belt, then hooked an arm around Simarn's.

"Let's go see what mettle of men we have," said Breea.

"Yes, my queen."

The title from Simarn was like a lash across Breea's heart. She didn't want another follower. She wanted a friend, now more than ever in her life. Simarn's eyes continued to rove the gathering night, her free hand resting on the haft of the crossbow at her hip. Breea ignored these signs of Simarn's battle readiness, and led the way across a work-bridge of rough planks that spanned the dry moat before the wall. Ahead, men laughed. The muscles of Simarn's arm tensed.

Breea paused. She didn't want Simarn shooting anyone. Fifty strides away she sensed a swale of land somewhat apart from the main body of the camp, and, within, a long campfire ringed by the warm presence of men. Through the smoky pall she could make out its orange glow.

Breea said to Simarn, "None will see us."

Simarn looked unsure.

Breea listened to the Tetr medallion, and called a breath of wind. She wove the summoned air into a pattern of concealing smoke and shifting unseen. Dark cloaked them, and a breeze whispered through their hair. Simarn shivered. Breea let a breath of warmth flow into the girl, and felt her relax.

They walked until the haze brightened with firelight, and the outlines of backlit humps resolved into the forms of men sitting on bags and pack-mule boxes. Breea walked aside to a piece of higher ground to study these men who had answered her call to war. Their scent on the air was sour. They lounged, talking and cursing, eating from wooden bowls with short knives or drinking from tankards. At one end of the long fire pit, two iron tripods straddled the coals supporting steaming cauldrons. A thick-limbed figure in a pale, filthy dress with ragged hair hiding the face went from man to man, retrieving bowls, going to the pots and ladling a heaping serving into each. A foot stuck out and the figure went sprawling in the dirt. Men laughed. Simarn's crossbow came up, but Breea put a hand on the weapon before Simarn armed it.

Breea watched the figure in the dirty dress. The grunt of pain from the figure had been no sound a girl would make. It was boy. Breea guided Simarn close behind the backs of the men on the near side of the fire. To a man they wore the black wool of Yasharn soldiers—including the boy under his ill-fitting dress.

"Git up, oh queen," said one of the men.

Breea had to restrain Simarn with force as the men laughed. For herself Breea wove a boundary at her core and the essence rising within subsided.

The boy rose and picked up the bowl he'd dropped. Breea saw through his ragged hair the streaks of tears down his humiliated face. He went to a pot and was reaching for the wooden ladle when a piece of firewood flew through the air and smacked into his hands. He yelped and the bowl dropped into the flames.

A man sitting by the brightest, warmest section of the fire bellowed, "Was you servin' me shit-dirt stew, girlie?"

Breea studied the speaker. He was a big man, powerful but gone fat, with a high voice. He wore a sash with a single, thin line of red. An officer, but low ranked. The insignia of the company on his left shoulder was so covered with filth it was unreadable in the firelight.

"No, sir," said the boy. "I naer would, sir."

The man sneered. "No sir, no sir. Git wine, girl! Or I'll make ye queen fer true."

The boy bunched the filthy skirt and walked away quickly. A sword licked out and the flat smacked his bottom hard. The boy fled with a gasp of pain. Men laughed loud and drunk and harsh.

Breea hissed in hatred as memories of SaKlu and the filth of the Rose tavern whirled before her. One of the men a couple strides in front of her turned to stare into the dark with a startled expression.

Breea knew he would see nothing, and thought that if this was an example of her army, then she would have to make an example of them. Pulling Simarn along with her, Breea ran around the circle to follow the boy.

They found him standing in hazy moonlight beside a laden cart, sniffing and wiping his face with the back of his sleeves. Breea walked up to him and put a hand on one broad shoulder. He yelped in terror, but did not try to escape.

Not intending to terrify him, Breea was unsure how to proceed. She didn't want to reveal who she was. Not yet. The boy's head turned to stare at the shifting dark that was her hand on his shoulder. He tried to move away, but Breea held him, feeling the muscles of his shoulder ripple like warm iron. The boy was heavy-weapon trained, and older than she had first thought, perhaps sixteen.

Simarn's bow clicked and the boy started at the sound.

Breea said to both of them, "Be still."

At her voice the boy sucked in a breath. Doubtless he had not expected a woman's voice. It gave her an idea. She released him, unbuckled her dagger belt, and handed it by feel to Simarn.

Away at the fire, the officer called, "Queen bitch! Worse for them that be late, girlie!"

"Where is the wine?" said Breea.

Wordless, the boy pointed to the cart where a massive tapped barrel sat beside a tall jug.

Breea said, "Take that off."

The boy seemed to understand and stripped quickly out of the dress. Clear of the shame, he stood straight, a little shorter than Breea, and though his eyes showed fear they also carried intense curiosity.

Breea wasn't sure what would happen next, and how many might die, so she asked the young soldier, "Are there any worthy in your company?"

The boy frowned.

Simarn said, "Answer your queen."

Like a jug being poured full with realization, the boy's eyes grew round, then horrified. His legs went soft and with a noise between despair and awe, he dropped hard to his knees.

Breea sighed. He would be of no use now. She walked to the cart and took the jug.

"Tettle," whispered the boy.

Breea turned back. "How will I know him?"

"No beard," said the boy.

Aside to Simarn, Breea said, "Stay with him."

"Yes, my queen," said Simarn.

Breea filled the jug, then walked back to the ring of men. Before stepping among them, she *listened* for the essence of the fire. It was far more powerful than the hearth fire she'd played with earlier. Respectful of its heat, she bound its essence to the earth, forging a woven path between them, letting cold stone draw down the heat of the flames until only faint coal remained. The men seemed too drunk to notice.

Breea unraveled all but a few strands of her cloaking weave and stepped among them. Their smell assaulted her. A sword flashed out for a swat, but the wielder overbalanced as it swept empty air. His neighbor cursed him and shoved the blade away where it had nearly taken him in the face. A man held a tankard in Breea's path, and she paused to pour. In the dark the man gave a nod of thanks, not quite looking at her. His eyes were bleary with drink, and his expression closed. Unlike the rest, the man was clean shaven, his grizzled hair cut short—Tettle, the man she would spare.

The officer on the other side of the fire ring bellowed, "Serve me, you bitch."

She moved on, but was stopped again by outthrust tankards. Unhurried, Breea poured a measure into each that was offered. The men seemed to enjoy the small rebellion of forcing their leader to drink after them. In the faint red light of the coals, no one saw who was serving them.

As Breea made her way around the fire ring, the officer's

lips shaped a tight cunning sneer. When she was close, he held his tankard in his left hand, close in to his chest, and waggled it to request drink. His right hand formed a great fat fist on his thigh which he let fall to the side to hide it from view.

As Breea began to pour, she looked into the man's eyes and released all boundaries on her power. The threads of her cloaking weave shredded and her skin shimmered alight. The officer's fist, raised to strike, trembled in the air as Breea's molten gaze burned into his soul. Behind Breea the fire roared as it caught the bloom of her essence-power. The officer squealed in terror and his bowels emptied in a noisy flush. His face spasmed in pain and he fell back off the crates that were his chair. On his back, he gurgled and spasmed, his face stretched with agony and livid fear while knotted fists clutched his uniform over his heart. A final breath wheezed from him, and he lay still, eyes staring.

Satisfied, if a little shocked, Breea turned from him to eighty faces gone white behind their beards. Essence rose from her glowing skin in faint whirls and the Tetr emerald on her breast shimmered like spring grass in the sun. Sweeping the assembly with her gaze, Breea realized that no one else need die. She turned to Tettle and walked to the man. His face was like an awed child's, mouth round like an O. Breea reached down and raised the hand that still held his tankard and poured the cup full. Holding his fingers to the handle so he wouldn't drop the wine, Breea turned to the men.

"Drink to your new captain," she said.

Slowly, they reacted. A few drank so fast they slopped wine over their faces. Others stared in blank awe. A man near raised his tankard, found it empty, then pretended to drink. Breea went to him and poured the man a dram. She gave him a nod, and he drank, trembling. One man with no tankard emptied his stew bowl and offered it. Others followed suit. In complete silence, Breea walked the ring, giving each a small measure of the remaining wine.

Tettle stood and roughly cleared his throat. He raised his tankard, and bellowed, "The queen!"

The company followed suit, more or less. Some seemed unable to stand.

Breea set the jug on the ground, looked at the stinking, fearful men, and said in a dark tone, "The One to your blades."

She turned and strode into the night, binding her power and vanishing from sight.

CHAPTER 10

Pray for Storm

VALIENA WATCHED TAUMEA USE THE ROPE TO walk up the cliff wall. His words rang in her mind with the force of prophecy. *A path forged in blood.* Her grip on the bow tightened as she remembered her thirteenth summer and the harrowing escape across the Timaret Plains from the Temple assassin sent to retrieve her. On the darkest night of that flight, Valiena had seen her destiny—a vision of a mountain in moonlight, and a mound of blood and flesh she boiled to feed an army—an army led by a girl. The mountain had been Limtir, and the girl—Breea. Valiena felt certain that the time of armies and blood was upon them. Breea would come, an army at her back. That knowledge gave Valiena the strength to face any foe. She thanked Opalah for life, love, and a straight path, then added heart's thanks for the gift of Anila and Spe. All she and Taumea need do was survive and protect the children until Breea found them.

The rope went taught and the apple baskets began to rise.

Valiena looked up and down the canyon, then checked her bowstring for wear or damage. She smoothed the notched arrow's fletching and found that a part of her was grateful for the whole harrowing journey, for within that time she'd come to know Taumea as few women knew their men. She wondered if what he thought of her had changed as well. She was not the same woman who had ridden out of Limtir with her best friend eight long months ago. She arched her back, stretching.

The time in the Abital ruins had been restful, and her body felt lean and powerful, like a horse in her prime. The thought brought memories and pain. Living without her mare Oletanan was a daily agony she struggled to ignore. To distance herself from fears about the fate of her dearest horse, she set herself to speculating about the kind of horse Taumea might have chosen for her and the girls. It was going to be good to ride once more.

The empty rope came sailing down, and after checking up and down the canyon, she set aside her bow and tied the rope to the their bundles. She stepped back and waved to Taumea as he peered down. He vanished and the packs rose.

When the rope came back down, it had a big loop tied in the end.

"Opalah bless," said Valiena, staring at the rope in concern.

She dropped her arrow into its quiver, and shouldered her bow. Gingerly she stepped into the loop and raised it around her backside. She backed up to see Taumea looking down at her. His teeth flashed as he grinned. She tossed her hair in defiance. When the slack began rising, her heart leapt. They'd done this once before when entering the canyons of the haunted city, but it had not gone well.

"Walk the wall, walk the wall," she muttered, and stepped up to the rock face.

The rope tightened and lifted her. It cut into her hips and she slid forward, banging her knees on the rough stone. She pushed away as she was lifted from the ground. After a few more painful encounters with the stone, she managed to get her feet against the rock face.

As she rose above the canyon floor, the view of dawn sky opened and she could see that Taumea had placed a saddle on the cliff edge to ease the rope over the rim. She was appalled to see a curl of smoke rise from the leather, but before she could take action, she was at the top and Taumea's arm was there. She gripped him with both hands, and he lifted her up and over the edge.

He called, "Halt!"

Valiena hugged him for a moment, then looked to see Anila standing before the warhorse that Taumea had used to raise her. The girl looked so tiny beside the animal, but it seemed to like her, lowering its head to gently sniff her shoulder. Her body was stiff with fright and wonder, but her face was determined. She looked to Taumea to see if she'd done right.

"Bring him," said Taumea in an approving tone.

Anila walked, and the warhorse followed obediently.

Taumea said under his breath, "He wasn't like that with

me."

"Moonlight upon us," said Valiena. "Arahal."

Taumea looked at her.

"Heart of the horse," she said. It had been the same with her and Oletanan. For most plainsfolk the bond happened only once in their lives. She felt tears starting, and to distract herself, pulled the saddle from the edge, looking at the damage the rope had done with an eye to mending the seat.

"We don't need it," said Taumea.

Valiena stopped. She knew the comment was his way of urging her to useful action. She stood and took in their situation as she would upon first entering a kitchen. An abandoned orchard surrounded them. To her right a string of mounts tied to a tree nosed about in the dry grass beneath it and scuffled with one another when one found an old apple. Beneath another tree, Spe lay tight against a blanket-wrapped figure that did not move. A league or so to the northeast, a column of black smoke billowed high into a blood-colored sky. Valiena felt a shiver tighten the skin of her back and neck.

Unshouldering her bow she looked to Taumea. He was gazing west, where snow-dusted peaks caught the red light of dawn like bloody teeth before a dark gray sky. He looked at her, and she nodded. The mountains would be their path— a path toward Breea.

Taumea said, "Two pack strings. We will shift mounts every other bell. We must make the hills by nightfall."

Anila came up to them with the warhorse behind her. It nuzzled her hair, and her eyes widened. Valiena laughed in gentle delight. Kneeling beside the girl, she said, "He likes you."

Anila turned stiffly to face the horse and he turned his

head to regard her with one brown eye.

"Come," said Valiena. "Let's be sure he is ready to run. Hold the reins in this way."

Valiena looped the leather through Anila's fingers.

"Now talk to him."

Anila was mute.

"It matters not what you say, but it won't hurt to tell him how beautiful he is. How strong and swift. Like the wind."

Anila looked up at the mention of wind.

Valiena stroked his forehead and watched the horse's reaction then ran her hand along his neck to his shoulder. He shifted a little, but was intent on Anila. The brown coat was hot and damp. Valiena held out her hand for Anila's, and guided the girl's hand up to the horse's shoulder. It was about as high as Anila could reach. At her touch the horse trembled, raised his head, and whinnied. Valiena knew it would happen and caught Anila as the girl stumbled back. The horse shook himself and took a few dancing steps, shod hooves loud on the sandy stone.

Two big tears rolled down Anila's cheeks and she trembled in Valiena's arms.

"He's yours now," said Valiena.

Anila's face changed. "Mine?"

"For ever more."

The girl stopped trembling and leaned forward. Valiena stood way and wiped her own cheeks.

Anila took a step toward the horse and he reciprocated. She raised her hands and the warhorse lowered his head into her arms.

Wind hissed through the dried grasses and set branches waving. There was a gasp from the girl's mother. She struggled to a sitting position clutching something to her chest. Spe pushed herself up, rubbing sleep from her eyes with dirty little fists.

Taumea said, "Let us move." He picked up his bow, slung it over his shoulder, and strode to the horses.

Valiena went to their pack bundles and untied them, rearranging the bedrolls and clothing and gear. She looked up to watch Anila walk to her mother with the warhorse in tow. The girl's mother hissed something and Anila stiffened. Spe shook her head in denial. Valiena noticed Taumea looking at her, and returned to her repacking, using blankets and rope to shape pack bags that could be draped over a horse. It was a task she was long accustomed to and she finished before Taumea was ready with the horses. She went to him and picked out an older though still spry mare for her first mount.

Valiena stroked the animal and checked its legs while asking in the language of her people where the mare had acquired her many battle scars.

"These are fair horse," said Valiena to Taumea. "Older than prime, but experienced. Why was there cavalry in Tilin?"

Taumea finished adjusting the saddle on a big gelding. "Their riders bedded in the Temple. Not a local garrison."

Valiena glanced at the column of smoke spreading across the sky. Twenty horse meant that in men at least, and Taumea spoke of their riders with calm detachment. That smoke was likely a pyre.

Taumea drew close with the horses between them and the girls.

"Scouts," he said. "Hunting us, most like. There were villagers flayed. And there were Soot."

Valiena looked at him in fear.

"Not a full ril. One I took," he said. "Another escaped."

Valiena said, "Scouts and Soot? Does that not herald the coming of a larger force?"

Taumea nodded, and she could see that he had been thinking the same thing.

He stroked the horse's flank and said, "We do not have Meric mounts, but we have many. We will outpace pursuit." In a lower tone he said, "If the mother cannot take the pace, we will need to decide what to do."

"How sick is she?" asked Valiena.

"Red lung," said Taumea.

"Opalah," said Valiena. "The girls should not be so close to her."

Taumea shook his head. "Their nature protects them, I think, for neither of them have it." He left the rest unsaid. He and Valiena were no Alach to resist the attack of a disease that could fell cities.

Taumea looked out through the branches at the mountains to the west. "It will be a ride worthy of song. I shall expect you to compose something suitable."

Valiena jabbed him in the ribs just like Breea used to do when they had been three inseparable friends running wild in the halls of Limtir. It reminded them both of Breea and how unsure was their path to find her. Silent, they loaded the horse.

———*∿∿*———

Valiena did not like the look of the High Path road. From her vantage on a low rise half a league away, she could see the stone track heading off for leagues in both directions, which meant that anyone with a similar vantage could see the same. Further, there did not seem to be an approach that gave good cover. Their mountain goal towered to where the sun was falling into the storm clouds behind the peaks. Before night fell they needed to be up among the steep-sided hills that rose abruptly beyond the road and rolled away west in smooth rising waves that grew nobbled spines as if cresting into the mountains. Valiena crept back a bit and turned to see if Taumea and the girls were visible. She knew approximately where they were in the low scrubland, but there was no sign of their approach. Out east, the sun still touched the land. There was no sign of the burning village Temple, but she felt sure they were being tracked from there. Eighteen horse left a unmistakable trail. To the southeast the red dunes around the ancient Alach city were a line of rich orange on the horizon that faded to gray as she watched. The sun was gone. Valiena blinked her tired eyes—strained all day from trying see any sign of an enemy before it saw her.

In the morning before they had set out, Taumea suggested that Valiena range ahead, and Valiena had understood. The girls were all. He must not leave their side. She had since exhausted four mounts in her scouting. Pushing aside her own fatigue, she slid forward through the dry grass hummocks to check the road once more—and froze.

A long line of black had appeared on the road from the north. Cavalry, moving briskly. As she watched the column pass along the road, she groaned. Every quarter league a black spot was left at the tail like droppings from the hind end of a caterpillar.

Valiena moved back, careful not to raise dust, and picked up her bow. Out of sight, she ran to her horse and led him away by the reins.

Following her own tracks, she made her way back to the shallow wash she'd used to come upon the rise. When there was no chance of her dust being visible from the road, she mounted. Leaning down by this horse's neck she whispered, "*Yeaf!*" The horse had learned in recent hours that this meant to gallop, but he was tired and reluctant. Valiena kicked his flanks and he bounded heavily forward.

Taumea appeared sooner than she expected, leading the string of mounts at a trot up the wash. He called to them in Yasharn, ordering a halt. The horses obeyed like the well-trained mounts they were. Directly behind him Anila rode her horse with her sister astride before her, the little girl somehow asleep against Anila despite the bouncing pace. After them Tiyha sat her horse like she was made of wood, shoulders curled, head down. Her skirts bunched up around her knees, showing rough woolen leggings above her winter sandals. One hand was a fist clutched at her belly. There was blood on her lips. Valiena shuddered at the thought of red lung and reined up beside Taumea.

"Cavalry on the road," she said. "They are leaving soldiers every quarter league."

He considered this, then asked, "Any sign of water?"

"No," said Valiena. "No pools, no streams."

"Buildings? Smoke?"

"None."

His head rose. "Their cavalry will have water."

Stealing water from Temple cavalry did not seem like a well-lit path, and Valiena realized that she hadn't told him how many there were. "I saw ten pa-hoc of them at least," she said.

"Then we shall drink quietly," said Taumea in a flat tone.

Valiena found herself smiling.

Taumea looked up the wash. "Any cover?"

Valiena shook her head. "The land shallows from here. There is a single hill ahead and then a long flat slope to the road."

Taumea dismounted, then lifted the girls down from Anila's horse.

The warhorse turned and pushed at the girl's hands, sniffing insistently.

Spe said, "He's hungry."

"Give him an apple," said Taumea.

Both girls looked up at him in surprise.

Their mother, still astride her horse, said in a wispy voice, "Azsark apple is not for beasts."

Taumea replied, "We have given the horses our water, but not enough, and no time to forage. Their strength is our life."

Valiena and Taumea had planned to feed the horses the Azsark apples from the start. Tiyha's haggard face went defiant then despairing. Valiena didn't know what to say to help Tiyha come to terms with the truth that these would be the last Azsark apples she would ever see. Never again would she return to her village—never again send her daughters to the Azsark for apples for their vicious Da. Taumea had not said it, but Valiena could tell from his manner that Da was no longer a threat to anyone.

Spe was watching her mother with big innocent eyes and Anila too. Even Anila's horse looked at her. Tiyha looked away from them all.

Taumea helped Valiena dismount. He mounted his own horse and signed, *Feed the horses,* then urged his mount into a gallop up the wash.

Valiena stroked the head of Anila's horse.

"Have you named him?" she asked.

Anila clenched her jaw, but Spe said, "He's Azsark!"

Anila looked like she wanted to curse her sister, but didn't contradict her. Valiena smiled, and wondered how Tiyha would take naming a "beast" after the tree.

"A wonderful name," said Valiena. "My horse's name is Oletanan. She's the fastest horse in all of Limtir but for one. Would you like to hear how we met?"

Both girls were intent on her face. "Come," she said, "I need your hands, and you can earn your story."

First Valiena untied Azsark from the lead. At this stage of the Arahal, a horse and rider were inseparable. She took the girls down the line of horses to those carrying the apple baskets. Azsark followed and began nibbling some dry grass close to Anila.

Valiena slung her bow across her chest and lifted an apple from a basket. With a cook's skill, she sliced it in half with her long Limtir dagger.

Seeing the girls' hungry looks, she said, "Your horse eats first." She handed half to Anila.

Before Anila could turn, Azsark's head descended over her shoulder. She raised the huge piece in both hands. There was a crunch and apple juice ran over Anila's hands.

"Keep your hands flat," said Valiena.

Azsark took another loud bite. Spe reached up and Anila lowered the dripping chunk of apple to her open hands. The warhorse's head followed the apple, felt it with his lips, then took a dainty bite. The sisters held the apple together as he ate.

When he was done, Valiena loaded the girls with giant apple halves, then walked up the line, sharing the story of the flash flood which had led her to find Oletanan as a foal.

Over her voice, the sound of crunching was loud, and apple scent filled the wash.

The horses' ears twitched and Valiena lifted her bow off her shoulder, setting an arrow to string. Both girls tensed and she saw Anila take a breath. Taumea appeared at the far bend in the wash, riding at a trot. Valiena put the arrow away, and briefly touched Anila to let her know all was well, then strode out to meet Taumea. She and Taumea tried to keep discussions of what was hunting them away from the girls.

He dismounted and walked his horse until they met. His face was grim.

"They are lighting watch fires," he said. "Patrols will begin as the light fails." He looked back and up at the black clouds beyond the first range of peaks.

"Taumea," said Valiena, voicing something which had nagged her for the past hour. "Why are they ahead of us here?"

"Would that those clouds would descend," he said. "Rain or snow, either would be welcome cover."

"Can we fly south?" asked Valiena.

Taumea turned back to her. "Did you see the barding on their mounts?"

Valiena hadn't noticed, but it was true that the cavalry had appeared universally black in color, which wasn't natural.

"Black is the barding of Kultash cavalry," said Taumea. "They are here for us. All ways will be watched."

Valiena bore down on her fear, amazed that her reaction wasn't worse. Being hunted by Temple assassins and Dauthaz had changed her view of danger. For some reason that reminded her of Breea.

She said, "Are they truly come for us? Kultash do not

obey the Temple."

Taumea said, "They will be of the Iplock Ulshan. The whole mounted battalion, it would seem. They may have decided that word of us was worthy of their attention, or perhaps the Dauthaz made passage through Iplock and set them alight, leading them here. The Temple may have forgotten what true Dauthaz are, but I doubt it is so with the Kultash. If an accurate report was made to them of that thing's nature, they may not know of us, yet they have blocked the way to the mountains. That implies foreknowledge of our intentions."

"Could they have captured Charlthon at his manor?" said Valiena. "We know of the mountain routes from him. It was the way Breea took."

Taumea went still, considering. "We shall wait for dark and see what may be discovered. No matter our path, we must not meet Kultash cavalry on open ground. Pray for storm."

—◦◊◦—

Anila stood where she could see the Limtir lord and lady but Azsark blocked her view of Ma. The listening tube was something Anila could do without Ma noticing, but it required focus, and even if Ma couldn't always feel Anila using the Breath, Ma could see it on Anila's face when she did. Since first meeting the lord and lady, Anila made certain to listen to what they had to say to each other, and made sure Spe could hear too. Something big and terrible was happening and Anila believed now that the lord and lady were trying to save everyone from its coming. Taumea's words at morning had etched themselves into her thoughts:

We're going to need everything those girls can do. She knew he meant the Breath of the Gods, and far down in her chest she hid the secret joy that his words brought. To be needed for the Breath was her deepest wish.

On the ride, when she had whispered to Spe that the two of them had to help the lady and lord, even to using the Breath, Spe had agreed so readily that Anila realized her little sister had already made the same decision. Spe didn't talk much, a lot less than the other girls her age in the village, but Spe thought about things a lot more than anyone knew. Anila laid a hand on Spe's head and looked down at her. Spe was frowning with her eyes closed, lips pouted out in concentration.

The Breath of the air shivered as if the whole sky had gotten a chill. Behind Azsark, Ma gasped.

Taumea and Valiena came walking up. Anila's heart pounded in fear of what the lord and lady would do in response to whatever Spe had done, but they walked past, continuing their conversation, merely nodding to her. Spe's face had relaxed into a tired, vaguely determined expression. Anila followed after the lord and lady, herding Spe along. A dread-filled glance at Ma showed not the sharp iron of her anger, but a shocked and haunted expression—and pain. Feeling guilty, Anila looked down. Everything they did seemed to cause Ma pain.

—◦◦◦—

"The dark is full," said Taumea.

He lay concealed with Valiena watching the line of faint orange flickers that marked the fires along the road. Every few minutes a fire would go dark for a moment as a figure passed in front of it. A cold breeze pressed at their faces, whipping the grasses around them.

Beside him Valiena remained silent. He leaned over and kissed her temple through the wool of her cloak hood. She crawled back from the top of the rise. Taumea followed and they walked down to the string of horses. It was a relief to get out of the wind.

Without a word Valiena untied the lead rope of a string of thirteen mounts from a stake they'd driven into the sand, then stood by. She did not like this plan. Taumea took stock of the mounts they would keep. Behind horses for him and Valiena's mount, the girls rode Azsark. Their two faces showed pale by moon- and starlight, eyes shining. Their mother, wrapped in thick blankets on the next horse, was invisible within the folds.

When the wind had come, the girls had refused Taumea's offer of blankets, asking him to give them to Ma. When he hesitated, Anila had reached down and put her hand on the side of his face to prove that they were warm— the gesture so trusting that it had warmed his heart for hours after.

He walked over to their horse and tugged off his gauntlet. He raised his hand to them. After a moment, their hands settled on his fingers like warm birds. He gave them a squeeze then started at the heat he felt through their skin. Warmth passed up his arm, and for a moment he was sure that their worried eyes had flared like sparks whirled in a gust of wind.

In wonder, he left them and walked to Valiena. He laid his warm hand upon her cheek, then slid it around the back of her neck and pulled her up into a kiss. Her lips were cold, and she made a little cry of affection and worry into his mouth as she wrapped arms about his chest in a fierce embrace.

"Opalah," she said when they broke the kiss. "You're warm."

"Truth," said Taumea. "A gift from the girls. You?"

"Getting cold," she said.

"Then I go."

Taumea wrapped his cloak about him, took the rope from her, and strode into the wind. The long string settled into a walk behind him.

Halfway across the moonlit plain, motes of chill struck his face and he looked up. Snow. Stars above the mountains were vanishing in line as though being extinguished by a rush of black water. The storm was coming down from the mountain. He glanced back across the dark plain, then quickened his pace.

Near the road, he hobbled the horses and approached. There was no need for stealth. The pair of Kultash warriors at the nearest fire were hunched over the flames, intent on keeping it lit. Taumea went back to the horses, took off his sword belt, and tied it on a saddle. He led a pair of the Temple horses south, well beyond the fire then up onto the hexagonal stones of the raised roadbed. He slashed a hole in the center of a blanket and put his head through. It covered his armor well, and he set out for the watch fire he'd scouted.

The sound of shod hooves on the road brought the Kultash warriors around, hands on hilts. Snow whipped past in the wind-thrashed firelight. Each Kultash wore a black coat of thick wool. Wide belts supported gently curved two-handed swords. Long dark scarves were wrapped around their helms, faces, and necks. Taumea walked to the edge of light, one arm up as though shielding his face from the wind.

He made repeated touches to forehead and sky and said in the way he'd practiced with Valiena, "Fresh mounts, holy sirs."

The warriors turned back to the fire, calling for him to bring them more wood. Taumea grinned. Quick as quick he tied his horses to low shrubs beside the Kultash animals then ran around to the wood pile. He grabbed a huge armload, dropped it at the warrior's feet, then, bowing and saluting, rushed to the warrior's mounts. Swiftly, he swapped saddles, then vanished down the road with two fed and watered Kultash horses.

Once out of sight and hearing, Taumea left the road and returned to the string of mounts. It had gone precisely as he had hoped. Smiling to himself, he tied the new horses to a shrub, then went still.

The world dimmed almost to complete pitch as though a god's shadow had covered the night. He looked up in time to see the last light of the moon smother behind a ragged edge of cloud. The decision to steal another set of horses had been swift and simple. The animals were life, and these two Kultash animals looked to have some Meric steed in their bloodlines. By feel, he untied another pair of Temple horses and made for the road once again.

The next pair of warriors ignored him completely as they worked to build a wall of wood upwind of their dying fire. Taumea exchanged the horses and slipped away.

It took some searching to locate the mounts. Without pause, he cut the remaining animals from the string and set them loose. With four new horses, he strode toward the star blaze that remained in the east. When he felt himself close to the place they had chosen to meet, he bent low to the ground and found Anila's silhouette atop Azsark against the stars of the eastern horizon.

Valiena was suddenly before him, come out to meet him. Breathless, she said, "The road."

Taumea couldn't fathom what he was seeing. The flickering fires along the road had begun to dim and wink out.

"Blood and martyrs. That's snow," he said.

They quick-stepped toward Anila and the horse string. They could hear the snow coming.

"Do we turn back?" asked Valiena.

"The mountains are our path," said Taumea—and the storm struck. Driven snow bit at his face with a hiss. The world went icy and utterly dark.

"I'll find the girls," called Taumea, and gave the bridles of the new horses to Valiena by feel.

Walking with the wind, he felt his way down the pack string, thinking hard. They needed to get into the hills, and they needed shelter. Already he could feel the slight crunch of collected snow beneath his boots. Moving past Valiena's mount with one hand on the rope connecting horses, he noticed a change in the wind—it had lessened before him. He reached blindly before him, but carefully, for if Azsark was there, he did not want to startle the stallion while standing in the path of a hind kick.

"Azsark?"

Instead of a horse, he touched a wall. His hand flashed to his sword hilt. There could be no wall here—they were on the open plain. He reached out and found it again, firm and oddly smooth under his glove. Above and to his left, two pairs of luminous eyes, one higher than the other, turned his way. The wall went soft and a breath of air puffed past. A hummed melody could be heard over the now distant wind.

Spe said in an immensely satisfied voice, "Storm."

"That it is," said Taumea, feeling dreamlike. "Yet not where we stand."

"That's Anila," said Spe.

"Ah. Good," said Taumea, coming up beside them in the dark. "Very good. In truth." He felt like laughing.

"I'm the storm," said Spe in a voice that indicated she wanted approval too.

"You are?" said Taumea.

"I prayed!"

When the full meaning of her cheerful declaration sank in, he muttered, "Blood and…" He cleared his throat. "I mean to say good, very good." This was exactly like traveling with Breea—revelations and elemental forces brought to heel. He grinned.

"How big can this…shelter be?"

Spe's sparkling eyes looked up at Anila, but neither answered. Either they did not know or this was a big as it got.

A few minutes later, Taumea was lifting Valiena in his arms and doing a little whirl in the snowy dark.

"They're weaving," he said, setting her down. "The storm is theirs."

"Opalah bless," said Valiena, breathless.

Using him as a windbreak, Valiena said, "We cannot take all these horses. We can't feed them."

"We need to cross the road," he said. "We can release the spares at first light."

Valiena said, "Let us use a Windrider remount."

Taumea considered, then said, "Show me."

In the dark, Valiena led their horses into a circle. She cried out in fear when she ran into Anila's woven circle, and

Taumea rushed to her, finding her trembling and on the verge of tears.

"I wanted to surprise you with that," he said.

"You did."

In a voice on the edge of despair, Anila begged forgiveness.

Valiena went to her and Taumea followed.

"Make it again," said Valiena in a soft but clear tone.

Anila trailed off. Spe's sparkling eyes looked back and up at her sister.

"Mighty of the trees," sang Anila in a cracked voice, and the world went quiet.

"Bright ways," said Valiena cheerfully. "It's lovely."

Anila broke into sobs and the ice-laden wind slammed into them. Valiena's voice murmured confidently and Anila gave querulous acknowledgment.

Working within the ring of horses, they shifted apple baskets, saddled the new mounts, and moved Tiyha as well as their gear and provisions, all by feel.

"This worked well," said Taumea.

"Windriders," said Valiena with pride, "often ride the night."

Taumea asked, "Can they navigate in a blizzard?"

"Like breathing," said Valiena. "The wind is your star."

"Indeed," said Taumea.

They released their unneeded Temple mounts, reluctant to see them go. Valiena spoke to each before she released it into the dark. Taumea coiled the long lead rope and put his head through the coil so that it lay across his chest. He drew his sword to use as a touching cane. Together they took the lead rope and stepped cautiously into the bitter wind.

Taumea measured the passage in strides, squinting into

the black wind for any sign of the Kultash until melted snow streamed down his face and down his neck.

The smell of smoke was suddenly strong. Valiena stumbled to a stop beside him, and he pulled down on the horse's bridle and pushed against its forehead. The horse halted then took a couple steps as the animal behind bumped into it, but Taumea held it back. He unlooped the rope across his chest and gave Valiena one end, then stalked forward with the other.

A hint of light flickered through the snowfall. He crept closer and almost fell over the edge of the raised roadbed of the High Path. Across the stone road, two Kultash soldiers could be seen working around a suffering fire. They were building a curved wall of interlinked firewood pieces upwind of the fire. Snow streamed thick through the firelight almost horizontal to the ground.

One of them poured something onto the fire and it flared. In the light, two black-barded horses showed to one side, their hind ends facing into the wind. Both were looking across the road directly at Taumea. He saluted their watchfulness and backed away. A sound caught his ear and he whipped back his hood to listen. It had sounded like a wolf howl. The Kultash might be recalling their watch. He checked the pull of his sword and dagger, then let the wind push him along the rope back to Valiena.

After coiling the rope once more, he said into her hood, "We go five hundred strides north. Then cross."

It was a slow, hard walk in total darkness. At the end of this stride count, Taumea used his sword to feel the way to the stones of the road. With his hands he felt along the stone way until he found a sandy dune that would let the horses walk up onto the road without fear of breaking their legs.

They crossed and he said into Valiena's hood, "Up into the hills. I will follow on."

Valiena's voice sounded bent double by strain. "Taumea. I cannot see. This may not be the route."

"There is no other path," said Taumea. "We must be free of the road."

"I cannot see," she said again.

"I can," said Anila's voice out of the dark.

"Azsark to lead," said Taumea without hesitation.

A few bells later, Taumea abandoned his watch on the road and trudged up the dark valley. The snow was falling as heavily as ever, blowing into his face. Despite the cold, he felt like a furnace. He found himself stepping through knee-high drifts. From what he remembered of the valley, he had a league of travel before having to worry about the valley branching. Without his noticing the night had gone from pitch to merely dark, and he knew the moon was shining through to light the white ground. It reminded him of his first winter in Limtir and Breea's night walks on snowshoes by cloud-filtered moonlight through the Gamanthea-Dur forest.

Somewhere beyond these mountains Breea was fighting. In the Alach city ruins, both he and Valiena had dreamed of her battles, though in the morning they could never recall exactly what or who their friend battled. Taumea needed to find her, for beyond the loyalty of true friendship, he was duty driven by oath to protect Breea. With a determined sigh, Taumea set his thoughts to what lay directly before him— how he might cross the mountains with the girls. This storm had poured its cold blanket on the high mountains for more than a day before Spe had called it down. The mountain passes that their ally Charlthon had described would be treacherous now if they were even reachable without snowshoes. Their plan had been to cross the pass that rumor identified as Breea's path once he had recovered from the wound received crossing the Leuvat Sea. Charlthon had told a story recounted by high-country miners that a woman with foot-long green fangs had nearly eaten them alive. The Temple had also heard the tale, and the arrival of Soot in the area had forced Taumea and Valiena to flee Charlthon's protection and run south to the canyon ruins of the buried city.

A cry came to his ears, and he threw back his hood, head up. There was nothing more. The snowfall had slackened, only lightly wetting his face. Turning a circle, he froze as a hot wash of calm smashed through him. A thousand paces away, down at the mouth of the valley, a cluster of lamps flickered in and out of vision. The Kultash weren't moving on.

Taumea drew his blunted sword. In long downhill strides he set out to meet the Kultash.

CHAPTER 11

Chosen

AS BREEA STRODE BACK TO THE WINE CART,
bitter thoughts troubled her. How could she save a nation
with such men? The Oregule made beasts of men, but here
were men who corrupted themselves. Most-like they would
fade into the night now, and that was best, for with their
heads that far into the barrel they would more than likely die
at the pace she intended to travel. Were all who joined her to
be like this? Would she be traveling with Batusha only? She
longed for the honest skill and dedication of the Tomeguard

back home, but home was dead.

At the cart she drew a dagger and slashed the barrel with an angry stroke, skipping aside as the wine streamed out. A vision of a river of blood swept her cold.

Breea shuddered, and sheathed her pulsing dagger.

"My queen?" said Simarn in a worried voice.

"What is it?" said Breea.

"The boy, my queen. He returned to the men."

Breea nodded, then realized Simarn might not be able to see her in the dark and said, "Yes."

Angry, and fearful of what she would find, she strode in cold moonlight toward the sound and firelight that seemed to be the heart of the muster. Soon she stepped into a loose stream of soldiers heading for the nearest muster blaze. Most took little notice of the two women among them, though one or two knelt, touching fingers to forehead when they recognized her. Most were young, carrying a single sack which hung from weapons over their shoulders. Some carried nothing, not even a weapon; others looked like overburdened mules with armor, bags, packs, and rolls and various weapons about their person, from spears to long-hafted battle-axes.

When she stepped into the broad ring of firelight cast by a head-high blaze, a stunned quiet spread before her, followed by a wave of obeisance and prostration. An Aska-Wuthos officer who had been directing men to a row of tables took a step toward her, peering in disbelief. His eyes widened, and in one motion he threw open his cloak, drew his saber, and dropped to one knee, touching the blade hilt to his forehead.

Coming up to him, she said in his language, "Rise."

He stood, sheathed his blade with a snap, then

straightened in the aspect of a statue. Breea's senses let her feel his racing heart, making the outward stillness he displayed impressive. A true officer. Disciplined and passionate. His armor under the cloak looked to be fashioned of polished brass and dark scales. She resisted the urge to reach out and feel their texture.

"Where are your commanders?" said Breea.

"My queen," said the soldier. "At the center." He pointed with a crisp gesture toward the next muster blaze, then returned to attention.

"Thank you," said Breea. After a moment, she said, "You may return to your duties."

"Aye, my queen." He turned and marched to the line of kneeling, prone, or bowing soldiers. Most had their heads lifted to peer at Breea.

"Up!" he shouted in accented Yasharn. "She's nowt your queen till you've put your mark on parchment and sworn body and soul to her."

A young soldier, not yet old enough to grow a beard, asked the officer something, and he said in a lower tone, "Aye. S'truth. Chosen she is, and so shall we be, in her Service."

A few steps into the dark and a touch of essence served to cloak her presence. Breea watched. The lines to each table moved slow but consistent as each recruit was questioned about his skills and current unit, then made to swear to obey the Chosen in all things. Finally, a clerk in gray robes took the man's name, and each made his mark beside it on a sheaf of parchment. The recruit was given a colored divot of wood and directed to one of the distant blazes glowing through the smoke haze. The process seemed organized, and the men looked sound enough.

Feeling better, Breea shed her essence-cloak and walked with her new men. It felt right to be seen, and after her encounter with the drunk company she found it rewarding to see signs of respect from hale men who had come to her call. Aska-Wuthos seemed to be the core of the muster, directing men and materials. Runner boys in blue tunics with a yellow sea-dragon emblem darted among the men, stopping to deliver small scrolls to Aska-Wuthos officers. Recruits walked singly or in groups, showing their colored divots of wood to Aska-Wuthos soldiers standing beneath torch pikes driven into the ground. The soldiers directed the recruits accordingly. Here and there she saw soldiers with laden pack animals, and fewer yet who rode their own horses. These men were given special instruction and directed away from the general flow.

In the dark between muster blazes, few took notice of Breea, but as she neared the heart of the muster the way was lit at frequent intervals with pike-mounted torches that flickered and smoked. In these brighter places a murmur of comment and bowing spread out from her. Simarn was her shadow, her bow loaded, the weapon drawing frowns and whispers. There were dozens of dialects of Yasharn and a few languages that Breea had never heard but could understand by way of the Tetr medallion. Assembly fields gave off a low murmur of voices punctuated by shouted orders and occasional laughter or music. Cook fires were being lit in ordered rows in these areas, and she could smell meat cooking. Breea wanted to go among them, and be with them as they ate, but she kept to the bearing given to her by the officer. After passing a few of these assembly areas, she wondered how many men they held and how many were answering the muster.

Ahead, half a dozen men in black coats belted over chainmail stood with legs braced and arms crossed. Their formation blocked the path. Curved two-handed swords were thrust through the belt at their waists. All were bearded. At twenty paces Breea paused, for they looked like Temple guards. The soldiers passing back and forth before them gave them a wide berth. Beyond lay an immense array of oiled-leather tents with dark figures moving among them. Eyeing the warriors, Breea closed to ten paces, then looked to either side. The tent array curved away in hazy moonlight in each direction as though the encampment shaped a circle. At each gap between tents another tall, black-coated warrior stood.

The six before her watched her with vivid gazes. Behind her a crowd of onlookers was gathering, whispering. Breea set her shoulders and strode forward. At five paces the six split aside like a door opening, three to a side. When Breea's boot passed an invisible threshold just before the first pair, the six leaned forward in a smooth half-bow, raising their left hands to touch foreheads, extending their arms upward, fingers pointing to the sky. They held that posture until she and Simarn were past.

Breea couldn't resist looking back and watched as the six swung closed the gap with measured steps. Where their chainmail glimmered at sleeve ends and at the thigh, it appeared to be twice as thick as normal mail, and fashioned in a knot-like pattern. She'd never seen anything like it. The cut of their coats left room to move, as did the bloused pant legs gathered just below the knee into tall, oiled boots. Not the same garb as Temple guard, and these men wore dignity like plate mail.

Breea whispered to Simarn, "Who are they, I wonder?"

When Simarn didn't answer, Breea looked at her. Simarn's gaze on the soldiers' backs was a whirl of fear and wonder—and awe.

Simarn flinched when she realized Breea was watching her.

"Kultash," said Simarn.

Breea didn't know what that meant, and she ignored the whispering Tetr medallion, for she was hurt by Simarn's flinching reaction to her. Was this what it meant to be Alach? To be feared by all? How much had Simarn seen of the death of the captain of the foul company? Breea touched the Tetr medallion, then snatched her hand away. She turned on her heel and strode for the center of the tent rings. Simarn ran to catch her.

Through the smoke haze a great round tent came into view, lit by torches and ringed by Batusha warriors resplendent in red lacquered armor. Their weapons were drawn. Before the tent's entrance two Batusha masters *chak'ood*, and two Kultash bowed, but Breea was staring at the fanged head of a Dauthaz dripping white blood down the haft of a spear that spiked the skull. It was fresh.

The heavy door curtain was thrust aside and the priest Arin stepped out. When Breea turned to him, he nearly bowed, but caught himself with a jerk, apparently remembering Breea's instructions for him to stop bowing. He chose a dignified *chak'ood* instead. Breea's order had been a joke at the time, but she liked being greeted with a simple salute rather than obeisance.

"Master," Arin said in a warm voice. He stepped aside, holding open the heavy door cloth.

Breea paused to look at him. The warmth of his voice was matched by the relief and pleasure in his eyes. He looked down as though embarrassed by her regard. Moved, Breea touched his shoulder as she passed into the dim warmth of the tent. It smelled of hot beeswax and men. She found herself in a candlelit partition, and paused. There was no clear path forward. She could hear voices before her in low argument.

"Arin," said Breea quietly. "Why are Batusha guarding this tent?"

Arin skipped past and held aside another curtain to the side. His eyes said the answer lay within.

Breea walked into the open lamplit heart of the tent as Arin called in a ringing voice, "Master Banea, Chosen of the One!"

A high, square table illuminated by four candelabras dominated the center of the space. On the left stood six Batusha warriors in beautiful red armor decorated in gold filigree. Together they turned to face her and slapped back-fists to palm. Master Planner Longat was there, along with Sabar, Ootha, and Neprawn. The other two weapons masters were men she'd fought with against the Dauthaz, but did not know their names. At the head of the table facing Breea stood a giant, bearded warrior in a black coat over unusually thick chainmail that looked almost woven.

First of the Kultash, whispered the medallion.

Breea met his gaze, and a humming thrill sang through her. She felt no weaving, but there was something in the man. Across his broad chest shimmered a sash of red-gold woven in patterns that seemed alive in the flickering candlelight. Breea's eyes dropped to the hilt of his curved sword, and followed the scabbard as far as she could see. She judged the blade alone to be twelve hands long. The double-handed hilt was wrapped in black leather and free of any adornment.

On the right side of the table opposite the Batusha masters stood five warriors dressed in the black coats and mail of Kultash. They regarded her with neutral facades. Each cut an impressive figure, even the graybeards, yet they seemed almost like children compared to their leader.

At the back wall there was movement—a figure rising from a chair with assistance from young Tam Beddig. The figure straightened and gingerly put back-fist to palm, his gaze enigmatic. Breea grinned. It was Scaukra. His blush was visible even in the candle and lantern light.

"*Anule*," she said.

Batusha relaxed. All eyes were upon her, and she was thrown back to the moment in the guild hall when her first act as the new Master of the Batusha Weapons Guild had been to lead them in a desperate street battle against the army of Temple guard sent to destroy them. It had been her first true battlefield and her first attempt to lead men. Unproven, she'd acted on impulse without expectation, and without plan. She still did not quite understand why Batusha had followed her, a woman, into battle that day.

This night was different, for she knew herself proven to the Batusha men, as their gazes affirmed—respectful, a touch awed, and—she stiffened. Ootha was staring at her breasts. Breea clenched her jaw in irritation, then smothered a grin. His gaze too was slightly awed, and seemed glazed with memory. There was no malice in his direct maleness. He'd seen her naked and glowing with essence-power, and apparently couldn't forget the sight. He felt her regard and ripped his gaze up from her chest to the level of her eyes without meeting them. His brother Sabar raised a hand to smack the back of Ootha's head, but stayed the hand when he found her watching. Breea almost giggled in nervous excitement. Here she stood before some of the deadliest warriors in all of Yash, yet in their hearts they were but men.

Except possibly this Kultash leader. He was as tall as Neprawn, but darker in every way. His gaze was cool, intent, and judging. Breea asked the Tetr medallion about him. Surprisingly, it knew only his name and title. It spoke of the Kultash whose dedication to a life of prayer through combat had made them legends across Yash and beyond. Beholden to no one, not even the High Priesthood, Kultash were said to take their orders directly from their god Het. Each Kultash lived according to the strictures of the Wisdom of the One. The circular array of tents outside was their camp pattern, and the tent she stood within was Ulshan—mobile sacred ground for battalion-scale Kultash gatherings. No Kultash army had accepted defeat since their order founding in the early centuries of the Yasharn realm. Breea's heart pounded with excitement. With such warriors at her side, saving Carsythe seemed suddenly possible, yet the man's manner was not one of an ally.

She adopted Ajalay's serious tone, and said to the Kultash, "I do not know you."

Before he could answer, Breea sensed someone enter. A feeling of violent intent bloomed behind her, and she whirled to find the youngest of the Aska-Wuthos brothers glaring with unconcealed hatred at the First of the Kultash.

Breea waited to see if the young man would stand down, but he seemed fixed in place, struggling to master himself.

To break the tension, Breea looked at Master Longat, and said, "How fares the muster?"

Longat turned to the table and waved a pudgy hand at a freshly drawn map. "Master, four ra-hoc are assembled."

Shocked, Breea stepped up to the table. "Four? Then, that is eight thousand men?"

"Twelve, Master," said Longat. "All the ra-hoc stand at full strength." His eyes sparkled with pleasure.

The young Aska-Wuthos strode to Breea's left, then took a knee, head bowed.

"Rise," she said in the Aska-Wuthos language.

At her use of his language, Breea felt the interest of the officers of the Kultash intensify and darken. Breea longed for Bay-ope. He would know how to teach her to handle these men. There was history here she did not know. She'd studied enough in her training to understand the dire consequences of going to war with a divided force.

The brother said, "Assembly of the fifth ra-hoc begins, my queen. We prepare ground for the sixth."

It did not seem possible. That would make fifteen thousand men, and the muster was only a few hours old. It made her giddy. Her first thought was to share the glory of it with Taumea and Valiena, and that put a knife in joy.

"Warrior," she said to the Aska-Wuthos, turning her mind from the fate of her friends. "You have fought for me, and are making me an army to break the siege of Carsythe. I owe you much, and yet I do not know your name."

A tremor seemed to pass through the young officer and his hatred bled away before pride.

He said with feeling, "Griv dal Wuthos, my queen."

"Griv dal Wuthos, please continue the muster."

Griv touched a knee to the ground, then strode out.

A man entered the chamber from a side curtain. He bowed deeply, then waited. He carried a scroll case, and was dressed in layers of thick gray wool. His fingers and the ends of his sleeves were stained with ink. Longat grunted and the man scurried forward. He pulled rolls from his case and set them on the table. Longat spread one open, smearing ink. His mouth curved down beneath his beard as he wiped his fingers on another sheet, but he had eyes only for the numbers. He dropped the sheet and gripped another, spreading it more carefully. Sabar took rocks from other sheets and weighted this one open on the table. Longat pushed the parchment to the center of the table, and the Kultash leaned in, murmuring to one another as their powerful hands drifted over the black ink, tapping entries. Batusha masters replied in kind. Their communication was so minimal that Breea could not follow it, but it was clear there was a plan against which all was being compared. Relief was like a flow of warm water over her that chilled as she realized that the First of the Kultash was looking at her with patient distain.

Like General Ohan, this was a man before whom she must not show weakness. Breea met his gaze with calm expectation. The thrill of that contact sang through her again. A part of her wanted to look away from the penetrating, judging regard, but she had gazed into the white eyes of Oregule. This man was nothing to them.

He blinked and said, "I am Sakuront Melayn, First of the Kultash."

"Why are you here?" said Breea.

Anger flashed through him, and Breea was pleased that her barb had found flesh. Despite the obvious fact that Sakuront was supporting the muster by allowing Batusha the use of the Kultash Ulshan, she did not like the way he watched her.

Sakuront said, "We await a sign."

Breea considered this, and assumed that he meant a sign

from god that she was Chosen of the One and that Het wished the Kultash to support her. It fascinated then angered her that all that had happened in recent days was yet deemed insufficient signs for the Kultash to act. Or was it inadequate evidence for this man to act? He was the pivot. The blessing of the Kultash for her quest could be key to the size of her growing army, but she would accept condescension from none.

"What would serve?" she said.

Sakuront said, "The One decides."

Breea nodded as though she accepted that. "So be it."

The skin around Sakuront's eyes tightened.

Breea's heart had begun to race, but she managed a straight tone. "Would your defeat in personal combat suffice?"

Conversation halted in the room.

In Sakuront's reply was a heavy mix of distain and boredom. "Name your champion."

Scaukra snorted a laugh, then coughed, leaning on Tam.

Ootha and Sabar looked at each other and muttered, "Blood and puss!"

Sakuront looked indifferent.

Breea asked him, "Do you abide by the new edicts?"

The man's bearded chin raised. "Nay. The Kultash abide the First Word."

"Good," said Breea. "I'd hate to for you to feel that I was breaking with Het's will by wielding blades."

Sakuront said, "There is no true edict against a woman holding a weapon."

Breea held back a smile. He still did not understand.

"High Priest Duyazen concurs," she said. To the Batusha masters she said, "Masters, will you clear this table from the floor?"

They did as she bade, exchanging looks of mingled excitement and raw concern. The five Kultash officers did not offer to help the Batusha move the table.

Breea turned to Simarn, who was at her shoulder. "My friend, will you disarm your bow? And keep it thus."

"Yes, my queen."

Breea took off the Tetr medallion and gave it to her, then gestured for her to move to the wall.

Breea faced Sakuront. "Sakuront Melayn, First of the Kultash, I am Breea Banea, First Sanis Scholar of Limtir, Master of the Batusha Weapons Guild, and I do challenge you."

"Nay!"

"In the name of Het," said Breea.

Sakuront drew back.

"By combat. To make His will known."

Sakuront stared, outrage building like an ocean wave.

She finished the challenge. "Name your weapon."

The First clenched his fists and his nostrils flared. He sucked in a deep breath as though to bellow.

In Breea fear spiked that he might explode in rage, but his eyes had already gone from rage to calculation as he figured how completely he had been outmaneuvered—trapped—into fighting a woman. The challenge in Het's name was writ in the First Word—a formal challenge between holy warriors—and could not be refused.

Sakuront impressed Breea by stating, "Staves."

The First walked backward five paces, pulled his scabbard out of his belt, then knelt with easy grace, sitting on his heels, hands resting on the scabbard across his thighs.

Breea stepped back an equal distance—though it took

more steps—and unbelted her daggers. She felt the loss of their sharp power, but her goal here was not to kill. Sakuront's choice of staves meant that neither was it his— she hoped.

Off to her left, Scaukra sent Tam to her. The boy saluted with a loud *chak'ood*. Breea held the dagger belt for him to take. He stared at the woven black leather and the emerald-hilted blades, then took them with nervous care. Before Breea turned from him, he looked up into her eyes. He had something to say.

She gave him a small smile, and he whispered, "Master Banea, Master Tafitamar says…" The boy swallowed, then dared to sidle close. Breea bent toward him and he whispered, "He says don't kill the First." Breea started to reassure him, but Tam wasn't finished. "Master Tafitamar says the First is not like Htaas. The First is much more dangerous, but he must not die."

Must not? Such wording stank of prophecy. What did Scaukra know? Breea nodded to Tam's words, though she was looking at Scaukra. Tam bowed and backed away.

Neprawn walked across the room toward the exit partition. The tall warrior turned at the curtain and *chak'ood* to her, shifted to nod crisply to Sakuront, then ducked through the curtain.

Tam's words swept about in Breea's mind. She wasn't sure what Scaukra's advice meant, but only days ago he had urged her to kill Htaas, the former Master of Batusha. Batusha now called her Master as a result. She'd barely defeated Htaas, and had been able to do so only through Scaukra's advice. However, she was not the same woman who had stumbled into a weapons guild, and taken their challenge to prove her skill until she was forced to fight for her life. She was Alach, and this was the time to be so.

Relaxing all her boundaries was a relief, and she nearly cried out in joy as essence-heat roared up within. Warmth flowed out, and the entire area became known to her—the cold night sky, thousands of men on the move, hundreds of fires—and before her a pool of ominous calm with Sakuront at its center. She'd never felt anything like it, yet it…Breea took a sudden breath. A sliver of fear lashed out and scored a cold blow across her confidence. Sakuront's peace reminded her more than anything of Taumea. In all her years of training, she had never bested Taumea unless he permitted the strike.

Quiet, urgent voices intruded on her thoughts and she listened to the arguing of the Batusha masters debating whether to allow the fight. The way they were talking, it seemed that most of them thought Sakuront the greatest warrior in all of Yash, if not the world. He'd beheaded the Dauthaz outside with a single stroke—from the draw. Breea's shoulders fell slightly. Had they no confidence in her? As they argued, neither her champions among them— who felt her invincible—nor those who seemed certain of losing their guild master, saw any profit in a duel with the First. The man was undefeated—in challenge and on the battlefield. Kings had fallen beneath the blade of Sakuront Melayn.

Biting her lip, Breea prepared her strategy. She would end it fast, surprising the First. He would not be prepared for her speed, nor the essence-strength she now wielded. If absolutely necessary, she would weave, but she wanted to win without resorting to that kind of combat. In essence-weaving she was a novice, but in fighting men far stronger than herself Breea knew herself to be a master, even without the power of essence. Now she needed a weapon.

Before she could ask, Arin burst through the door curtain. He looked between Sakuront and Breea, then walked briskly to her. Breea eyed him coldly, for she would accept no counterargument. He did not quail beneath her glare. His face was composed and his eyes flashed with something like pride and thrilled expectation. In Breea's heart some of the confidence stolen by the doubts of the masters returned to her.

"The Will of the One is with you," said Arin. "It is a sign. All shall witness."

Neprawn came through the cloth carrying half a dozen fighting staves of varied length. Breathing hard, he approached Arin with the weapons across his arms. The priest selected one, intoned a short verse, and presented the staff to Breea. She touched it, but did not like the grain. He presented another, but it felt too light.

"The dark one," said Breea.

Dubious but obedient, Arin took the longest staff from Neprawn's arms and handed it to Breea. The weight was astonishing, yet with the heft came a flow of motion that made Breea's heart skip. Grinning, she ran her fingers over the smooth surface. She could see no grain.

"What wood is this?" she asked.

Arin said, "Master, this is Path Maker."

"The weapon or the wood?"

"The weapon, Master. It is an old guild weapon, said to have been the Master's staff when the guild still wandered." At her curious look he said, "Hundreds of winters past."

"I shall endeavor to be worthy of its history," said Breea.

It took an act of will to quell her urge to whirl the weapon. She rolled her shoulders and breathed deep to test the flesh of her still tender back. Twinges of pain answered.

Breea set one end by her right toe and held the staff vertical with her right hand, elbow tucked to her side. None here would know, but it was the attention stance of Limtir gateguard. This night she intended to earn herself an army of the finest warriors in Yash. To do so she would honor the men who had trained her since birth in the arts of battle, many of whom were now dead at an Oregule's hands. She gripped the staff tight. Sakuront would fall because he must. She would not fail her teachers, nor fail to bring an army worthy of the Meric people. This battle in a holy tent by candle flame was a test of all her worth.

The Batusha masters quieted as they realized what staff she held. They drifted around the rim of the room to stand behind her. Breea ignored them, and ignored Arin as he sang his blessing verses. There was nothing now but her and the arrogant giant who waited.

Eight tent flaps opened around the chamber edge and Kultash warriors took station around the perimeter. Breea wondered if they were there to keep the proceedings undisturbed or to prevent her from fleeing. A white-haired Kultash officer entered from the main entrance. He walked with formal ceremony, and carried a staff of lustrous, dark-red wood vertical before him. A chill flitted over Breea's skin. The staff was made of Gamanthea-Dur heartwood. Sakuront stood. The staff-bearing Kultash walked to the center of the room, turned with crisp precision, then approached Sakuront. The man touched the staff to his forehead, then held it out. Sakuront held out his sword in turn. Each man gripped the offered weapon and released the one he held.

Impatient, Breea stepped forward and Arin hopped out

of her way. Sakuront moved to meet her.

Path Maker hummed in her hand—like a song. A song of battle. Each of her steps made a ripple of change through the essence about her. Sakuront lazily brought his staff to guard. Breea paused, feeling her heartbeat running like a drum—like the drums of the crew aboard her friend Etrya's ship *Halisheen*. Raising her left hand to her staff, she felt power coursing up her arm, flowing into the air. She waved the staff around, amazed by the sensations.

Sakuront was almost upon her, and she could feel his coming like the force of water at the lip of a waterfall—smooth and unstoppable—unless you were a rock. Sakuront struck, his staff a blur. Breea moved Path Maker into its path, stopping it dead with a crack that echoed through earth and sky. Everyone within hearing flinched. Sakuront took a step back, his eyes reassessing. Such a blow would have driven most men to earth.

Pleased, Breea danced back out of reach, and set Path Maker in motion. Sakuront's strike had failed because in that moment she had been linked to the bones of the world. To strike her had been to strike bedrock. Her staff hummed like the wings of a hornet—a very big hornet. Sakuront circled, his staff shifting in response to her pattern. Breea broke the cycle without warning, attacking, using her speed to power past his guard. His lack of guard was a trap. Her strike met air and she felt a blow aimed at her center. Only by force of essence was she able to bring her staff in to parry. His blow was like being hit by a falling tree, and Breea went flying, landing hard and tumbling in the dirt.

Sakuront was upon her in an instant, weapon arcing down. With Path Maker she deflected the blow. Despite redirecting most of the force, she was pounded into the ground. On her back, Breea twisted and defended as Sakuront rained blows. None found their mark, and Breea was getting angry. Heat burned in her chest, growing with each parry. Power bloomed, and each of her parries grew in ferocity. Crack-cr*ack—crack!* Sakuront's calm wavered as his staff was struck aside, torn from one hand. The moment gave Breea a chance, and she rolled, using her staff to lever herself upright. It nearly cost her the battle. Sakuront's staff clipped her scalp, tearing hair as it passed, and Breea flashed to memory of Lupazg the Oregule cutting through her hair with his black sword. With a cry of rage and terror, Breea struck blindly, then found herself on hands and knees. Sakuront sat on his rear twenty feet away, legs splayed, panting, nose and mouth bleeding. The cloth of the whole tent was billowing—most of the candles blown out—but Breea was her own light now. Baring her teeth, she stood. Sakuront scrambled to rise, stumbling as he found his limbs not responding as he expected.

Breea attacked, calling upon earth and sky, whipping Path Maker in a great scything blow. Sakuront bellowed, swinging to parry. The weapons met with a sound like the world splitting in half. Pain stabbed Breea's hands and she stumbled backward.

Path Maker was gone. Her hands were a bloody mess of flesh and splintered wood. A few strides away Sakuront groaned, bending over. His hands were the same, dripping blood onto the cold, dry dirt.

He looked up. Breea could feel his fury. Though her own wrathful power desired more than anything to rise and crush him, she bore down on the battle hunger. This was a test of wills as much as skill. He must stand down.

The First of the Kultash straightened, then advanced.

"No!" cried Breea. She raised a leg and slammed her boot to the ground. A ripple of earth tossed dirt and small rocks out in a wave. The First kept coming. Breea strode to meet him, power singing through her like storm winds. Sakuront attacked, blood flying from his hands. Breea could feel his intent, and ducked, stepping in. Both of her fists struck him in the chest, but lightly. The power of the blow lay in her will—driven by earth, wind, and inner fire—and it smashed into his inner calm. Sakuront stumbled back and fell, landing on his rear. Breea stepped in and slapped a bloody hand on his forehead. She forced his head back and looked into his eyes.

Sakuront shuddered. By degrees his eyes grew desperate. Then for a long moment they both froze.

Sakuront said, "Chosen!"

Breea stepped back, and his head fell forward. She blinked at the vision they'd shared in the frozen moment. With halting steps she came forward, then knelt before him.

After a while, she said, "You will need your hands."

She wove a curative pattern about her own, then gathered his and let the blue mist whirl about them both. Calm settled him, and his head came up. His dark eyes searched her face, then looked at the blue light in the air about their hands.

Sakuront's voice rumbled, "Aye."

CHAPTER 12

Protect

IN THE DARK, SNOW CRUNCHED SOFTLY UNDER Taumea's boots. He went down as quickly as he could, using the lamps of the Kultash below to orient and circle wide to the right of the road south of the warriors. A hundred paces away, a group of six lantern-bearing Kultash had left the group and were striding up the valley, lamps held out low to follow a path through the fresh snow made by horses— Valiena's trail. Two lanterns remained with the horses on the road, though Taumea could not tell how many men remained there. He stepped up onto the raised stone road, then approached.

A sense of danger stilled his motion. Taumea settled into the low stance of Cat Straddles Water. The wind pushed and buffeted, but failed to move him. The horses were twenty strides away. Lamplight moved and flickered on the snow-coated paving stones through their legs. For long breaths he watched and listened. When he saw what he was looking for, he made no motion, and stared into the dark beside the road a few strides ahead until it happened again—a puff of brighter dark that caught the lamplight before being whipped away. A sentry's breath ten strides away. The Kultash were hunting—showing caution and intelligence—operating in groups, using almost-hidden sentries. A stab of regret hit for the necessity of killing such warriors, but Taumea let it pass. This path was forged in blood.

Careful to keep his blade edge-on to the light to avoid reflections, Taumea worked the damaged sword back into its scabbard. He moved to the left to silhouette the figure against the shifting lamp glow beyond the horses. The man was kneeling in the snow beside the road, back to the wind. Taumea imagined his head swinging back and forth, peering into the dark.

Low to the ground, Taumea crept forward, pausing when he sensed the man might be looking his way. At three paces Taumea gathered himself and waited. A horse nickered, and the man's head turned to look up the road. Like a specter, Taumea rose and stalked close. His hands snaked around to the man's chin and yanked it back, then jerked upright with a savage pull that lifted the warrior from the ground. The man's neck went with a pop that left the head slack in Taumea's grip. He let the body settle gently to the snow, avoiding any clink of sword or helm. Taumea pulled off his gloves and felt for the man's sword belt, unbuckling it by feel as he watched the horses shift in the dim light ten paces away. In a few moments he'd covered the body with his cloak and wore the Kultash warrior's coat. It was heavy and warm, cut to allow good motion on most sword arcs. The Kultash sword belt went over its folds, then he unhooked the man's helm. It fit well enough, lined with something soft and thick, though heavy with a chain camail to protect the neck. Taumea lay his Limtir sword and belt on the body, then pulled the long Limtir dagger off the belt and tucked it snug in the small of his back through the Kultash belt. By feel he checked that he could draw the dagger easily, then strung his bow and set it and the quiver across the body. A quick examination of the man's armor revealed thick chainmail from shoulders to midthigh but no armor below that, though the forward part of the man's high boots felt reinforced. Taumea stood and drew the Kultash sword. Its draw was long, requiring him to stretch to clear the tip of the sheath. It had fair balance, heavier at the end than was ideal, but wielded with two hands it was capable enough. He tested up and down the edge with his thumb. Sharp.

Blade in hand, Taumea strode forward and knelt, peering under the horses. There were four Kultash warriors and two servants. Likely there was another sentry on the road to the north. More than he'd thought. It looked like the Kultash were pulling their men off the road. Two of the warriors held lanterns while the servant stood by with handfuls of reins. All were facing upvalley, watching the ascent of the six above. For eleven Kultash, he needed to winnow their numbers before crossing blades. He walked with swift strides back down the road to the dead sentry, retrieved bow and quiver, then scrambled up the slope into the valley until he had a clear view of both the men below and those above. By feel of the fletching, he selected an arrow with a wide hunting point, and set it a-string. After a moment anticipating their reaction to a bow attack from the dark, he decided that the important question was how many arrows he could send into them before they realized that the light of their lanterns held death rather than safety.

Taumea drew, aiming for a warrior on the road. Judging the wind by its feel on his face and via the drift of snow through their lamplight, he let fly.

The Kultash cried out and fell to the stones as his knee gave way. In shock, he and his fellows stared at the arrow clean through his knee. Blades flashed out and the Kultash faced the direction from which the arrow had come—exactly as Taumea expected. His already drawn bow snapped, and a bodkin-tipped armor-piercing arrow struck. A Kultash toppled back, clawing at the shaft through his heart. The men above were shouting to know what was happening. Taumea drew his bow once more, and he took the first on the road to reply with a shaft through the throat. The man fell and his lantern shattered on the stones. The last soldier handed his lantern pole to a servant, and the smart man tossed it away. In the light of the guttering lamp, the Kultash raised his sword over the servant, who cringed back. Taumea dropped both men with two swift arrows, then put an armor-piercing shaft into the chest of the last warrior as the man tried to take cover. He dropped among the horse as the spilled lantern oil flame stuttered out. Taumea nocked and drew, swinging to the soldiers dashing down the hill.

The darkness from below stalled their descent. Taumea could hear them talking, arguing. Before they decided, he put an arrow into the face of the man who seemed to lead them. As he went down, the rest threw their lanterns in Taumea's direction, charging after. Darkness closed about them as the lights sailed, and Taumea released two arrows blind into their midst.

Two lanterns flickered out as they landed in the snow, but one hit open ground and burst in a flare of light. Taumea was already running and slipping downhill, but by the Kultash's battle cries, they had caught sight of him.

Near the road he heard what he feared—the ring of horseshoes on stone. Dropping his bow and sweeping the Kultash sword from its scabbard, Taumea scrambled forward in the dark, feeling for the road. The horse's footfalls were hesitant in the darkness. Its rider cursed and bellowed for it to run. Taumea found the roadbed. Swinging the two-handed sword at leg height, he leapt into the rider's path. The blade bit and the horse screamed. Its motion knocked Taumea aside and tore the Kultash blade from his grip. He hit the road hard, as did the horse. The rider's cry cut off as he too slammed onto the stone roadbed.

It was no longer completely dark—moonlight seeped through the clouds and made grays of the black. A quick check found a single arrow in his quiver, the rest gone in his tumble. His bow lay in the snow somewhere off the road.

Shouts heralded the arrival of the Kultash from above. Taumea drew his Limtir fighting dagger. There were five warriors, spreading out, talking to one another, coordinating and lining up by the sounds of their voices, whipping their swords through the air before them. They walked forward, and Taumea dropped low. The near man's sword swept past and Taumea rolled into the man's legs and struck upward with his dagger, shoving hard, sinking the blade to the hilt in the man's groin. Hot blood doused Taumea's hand as the man managed a single sword stroke downward, which Taumea took on his back. Limtir armor stopped the cut, but the force smashed the air from Taumea's lungs. In agony he reached up and gripped the sword's guard to halt another strike, and twisted his dagger. The man squealed, quivering, and collapsed aside. Gasping to regain his breath, Taumea rose with the man's blade in hand. He had not expected the man, any man, to be able to react with such skill and power after being knifed in the groin with a long dagger.

Shadows approached from two sides, calling to the downed man. Taumea took a knee with the sword vertical before him, the haft held at his center. He deepened his breath against the pain, and, with care, felt for his dagger sheath, slid the blade in, then gripped his sword with two hands. Kultash approached, voices questing, blades whistling as they sought to clear the air before them. Taumea let his breath deepen and slow, listening to the fear edging their voices.

The downed man beside him moaned, and the warrior to Taumea's left said, "Hanin? Ye there?"

Taumea rose into a high crouch, dropping his blade tip left, then lunged that way, extending his arms in a straight thrust at the voice. The blade hit hard, but did not pierce the man's mail. He grunted and parried, and his sword crashed into Taumea's, knocking it aside. Taumea let his blade flow with the parry, but kept his long stance, thigh horizontal. He dropped his blade's tip, disengaging from the man's weapon, and with his right hand swept his blade back the other direction low and hard into the leg of the man coming up from the right. The sword bit deep and the soldier screamed. Taumea lifted his blade back over his head in time to catch the leftmost Kultash's next attack. Taumea rose, whipping his blade around in an arc to hit where he judged the man's arms should be after the parry. His blade rang on mail punctuated by the sound of cracking bone. The man grunted but did not cry out until Taumea's blade sliced across his face as Taumea slid past him. The Kultash bellowed almost in Taumea's ear, and lunged, knocking Taumea off-balance. They hit the snow in a tangle.

Taumea let his sword go and found the Kultash's throat with one hand, squeezing his fingers into the flesh. The man gagged, but had only one functional hand to fight with. It gripped Taumea's wrist, wrenching to disengage the digging fingers. Taumea's other hand groped for his dagger, drew it, and parried the downstroke of yet another Kultash standing above them. Taumea let go of the throat and stabbed it, the blade passing through soft flesh like water. Taumea rose inside the standing warrior's next stroke and thrust his dagger up under the man's chin, but found it stopped by a full camail across the man's throat. The Kultash's helmet slammed into Taumea's as the warrior head-butted Taumea, doing neither of them damage but giving Taumea time to wrap a hand around the back of the man's head and pull. The Kultash reared away to break the grip, opening his face to Taumea's dagger, which drove through an eye. Taumea wrenched his blade free and hopped to get his feet under him, dagger at high guard.

There was no one there. Over the wind he heard a man groaning but none were standing. With swift precision, Taumea put each to death. As he rose from quieting the last, it felt as though the wind had swept all sound from the world but its whispering hiss. A fresh shroud of heavy snow came riding its breath, pattering against Taumea's helm. The cloud cover thickened and dark obscured the already dim battlefield. He would need to relight a lantern to find his arrows and bow and gather a few Kultash quivers.

Later, wearing his cloak over the Kultash coat and helm, Taumea stepped up the valley in the thickening snow. At his waist a Kultash blade rode beside his Limtir weapon. His unstrung bow he carried in one hand and in the other a lamp pole, resting over his shoulder. The unlit lamp swung with his strides. Pausing, he transferred the bow to the lamp pole hand, then scooped a handful of fresh snow, squeezed it into a block, and popped it into his mouth, melting it to drink as he checked his back trail. They would come, if not in the next bell, then tomorrow or the day following. He turned and strode upward, thinking back to the years before Limtir and the price he had extracted from the invaders of his homeland—and the name they had given him. So would it be with the Kultash.

It was long into the night before he caught a scent which told him the girls were near. The snow had grown waist deep and he had begun to worry about avalanches from the steep-sided hills when a whiff of smoke brought him to a halt. The valley had narrowed, and with the whole world covered in snow the light had gone gray in the light of the moon through the clouds. He'd seen through fitful gaps in the curtain of snow that the left side of the valley had turned to rugged cliff. With the set of the wind, at their base would be the best chance of shelter. He crossed to that side of the valley and found the smoke scent again, and sign of a horse's passage. It led to a narrow maze of snow-draped boulders overhung with laden pine boughs. Following his nose, he found the way blocked by a bulk of darkness that raised its head and gave a warning chuffle.

"Ho, Azsark," said Taumea, offering an open hand.

The horse sniffed him then shook his head free of collected snow. Azsark did not like the scent of blood. Taumea spoke soothingly and patted and stroked him, then sidled past, causing snow to slide from the blanket that had been draped over the horse's back. Behind Azsark the other three horses stood in a wide space open to the sky. All appeared to be sleeping and took little notice of his passage. The snow here had been trampled a good deal, and trails led to the far side where warm firelight shimmered through the snowfall.

The girls sat near the fire under the piece of sailcloth Taumea had bought off a merchant's cart on the road after leaving Charlthon's country home months ago. Valiena's stewpot hung over a cheerful fire and the scent of sage tickled his nose on the cold air. Each girl had a steaming bowl in her lap, but they were staring at him instead of eating. Valiena ran out to him and they embraced. He suppressed a grunt of pain as her strong arms pressed against his back where the Kultash had struck. Valiena pulled back, blinking as snow landed on her face. Her hand went to his cheek, then up to touch the Kultash helm under his cloak hood. Wordless, she took his hand to guide him under the sailcloth. He felt a tremor in her grip. She knew what he'd done.

Under the edge of the tarp, he set his bow and the lantern pole on the fresh pine boughs beside Valiena's bow. Taumea took off his cloak, gave it a shake beyond the shelter, then folded it for a seat near the fire where Valiena had brushed the snow clear, revealing a flat slab of rock. Both of the girls watched him with wide eyes as he unbuckled his belt and set his swords beside the bows. Lastly he took off coat and armor. With a grunt and a sigh, he settled cross-legged onto his cloak, then unbuckled the Kultash helm, setting it by the weapons. Tiyha lay asleep at the back of the shelter on a bed of boughs. The weight of snow was pushing the shelter cloth down on her. Taumea had many good memories of mornings waking under a blanket of snow, but he doubted Tiyha would feel the same. With the Kultash scabbard he lifted and shook the cloth until the snow slid off, then settled back beside the fire. Snow fell soft in the firelight. The spot among the tall stones was well sheltered, ringed by twisted pines. This was the kind of special place Breea favored, and like her someone had left a wood cache.

When his stomach grumbled, it sounded loud enough to echo.

Anila raised her bowl, offering to him. There were only two bowls.

"No, lass," said Taumea, pushing it back to her gently. "You finish."

She didn't respond, staring at his bloodstained fingers touching hers. He'd washed his hands as best he could in the snow, but they looked grisly. Neither girl was eating, staring at him. They seemed to sense something had happened, or perhaps it was the Kultash coat, or the blood which stained it.

"Eat," commanded Taumea, and both girls turned to their spoons.

Valiena came over and settled next to him.

"A good place," he said, accepting a slice of apple from her. "How did you find it?"

"Azsark led us," she said.

Anila glanced up at them then back to her bowl.

Taumea signed to Valiena, *Girl or horse led?*

Valiena shrugged and tossed her hair as though to say, *Does it matter?*

Taumea grunted and helped himself to a wineskin warming beside the fire. After he drank, Valiena took his bloody hands in hers. The cuff of his shirts and woolens were still sticky with the scent of blood.

"Let me wash them," she said.

"Don't waste the wine," he said.

Valiena flipped her hair with irritated forbearance.

He grinned, and she jabbed him in the ribs. She retrieved a waterskin, a cloth, and a sprig of dried, sharp-scented herb. She cleaned his hands, then rubbed them thoroughly with the herb until it turned to powder. She held his hands then, caressing them as snowflakes whirling in on the wind landed and melted on his skin. Her fingers pressed a series of signs into one palm.

Tilting his head, Taumea said, "I'm your fishmonger?"

"Protector, you oaf," said Valiena.

He chuckled and kissed her, then held his hand to the firelight. "This is *protect* or *guard*. And with this you indicate the target, or this for a group."

"Seems simpler to combine them," said Valiena.

"That's the sign for fish," he said in a flat voice.

"Liar," she said.

He couldn't hold back an unrepentant grin, and said, "Anila is done."

After Taumea had eaten and the girls were sleeping beside their mother, Taumea retrieved the whetstones the blacksmith had given him. A burning stick from the fire served to light the Kultash lantern. He donned the Kultash coat and his Limtir cloak, then took up his Limtir sword. Valiena followed him out into the snow.

To her he said, "Sleep."

Valiena asked, "And you?"

"It will be dawn soon."

She looked at him for a moment, then returned to the shelter. Taumea walked to a spot he'd seen earlier where pine branches and stone conspired to create an ideal lookout sheltered from the weather. After kicking and brushing the snow from lower rocks, he climbed up to the spot. He settled against the tree, satisfied. As expected, the vantage afforded a view of both the protected glade and the near end of the winding path to the camp. The lantern pole he wedged between stones to hang beside him. It would make him a target for anyone with a bow, but given how the snow continued to pour down, he doubted any could reach them, and he needed the light to work on his sword.

Back under the shelter cloth, Anila watched Taumea's lamp shimmer through the snowfall from where he had climbed up the rocks. After a minute she caught the sound of stone sliding across steel. She raised her head to listen, then held her hand to the fire and made the sign *protect*. Spe's hand rose beside hers, imitating. Anila looked down and saw Spe's big eyes looking up at her. Anila nodded. Spe heaved a sigh and snuggled closer to Anila. Anila wrapped her arm around Spe and listened to the storm beyond the glade, and the sound of the Limtir lord sharpening his blade.

CHAPTER 13

What She Cannot

THE BLUE RADIANCE OF BREEA'S HEALING FELL
away from her hands, revealing tender pink skin. The wood
splinters were gone, consumed by the weave. Breea stood
from Sakuront and looked about the dark tent. Most of the
candles were out, and every man in the space was kneeling.
She was the brightest thing in the room, with light streaming
out through the rents in her dirty, once white blouse. Closing
her eyes, she let essence-heat soothe the pain in her wounded
scalp and the torn flesh in her back where the incompletely

healed skin had ruptured. The heat waxed to searing, and she found that she was channeling heat from deep in the ground. Startled, she wove a boundary at her core. Pain returned as the glow left her skin.

When she was sure of her voice, she said, "Bring the planning table."

Half a bell later, a frustrated quiet had settled over the council of officers standing shoulder to shoulder around three sides of the big table. Breea, in her ragged dress, stood alone at the fourth side with her fists on her hips. When the candles had been relit, argument had been kindled. Few had voiced plans in agreement with one another, but all stood firm against Breea's desires.

Sakuront alone withheld comment, gazing down at them all, his dark face cool with the restraint one bestows upon children.

"Twenty leagues a day," she said.

Pressed lips and covert glares met her repeated assertion.

"We leave tonight."

The men erupted in exclamations, shaking their heads, hands pounding the table with proclamations of impossibility.

Breea weathered the protests, but when they began arguing with one another about the degree of impossibility, she said in a conversational tone, "Do you know what an Oregule is?"

There must have been something of the Alach in her voice, for as one they quieted. Across the table from her, one corner of Sakuront's mustache twitched, but she couldn't tell if it was a sneer or half a grin.

Breea said, "The one that destroyed Limtir..." She paused as loss and rage ripped through her, crushing her voice. She noted how men's eyes widened, a few exchanging glances of amazement—or was it pleasure?—at Limtir's fall.

Raising her gaze to Sakuront, she said, "It stood six hands taller than you." There was no mustache twitch. "Dauthaz are their *servants*. Oregule make them out of men, twisting soul and body until nothing remains but vile cold." Here and there fists clenched and jaws tightened as warriors remembered fighting Dauthaz. A few glanced at Sakuront as though sizing up something worse than him.

Breea said, "The Oregule that infested the High Temple was the second that I have faced."

"Nay," whispered a Kultash.

Another said, "No such thing has ruled Yash."

Fear hid in the shadows of their disbelief, but before she could rise to slay their ignorance, Sakuront said, "Has any questioned my call?"

"Nay!" said the Kultash men in unison. "We Serve."

"Hmh," grunted Sakuront, communicating in the sound an entire realm of disappointment.

Breea was amazed to see the officers pondering—eyes darting as though searching for something they had missed.

One, a thin, gray-bearded warrior with wise though chilling eyes, glanced at the First in complicit frustration and said, "First, upon what sign did you issue the call?"

Sakuront said nothing for a moment, then folded his arms across his chest. "Upon the sign of corruption."

Breea asked the medallion what this meant. Its answer left her cold.

Another, among the youngest, asked, "Not upon conversion?"

The graybeard said to him, "In what age have we bowed

to the Temple's whim?"

"None, wisdom," replied the warrior.

The graybeard said to Sakuront, "First, what corruption?"

Sakuront stared at Breea until all the men turned to her.

"The Temple Oregule," she said.

Sakuront leaned back in confirmation, and Breea watched his fellows struggle with the revelation that they had been called together to cleanse the Temple—to slay every living thing within its walls.

The Yasharn army officers at the table withheld comment in respectful silence, as did the Batusha masters.

Into the silence Breea said, "Their name means *Life Bane*, and another leads the Kaul Kaul nation. You have heard of the siege of Carsythe?"

Small nods around the table, their faces struggling back to the present.

"I have seen it," she said. "A storm over the city, and an ocean of Kaul crashing upon her walls. The city cannot stand, for what leads the Kaul Kaul has knowledge of Legend Time warfare. It is building siege towers of Gamanthea-Dur to top the outer bastion."

She had their full attention, and decided not to tell them of the Urdjra. It was too much to believe.

Remembering the eyes of the Oregule in her vision, she paused, feeling vulnerable.

"I alone," she said, "cannot meet the power of this beast. When I fought the spider in the Temple…I failed."

Breea turned to Simarn. "She saved me. This girl stood before the cold might of the ancient enemy and cut it down with a single bolt from her bow. Without her I was lost, and with me—your city, your realm—*lost*. Carsythe stands before another, and she too will be lost without your aid. I need men who will…" She gripped a dagger hilt as emotion took her voice. Candle flames swayed as ripples of essence pulsed out from her.

The warriors frowned, nervous and unsure.

Sabar looked up from the candle he'd been watching and said, "Do not tell Master Banea what she cannot." His grin, accented by an old scar across his lips, held a touch of worship.

Breea mastered her emotion and said, "We set out this night. Walk if we must. Carsythe cannot fall."

No one objected, and she knew the next question to be asked. Feeling grateful for all her martial studies at Limtir, she said, "What order of march do you advise?"

Master Longat lay a hand on the table, but Sakuront spoke first.

"We shall be the vanguard."

Longat looked up at Sakuront with a sour expression, but before he spoke, he checked Breea's reaction.

Inclined to agree with Sakuront, she held her tongue while she considered. The greatest advantage would be that no one in Yash would challenge their passage with Kultash leading, yet it meant that every other unit would be eating Kultash dust. If they crossed into Mericsland with a Kultash vanguard, it would seem an act of war. She wondered if Sakuront's declaration had been given in aid of speed, or simply that Kultash would brook no one to ride before them.

"Through Yash," she said, "the Kultash shall forge our path."

The Kultash leaders seemed well satisfied with that.

"In Mericsland," said Breea. "Batusha and the Aska-Wuthos will take the van."

Ootha elbowed Sabar, unable to hold down a smirking grin. The Kultash men stiffened their backs, but didn't object. Sakuront stared at her in his cool way. Despite the vision that had shaken them both, his demeanor had changed little.   Among the whirling sights of the vision she remembered Sakuront's hands cradling a child's broken skull. How they were linked and what it meant to her she did not know, but her heart raced.

Master Longat signaled to a clerk who was standing ready at the edge of the chamber. The man ducked through a partition and returned with a scribe's tray. The scribe set the tray upon the table, drew two candles near to him, checked the tip of a quill, uncapped his ink, and stood ready.

"Precedence of march for the Army of the Chosen," said Master Longat.

The scribe's quill tip danced across the parchment.

Breea stood away as the officers of her army began enumerating unit placements. Her army. It felt like a vision made true, and was somewhat eerie. Perhaps this was what it meant to be Alach, weaving change into the world at a pace that made it unrecognizable day to day. The flame within felt…ready. Her right hand traced the medallion scars on her chest, and the essence of the air trembled. Candles on the table flickered and the conversation there paused a fraction before continuing.

A horn sang out beyond the tent, sounding to Breea like the deep-chested mountain wolves of her home range. Master Longat cut his next statement in midphrase, for Sakuront had walked around the table. The other Kultash fell into line behind him. Breea frowned. Clearly the planning was incomplete. Why were the Kultash leaving?

Arin stepped up to Breea and said, "Night prayer."

Breea took a deep breath to control her impatience. Longat at least was not pausing, working through the order of march with the Aska-Wuthos.

"Will they return?" she asked Arin.

The priest said, "Master, have you witnessed the Kultash at prayer?"

"There is something to watch?"

"Master, you may wish to witness."

Sensing a change in the movement of men in the camp outside the Ulshan, Breea said, "Lead."

When they stepped out of the tent, the sound and motion of thousands of swords being drawn shocked her into drawing both of her daggers.

Sakuront stood five strides from the tent entrance, his blade held aloft with one hand. A line of Kultash stood in the same attitude down the avenue between tents. It was the same all around the Ulshan, every space among the leather tents filled with Kultash facing outward, swords high. The Batusha warriors around the Ulshan had backed up to the tent cloth, keeping out of the way. Breea put her blades away.

The Kultash raised their other hand to the high swords, and the blades swept down in a unified strike that cut the air with a swish that was almost a roar. Breea felt a chill of wonder. After a breath, the blades flashed through a cut up and across the body. They began then, in earnest.

Breea stepped forward, drawn by the unity of motion as the bitter night air hissed and sighed with the passage of three thousand blades in continuous motion. Around Sakuront, slivers of metallic fire came and went as his great sword caught and threw off the torchlight. Breea longed for a sword to join them—join Sakuront. She could sense essence-power in the weaving of his blade. Her dagger hilts sparkled as her heart raced to the grace of the purity of his motion.

Then they were done, and their blades drifted down from high. The world seemed to settle. The power about Sakuront unraveled into a pool of calm. He stood thus, head bowed and sword at rest, blade tip less than a hand from the ground in front of him. With a flick of steel and smooth double sweep, he returned his weapon to its sheath. When he turned, he found Breea watching him.

The First of the Kultash paused, then touched his forehead and opened his fingers to her, rather than the sky. With his officers, he reentered the tent.

Breea began to thank Arin for having her witness the Kultash at prayer, but the priest's eyes were wide like they got whenever she did something unexpected. She waited for him to explain, but he looked to be wrestling with the import of whatever he'd seen. Doubtless he would tell her later.

Breea took Simarn's arm and walked back into the tent. The girl's eyes were glazed and her breath a little rapid, though Breea felt a darkness behind the stunned gaze. At the threshold of the inner chamber, Breea stopped in place and looked into Simarn's eyes. There was a rage boiling in the young woman that Breea recognized, for she held that savage feeling within as well—a hatred of the cruel, a burning desire to cut down the enemy—whoever and whatever they may be. Dori had said as much. *She is like you in war.* But in Simarn there was more than hatred—there was hunger.

In a quiet and somewhat ominous tone, Breea said, "Would you like to be able to blade-dance like that?"

Simarn nodded.

"Good," said Breea. "I need a new sparring partner."

Simarn's face paled, and her face fell toward hopeless fright.

Breea refrained from rolling her eyes, and said, "First lesson. Know when the teacher is teasing you."

Simarn looked down, abashed, and said, "Yes, my queen."

"Second lesson," said Breea. "Look up. Always. Your toes are not the enemy."

Simarn raised her head. After a breath, humor touched her lips, and though it didn't linger, it was enough. Breea set a hand on Simarn's shoulder and gave it a squeeze.

As they entered the inner chamber, a line of boys came streaming out, their faces so determined to their task that most barely glanced at Breea in passing. Partition cloths had been rolled up around some of the perimeter, revealing clerks in gray robes standing at work on tall tables. Boys and young men in the livery of various units came and went with parchment, or stood waiting to receive notes hastily sealed with wax. At the central table more clerks came and went, passing orders written and verbal to the outer ring. Batusha boys hovered, ready, dashing away after a few curt words. Neprawn noted Breea's arrival and *chak'ood*. Batusha followed, then everyone else was bowing or kneeling.

Embarrassed to have halted all their work, Breea said, "Tomes, don't stop for me."

Talk began again, though quieter. Longat beckoned to Neprawn. The tall warrior listened to the planner, then strode over to Breea and *chak'ood*.

"Master, Planner Longat requests your blessing of the plan."

Breea walked up to the table.

Master Longat saluted her, then presented a freshly written sheet. She studied it, needing no help from the Tetr medallion.

Longat swept aside sheaves of parchment, revealing an impressively detailed map of Yash. His fingers ran along fresh black dots that marked a route east across the realm, then south around the end of the mountain range which bordered much of the western shore of the Leuvat Sea. At the southern extreme of the mountains, a town's name brought a smile to Breea's face: Venth, the hometown of captain Etrya Finwall, the first person Breea had met other than Ajalay who could weave essence. The route passed Venth then moved up the west coast of the Leuvat Sea past Iplock and all the way to Twinport and the border with Mericsland. She leaned out over the table and pushed away papers covering the north-central regions of Yash.

"Why not a northern route?"

"Snow and ice, Master. The High Path from Aska to Twinport will be treachery itself. No road for shod horse."

"How many horses do we have?"

"Twelve thousand, Master. Not even General Ohan's writ can pry out more. On the fair side, it also brought something over a thousand mules. A blessing."

"Mules?" asked Breea.

"Army stock, Master. Tough, eat only what they need, and trained. Better than carts where the stones end, and faster than oxen." He waggled his head a little, and said, "Not as good eating."

Breea ignored his last observation and looked up at Sakuront. "The Kultash have their own supply?"

Sakuront nodded.

She took his simple answer to mean they did and could

travel at speed. She read through the order of march, counting. Abruptly she pushed the order of march toward Longat.

"This is all?"

"Aye," said Longat.

"This leaves the bulk of the army behind. And the supply."

He looked pained. "Master, what you ask…"

Breea looked at the other Batusha masters. Their gazes were uniform in conviction, though most averted their eyes when hers touched them. Sakuront was quiet.

She took a deep breath, then let it out through her nose. From what she'd seen of his character, if he believed another plan was possible he would speak.

"Six thousand," she said. "Half of that Kultash. Who else?"

"We are selecting the finest, my queen," said an Aska-Wuthos.

Longat added, "Three horse to a man, Master, will grant us speed. We will go without shelter, and supply enough only to achieve the next city."

"That is well," said Breea, still struggling to suppress her disappointment at leaving more than half her force behind. "The main body then will follow? At what speed?"

Longat said carefully, "With Het's blessing and proper guidance—upon the High Road they should stride eight leagues a day."

Breea chewed her lip as she calculated the main body's arrival in Mericsland.

"Spring. They will not arrive until spring." She felt like pounding the table.

No one said a word. They even seemed to be breathing

quietly. Breea did her best to check her emotion. This was a test, and they were the judges, watching for the quality of her mettle. It was a test as well of trust—hers of them, and they of her judgment.

Six thousand warriors of quality. Mounted. She turned it over in her mind, then studied the map. Taking the High Road down to Venth and around the mountains added a hundred leagues to the journey. Her gaze drifted northward. Along the western slopes of the mountains a large blank lay upon the map—the Haunted Lands. Not even the rivers were drawn there, and certainly not the pass she'd used to cross the mountains. The first significant city west of the region was Gimlek. It was sure to be one of the cities she'd avoided in her cross-country walk to the capital.

"How good are the roads to Gimlek?" she asked.

Heads bent over the table, and Longat said with a frown, "Passable. Though half as wide as the High Path. Master—"

Breea said, "There is a fleet at Iplock."

She saw the light of interest dawn in their faces.

"Aye," said Longat. "But Gimlek—"

Breea cut him off. "The shortest path to Iplock"—she pulled a dagger and drew its tip across the map—"is across the mountains here. There is a path."

"Master," said Longat, his pudgy fingers making negation motions over the unlabeled region. "We cannot…" He stopped as though realizing what he'd said. The planner's fingers curled back into a fist, then withdrew.

Sakuront said to the Kultash officers, "Mount."

Chapter 14

Little Breeas

TAUMEA WOKE WITH A START AND CAUGHT THE whetstone as it slipped off his lap. Dawn was well advanced and the world had changed shape with another seven hands of snow. He had not intended to sleep, but felt no alarm. This place settled a man like the Nesua Oduuhn forest in Limtir Valley. A light snow mist was falling, and he could see out over the rounded white boulderscape to the valley beyond. In the glade Valiena was trying to heave snow off the sagging shelter. Below Taumea the horses shifted in wells of snow that came to their chests. A bird looking for breakfast among the branches to his side made him think of Breea. Doubtless she would know its name, and what it ate. He rubbed his hands and closed the folds of his cloak. It seemed that the sisters' gift of essence-warmth was gone, for he was chilled through. He rolled his shoulders, feeling the bruises of combat, especially across his back where the Kultash blow had landed. Taumea examined the progress he'd made to re-edge his sword, then slid it into the sheath. He plucked the lantern pole from its spot in the rocks, noting that tallow remained, which was odd as he did not recall blowing it out.

He slid down the rocks, half buried in a little avalanche of his own making. Azsark backed out of the narrow channel to the left, pushing a great pile of fresh snow along with his rump. The horse turned and strode past Taumea, breasting its way through the drift. The other horses fell into line behind him, and Taumea followed in the channel they made. He heard the girls talking in excited chirps as Azsark pushed his head under the low sailcloth. Taumea waded past Azsark and kissed Valiena.

"You slept," she said, studying his face.

They both turned as Spe emerged from the shelter and gasped, staring up at the edge of the snow higher than her head. With a squeak of excitement she leapt forward and vanished completely into the drift. No one moved for a stunned second, then Taumea and Valiena strode for her. There was an explosion of white and they found themselves covered with snow. Before them Spe stood in a circle cleared of snow, her face serious with concern and a little fear that all was not right with this. Taumea and Valiena shook out their hair, and dug snow out from where it had gone down their necks.

Azsark's head emerged from the shelter with Anila hugging it. The horse's head rose up, lifting her in the air. When his head was horizontal, Anila clambered over it and down his neck. Straddling his neck facing backward with her skirt pushed up to her knees, she dusted snow off his withers and shook the blanket, dislodging the rest. She turned around on his back and looked at the world from her high vantage. Her eyes were shining with interest, cheeks ruddy from the cold air and her efforts.

"Fair morn," said Taumea.

She blushed a fiery red, but looked proud.

A great poof of snow went flying into the air out over the glade, and Spe squealed in delight. She ran forward whirling her arms and another cloud of snow exploded out from her. The horses moved to paw at the browse she'd exposed, and Taumea grunted.

"Little Breeas," he muttered to Valiena.

"Opalah," said Valiena in agreement.

Tiyha's angry voice called from under the shelter, "Spedora!"

Spe spun about, hands clutched to her chest in fear.

In Taumea, anger flashed cold and his gaze tracked around to the shelter. Valiena laid a staying hand against him, then ducked under the shelter, calling softly to Tiyha.

Taumea walked to Spe. Her eyes were fixed on the dark edge leading under the sailcloth. When Taumea picked her up, she flinched.

He set her on Azsark's back in front of Anila, and said, "That's a fair thing you did for the horses, Spe. Can't eat apple for every meal."

After a bit, she frowned and said, "Can!"

Taumea chuckled. "Truth. Yet better if they don't."

Valiena reemerged, her face worried. She asked Taumea, "Have we time for first meal?"

Taumea looked up. The cliff that backed the glade rose sheer into heavy gray cloud belly. The day felt of more snow. He thought back to the actions of the Kultash—their determination, and their skill. Hunting Dauthaz was all to them, and now they had one, or so they would think. To their mind the only thing capable of slaying them in force would be Dauthaz. He had given their crusade true reason, and their conviction fuel in the form of vengeance.

"We eat in the saddle," he said.

——✸✸✸——

Leaving the glade, no one spoke. It felt like leaving the home of a friend. They entered the narrow way leading out following the trail plowed by Azsark, only to find the channel blocked by a drift that topped the boulders. There could be an army of Kultash in the valley beyond and none would know of the glade. Taumea slid off his horse and struggled back through the deep snow to Valiena, who sat her horse looking cold and sad under her cloak hood, her bow strung and armed in her lap.

"The way is blocked by drift," said Taumea.

Valiena brightened. "We stay?" she asked.

He understood her sadness, and set his gloved hand on her thigh.

"No. I want to ask Spe to clear the way."

Valiena glanced ahead at Tiyha's hunched back, and nodded. She slipped off her horse and the two of them walked up to the girls' mother.

"Tiyha," said Taumea.

The woman turned red-rimmed eyes his way. She looked like she was in pain.

"We need your girls to clear the path," said Taumea.

Despair seemed to be her main reaction.

"As you say, m'lord," she said and dropped her gaze.

Taumea turned and worked his way through the churned snow to Azsark, where he could hear the girls in whispered conversation. They went quiet as he came up to them.

"You heard?" he asked.

They looked scared and caught, which puzzled him, but after he merely waited for an answer, Anila nodded.

"Good. What do you need?"

They seemed unsure how to answer such a question and Taumea clarified, "Shall I carry you to the front?"

Spe grinned and looked up at Anila, asking with her gaze if they could do that.

In a quiet voice Anila said, "We can Breathe from here."

Spe pouted.

Taumea said, "Then begin." He added, "Gently. We may need your gifts much today."

Anila's face went hopeful, then she looked down, embarrassed.

"Aye, m'lord," she mumbled like her mother.

Taumea put his back to the boulder behind him and turned his head to the snowdrift to give them a sense of privacy, but he watched from the corner of his eye.

Anila straightened her back and said, "May all I say and all I think…"

Spe's face went focused and Taumea stiffened as a breeze flowed past him. His heart began to beat with the thrill of being so near their weaving.

"…be in harmony with thee," said Anila. Wind gusted

and snow dust filled the air.

"Breath within," she said, and laid a hand on Spe's chest. Spe relaxed, leaning back into Anila, and the wind calmed. Snow settled.

Anila closed her eyes and said, "Breath beyond."

Air flowed down in front of Taumea's horse, whirling with snow.

Spe's hands came up, palms out.

Anila leaned forward, and said, "Mighty of the trees."

Spe pushed, and the whole drift vanished.

Taumea peered through the clearing cloud and saw the trail open as far as he could see. Azsark whinnied, and shook his ears.

"That was well done," said Taumea, and patted each of their legs. He pretended not to see the tears brimming in Anila's eyes at the praise. Spe looked a little dazed, her hands rubbing the center of her chest. Taumea walked forward and mounted.

By the time they reached the edge of the boulder field, the wind had risen. Before them, blowing snow hissed over sculpted drifts lining the valley floor. Their tracks in the night leading to the sheltering boulders had been wiped clear, and as far as he could see nothing else had passed. Azsark came up beside him and he looked at the girls. Anila wouldn't meet his gaze, but she was staring at his horse's neck, awaiting his word.

"Make your shield," he said.

Anila sung softly and the wind vanished around them. Taumea felt warmer instantly. He looked back. Valiena was twisted in the saddle looking down the valley for any enemy, but there was only snow and wind and low gray cloud which hid the hilltops around them. Tiyha was staring at Anila's back, but Taumea could not guess what the woman was thinking. Before he could urge his mount ahead, Azsark walked upslope, breaking through a wind crust on the first drift. Taumea directed his horse into line behind and their ascent into the mountains continued.

As they went, Taumea ate cold baked yam that Valiena had parceled out to everyone before setting out. She had a good supply of the roots, he knew, having dug most of them with her, but foraging would be impossible as they crossed the mountains, and was another reason to keep moving.

The next snowfall began before midday. The air grew colder yet, and the flakes streamed past like a flowing river. Anila's shield kept most of it from their backs, and Taumea knew that without the girls crossing the mountains would be impossible. It might not be doable even with them. There was no other path, however, not with the entire Iplock garrison of Kultash below. Taumea knew how he'd proceed with a winter hunt in these conditions, and hoped the Kultash were less capable. He checked his group's back trail continually, noting that Valiena was doing the same.

By early afternoon they had climbed into the clouds, the temperature had dropped further, and ice was forming on Taumea's beard from his breath. He was walking his horse, working hard to keep pace with Azsark as the horse plowed through the drifts, seemingly tireless. Taumea had no doubt that the animal was borrowing strength from his riders like Letet could from Breea, but he wondered where the horse was leading them. What did it know? Or were the girls following some scent only they could detect? Each time there had been a split in the valley, Azsark had led them to the right, often into a lesser branch so that Taumea was sure they were no longer on the main channel. That would be a problem if this route did not lead to a traversable pass.

The light had changed, indicating that the sun had passed beyond the peaks above. They would need shelter soon. The valley had narrowed and grown steep. Azsark had taken to traversing back and forth up its length. The relentless wind kept much of the snow from settling, but still it deepened, and Azsark slowed. By Taumea's sense of way, the valley they followed was heading northwest. Big wind-scoured boulders dotted the sloped ground like stones in a river; long drifts of snow gathered behind.

Without asking, Spe cleared a path through these. Before each, Anila let her sheltering weave fade. The wind that hit then was bitter enough to hurt, the snow in its grip like a stinging rasp against any exposed skin. The one consolation Taumea felt was that no one could follow them in this.

He looked back and saw Valiena falling behind as she walked her own horse. Taumea called to the girls to wait, and went down to his wife.

Valiena was panting as she came up, and leaned heavily against him for a while. She stood on her own, pushing back her ice-rimmed hood far enough to look up at Taumea.

He cupped the side of her head with a gloved hand, then turned and went back up the line.

To the girls he said, "We need shelter. Dark is coming."

Anila looked at him, pale with exhaustion. Sweat glistened on her face.

Taumea didn't know how to put the question so he just asked, "Where are we going?"

Spe pointed uphill. Taumea turned, and stumbled back a step.

Pale through the snowfall, twin gatehouse towers loomed, fashioned in the same soaring style as Limtir's, but as he stared he came to realize that this was a ruin—the gatehouse arches broken and yawning empty of doors. Gnarled, ice-crusted pines grew from cracks in the ramparts to either side.

Valiena came scrambling through the snow beside the horses, bumping into Taumea. She took his hand and held it to her chest, heaving great puffs of misty air. He squeezed her hands. Azsark shivered and started walking, head low.

Within the gatehouse tunnel, snow fell in straight curtains shaped by the broken ceiling, piling in tall drifts beneath. Taumea used a coal from Valiena's fire bag to light his lantern and took the lead. The way was rugged with mounds of rubble, ice, and snowdrifts, but not impassable with careful leading of the horse.

They emerged into a courtyard smaller than Limtir's, but of the same design. A massive ruin stood ringed by open courtyard. Taumea mounted to be able to see over the deep layer of snow which filled the space. Wind whirled snow about, though gentler here than in the open. The damage to this other library was softened by the smooth, thick blanket of snow. That it had once been as tall as Limtir seemed clear. Directly to his left the main rampart led to a cliff where a frozen waterfall hung, vanishing into a gap where the wall met the rock face. In the other direction, the wall met another cliff riddled with six levels of tall, empty windows. What lay behind the main building was impossible to make out through the snowfall.

Calm settled over him as he worked his way through thrilling thoughts. A fortified library built by the hands who had raised Limtir would possess the same features. The makers of Limtir had been subtle and wise in the ways of people and warfare. There would be secret tunnels leading to escape routes through the stone of its foundations.

Along the inner face of the wall to his right, the wind had scoured the snow almost to the stone of the courtyard, and Taumea led the horses along this path to the windowed cliff. At the corner of the walls, the eddy of wind had deposited snow almost to the top of high doors set in its face. Taumea pushed the top off the snow blockage, and crawled through. The room beyond felt like a haven though it smelled faintly of bird droppings. There were cliff swallow nests all around the high rim of the chamber. He turned and kicked snow out of the doorway.

"I can help," said Spe in a tired voice.

Taumea said, "No, lass. This one I can do myself." To Valiena he said, "Room for the horses in the first chamber."

Valiena's shoulders settled with relief.

Soon he was able to lead his horse within. Back outside, he took Spe in one arm and Anila in the other and carried them inside. Azsark followed. Valiena entered with Tiyha still mounted, then helped her off the horse and settled her near her daughters. Taumea and Valiena went back outside. The cold was growing intense as the light faded from the clouds. In quiet accord they halted and stared at the ancient ruin, so like Limtir. The sweeping eaves were broken and only three levels of the building remained.

Neither of them voiced their deepest worry—that this would be the fate of Limtir, that their own mountain fastness of knowledge and security had fallen—now on its way to ruin.

Taumea set the thoughts aside, and said, "Wayfeast?"

"Have we any wood?" asked Valiena, wiping at the tears on her face.

He looked up at the trees on the high rampart above

them. One or two were snags only.

"Soon we will," he said. "Use the lantern and see if further chambers are safe. The deeper we can get, the warmer it will be. Val, this is another Limtir."

She nodded, but hadn't made the leap to his thoughts.

"There will be deep wells for water," he said, waiting to see if she would think of the rest.

It took her no time to finish the thought, "Opalah—could there be a way?"

"We shall look."

Valiena hugged him, and he could feel her trembling, though from cold or emotion he could not tell. He held her until she relinquished the hold. She took up the reins of her horse and led it inside. Taumea went to the packhorse and pulled off the Kultash blade. He made his way to the drifted base of a long straight stair that went up the inside of the wall.

On the top of the wall, he gripped a rime-coated pine against the ferocious wind and looked down the narrow valley where they had come. He couldn't see far, but nothing but snow moved there. Staying low, boots crunching through rime and snow, he made his way to the first snag. Careful of his footing, he swung the Kultash blade, lopping off a limb with a ringing crack. He tossed the branch over the inside edge and swung for the next.

He worked with a growing sense that he was not alone. He spent a moment surveying the dim courtyard, and then the ruined library. Even broken, the building's massive walls and galleries of windows spoke of a majesty and sense of beauty not seen since the Legend Time. With the deep snow cover he couldn't tell if any of the interior rooms were intact, but even with multiple levels collapsed above, he guessed there might be some. The building had been built on a fortress scale.

Where he stood the gnarled pines spaced along the wall reminded him of sentries, their roots growing into the rocks, filling cracks as though holding the wall together. The trees looked ancient, and as old as the wall itself. Feeling as though he might have committed a desecration, Taumea gently brushed snow and rime from the weathered bole of the snag he had decimated, then put his hand upon the ancient trunk.

"Forgive me," he said. "We…we are of Limtir, and are in dire need."

There was no change. The bitter wind tugged at him, working its way into every gap in his clothing. He quickly made his way down the length of the ice-rimed wall to the next snag. He looked back but all he saw were trees and the snow rushing past. He lifted the Kultash sword and began.

Finished, he leaned through a stone merlon of the crenelated wall and checked the darkened snowscape of the valley floor below. The scent of pine filled his nose, unaffected by the wind. Thoughtful, Taumea looked about, then patted the stone. A season past he would have thought the sensation an imagining, but on this journey he had learned to believe in the unseen essence. In his heart he knew that the pines were offering to keep watch for him.

"My thanks," he said, then sheathed his blade and made his way back along the wall and down the stair.

Working in near darkness, he filled his arms with pieces of pine. He dropped them in the first chamber, noticing that the horses were no longer there. He went out for more. Returning with arms laden to the chin, he was pleased to see the warm light of the lantern appear in the doorway. Valiena stood in its light, the lantern pole in one hand, and her armed bow in the other.

She backed out of his way as he entered.

"I found candles," she said.

Taumea grunted and said, "Lead on."

The doorways they passed were arched, their borders carved with the likeness of plants and animals. The floors were dry and the air warming as they went. In a room almost too big for the lantern to light they came to the unsaddled horses, and Taumea could smell apple on the air. It reminded him of the scent of pine on the wall.

Azsark and the other horses turned and walked toward Valiena's light with hungry looks. They needed more fodder than apple. Taumea started to ask about them, but Valiena led him to a side chamber where one of the horse blankets had been hung over the entrance. Valiena held it aside and Taumea walked into a small room dominated by a stone table where all their gear was piled, well lit by dark wax candles in four corroded candelabras set at the table corners. Thick dust on the floor muffled his bootfalls. The walls were lined with tall hearths. Tiyha and Anila were scraping one clean. Taumea delivered the wood beside them, then peered into the big opening at the back of the room that looked like a window to nowhere. A shaft ran up and down within.

"As with Limtir," he said.

Valiena joined him and said, "Yes, a warming and finishing chamber for the hall beyond. The kitchens will be below."

While Valiena made a fire and prepared to make the first hot meal in days, Taumea removed his armor, placing it on the table, grinning when Spe's face appeared in a nest of blankets among the gear. She blinked at him with sleepy eyes. Free of the weight of armor, he stretched, reaching high, then down, touching fingers to the floor. That wasn't good. He should be able to touch palms. He took off his wool surcoat and in shirt only began the slow combat form of Turtle Aims to Fly.

Spe watched with an unblinking gaze, then vanished under the covers. A second later he heard her whisper from the other side of the table, "Ani! The lord is dancing!"

It felt good to move unhindered. Having taken measure of the area to move, Taumea closed his eyes, letting the flow warm his muscles and ease his thoughts as the weapons masters of Limtir had taught him.

A bell later he was sitting cross-legged on the floor. He surfaced from his deep focus and became aware of the fire crackling. The scent of rabbit stew with sage urged him to motion. He rose, and Valiena went to the pot with one of their wooden bowls. Spe was asleep in her blanket nest on the table. Anila and Tiyha sat on thick pine limbs beside the fire. The sweat of practice was cooling Taumea quickly, so he sat with them near the warmth. Valiena handed him a brimming bowl. How she had managed to save a rabbit all this time, and where she'd kept it, was a mystery he simply accepted. Her way with food was like Alach weaving to him. He looked his thanks to her and set to.

After he was done, Valiena knelt behind him and her hands settled warm on his shoulders. He sat straight with hands on knees. Her fingers dug into his shoulder muscles, and he groaned. When she found the bruised places he shook his head, and her hands worked around them gently. Pushing him forward, she started on his back, but he flinched.

"Turn around," said Valiena.

He did and she followed, then lifted his shirt in the light

of the fire.

"Moonless night…"

Taumea held still as her fingers explored around the tender area of the Kultash blow.

Spe emerged from her blankets and let herself down from the table. She ran around to the fire side to look. Taumea reached for his shirt. There was no point in being a spectacle. He raised the shirt to slip it over his head then flinched as two searing little hands touched the wound.

"Blood and martyrs!" He craned his head around.

Spe was on her knees leaning forward, arms straight out, eyes bright like the fire behind her. He decided not to move, then regretted the decision as essence-fire burned into him.

Then her hands were gone. He shuddered.

"Spe," said Valiena in a serious tone, "what did you do?"

Taumea took a tentative breath, then straightened, filling his lungs. He turned around and sat on his heels. Spe was looking worried. She looked at Taumea for reassurance, and he nodded to her.

"Tell her," he said, inclining his head toward Valiena.

"I Breathed to him," said Spe.

Valiena looked awed. Beside her Tiyha took a breath as though to scold, but Spe cried out, "Anila did it for me when I hurt!"

"It worked, lass," said Taumea. He rolled his shoulders and flexed his back with almost no pain. Tiyha's eyes seemed drawn to his musculature against her will, and Taumea saw Valiena smother a knowing grin. He felt warm and powerful. It seemed a shame to waste the strength the little Alach had given him. He stood and donned his shirt. Spe was avoiding looking at her mother.

Taumea said, "I am grateful for your Breath, Spe. My

pain is gone. That is a useful skill."

He gave Tiyha a curt, respectful nod of thanks. The girls' mother looked confused.

"Have you more of those candles?" he asked Valiena.

"Hundreds," she said. "Feast hall lighting. Linen and setting rooms to either sides. We could feast off crockery if had we a way to wash."

Taking up the lantern, she led him out of the room to another chamber in the same wall. Deep shelves were cut into the stone walls. Stacks upon stacks of dishes lay under thick coats of grime. Upon one shelf, rows of dust-covered candles lay in neat array.

"I'm going to search for a way through the mountains," said Taumea as he knocked dust from candles and inserted them into a candelabra. "We need the mother to accept their weaving. We have a long path and foes like hounds."

Valiena said, "All you need do is remove your shirt, warrior."

Taumea didn't comment on her teasing. His thoughts were on how to explain his experience with the trees.

"On the wall," he said, "it smelled of pine."

"The fire the wood has made is like sun in the grass," said Valiena.

Taumea smiled to hear her plainsfolk talk, but he shook his head. "In the wind," he said, "there should have been no scent."

Valiena frowned a little, not understanding. She reached up and traced the side of his face with her fingers.

He said, "I think they will keep watch for us tonight."

"Who will?"

"The wall. The pines. They told to me, Val, of their watchfulness."

"On our behalf?" asked Valiena.

"Yes," said Taumea.

Serious, Valiena said, "Did you give thanks?"

"I did."

"How did you know to do so?"

He quirked a grin at her. "I may have been taught a few things by my woman over the seasons."

Valiena looked pleased, then asked, "Can we stay here?"

"No," he said with regret, and touched her face as she had touched him. "I kicked the hive with both boots. They are coming. They are all coming."

Valiena's eyes went cool, her face etched in hardship. "Then kill them all, Taumea."

Using the native language of his people, he took oath upon her desire.

Valiena blanched.

Taumea said, "You cannot know this tongue."

"In your sleep," said Valiena. "Long ago."

Taumea drew himself up. "It is the pledge of a dead race." He drew his sword and held it to the candlelight for her to see.

In Limtiric, he said, "Your words upon my blade. Do sing."

CHAPTER 15

The High Path

IN THE DARK, THE APPROACHING CLATTER-ROAR
of twenty thousand hooves against the stones of the High
Path was a river of sound that flowed over Breea where she
waited out of sight.

The mount Neprawn had given her trembled, muscles
twitching with the desire to gallop. Her boundaries were
knotted tight so as not to betray her presence through her
daggers, but the horse could feel how she felt—the singing

thrill of setting out.

Breea bent forward to speak into his ear. "Does the sound excite you, Balor?"

He tossed his head.

She stroked his neck. "*Ooth, ooth, r'hame.* The time for charging will come."

Sakuront came riding up the road, backlit by two mounted warriors bearing spear-tipped lantern poles draped with ribbons of cloth. Behind them rode an officer vanguard six wide, their gold and silver sashes flashing yellow and orange in the light of the lanterns. Down the flanks of the column every sixth soldier bore a lantern pole that illuminated the edges of the road. The riders between the lanterns had bow cases and capped quivers hanging from their saddles. After twenty-four rows of the vanguard, triple rows of saber cavalry alternated with rows of servants riding mules to which were tied spare mounts and two baggage-bearing mules. The Kultash seemed never to end. Was this what three thousand cavalry looked like? Breea sat back in the saddle and fingered her dagger hilts.

After the rows of ordered cavalry came disorganized Batusha. They rode in no particular order, the younger warriors laughing at one another as they cursed their mule mounts. Each man led a string of three laden mules, often with an aspirant boy or two sitting on the bags. Simarn and Dori were somewhere among them, leading Breea's own baggage, but the night was too dark to see the young women among the throng of warriors and mules. Breea ran fingers over the expensive cloth of her split skirt. It was comfortable and the seamstress had been wise in the way of mounted garments, for the shape let Breea sit a horse with ease.

After Batusha marched the Aska-Wuthos. To a man they

had refused to ride, their officers resolute in their ability to outlast any horse. Breea nodded in admiration for the unity of their strides as they kept easy pace with the mounted host. Each bore a turtleshell shield, two light spears, and a pack. Some carried bags, other weapons, and more or less armor. They strode in unison, but their outfitting was personal. What had prompted Duyazen to send them with her? Did he not need them? Or had he seen her need as the greater?

After this came unit after unit of Yasharn—first an array of mounted spearmen, then bow, long-ax, and units of shield-bearing heavy infantry nervous on their mounts. Here and there Batusha masters and Aska-Wuthos officers rode within the column, peeling away to gallop up and down the line to deal with issues which threatened to slow the force. Any man or beast that could not continue was sent back to the field of muster.

Breea urged Balor to a walk and rode back along the way until she found the line still leaving the smoke-shrouded muster fields outside the city. Here mounted units cobbled together of random soldiers were each led by a Yasharn officer recruit.

"Tomes," said Breea, looking back. Her army spread for more than a league down the High Path. At the far end the Kultash lanterns vanished into the distance like a river of stars.

An angry bellowing brought her attention to the flickering cloud of torchlit smoke and dust out of which men and horses flowed. Here and there smaller figures dashed in and out of vision. Breea urged Balor closer and recognized Master Longat's voice. To one side a contingent of Yasharn cavalry waited, standing in groups and commenting on the march or checking their gear by torchlight—the rear guard.

From the din Longat's voice bellowed, "Het's blood, you gutter-supping apple-squire! Where is the grain?"

At Breea's urging Balor walked forward, parting the flow of mules and men. Longat was standing before a cringing man who wore a gray woolen uniform like many of the others watching the scene. A young Batusha warrior held a lantern pole that lit the work of a scribe standing at a portable desk, who was keeping his head bowed to his work.

Longat said, "I'll have grain, or I'll have your skin for a shawl!" One hand settled on a dagger hilt.

"Lord, sir," said the man and looked about for support, or escape.

"Master Planner Longat," said the lantern-holding warrior.

"*Master*," said the man, "Planner, sir, I was told ye needed palisade pole, an' shovels fer moats."

"By who?"

"Provisioner, sir." He held out a square of parchment.

Longat ignored the proffered writ and looked back across the muster fields as though expecting his most foul enemy to appear through the night smoke. Shaking his head, he noticed Breea at the edge of the lantern light. Whirling, he *chak'ood*. Every Yasharn in sight knelt.

Breea dismounted and walked up to the master planner. He was covered with dust and sweating despite the cold air. He looked tired, though his eyes blazed in his round, bearded face.

"Master Longat," said Breea. "An honest mistake I am sure. Our other supply is in order?"

Longat was clearly not sure the mistake was honest, but he said, "Master, bereft of the grain, the remaining supply is staged and has begun to depart." He swung his glower over the assembled supplymen. There was a surge of movement as they rose and got to work. Longat watched for a moment, then turned to Breea.

She asked, "What unit is the rear guard?"

"Anthem lancers, Master."

To a Batusha boy standing ready beside the scribe, Breea said, "Ask the lancer officer to join us." The boy dashed off. Breea was not surprised that he seemed to know exactly where the lancers were despite them being out of sight. She would have to ask Scaukra about the command structure within the young aspirants, what their true duties were. There were layers to Batusha.

The Anthem officer strode into the light, a conical helm beneath one arm, breastplate flickering with reflected torchlight, a saber swinging against his armored thigh.

Bay-ope had taught her that four things moved working men to their tasks: force, authority, respect, and love. With the provisioner that Longat seemed ready to kill, she might wield two of them.

The lancer bowed to Breea, and said, "Pa-hoc Hean Grent. In Service."

A pa-hoc? Breea nodded. A hundred lancers would be sufficient force.

"Hean Grent," said Breea. "From the provisioner we require—" She turned to Longat.

"A thousand med of grain," said Longat.

"Upon Lord General Ohan's writ," said Breea.

Grent's eyebrows flicked up.

"Chosen," he said. "Your word is law."

He bowed and took two steps back before he turned neatly on his heel. Longat flicked a hand at the gray-clad supply man for him to follow. Longat looked about, resting his hand upon his dagger hilt with clear menace. Men who had paused to watch surged into motion, the mules following with less enthusiasm as though they too were fascinated by the Chosen.

Breea was staring after Grent. His courtly manner had impressed her, but his words had shaken her.

Longat stood in quiet attention, waiting to see if she required anything else from him. She found that she wanted to praise him for all his efforts.

"Master Longat," she said, "The column is..." Thought deserted her as she saw it reach before her into the night.

He blinked, waiting.

"Long," said Breea.

"Aye, Master." His expression was flat.

Breea blushed. Feeling impulsive, she reached out to touch his chest and sent a small surge of essence through her fingers.

Longat gasped.

"Oh," he said. "You bless me."

He blinked and two tears ran down each side of his nose.

Moved by his reaction, Breea did not know how to reply. She bowed instead, then turned to her horse.

"Master?" said Longat.

"Yes?"

"If this assemblage is to become a force capable enough to meet you by spring, it will need a heavy hand and a sharp point."

He was probably right. The finest units were riding with her. She understood what he was proposing. With Longat in command she could trust that the force would be there to reinforce her soonest.

"We shall miss your wisdom until the spring, Master

Planner."

Master Longat *chak'ood*, and looked like he might blink another tear.

Breea smiled at him then mounted and looked out at the city of Yash. In the cold dark above the flickering haze of the muster fields, a point of deep yellow sparkled—the Temple orb.

"We go," she said to it, not knowing if it was simply the orb she spoke to, or some power beyond the crystal. That uncertainty reminded her what the Meric emissary Ierra Dometea had said back on the Timaret Plain when she had first left Limtir. *A broad hand moves again in the lives of men...Beasts of Legend rise. Urdjra in the north, the wolf at Limtir. The gods are stirring.*

Like then, she was again riding away from her friends to traverse the world in answer to another call. The solitary ache of it crushed some the wonder of the night's events. The clash within was confusing—and familiar. Perhaps this was what being a prophecy felt like.

Men were slowing in their work to look at her. Breea sat straighter in the saddle and sent her thought and voice to the orb. "Hold the city. Return kindness and wisdom to its rulership."

On the road a few bells later, the dawn was being smothered in darkening cloud. Breea sensed that snow was coming and though she would welcome sight of it, she feared what it would mean for the pace of the army. Since first light she'd ridden beside the supply section of the column, having discovered that wherever she rode raised the spirits and pace of the men within sight.

A welcoming cry went up from the tail of the line, and Breea twisted to look back. Rows of sack-laden mules were coming up the way at a fast trot, followed by what looked like rows of perfectly straight grain stalks tipped with silver seeds. Breea turned Balor and waited for them. The supply men riding their mules turned to watch her as they passed.

Pa-hoc leader Grent called an order and the lances tilted toward Breea as they passed. Breea saluted them with a dagger raised high, and set it sparkling. This caused some disorder in their salute as the men shouted in wonder.

The road was empty behind them. The army was complete, and on the move. Joy burned through her like essence-fire. Breea sheathed her dagger and wheeled Balor.

"*Yeaf!*" she called to him, and Balor leapt forward.

Her galloping up the column started a shout among the men that became a rolling wave of voice that paced her up its length. At the head, Sakuront turned to watch her gallop past.

To her left, open fields spread across the narrow floodplain to the foot of the rugged hills she had traversed on her way to the city. Somewhere up there would be the ruin where Scholar Baile had given her shelter. She turned Balor to the hills.

With open space to run, Balor stretched out and Breea flashed to running Letet through the Su forest on the Valley Road below Limtir. The wind of their passage whisked away homesick tears.

Nearing the slope, Balor slowed, skirting boulders that sat at the edge of the fields like the toes of the ridge. Breea touched Balor's neck and unbound her power. His hooves dug in and he charged up the hill. Leaning forward she put both her hands on Balor's neck. They flew up the hillside following its contours and dodging past boulders so near that Breea could have touched them.

At the top Breea shouted and Balor reared with a bellowing neigh. Breea caught herself with fistfuls of Balor's mane, then hugging his neck as his forehooves pumped the air. He dropped back down and danced forward, ready to go again, but Breea eased him around in a circle by touch. Both of them were breathing hard as he settled into a walk along the broad spine of the ridge. With care, Breea let their connection fade, stroking his neck and praising him. Sitting back, she became aware of a distant roar. It came from below, on the road. The army was cheering.

Breea drew a dagger and let all her affection for these men who had chosen to fight with her flow into the blade. Emerald green burst into the air around the blade, flashing like sunlight on water.

Seconds later the cheer crested and the Kultash wolf-horns howled. She smiled in awe at the whole long length of her army. Beyond them the great Yash River looked like a ribbon of dark iron as it reflected the stormy sky.

Balor's step faltered and Breea looked ahead. Twenty strides away a gaunt man in a sheepskin coat gaped at her. Around him sheep stared at her with similar expressions. She sheathed her sparkling blade and stroked Balor's neck to let him know that the figure was a friend.

"Greetings of a fair morn, scholar," she said.

Sighn Baile bowed and knelt all at once.

Breea slid from Balor's back and walked up to the scholar. Balor followed her like a dog.

"Scholar Baile," said Breea fondly, and took a knee in front of him.

His head rose, stopping as his eyes came level with the Tetr medallion on her chest.

"Tetr-Sanis," he said in wonder.

"I wear the medallion," said Breea. "But Ajalay is Tetr."

Sighn's head came up, and Breea saw again that sharp, inquisitive face she had been so grateful to meet on her terrible walk to the city.

"Scholar," she said. "You can return to Yash. The Temple has fallen. Ajalay is there, and Bay-ope. Duyazen is high priest once more. Your college can begin again."

Sighn looked over her shoulder toward the western horizon where the city lay and said, "I have had all I can learn of Yash. I wish to return home, Tetr."

Heart's agony spiked Breea's chest.

"Scholar Baile," she said, "Limtir has fallen to the Oregule."

Sighn's face went slack with the look of a man who has lost the last treasure of his heart.

In Breea, rage at the Oregule bloomed. Waxing light from her blades seemed to cut the air about her into sparkling fragments. Sighn took a step back and she closed her eyes to shield him from their fire. When she had bound her emotion, she opened her eyes to find him frowning.

"Where are you going?" he asked, "if not to retake Limtir?" He waved a hand at the army below.

"I am marching to battle another of the Oregule," said Breea. "I intend to break the siege of Carsythe and slay the beast that leads the Kaul nation."

The breath left Sighn in a wheeze. He blinked a few times, then his eyebrows went up.

"That I must see," he said.

Breea embraced him.

"Ah girl," he said, patting her back. "We have some stories for Limtir hearth-nights to come, have we not?"

Breea stepped back and wiped her eyes.

"Yes," she said with more darkness than she had intended.

Sighn had no belongings he wished to take and mounted Balor behind her with a nimble hop.

As they rode down the steep hillside, Sighn asked, "That black barding. Kultash?"

"Yes," said Breea.

After absorbing this, he asked, "The green light and the gold? That was you?"

"The green," she said.

"The wind as well, then."

"No," said Breea. "You felt the wind here?"

"Tomes, Tetr, it gave my sheep visions."

Breea giggled at the thought, and basked in the sense of home Sighn brought to her. A sheep called out. It sounded worried. She looked up to where a few of the animals stood watching them descend. She felt Sighn twisting to look. He heaved a sigh.

"I can arrange a shepherd for them," she said.

"No, no," said Sighn. "Let them live free for a while. There are no wolves here and their owner will seek them when I fail to appear. Should already have brought them down. So tell me, Tetr Banea, how did you convert Yash's most ancient and devout warriorhood to the cause of Limtir?"

The cause of Limtir. Breea had not thought of her quest in those terms. She liked it. And it was true, she was a traveling scholar, only her knowledge was that of the essence and of battle. She was, in truth, an Alach scholar of Limtir.

To Sighn's question she said, "I caused the High Temple to collapse, and defeated the First of the Kultash in single combat."

She felt Sighn go still, and grinned to think of his bright eyes blinking in shock—then he started laughing, the same whooping cackle he'd made at their first meeting when Breea had told him of essence and weaving. Balor flicked his ears back in irritation, and Breea started to laugh as well, though she had no idea why. Sighn's bony fingers shaking on her shoulders in uncontrolled mirth was the most comforting thing she'd known in an age of moons.

In the chill morning, a faint mist drifted with the army—their breath, and steam from the horses' bodies. Breea took Sighn to the Batusha section of the column. The company saluted her as Balor joined the flow. She asked the nearest Batusha warrior for a horse for Scholar Baile.

While they waited in the noise of the column's movement, Simarn urged her mount over to Breea. Neprawn followed, along with Sabar and Ootha. Scaukra watched from a distance. He looked pale in the gray morning.

As Neprawn approached, Breea could feel the rotten chill of the Oregule medallion from a saddlebag on his mount.

Pulling her attention from the vile thing, Breea called to Simarn over the clatter of hooves, "You are well?"

The young woman nodded, but the set of her face was forlorn. She wore a red cloak lined in black fur with the Batusha Weapons Guild starburst of blades in gold upon the back. All the masters Breea could see wore cloaks of the same design except Neprawn, who wore a dull red shearling cloak like the regular warriors.

A gray-clad supply man rode up with a horse on a short lead. Sighn motioned him over, and an impressed murmur accompanied Sighn's neat shift from Balor to the new horse.

To Breea it wasn't much of a maneuver, but Batusha were new to horseback.

"Knowledge grace you, Tetr-Sanis," said Sighn in thanks, and bowed straight-backed, from the waist.

Every man and boy in sight was watching the exchange—and looking at her with something near worship. She felt both warmed and embarrassed by their regard. Warriors had been watching her since she was little, and their looks, whether admiring, jealous, or lustful, had been relatively easy to bear. Something different was expected of her now. Bay-ope would say something to make them laugh. Ajalay would perform some act with imperial dignity to heighten their respect, but Breea could think only of wishing Simarn more joyful.

"Master Neprawn," she said. "Please consider Simarn a Batusha aspirant. Under your tutelage, if you will."

Neprawn *chak'ood*. He also blushed.

Breea's next statement quelled the secret smiles among the men who had overheard. "The Oregule Slayer is to be trained as my personal guard."

Simarn swallowed.

"Master," said Neprawn, "your word is law."

She looked at him sharply but his eyes were lowered. Where had that saying come from, and why did everyone suddenly know of it? Feeling irritated she looked to Sighn to see how he took the saying and found the old scholar wearing an amazed expression as he looked over the Batusha men. He noticed her looking at him and bowed again from the waist.

Sighing inwardly, Breea took Balor off the road and kicked him into a lope up the column. Travelers who had cleared off the road blocked the way so Breea rode out into the fields. Sighn's obeisance had lodged a spike of loneliness in her chest. He'd done it for her to show his respect before the men, but his honoring of her also made a wall between them.

Stroking Balor's neck, she asked him, "Am I fated to ride alone?"

A voice of memory said, *You are the hope of all*—the words of High Scholar Hegen in the ancient city of Sherishin, who had known her parents and apparently more of Breea's destiny than anyone else other than Lord Keharna. There seemed always something that forced her away from certain knowledge of her fate. In Sherishin it had been the Temple Soot assassins who had tracked her and Valiena and Taumea. There had been no time to talk to Hegen before they rushed off away to sail across the Leuvat Sea. Now there was Carsythe to save. Looking at her army she saw thousands of faces watching her, and it came to her that part of what disturbed her so in their looks was their belief, and their trust.

Balor wanted to run. Breea gave him leave and they raced over the fallow fields leaping stone walls until they came even with the head of the column. Breea guided Balor back onto the road, matching pace with Sakuront's mount. The First rode aside to give her a place beside him, and when she had taken it, he raised his hand, then swept it forward.

Wolf-horns sang and the Kultash moved into a trot. Without being asked, Balor matched pace with Sakuront's huge steed. Breea settled into Balor's trotting gait and watched the lowering clouds.

Go away, Breea thought to the weather.

At home in Limtir, after Ajalay had taught Breea to listen to the essence, the mountain forests had begun to act to her will, though she'd had no sense of why or how. The last had been on her flight from Lupazg, when the meadow grasses had unbent, concealing her path. The memory of her first sight of Lupazg sent slivers of ice up her right arm—the arm that had driven a blue steel dagger through the beast's eye. Deliberately Breea lifted her right hand. Two fingers marked by Oregule. The first showed a scar in the shape of a wolf print, and on the next the eight eyes of a spider were picked out in fresh pink scar tissue. The perfection of their placement on her fingertips felt ordained.

Breea clenched the fist, then wove a boundary against the hatred which threatened to roar up within. To calm herself, she set her thought against the problem of the storm.

Captain Etrya Finwall, who had given Breea passage over the Leuvat Sea on her journey into Yash, had taught Breea how to feel and call the wind. The sea captain's ability with the air was direct. It wasn't weaving, at least not as the books taught. All Etrya had lacked to shape a storm was sufficient strength of essence.

Strength I have, thought Breea.

To the medallion she thought, *Speak to me of the air,* but beyond Legend Time history and stories of what it called *storm weaving*, the medallion could tell her little of how to weave the air on such a scale. The emerald seemed to be a tool more of linguistic and political knowledge and small practical weaving—sensing whether a man was lying, weaving the voice to various effects, and a few weaves that were useful for a traveler such as making fire and cleansing water. It knew everything of weaving that Ajalay had studied while wearing it—the Abitalen histories, and the weaves of war that the she had used to strike at Lupazg the Oregule in the halls of Limtir. There was much of the governance of

Limtir and some limited instruction on weaving the deep essence of the world, but nothing about wind.

After three bells at a trot, Sakuront raised his hand and the Kultash wolf-horns signaled. The Kultash host settled back to a walk. After twenty horse strides, he swung down from his mount and the horns sang again. Breea looked back and saw the Kultash swing from their mounts on the left side and in two strides were leading their horses by a short length of rein. It was an impressive maneuver, as none of the horses broke stride. Breea dismounted on the right so that she was walking beside Sakuront between their horses.

The road rounded a long bend beside the river and a league ahead a city wall came into view. The sight of it was not a comfort. By the map this was Umenk, a city only a tenth the size of Yash, which was yet immense in Breea's experience. A smoke haze filled the air beyond the wall, rising to blend with the storm-gray sky. Even at this distance she could see that the wall was high and well maintained. That meant an active garrison—a bad place to get snared by whatever Dauthaz the Oregule may have sent to rule here.

"I do not think we should enter Umenk," said Breea.

Sakuront's cool face turned to her and she waited for his objection. Instead, he made a summoning gesture over his shoulder. Two officers came running.

Sakuront said, "We will skirt Umenk on the Grain Road."

"We Serve," said the men and ran back.

Sakuront mounted. Breea slowed her stride, letting Balor walk past, then swung up to his back thinking about the vision she'd shared with the First in their duel. She had felt deep emotion within the man as powerful as his body, and she knew that he had touched the molten essence at her center. Yet, any kinship between them felt tenuous, as though their souls were made of different essence. Was it then the vision which led him to trust her word, or did he also feel that Umenk was a trap?

Wolf-horns called the signal to mount. A few horse strides on they signaled again—a new call Breea had not heard before. Sakuront's horse stepped into a trot, and Balor leapt forward. Breea had to hold him back from racing ahead. The First's horse took no notice, not even a flick of ear. Balor's tail swished and his ears flicked back. Breea grinned and stroked his neck until he calmed.

A command sang out behind. Breea turned. The six-horse phalanx was changing shape with dance-like coordination. The central four of the first two rows had followed Breea and Sakuront into a trot, while the remaining pair on each side remained at a walk, then flowed in behind them into a new four-row that stepped up to the new pace. The gliding motion flowed like a wave down the column as if the army were a river entering a narrow canyon. The maneuver's grace and discipline sparked a desire to see these men in battle, and she wondered at herself. Remembrance of the singing joy she'd felt defending Batusha Guild Hall set her blade gems sparkling. Sakuront's gaze whipped around to them, then up to her face. She stared ahead, unwilling to look at him, unsure what her eyes would reveal. To kill with such focused ease—the power and thrill of it made her heartsick. Sakuront returned his attention to the road. Breea smiled as she realized that Sakuront's aloofness was a sham. He was watching her closely, and it pleased her to see that he took the light of her daggers as the warning it usually was.

Half a bell later, Sakuront slowed the army to a walk, then raised an arm to the northeast. He rode off the fitted stones of the High Path and onto a narrower road of packed gravel which led away at an angle. It ran straight through winter fields toward a broad cleft in the ridge north of the city. Breea found her shoulders relaxing as the sharp roar of hoof-metal on stone was replaced by a softer clatter. She looked back. Four horses abreast was the perfect width for this road. Had the rest of the army followed the Kultash example? Should she go look? Bay-ope would not. He would wait for his officers to report trouble, so she settled in the saddle and tried to ignore the sharp longing for her friends that thoughts of Bay-ope had sparked.

The city had noted their approach, and the top of Umenk's wall had grown a dark line of observers.

The gravel road took them northeast toward a crossroads where the Grain Road met a paved High Path heading north out of Umenk. The north side of the city wall came slowly into view. Near its center, a squat gatehouse straddled the northern High Path. All traffic on the road was into the city, fleeing the storm—while she was leading her army directly into its teeth. Doubt reared before her. The army was not equipped to sleep in the open. They would need to ride and walk all night—into a snowstorm.

Raising a hand to the Tetr-Sanis medallion, she traced the open book pattern carved into the emerald's face.

"What city lies next on this road?"

"Hamelgeer," said Sakuront.

Breea waited to see if he would offer detail, but he said nothing. Irritated, she looked toward Umenk. The city's dark wall felt hostile. Cold. A shock ran through her as she scented essence-rot—Oregule or Dauthaz, she could not tell. The air about her began to shimmer as essence-fire billowed up within. Balor tossed his head, feeling her power, wanting to run. Sparks whirled about her dagger hilts like green fireflies.

"Chosen," said Sakuront in a clear voice, breaking the rising tide of her anger.

She turned to him. When their eyes met, he blinked and the muscles of his neck flinched as he quelled a desire to look away. His dark eyes held hers as though proving to both of them that he could face whatever it was men saw in her gaze when the essence burned within. He broke the look and cast his gaze across Umenk's wall.

"A spider's nest," he said. His gaze swung back to her. "Hamelgeer has fodder, and houses enough to bed the host."

A spider's nest. The comment made her wonder what Sakuront knew of the Oregule spider that had ruled the High Temple. Could he sense the beast eyes watching them now from Umenk's wall? Or perhaps he meant simply that the city held snares and delay. No matter his knowledge, it settled Breea that Sakuront accepted her decision to pass the city, and, more, the First did not want her to attack the place. Breea took a breath and let it out slowly. She nodded.

—◦◦◦—

Dori shifted her weight to ease the discomfort of the saddle, but it hurt no matter what she did. She wasn't alone. The Batusha men and boys never spoke of it, but she saw them trying to ease the same pains. Without her ladyship near, Dori felt like a mouse in a house of cats. She felt safe enough, yet the way these men eyed her brought to the fore how utterly helpless she was. They didn't leer or make lewd comments. They just watched, making her feel like an especially fascinating part of a stage play. Simarn gathered even greater interest, but the looks toward her were darker and Dori heard low talk naming the girl everything from Sweet Death to the Oregule Slayer and one that was gaining favor: Neprawn's Doom. Those who liked that kind of banter were careful, though, never to voice the jest when Neprawn was near.

Neprawn the Tall seemed to be one of the more powerful guild masters. Dori had witnessed other guild masters listening to his words and even obeying him. After her ladyship's morning instruction to Neprawn that he teach Simarn to fight, he had spent three bells with her. Dori liked his stern but attentive kindness—helping Simarn learn to guide her horse and teaching her how to check and oil her crossbow. No one talked to Dori except Tam. She looked around, but the Batusha aspirant was nowhere near. He seemed always on the move, executing the orders of older warriors with deferential speed. She remembered the strength of his arm in the streets of Yash. On their dash to the Temple he hadn't bent the slightest bit, even when she had to lean heavily on him. She tried to imagine what he looked like under his jerkin, then looked down to hide her flushing face.

No one noticed. Chill wet struck against her face and she looked at the sky. After passing Umenk the road had run north and climbed to the flat top of the highlands, where a chill breeze had swept upon the army as though to hold it back. Light snow had begun soon after and there had been much debate among the warriors on the depth of snow they would see.

This felt to Dori like a storm finding is balance before pouring Het's wrath upon the land. Big flakes of snow whirled down as the wind grew teeth. Men threw cloaks across their chests and pulled hoods forward, hiding grim expressions. A call to light lamps sang down the column. Dori looked up to watch the activity for a moment, then folded in on herself, crossing her arms under her woolen cloak against the chill that was seeping into her. Loss welled in her heart, though she had no thought of why. Alone and saddlesore, she shivered as the wind wrapped its cold hand about her. Her mule stepped on as dark cloaked the world and the sky fell in pieces of white.

An endless misery later, her cloak was shaken before a heavy weight fell across her back and shoulders. Fearful, she sat up. The air was thick with snow, and man and horse were ghostly, lantern-lit shapes all about her. Hoof noise was muted and accented by a hiss of splashed wet snow. Beside Dori, her ladyship leaned over from her warhorse and arranged her ladyship's own bear-fur cloak across Dori's shoulders.

"I—I—" stammered Dori, trying to object through chattering teeth.

"Hush," said her ladyship, and put a hand on Dori's chest.

Heat flowed from the hand and Dori cried out. Men turned to look, dislodging snow from heads and backs. Warmth seared through Dori's body, burning out the cold. Her hands and feet felt afire. The flow stopped, leaving a warm glow. As the hand withdrew, Dori gripped it with profound emotion, then broke into a weeping she could not control. It felt as though the heat had burned away all barriers within and a welter of feelings overflowed within her. Her ladyship held her hand until the flood subsided.

Feeling cleansed, Dori quickly released her ladyship's hand. The lady gently lifted the bear-fur cloak hood over

Dori's head—then she was gone. Dori heard her voice behind in query and the voices of Batusha lifting in cheer as they answered her.

Dori held the cloak close about her though she was not cold.

CHAPTER 16

Hunt Me Not

THE PINEWOOD COALS WERE SETTLING IN THEIR own ash before Anila rose from her blankets and slipped out of the room. In the empty feast hall, she paused to listen to the air. Horse breath was the only sound. The Limtir lord was out exploring the ruin while everyone else slept, but she had no sense of him.

Following the scent of snow and pine, she padded down empty halls until she came to the room of bird nests. Fresh snow had covered everyone's tracks, and shaped a luminous white fan inside the door. Outside, the snow glowed in cloud-filtered moonlight. She looked back. The halls were dark and quiet.

Anila stepped forward, flinching at the squeak of snow beneath her winter sandals. Shaping a little air between lips and throat, she whispered it to her feet. Her steps after were no louder than the feather-sigh of falling snow.

Out under the luminous clouds the new snow came to her waist but it was soft. She pushed through it to the stair. The scent of tree sap and old pain led up the wall.

"Breath within," she whispered, then began the long climb.

Much of the stair was blown free of snow as though a path had been cleared for her. She kept as far from the open edge as she could. In places she had to climb over drifts. For these she used the Limtir lord's frozen footsteps, but each of these icy traverses left her trembling.

At the top she stared at the big pine which guarded the landing. Broken limbs and twisted branches gave it a shape that was somehow beautiful. It endured, and in the shape of this there was grace. She walked up and put a hand upon its flank. Snow on the bark melted around her fingers.

—◦◊◦—

Taumea held the candelabra high, peering through the graven arch into the room. The floor of the chamber was littered with crumbling weapons and disintegrating armor. At his feet overlapping layers of rust lay across the entry. A closer look by candlelight revealed that they had been chainmail surcoats. This room had seen a last stand. He stepped over the ancient armor, boots crunching on rusted sword flakes. The chamber had no obvious exit and there were no bones. He walked to the back wall. The stone was cracked in whorled patterns. He touched the pattern and pieces fell off with a dry clatter. With his light he looked high, then bent to examine the ground. Tiny sparkles lay amid the dust and grit. He licked a finger and touched it to the dirt. Holding the tip close to the candles he could see what looked like bits of colored glass. Not glass—shattered gemstone.

"They come," said a voice in his ear.

With a shocked bellow, Taumea dropped the candles and leapt back, ripping sword and dagger from their scabbards. Blades ready, he looked about for the source of the voice. Light danced wild on the walls from the few candles still lit burning sideways. He crouched and righted the stand, then turned carefully in all directions. When nothing else happened, he sheathed his dagger and relit the other candles. Sword in hand he took the candelabra out into the hall to look up and down the way. Firelight reflected in small glints from the scattered trail of ancient armor and weapons he'd followed to the chamber—a running battle to a room with no exit. His tracks looked to be the first boots to walk the hall since.

A breath of wind touched his face. It smelled of pine and...

"Anila?"

A meek voice replied from the air, "Yes?"

Taumea would have laughed, but for what she'd said before. "Who comes?"

"Kuthashk."

"Where?"

"They come." She sounded distant, not herself.

"Anila, how far?"

"Soon," she said. "The trees say soon."

Taumea froze. "The pines?"

"Yes, m'lord."

"Anila, where are you?"

"Haltir."

Taumea's breath caught. The name of this place was the Library of Haltir. He looked back into the room where a hundred ancient Tomeguard had died defending their home. Memories of Lupazg's attack on Limtir bled in his vision. The last bastions of the Legend Time knowledge did not seem to fare well.

Regaining the moment, he said, "Where in Haltir?"

"Outside," said Anila.

"The outer wall?"

"Yes."

"Anila, we need a path out of Haltir. I am in a room—"

In a terrified voice, Anila said, "I see them."

"Wake Valiena. I am coming."

———

Leaning on a branch of the pine, Anila watched the dual line of sparks move up the steep valley floor. Behind her, boots crunched on snow and she turned to see the lord Taumea running up the icy stair taking the steps three at a time. He flew across the landing and slapped hands against the parapet to stop his rush, boots sliding. His breath caught at the sight of the sparkling lines.

As he exhaled, calm flowed off him like a cool wave. Anila gasped. Lord Taumea had the Breath! She could feel Spe's Breath radiating from him, but this was something else, a chilling purity that felt like being bathed in water from the deep well in the Azsark larder. She felt safe as fear released its grip on her heart, though the calm created a chill at the same time. His gaze turned to her, then rose to the pine, and he looked for a moment at the wisps of moonlit steam rising from its branches.

"My thanks for the warning," he said.

Anila couldn't tell if he was talking to her or to the tree.

The lord stepped up to her and went to a knee. "Anila, is there a way to escape from Haltir? A secret path."

The scent of pine overwhelmed her. Through the roar of a waterfall, clinks of iron on stone fell sharp on the air. In a brightly lit tunnel, twenty noblemen and a lady watched people hammering symbols into the archway of a long tunnel. Their clothing was fine, beautiful even, but strangely cut. The woman turned to look at Anila with eyes that were the deep green of pine needles, and Anila almost wept to realize that the woman was, in some god-like way, the pine tree itself.

The lady's lips moved and Anila found herself speaking. "Follow the water, maker."

Anila felt a wash of heat across her face as knowings rushed through her. She blinked and found that she was looking down the parapet at the frozen waterfall on the cliff where the wall ended.

Anila said, "A way was made. But…the…she says the locks are broken."

"So we could be followed?"

Anila didn't answer. She was remembering what else the lady of the pine had shown her. Her gaze fell to the hilt of the lord's sword.

"Can they help?" asked lord Taumea.

Anila could feel the pines extending their will. Faint cries came on the cold night air from out beyond the wall in the valley below.

"They are," said Anila.

The sparkles had bunched up, forming rings. Some of the specks of light went out.

The lord Taumea watched with her for a moment, then asked, "Anila, can you find the tunnel through the mountains?"

Anila wasn't sure, but she would do anything not to disappoint him.

"Yes, m'lord."

"Good," he said. "I need you to lead Tiyha and Spe and Valiena away from here, through the mountains. Will you do that for me?"

Anila could only think that if they left him behind, she might never see him again. The thought made her belly seize. Tears came unbidden.

The Limtir lord looked pained, and laid a hand on the side of her face. A mix of Spe's heat and his calm flowed through her. Her Breath roared in response—billowing strength. Steam started coming off her skirt where snow had melted it wet.

She said, "I will, my lord."

The lord's cheek quirked in admiration. Anila looked down, unable to face his approval for it made her heart hurt so wonderfully it was frightening. She gasped as he swept her up with one arm and set off down the stair. At the bottom he waded back through the snow into the bird nest room, where a candelabra flickered on the floor. He swept it up with his other hand. Walking fast enough to put out most of the candles, he carried her all the way back to the hearth chamber next to the big room.

It was warm within, lit by faint coal-light. The lady rose from beside the fire. Anila's Breath was full upon her and the breeze of her arrival caused a few sparks to whirl as the coals shifted. The flare of light showed the lady armed with bow and arrow, though she did not look alarmed until she saw Anila on the lord's arm. Anila dropped her face in shame for having sneaked away, and wriggled to slip off the Limtir lord's arm. He let her down.

Spe stood abruptly from her nest of blankets on the stone table. She hopped to the edge of the table, crawled over the edge, and let herself down with a grunt, then came running.

She smacked into Anila, hugging, then looked up.

"You smell like a tree."

Anila didn't answer. She was watching the Limtir lord hand-talk with the lady and caught the protect sign as his hands gestured. He took off his sword and the lady helped him put on the thick Kultash coat over the scale armor he always wore. He belted the coat with the Kultash blade, then donned the Kultash helm.

The lord turned to Anila.

"Is the tunnel through the mountain tall enough for the horses?"

Fear smashed down and Anila spun to look out the chamber door at the horses. They couldn't leave without Azsark. That would be worse than everything else.

Her fear was eased by the weight of a hand on her shoulder—its heat and chill making her shiver. She looked up into eyes that reminded her of the promise she'd given at the pine. His face was different now—calm, but in a terrifying way.

She felt him looking at her as though he were fixing her

features in his memory. He turned to the lady. Anila followed his gaze and was shocked to see the lady reflecting his terrible calm, somehow blessing what Anila sensed would be deeds of blood and ending too horrible to think upon. The lady lit a candle in the hearth and brought it to him. No words were said between them, but Anila felt a ripple in the cool flow of his Breath. He turned and strode from the room, sheltering the candle flame with one hand.

The sound of his boots faded. Anila touched her shoulder where his hand had lain, then looked down at Spe. Spe was scared, but like always she looked to Anila to judge how scared to be. Anila put a hand on Spe's shoulder and whispered a wisp of warm Breath to her. Spe relaxed.

The lady was lighting candles. In their light her face was severe, with eyes that did not seem to see what was before her. Anila knew the look—Ma had looked that way for as long as Anila could remember.

The candle in the lady's hand trembled, dripping wax, not reaching to the next taper.

Anila walked around the table to her. Spe followed along.

Anila said, "The pines will help him."

The lady Valiena gentled and she set a hand on Anila's headscarf. "Opalah bless you. You have truth—it is the Kultash who need to fear. We need more candles. Run to the next room and gather a big armful? Be swift."

Anila took the candle the lady offered and rushed out into the big room with Spe keeping pace beside her. In the storeroom Anila grabbed candles by two and threes, stacking them like firewood across Spe's arms, then in her own. Azsark clopped over and stood in the doorway.

When they had candles to their chins, they turned to

leave, but Azsark wouldn't get out of the doorway. Anila walked up him to force him back. He touched her face with this nose, making her giggle and turn away.

Spe said, "Move, big apple seed. We're in a hurry!"

Azsark's massive head dipped to sniff Spe's headscarf, and she froze. Then he backed out. Spe looked at Anila with an amazed *he obeyed me!* look. They followed the horse out into the room, then dashed back to the hearth room trying not to spill candles.

Inside, the lady took their armloads and piled the tapers on the table. "Thank you. Gather the horses. Use an apple. Bring light so they can see you."

Spe ran to her basket and hefted an apple larger than her head from the hay. The lady took down the blanket that hung across the doorway. Spe went out into the dark hall, but Anila watched the lady go to the hearth and kneel beside Ma's sleeping shape. The lady touched Ma and spoke in a soft but urgent tone. Ma mumbled agreement and the lady helped Ma rise.

Anila followed her sister out into the big room. She didn't need candles to know where Spe was. She'd known where Spe was at all times before she'd even been born, and Spe had known where Anila was before Spe could say Anila's name.

Coming up to Spe, Anila said, "Hold this," and offered the candle while putting a hand under the apple.

"No," said Spe, clutching the fruit.

"They have to see it," said Anila.

Spe shifted her grip and maneuvered the apple so that it was a little higher than her head, braced with her cheek.

Anila held the candle beside the green-gold fruit and called, "Apple!"

Beside them Azsark neighed with a deep roll. His call made Anila cringe, but it also sent a thrill through her.

A clatter of hooves came so fast that Anila took a nervous step back. Spe wobbled, and Anila helped her lower the apple. They turned to go back, but Anila stopped. Spe continued toward the light, intent on her apple. The doorway to the hearth room was like a patch of sunlight glowing in the dark. Horse scent surrounded her. Everything was as clear as rainwater, and a deep sense told Anila that she would never forget this. Azsark nibbled at her hair, and she took off after Spe. The horses moved after her in a clatter of iron on flagstone.

The lady looked up as Anila and Spe stepped into the room. Horse heads filled the doorway behind them.

"True horsewomen," said the lady with a warm smile. "Bring the apple."

Spe brought it to the lady, who cut it into pieces with swift strokes, then swept the pile onto a cloth. The lady gestured for Anila to come then lifted the cloth corners and handed the bundle to Anila.

"For each, a piece, before I place the bridle."

After the lady had reins and bits on each horse, she led one into the room up beside the table. She climbed onto the table, arranged a folded blanket on the animal's back, then hefted one of the packs up onto the horse's back. It stepped away when it felt the weight and the pack almost fell to the floor. The woman leaned forward to grab the reins while balancing the pack with the other hand. Anila rushed around and pushed on the warhorse's belly with all her strength.

The warhorse ignored her until Azsark gave an ominous nicker from the doorway. The reluctant war horse tossed his head and sidled back to the table. Valiena praised the horse in a tone that was both soft and strong, almost like Ma used to use when she was teaching them about the Azsark tree. The lady caught Anila's attention, and pointed to the warhorse's ears, which had been back and were now relaxed.

Anila nodded that she understood and grabbed the ropes that the lady passed down to her over the horse, then ducked under him to hand them up to the lady's waiting hands.

When the pack was secure, the lady handed her the reins. Spe wanted to help and rushed over to grip the ends dangling from Anila's hands.

"Come," she said, and walked forward with Spe. "This way."

The laden horse followed them around the table without resistance. With pride they led him outside. Azsark stood to one side of the door, candlelight from the room painting his chest and head. The next horse was docile under his gaze as Anila brought the animal up to the table. She risked a quick look at Ma to see if Ma had noticed how much use Anila was able to be, but Ma was intent on folding blankets with one hand. The other clutched the red gem to her chest. A wave of sadness crested and broke over Anila. It left her trembling, tears brimming in her eyes.

Spe gasped. Anila felt it too, a Breath of calm savagery on the air, strong with the scent of pine—the lord was fighting and the trees were helping him.

Neither Ma nor the lady appeared to feel it, and Anila decided not to tell them. The lady might run off with her bow if she knew the lord was in battle, and he had told Anila take everyone away through the mountains. For Spe, Anila made a little motion with one hand—*don't say anything.* Spe clenched her jaw—her sign that nothing would pass her lips.

The weight of the decision settled over Anila like a

heavy blanket of snow, and with it came understanding—everyone's life now depended on her.

She dropped the reins and walked out past the horses and into the dark of the big chamber. Back in the hearth room, the lady's voice came faintly as she discussed the packing with Ma. The scrape of Spe's winter sandals came up from behind and a warm shoulder nestled against Anila's hip.

Follow the water.

What did it mean? Azsark's hooves clopped dull on the dust-covered stone causing echoes to dance between the chamber walls. His head came down over her shoulder.

She stroked his warm winter coat and said up into his ear, "What water?"

Azsark's breath blew over her hands. Breath. Anila smiled and nuzzled her cheek against his. She stepped forward, putting a hand on his nose to keep him from following. She felt Spe clutch at her hand, but didn't return the grip. Spe let go.

Anila walked into the dark, then halted and closed her eyes. Feeling inward, she touched the Breath of the Gods burning deep in her chest. It bloomed and whirled up. It felt so good all she wanted to do was bask in its warmth.

She recalled her purpose. Anila took in a long breath through her nose. The air smelled of stone and dust—and one cool thread—the scent of rock-born water.

With profound relief Anila clutched her hands to her chest and said, "May the tree bless."

She skipped back to Spe, took her sister's hand, and ran back to the hearth room. Ma and the lady Valiena looked up at them.

Anila said, "I know the way."

———◊◊◊———

Taumea strode down the moonlit slope, boots breaking through wind crust on the snowdrifts. A pine-scented breeze rose about with him, whipping snow down the moonlit valley floor like pale horse tails lashing in the wind. He tested the pull of his blades and rolled his shoulders, breathing the ice-laden air in deep drafts.

Downslope in the moonlight, the Kultash seemed to have steadied. There were no more cries, though by their lanterns they remained in two defensive rings one above the other down the valley, each at least fifty men strong. A pa-hoc of Kultash.

Taumea felt the battle calm settling over him, and for a moment he regretted not bringing his Limtir sword. If he were to fall here, it should be a Limtir blade that he held. His father's words hissed out of deep memory: *You cannot fall.*

The piney wind howled past Taumea, angry and knife-sharp. It hit the first ring of warriors and their line bent under the weight of slashing air. Lamps winked out.

The men before him had their heads down, arms up to shelter their faces. Taumea drew his Limtir dagger.

The gloved fingers of his left hand stroked up the blade as he intoned, "Do sing."

For the space of a stride he felt himself back in the forests of his homeland—a boy with a blood-crusted blade stalking invaders. Then he was among them. The first Kultash died from a powerful two-handed thrust that rammed Limtir steel through Kultash chainmail and split the man's heart. From the belt of the sagging body Taumea drew a second dagger. A warrior beside the man dropped his arm to squint into the wind and received the blade through the eye, uttering an aborted cry as the weapon went to the hilt through his skull.

Taumea stepped over the bodies and went low, rising to drive his blades up into the groins of two Kultash in the next ring. As both cried out, Taumea drove them back, trapping their arms and swords against their bodies with the force of his rush. The two fell back and Taumea leapt over them, ice-wind pushing him into open space beyond where a knot of three Kultash officers struggled to face the wind. Charging for the man on the left, Taumea dropped the Kultash dagger and drew his sword one handed. He parried the man's attack, and blade-crash pierced the wind howl. Faces in the rings turned as Taumea kicked the officer high in the gut, knocking him off his feet. The middle Kultash raised his sword two handed, staggering under the force of the wind. Taumea swept in under the blow, driving his dagger up beneath the man's chin.

As the third scrambled around to attack, Taumea's sword cut across his face. The circle contracted as shocked Kultash rushed to the aid of their officers. Taumea took two steps downhill and leapt. In the air, he parried the sword of the warrior in his path and slammed a knee into the man's chest. Ribs snapped and the Kultash fell back into the downhill-facing outer ring of men, sending them stumbling.

Taumea knifed another as he slipped through their ranks and sped down the slope in a flurry of dark snow.

He dodged to his left and whirled with blades raised. There was no pursuit. Pine wind sang past him but from it he felt no chill. He sheathed his dagger, and walked toward the motes of yellow that were the lamps of the next ring. Curls of wind-driven snow leapt from the peaks of drifts and whipped into the eyes of the ring.

Still, blades rose at his approach. Taumea turned his

back to the blades. With the wind in his face, he stepped back and sidled downslope holding his Kultash sword high as though expecting attack from above where not even a single lantern still glowed. The ring behind him parted and he stepped back into their ranks. He kept going, pushing backward through the defensive lines until a firm hand on his back stopped his progress.

"Hold," said a powerful voice over the wind, and Taumea knew he'd found his mark. This was the man he had come to kill—the pa-hoc leader.

Taumea reversed his sword and thrust back with all his power. The man voiced a growling grunt as the sword tip parted mail links, scoring flesh, though not quite piercing through. The Kultash leader stumbled back and Taumea sensed the man reaching for his sword. Taumea gave a ferocious heave back, pushing the blade past the mail and into the man. The officer grunted in agony and went over backward. Taumea fell back with him. The officer hit the snow and Taumea landed hard upon him, using his weight to drive the Kultash blade clear through the man's body and into the frozen ground below. The man's cry was cut as Taumea whirled and drove his dagger through the officer's throat.

A figure loomed and Taumea rolled aside as a sword strike flickered past. From the ground Taumea kicked the man's knee, sending him staggering down the hill. More were closing. No hesitation in these men, and Taumea knew he was facing the veteran core of this pa-hoc. Snatching the dead officer's sword from its sheath, Taumea whipped it across the legs of another attacker then used his dagger to parry a powerful strike that knocked him back. He used the motion to roll backward into another attacking Kultash. The

Limtir dagger slashed the man's thigh to the bone and gave Taumea the space to stand. More came.

"There!" he cried in Yasharn, pointing through the driven snow at the fallen figure he'd slashed.

In the second it took for the warriors to hear his accented Yasharn and realize the lie, Taumea had closed with the closest, driving the stolen officer's sword through the face guard of the warrior, followed by two quick savage swings against the mailed necks of another pair. A sword crashed into Taumea's helm from behind, ripping it from his head and staggering him forward. At the same time another blade bit into his leg armor from the side and he felt the searing sting of steel biting into his thigh.

They attack as one, thought Taumea.

He ran, parrying blows with sword and dagger, taking a slash across his armored back. Wind roared him free of the ring, and he stumbled ahead through the drifts with its helpful hand. He looked back. Dark shapes emerged against the pale night snow, following his trail through the drifts.

With a grim smile, Taumea whirled and ran, blazing an obvious trail. When the dark figures were out of sight, he turned and made a long leap downhill. Landing in a drift, he rose and ran downhill with the wind until he was sure he was invisible from his track across the valley, then curved his path back toward the other side, moving as fast as he could. The wind was gentle about him, warm with knowing. It seemed the pines knew his intent.

"Unending thanks," said Taumea to the wind.

When he reached the tracks marking the Kultash path up the slope, he followed it up until figures came to view in the light of the moon-glowing sky. A cluster of eight Kultash stood around their dead officer. The rest seemed to have followed Taumea's fleeing trail. One man knelt and lantern light flickered. He set the lantern on the officer's chest and turned the wick. Waxing light outlined the men. The sword through the man's gut had been removed. Curved greatswords were drawn and raised to the sky. A chanted litany came on the breeze.

Taumea went forward, wind rising about him. He drew his dagger and a hissing gust of wind surged to drown the Kultash song. The lantern on the officer's chest fell over and rolled off his chest, flickering out. Taumea charged.

His blade slashed three times and three men toppled, the backs of their knees sliced open. Then he was gone, leaping downhill. Cries of rage followed him.

⚉

Taumea found he was shivering on his back. A heavy weight impeded his breathing. The side of his face was numb with cold. There was light beyond his eyelids. One eye opened. His face lay against an icy stone wall that rose to a jagged bit of blue sky with wispy clouds sailing past—the broken archway of Haltir's gatehouse. He ached with cold, felt his toes and buttocks numb within its grip. Elsewhere, half a dozen sharper agonies were like spikes of pain pressing into him. With a heave, he shifted the Kultash body off him and managed to sit up. After a look about, he pulled off a glove and with a shaking hand felt around the eye that wouldn't open. The eye was crusted closed with blood. He found the source in a gash above this right temple—the blow that had laid him down. He picked and wiped at the eye until he could blink it free. He stood. Bodies lay like sacks of black grain under the arch. Downslope, the valley remained in blue shadow. Clusters of snow-dusted bodies marked his long retreat up the slope. The air was still, and bitter cold. Motion caught his eye and his heart surged, but it showed itself to be a mountain raven hopping among the bodies. The sight of a hundred dead men brought a chill to his heart. The knowledge that it had been necessary did nothing to warm him. A faint taste of pine coated the roof of his mouth, but the scent was gone from the air.

Taumea bent and pulled his dagger from the side of the Kultash warrior at his feet. The man groaned and opened his eyes. Taumea dropped, slamming a knee down on the man's chest. The steaming Limtir dagger flashed through the man's gray beard, but Taumea held the cut. The old warrior was glaring up at him, undefeated in spirit. In Taumea admiration was swept aside by bitterness.

Taumea growled in the Yasharn Valiena had taught him, "We are not the enemy!"

"Dauthaz be damned!" swore the warrior in quick response.

Feeling defeated, Taumea sat back on a hard block of stone. Shivering, he studied the old Kultash, then leaned forward and held the bloodstained haft of his dagger so the man could see its gold inlay of a ring of weapons about an open book.

Taumea asked, "Know you this?"

The old man sneered, though his eyes betrayed a touch of shock.

"Et Limtir," said Taumea. "We know Dauthaz blood..." He did not know the word for *white*. He swept up a handful of snow, shoving it toward the warrior.

"Dauthaz blood."

He tossed it aside and wiped at the wound on his head.

He held his fingers up, bloody red and trembling with exhaustion and cold.

"My blood!"

The old warrior stared at the fingers and did not answer.

Taumea leaned back and angrily wiped his hand and then his dagger on the coat of a nearby body, noting that the dead man's beard was streaked with gray. The last to fall had been their eldest and best. At the end, when the will of the pines had failed, Taumea had stood alone against their blades. Incredible warriors—as fine with the sword as elite Tomeguard. The fight had been the most savage and desperate of his life since boyhood.

Taumea sheathed his dagger. The act settled him. He stood and unbelted the dead warrior's belt, then wrestled the thick coat off the figure. With respect, Taumea spread it over the living warrior. The man frowned. Taumea unbelted the Kultash sword belt from his waist, pulled his Limtir dagger sheath from it, and slid it into the top of his right boot. Stiffly, he took off his slashed Kultash coat and dropped it over the man's legs. The old warrior stared at Taumea's dented Limtir scale-mail, perhaps remembering his own futile attempts to pierce that armor.

"Hunt me not," said Taumea, and limped away to find the girls.

CHAPTER 17

A Wall is a Wall

BREEA CLOSED THE BOOK OF BATTLE WEAVING. There wasn't light enough left in the day to read, and the more she learned the angrier she became. What she had gleaned from this tome over the last two hundred leagues of travel was like a boot to the belly. Ajalay had been too cautious, too secretive. Had the Tetr-Sanis deigned to actually teach Breea how to wield the essence in combat, much would have been different. Breea turned and stuffed the book into a saddlebag, then sat with arms crossed, fuming. She felt Sakuront eyeing her without turning his head. He knew by now that the book frustrated her, but never asked what it was she studied. She wasn't sure whether she was grateful or frustrated by his silence. For certain, she knew that if she ever found the Alach children that Duyazen swore were prophesied, she would not hesitate to teach them everything she knew. To turn her thoughts, she looked at the lovely pine woods draped in snow, then up into the clear cold sky.

The sun had been down for half a bell. All that remained was a radiant western sky which spread wheat-colored light through the tops of the snowy pines and made the distant smear of smoke above Gimlek almost beautiful. The warm light in bitter-cold air reminded Breea of home. Home, where the corpses of friends and family lay rotting and unburied. Home—where Lupazg ruled.

Before her hatred could ignite the fire within, Breea urged Balor ahead and gave him his head. As he tested his freedom, Breea leaned forward. She felt Balor's stride lengthen, and his ears turned back her way as though to ask, *Can I? Truly?* Breea grinned and rose in the saddle. She pressed his flanks with her knees. Balor understood and leapt forward as though his intent was to fly. Their link deepened and she could feel his heart beating counterpart to the rapid patter-crunch of his hooves on the snowy stones of the High Path. She let the power flow and Balor ran as he never had. His hooves carved through the snow, occasionally striking sparks from the road that made flickers of light against the trunks of the trees in the deepening evening.

Breea sang out like her friend Valiena, "Aie leeleeleee!"

The bass growl that answered sent ice raking down her back. A glance showed a beast racing after her, twenty paces behind. It was shaped like a wolf, black furred, white eyed, and immense, though smaller than Lupazg's wolf form—Dauthaz, not Oregule. Breea returned her attention to the road as it curved through the forest. The image of luminous white eyes and bared fangs remained, slashing fear through the heat of her essence-self.

Motion to her left sent another wave of ice through her. A second wolf was pacing them through the forest. She looked right and saw two more. They were matching Balor's gallop through the trees! The thing behind was not catching her because it was not yet ready to take her down.

The fear that spiked her burned away as Breea released all her boundaries. Light sprang from her skin and the emerald light from her dagger hilts cast a green glow into the forest to either side. The wolves leapt way as though fearing she would attack. Their reaction spurred both hope and terror. Hope because they feared her, and terror because they knew what she was—and they were not retreating.

"*Yeaf!*" cried Breea, and Balor found in himself greater speed, riding the hot flow of Breea's power.

The road became a blur and trees flickered past like the pillars of an endless hall. It was a pace the wolves could not match, but it was also one that Breea knew Balor would not be able to hold. She could feel his fear and his anger. He would fight, but against a pack of such beasts he would have no hope. They were more than half his size. She must face them where she could defend Balor. The road curved back and Breea leaned with Balor around the bend. She could feel the pursuit sixty paces behind, eight of them.

If they were hunting her like a pack—the thought came too late. Cold rushed in from both sides as a pair of Dauthaz beasts attacked from the front. Balor put his head down and met the first head to head as its jaws sought his throat. The shock of the collision rippled through her, as Breea drew a dagger and slipped over to Balor's left side. The jaws of the second wolf snapped on air as it passed over Balor's back. Breea stabbed up with her scintillating blade and gutted the beast in passing. In the same moment Balor crumbled. Breea hit the road, feeling bones give with deep cracks. She tumbled and slid down the road with Balor and the first wolf in a violent tumult of agony. Come to rest tangled in the legs of her dead horse, she screamed and reached for power. The deep essence of the world answered her call and surged up toward her.

Back up the road, the gutted wolf rose on weak legs and struggled toward her, dragging its intestines. Quick as she could, she wove as the battle tome had instructed.

Wolves came rushing. With her one uninjured arm Breea scrabbled for her remaining blade. The motion ground bone ends within her, but power and pain within were indistinguishable now. Breea yanked the weapon free. Claws scraped stone and flung snow as the Dauthaz scrambled away from the blade's piercing light. The gutted wolf flinched in the light but kept coming. Breea met its savage gaze and readied herself, weaving a focus. Dauthaz jaws opened to strike.

"Burn," she growled.

Earth essence erupted from the ground about her. Snow flashed to water and the Dauthaz wolf burst into flame. It reared and twisted to land flaming beside her, legs thrashing. Breea flipped her dagger in her hand and stabbed the shimmering weapon down into the thing's broad side. The blade sheared through rib and flesh, opening the beast's pale heart. It snapped at her hand—dying in the effort.

White blood boiled upon the stones. Though her skin felt cool, Breea's clothing was smoking and she choked on the stench of burning fur and the essence-rot of Dauthaz. Through steam and smoke she caught glimpses of the remaining beasts as they circled and paced. Breea looked at Balor. His skull was distorted, broken. Through her teeth, Breea cursed the Dauthaz and began weaving fire.

Flames roared, consuming the bodies beside her, and flowed into the sky. Calling to the wind, she bent the column of essence-fire over to the ground like a flower stem bending in a storm. The heat of the earth—bound by her rage—enveloped a Dauthaz wolf. It screamed as it burst into flame and sprinted away—flaming through the forest.

The pack retreated, melting into the dark. Breea concentrated on a healing weave.

The ringing crash of a massive horse's shoes on stone made its way into her awareness. She raised her head and looked through a haze of blue and green tinted smoke and steam to see Sakuront wheeling his mount, looking for the enemy. His sword flashed in the light of her weaving and looked long and effective.

I need a longer blade, she thought, and collapsed into darkness.

―⟨ν/ν⟩―

A deep susurration trembled the air.

Voices, thought Breea.

She was on her back staring at a star-filled sky turning gray in the east. The stench of char and death stained every breath. The air was warm, and the stones beneath her were hot through her clothing. The ache of her body was deep.

Afraid of what she would find, she tested in small increments, turning her head and flexing her hands. One hand still held a dagger.

A ring of men surrounded her. They stood at three paces, shoulder to shoulder, facing outward. By their silhouettes they were Batusha warriors. She looked fondly at their backs, then *listened*. Beyond the Batusha men she felt ring upon ring of kneeling men, more than a thousand strong. Their chant resonated in Breea's chest almost like Bay-ope's drum-deep voice. It lent her strength. Time to get moving.

When she tried to sit up, piercing agony told her that bones shattered in her fall were insufficiently knitted. The left side of her body felt a shambles—shooting pain in shoulder, thigh, and ribs. She lay back to let it subside.

When the worst of it had faded, she muttered to the sky, "I should have studied healing."

With focused intent, she gathered strands of inner fire and set them into subtle motion. The weaving took many bells and took everything she had learned from the tome of healing weaves and in assisting Yavay'adil as he restored Batusha and Limtir warriors during the battle for the capital. After it was done, her inner fire was banked and she basked in the absence of agony. If not for the burn stench and a ravenous hunger, she would have simply closed her eyes and slept on the hot stones.

Instead she rolled and used her right arm to sit up. Her bones throbbed with a deep ache, but it was bearable. She was sound, but knew the healing was incomplete. The thought of what it would take to mount and ride reminded her that she lay in the ashes of dear, valorous Balor. Her head dropped and she shook—the sound of her mourning drowned by the flowing chorus of the Kultash.

Wiping her face, she tried to stand. It took a call to the essence to achieve. The dagger in her hand flared, and the ring of Batusha warriors turned in surprise. The relief in their faces was solace for the loss of…much. The shortest of them was revealed to be Simarn in Batusha cloak and armor. The girl's eyes were wild with joy and worry as she clutched her black crossbow to her breast. Breea motioned her over. Simarn rushed to obey.

Breea looked at the crossbow. "Disarm that," she said. "I need your arm. On my right."

As Simarn disarmed the bow and moved to Breea's side to support her, heavy boots approached and the Batusha ring parted to admit Sakuront. He stopped at the edge of the warm air rising from the paving stones. He touched his forehead with his right hand and then swept forearm down before him in an arc until his fingers pointed at her belly, palm toward her face. From the depths of his coat he pulled the dagger Breea had lost in the battle. Without ceremony he extended it hilt first.

With Simarn's aid, Breea limped up to him and took the blade, sheathing it with care. Even that small motion raised pain in her shoulder.

"Chosen," said the First. "Your fire consumed…it."

"Dauthaz," said Breea.

He nodded at her confirmation. "We hunt the remaining, but they do not allow us to close with them."

"They hunt me."

His jaw tightened, but she couldn't tell what he was thinking. Did Dauthaz hunting her worry him? Or was he upset because she had almost died? She almost asked, but thought it unlikely he would answer.

The First said, "Another mount is saddled for the

Chosen."

Breea tested more weight on her left leg and winced. It would be agony to ride, but weaving could relieve that pain.

Sakuront glanced at her leg, then said, "Pa-hoc Hean Grent holds a company of infantry who claim to have your blessing."

"Infantry?" asked Breea.

"Armored strikers," said Sakuront. "Spear and long-shield. Their standard bears a broken barrel. They claim allegiance to none but you. They come from Yash with wagon."

Breea understood his thinking. If she could not ride a horse, perhaps she could ride a wagon. But who were these men? A broken barrel reminded her of the wine barrel she had split open. Was this the foul company she had encountered on the muster field?

"They followed from Yash with a wagon?"

"A twelve-ox hay cart," said Sakuront.

Breea looked up into his eyes, but his face was impassive. The First of the Kultash did not jest—which made the journey of these men a true and impressive feat, also beyond understanding after what she did to their officer.

Sakuront asked, "Have they your blessing?"

Breea considered. If the men of that foul company had taken her final words to heart, then they might think it so, for had not the Chosen of the One told them, *The One to your blades*?

"In word," she said. "Not in spirit. I spoke in scorn."

Sakuront said, "They shall be left beside the road."

"Don't kill them," said Breea.

"No, Chosen. Their cart only shall be brought." He turned and walked away.

Breea had no desire to see those men. Yet how had they paced cavalry with an oxcart? This required understanding.

"First!" she called. "I wish to see them."

"Chosen," acknowledged Sakuront, and strode down a row between his kneeling men.

She watched him go, amazed. He had just spoken more words to her here than in the last tenday. Had he seen her weave flame against the Dauthaz? Breea heaved a sigh. He must have, and knew now what she was—an Alach like the old stories. A corner of her mouth quirked a grin and she shook her head. What it took to impress this man!

The eastern sky had grown pale over the pine forest and Breea realized that the Kultash had been singing for her all through the night. She blinked away the emotion that rose with the knowledge.

She listened to the cadence of song, recognizing the language as High Yasharn. The strength of their belief rolled over her. A powerful urge to weave that belief, to wield it, set her heart racing. The immensity of what weaving could be rushed through her, then left her feeling like a humbled child before the scope of her ignorance. There was nothing for it but to study and practice—this she knew from a lifetime of such. Now she needed sustenance.

"Do you have anything to eat?" she asked Simarn.

The girl returned a blank stare, then shook her head.

"I need to eat," said Breea.

A sharp-eared Batusha warrior bent forward to the ear of a Batusha aspirant. The boy slapped gauntleted back-fist to palm and sprinted away. In the predawn light, Breea noted that the young aspirant was in full chainmail with leather greaves and breastplate and a short sword—battle gear. She needed to find the Dauthaz before they attacked again. With

Simarn's help, she knelt on the dark flagstone of the road, careful of her tender bones, and placed her right palm on the rock. She *listened*, letting her senses ride the currents of essence within the earth. Gradually an image of the landscape formed in her mind, but it was an earth view—water seeping and root patterns, deep warmth and surface chill. Pressing her hand into the warm stone, she felt for more. Spots of fast warmth were the heartbeats of ground-dwelling animals. Farther out in the forest the thrum of hoofbeats was muffled by needle duff. At the edge of awareness she touched what she sought, the cold essence of ruined souls. The Dauthaz were all together on a rocky hill beyond the limit of Kultash patrols. To Breea's earth senses they felt like a cap of sickly snow on the hillock.

She quelled a desire to threaten and goad them into attack and so be done with them. For now they were far away, and she needed time to recover. Simarn helped her stand. Her senses felt flat and limited after experiencing the earth sight. If this was what the land felt like here, what must listening be like in the Nesua Oduuhn forest in the Limtir Valley? Or on Limtir Mountain itself?

"One day," she vowed.

Outside Batusha's protective circle, a pair of men's voices sang out in harmonic command and the chanting of the thousand warriors ended. Breea limped to the edge of the Batusha ring. She touched the shoulders of two red-cloaked Batusha masters and they stepped aside, faced inward, and *chak'ood*. Two Kultash standing beyond turned at the sound. Both were taller than her, narrow of face and dark bearded. They held their chins at an angle that struck Breea as self-righteousness tempered by cautious respect. Neither had witnessed her defeat of Sakuront, but would surely have heard the tale. Both wore sashes of woven silver which were catching color from the dawn behind Breea, reminding her of the flanks of lake trout. The medallion told her that the sash identified them as war-campaign priests, and they were the core of Kultash spirituality on the march.

"Sond-hean," said Breea, naming the men by their Kultash title. "Your song was a blessing. I thank you."

They gave a slight bow in unison, eyes lidded. Breea's gaze hardened. Her thanks had been sincere, not something to be met with concealed contempt. Breea consulted the Tetr-Sanis emerald, and spoke in High Yasharn, the language of their book of faith, *The Wisdom of the One.*

"The Litany of Purity was a choice most appropriate."

Both dropped their chins in surprise at her knowledge, then lifted them again to recover their dignity.

Breea added, "I am sure the grace of your voices was an agony for the rotted souls of the Dauthaz wolves where they watch from the crest of yon hill."

The two resisted turning to look in the direction her eyes had indicated, but dozens of their kneeling brethren turned their heads to peer through the forest. The sond-hean bowed in response, deeper this time, but it lacked the coordination of their first bow. Their eyes had lost focus as thoughts and questions whirled. They were off-balance, reassessing her. Breea was content, and silently thanked Ajalay for the gift of the emerald. She turned from them and reentered the Batusha ring.

The crunching of small boots through snow announced a gaggle of Batusha boys approaching at full gallop from the far side. Batusha men made a hole for them and they tumbled in, carrying a folding wooden chair and sections of a tabletop with separate legs, as well as sacks of food, bottles woven round with thick grass stems, and an air of thrilled importance. They balked at the heat and smell of the blackened bones in the center, clumping up behind one another, peering around. Oldest among them was Tam, who stood at the back. He frowned then urged them on with a few kicks. In a surge they circled round to Breea. One or two tried to *chak'ood*, nearly dropping their burdens. A sharp word from Tam set them to constructing the table and placing their goods. More than one cast big-eyed looks at the center of the ring, Tam included. The warmth without fire seemed to unnerve the boys, as did the pair of cracked wolf skulls as large as horses' heads.

Dori strode up and Breea was so glad to see her that she stepped away from Simarn's support and gave the girl a hug. Mortified and pleased, Dori blushed. Breea sat in the unfolded chair, which was almost like a throne though it lacked a back, then tore into the food without hesitation. As she gulped some excellent wine to wash down bread and meat, Breea watched Dori herd the boys away, excepting Tam. Dori and the boy moved around each other with mutual deference, avoiding each other's eyes. Breea grinned.

Outside the ring, the Kultash host rose. She could feel their movement as they formed columns and marched back up the road. Some few hundred remained in the trees, however.

Guarding me, she thought.

Her Alach hearing caught orders to seek out a hill to the west. She paused her eating. Would they scout with sufficient force? A group of twenty took off at a run.

Should she have spoken? Why had she not? Breea found herself reflecting on the decision as her father had taught her, and the warm memories of his work to prepare her to rule were slashed open by a vision of his death. Breea wrenched her thoughts back to how to handle the Kultash. Should their patrol be slaughtered, they would know better what it was they faced. Would she then own the deaths for not speaking out? Had she told them to double their party strength, would they have obeyed? Even if they had, they would resent her interference, perhaps deeply. Better to let them follow their own path and learn from the consequence. But who would learn? Only the living. The rest would be dead. She rubbed her thigh where deep pain throbbed.

Were I unwounded, I would ride with them, she thought.

Yet she could not. The demands of her purpose took precedence. She must heal and continue ahead. Men would likely die for her inability to meet Dauthaz and Oregule in direct combat without becoming direly wounded. Balor already had. The harsh truth of such thinking quelled some of her need for food, yet healing herself made a hunger she could not ignore, and she continued to eat.

Once hunger had relaxed the set of its jaws, Breea sat straight and considered the Dauthaz further. They might not engage the Kultash. It depended on the depth of their purpose. They had hunted her like a young doe, waiting for the moment she left the protective herd, then drove her into the jaws of their fellows. Wolf tactics. Possibly they could be drawn into a similar attack on the ground of her choosing. Yet to hunt them would make delay—and to leave them granted them the choice of time and ground for another attack. Were these wolves sent by Lupazg or was there an Oregule in Gimlek? That thought drove her to stand—her next froze her in place—why had her essence-hot daggers not shredded the weaves binding their flesh as her strikes had done to the Dauthaz in Yash? These things were something new. She needed to consult with Sakuront and the chief masters of Batusha. Turning, she found Simarn and Dori close beside, ready to assist her, and accepted their aid, in part simply to bask in their care.

The bellow of an ox brought her up. The sound reverberated deep in her chest. After it faded, the distant grind of metal-bound cart wheels carried over the tramp of Kultash boots. First would be the mystery of the swift oxen. A little giggle rose as she imagined galloping oxen.

"Neprawn," she said.

He stepped before her and *chak'ood* with his gaze level over her head—full attention.

"*Anule*," said Breea, wondering why he was being so formal. "I wish to meet that company away from this." She indicated the burned place upon the stones.

"Your word," said Neprawn. He lifted his voice. "On the Master! Guard hand."

The circle of Batusha men broke and flowed around Breea into a three-deep rank nine men across that shaped an arc which backed and flanked her.

Breea wove power into her pain-killing patterns then bade Dori to step aside. Batusha made a hole in their ranks to one side and the young woman scurried away. Simarn stood stiff, as though anticipating a blow. Breea pointed at the ground behind her left shoulder. The girl's relief at not being sent away was so clear that Breea almost spoke to reassure her, but held comment. Simarn was Batusha now—an aspirant. The young woman stepped into position with fierce determination. Battle-wild blazed in her eyes as she scanned the open road before them.

Breea wondered, *Is that what men see in my eyes? Or something even worse?*

She set the thought aside and strode down the road to see what fast oxen looked like. Batusha followed in a way so as to cup her in the palm of their formation. The perfect unity of their strides at her back lent a sensation of strength and power she'd not felt simply riding at the head of the column. Batusha's support was personal. And more, something had changed as a result of this encounter with Dauthaz.

Kultash columns had walked off the High Path stones to give the road to the approaching cart. At some signal invisible to Breea, the Kultash columns faced inward then drew their two-handed swords. The blades settled forward into a bristling line down either side of the road. The cart slowed to halt. Quiet gripped the morning.

Fifty paces from Breea, Sakuront rode his horse out in front of the first oxen. Oxen? Was she seeing truth? They were giants.

Sakuront dismounted as she approached. A Kultash warrior ran from the side and led the horse away. The First stood like a pillar of latent threat in the middle of the road until she stopped before him. When their gazes touched, a thrill scythed through her. Was he angry at her for making him wait as she ate? Had he forgotten who's army this was? Breea unbound her power and let it billow up within. Sakuront saluted her in his way, touching forehead then sweeping his hand down to show her his palm. The formality and offering in the motion touched her heart and her hand drifted up to the Tetr emerald.

Sakuront stepped aside. Breea stood for a moment, recovering from the revelation that the First was a man equal to her Alach nature.

Ten paces away a young man had prostrated himself beside a pair of the biggest oxen Breea had ever seen. Long of leg with massive forequarters, they were to regular oxen what Sakuront's mount was to regular horses. Ice hung from their shaggy bellies and they held their heads low, snot slipping to the snowy road in strings. The deep draft of their breathing was making a cloud about them. They looked exhausted. Astride the leftmost a boy of five or six in dark wool clothing sewn from an old Yasharn infantry uniform sat with gaping mouth—eyes riveted on Sakuront and Breea. His dirty face was streaked with old tear tracks. Why was there a little boy with an infantry company?

Behind him five teams of the giant animals led to an immense, high-sided cart, the largest Breea had ever seen. On the footboards of its broad driver's seat a man was on his knees, bowed down with his head upon the wood. He wore a black wool infantry uniform, its filth visible at distance.

Breea walked past the young man prostrate beside the first ox. He was the one who had been so brutally humiliated by his company on the field of muster, and he was trembling. Terrified.

Not of me, she thought, and glanced at the unwavering hedge of Kultash swords along the near side of the road. What must it mean for a Kultash company to draw blades?

Breea strode down the line of oxen with Sakuront and Batusha making a column behind her. She stooped before the cart. As she suspected, the man on the driver's bench was Tettle, the man she'd declared captain of this company.

"Captain Tettle," she said. "Descend."

"Aye, queen!"

He slid to the end of the bench and leapt down, landing with surprising lightness. A long straight sword swung at his side. He dropped to both knees before her, chin to chest.

"Stand, please," said Breea.

Tettle rose. His black uniform bore a new insignia on the left shoulder, a hand-sewn brown wine barrel split at the base. He kept his eyes lowered. There were shadows under them, and his face was drawn in lines of toil, but he was clean shaven with no more than a day's growth darkening his jaw. He smelled bad, but there was no scent of wine or spirit about him. A different smell bothered her, something rotten, but she did not think it came off Tettle.

There was movement in the wagon and Breea saw multiple sets of eyes peering out at her through vertical slats in the cart side. The eyes were in small faces, women and children. Did these men bring families to war? Or was this an ox-borne brothel?

Green light scythed into the air about her. Tettle stumbled back then dropped to his knees. He bent forward, thumping elbows and forearms in the snow in prostration.

He cried, "We Serve!"

When she did not respond, his fists clenched as he steeled himself for her judgment. He clearly remembered what had happened to the prior captain.

Breea strode past him down the long cart. The thing was immense, with wheels as tall as her head. At the rear two columns of fifty men who had been following the cart blanched at the sight of her shimmering form, then knelt with hasty deference. The back of the cart had been rigged with a slatted door of thick wood, and Breea realized that the entire thing was set up like a siege engine. The wood of its high sides was heavy enough to stop any arrow, and periodic open slots between vertical slats were set at a height that would make for easy bow work.

"Open," she called. "Everyone out."

A wailing began inside, and Breea stilled her anger. The

light of her daggers faded and she reached up toward the gate. Sakuront was quicker and threw open the wide door.

Two lamps within showed the interior was more than half filled with gear. A roof of old canvas sheltered stacked shields, sacks of provisions, half a hundred spears, barrels of weapons, bundles of arrows, unstrung bows, and neatly stacked firewood. Clothing was draped throughout, and everywhere there was a flat space there were blankets and bedrolls. On one side a small black stove had its pipe wired up the side of the cart. Through it all peered near a dozen women's faces. A girl child's wailing stilled when she saw Breea peering in. The women looked deeply afraid, yet hard as well, with faces well tanned and set in lines of resignation and forbearance. Yet unlike the women Breea had seen in the taverns of Yash, they did not look broken, merely worn by hard life. Their eyes flicked between bloodstained and sooty Breea, armored Simarn, and the tower of Sakuront behind them. Wonder and curiosity began to supplant fear.

"Captain Tettle," said Breea in a quiet voice.

He came running, then stood to attention. He glanced inside and his face flushed with embarrassment and what could have been real concern.

Breea asked, "Who is this?"

"Queen," he said. "Our wives and.. servants."

"Servants," echoed Breea in a cold voice.

"Cooks, and washerwomen."

She looked at his dirty uniform. Not much washing going on.

Breea said, "I do not condone the bringing of women and children to war."

Captain Tettle expressly did not look at young Simarn there beside Breea. Before Breea could say more, the smell of rot distracted her, and she turned to the cart, wrinkling her nose. Were there injured in there with wounds gone foul?

"What is that smell, captain?"

Strangely, he looked pleased by the question.

"Queen," he said, and ducked under the high bed of the cart.

Breea bent over and saw that even more gear was slung beneath the cart. Tettle cut a sack from a ring and brought it out. Breea stepped back from the stench, her daggers throbbing bright. Twined with the scent of flesh rot was the chill corruption of Dauthaz.

Tettle dumped the sack and a pale skull rolled onto the stones. Flesh that had been slashed, beaten, and pierced was rotting off the bone, but nothing could obscure the glinting eyes of a spider where a man's should be.

"Queen," said Tettle. "A fiveday north from Umenk, this beastie came a-riding hard upon us. Het's cold wrath had made a white waste of the road, and this one was lost like a...spider in a snowstorm." He grinned at his own joke. "It had all the look of a man, and was riding our track through snow so deep we'd not seen the stone of the High Path for two days, but nothing stops Lillhup ox, queen. Long as you got feed, they'll plow stone."

Breea marveled at Tettle's sudden storytelling. The women and kids in the cart were moving up to listen.

"His horse was spent, and night was coming. We welcomed a man in Umenk Temple garb, and offered him wine and meat, but he refused, which we owed to him being priestly. He seemed mighty set on getting up the road, asking if we knew our way and if the ox could run. We assured that we did and they could, if Het willed it. Karla lights a lantern, 'cause she's got a nose can scent trouble over the horizon.

Umenk, he goes still in the light. Takes our measure; fifty walking behind and fifty aboard cart, as is our way, then orders 'Down!' Down to the snow, women and pups included. 'Why?' says I. 'Het's will,' says he, and lays a hand to his hilt. By Karla's lantern I sees on his fingers…more than rings! 'Well,' says I, 'Can't argue with Het's will,' and I gives the signal for us to dismount the cart."

Behind Breea, a man's voice called out. "And to arms!"

Tettle gave a knowing nod. "Aye, that signal too, my queen. That signal too. Every man of us tumbles down, women too, but with shield and all. I grip me own and leap after. And there he stands within, looking like he's king o' the cart with us behind and ice in our teeth as Het's wrath howls on. Then I whistles the teams a-stop. Down he comes, blade out to take us all."

Tettle raised his voice. "What's the cry?"

"Wall!" thundered a hundred men's voices.

Breea jumped and couldn't keep from grinning.

Tettle continued. "And none too quick, for he moved like death's own spear. Cleaved my shield, he did, and two more besides. But a wall's a wall, and we closed up till his sword snapped in his hand. Came then, he did, with tooth and fang, face gone white and full of eyes. But a wall is a wall, and he not made to climb it." Tettle gave Breea a short bow to conclude.

"How many did you lose?" asked Breea.

"Queen? None, my queen. Battered may, but we shed no blood for this." He waved a dismissive hand at the Dauthaz skull.

The throng of infantry warriors had risen from their knees during Tettle's tale and approached, but not too closely. Each wore a shield on his back, a massive rectangle of black wood and tarnished bronze, shaped to cup the warrior who held it in a protecting curve. What strength must that Dauthaz have wieled to cleave such shields, and what men to hold the line before such ferocity. In the shadows of early dawn their eyes reflected the cart lamps like flecks of dull amber set in shaggy-bearded faces that were almost childlike in their wonder and fear of Breea. The Broken Barrel Company looked like a crowd of upright bears and smelled far, far worse. For a moment a distant flute sang of battle. Breea nodded. They would do.

"You will take final post in the column."

Tettle dropped to both knees in the snow and said with emotion, "Queen. Aye. We Serve!"

The Broken Barrel Company knelt and followed his example in a discordant chorus.

Sakuront lifted his arm in sign and a thousand Kultash blades returned smoothly to their sheaths. Calls rippled up and down the line, horns blew, and the Kultash warriors set out once more, back up the road.

With a glance at Sakuront, Breea walked the opposite way. The First followed at her shoulder. Batusha made a path for them, then closed up behind. Ahead, by the light of a lantern held between the lead ox team, Breea saw the little boy standing on his mount's massive shoulders, looking down into the light. The boy made a huffing sound then slid down the bull's neck, catching one great horn and swinging for a moment before dropping to the ground. There was talk, and the boy's voice rose in whine of wordless complaint.

A young man's voice said in response, "You ride Slayer, his yoke is yourn. Get the tack bag. We'll move soon. Fleet!"

The little boy came running out from under the ox's neck

and slid to a halt four strides away. The boy's eyes were riveted on Sakuront, the sullen expression gone slack with surprise and shock. The First stepped around the boy without pause and his black cloak brushed across him.

Breea looked over her shoulder at the boy. The boy mimed a sword salute, and said with profound admiration, "First."

"Het's hounds, Beelt," said the older voice. "Do what you're tol—" The voice cut off as Breea and Sakuront strode past the last draft team.

"Rust," said Beelt, "the First!" as if that explained everything.

After a breath, Rust replied in a whisper that only Breea's hearing could catch. "Aye, and that be my queen."

Breea grinned with a little pride, then sobered and flicked a look up at Sakuront. It was hard to tell in the dim light but she had the sense that his expression was both soft and dark, and she guessed that he was looking into the vision that bound them. Breea stopped her hand before it rose to touch his arm.

Behind, Kultash horns signaled the call to mount. Their sound made Breea think of the Dauthaz wolves. What was the fate of the warriors who had gone to investigate the hill? She was about to kneel in the snow to listen to the land when a pair of Kultash warriors brought up Sakuront's horse and a second mount nearly as massive. Both animals wore armor over the long black Kultash barding. Breea recognized the second horse as the mare Fahri, Sakuront's third spare mount.

"You bless me," said Breea to the First as she accepted the reins from a bowing Kultash warrior.

Sakuront's cool aloofness was back, and he said nothing.

Watching Fahri's ears Breea stepped beside her neck, crooning softly in Breowic. Her voice was strangled by a surge of sadness for lost Balor. Anger followed, and she stepped back, handing the reins back to the Kultash warrior.

Breea knelt in the snow and touched the road ice. It melted away before her anger and she pressed her hand to the stone.

The wolves were no longer upon the hill. Hoofbeats trembled faintly upon the ground, likely the men who were sent to investigate the hill. Calling upon the flame, she poured her power into the stones and hunted through the land for the chill that was more than winter cold. When she found it, she snarled with hatred.

Above her, Sakuront's sword whispered from its sheath and his boots stepped into a wider stance. His response to her anger made her feel momentarily warm, though the sense of Dauthaz was too foul to let her relax. She stood, gasping at the piercing agony that lanced out from her barely healed thigh bone. Simarn started toward her from the arc of Batusha warriors, but a hand stayed her. Breea *listened* to her own essence and found that wielding her flame to listen to the land had burned away her pain-killing weaves.

Through clenched teeth she said, "They have circled to the rear. Eight of them."

Sakuront put his sword away, and did not ask how she knew. Breea wove a more powerful weave to ease her pain. Truly, she needed to read more of healing than of war.

Rubbing her thigh, she said with resignation, "I must ride the cart."

"Yan," said the First, and one of the men who had brought the horses stepped up. "Two pa-hoc, rear guard, spear and bow."

"No," said Breea. "Put no more men in their path. They are hunting me. I will ride the cart."

"As you will."

"Thank you," said Breea. "To Gimlek?"

"Yes," said Sakuront. "*Par oot.*"

Trotting pace. Breea nodded. "Hean Grent of the lancers should know what opposes us."

"I will see to it," said Sakuront.

He mounted and Breea looked up at the towering figure he made against the starry sky. Night was full upon them.

"The One to your blades, Chosen," said Sakuront.

Before she could reply his horse leapt away, snow and ice flying from its hooves. The ground trembled under its tread. Such a horse could meet a Dauthaz on the field, perhaps even two, but against eight only Alach strength would serve. A vision of what the Dauthaz wolves could do to her army at night set the hilt stones of her daggers flashing.

Abruptly she strode back up the road toward the oxcart. Batusha warriors leapt aside to make way for her, then followed close.

Horns howled and officers bellowed. The army was preparing to march. Breea could feel them flowing and swirling like conifer needles in a stream as she limped through churned snow covering the road toward the oxcart.

Directly ahead the dirty yellow light from a smoky lantern outlined the boy Rust kneeling in the snow beneath the yoke of the first of team. He pounded furiously with a hammer. Beelt stood beside him, peering up at Rust's work.

Captain Tettle's voice called from the cart, "Lill...*hup!*"

Ox heads rose from their drooping positions and the yoke rose out of Rust's reach.

"Hounds!" he said, and dropped his hammer into a leather sack at his feet.

Beelt leapt for the oxbow around Slayer's neck, caught it, then seemed to float hand over hand up over yoke. He scrambled up the animal's neck and whirled to land astride its massive shoulders.

On the other side, Rust had the lantern in one hand and the leather tool sack in his teeth as he stepped onto the hauling tongue between the oxen and leapt to the back of the other animal. Squirming astride, he raised the lantern and took the sack from his teeth.

From the cart Tettle called, "Hup!"

The oxen leaned into their yokes and began walking. Beelt looked at Rust, who nodded.

The little boy gave Slayer's shoulder a pat on the right side behind the yoke and said in a firm tone, "Ai. Ai."

Slayer and his partner ox turned to their left. Breea held her ground as they turned in front of her, passing almost within touch. Beelt noticed her at the last moment and his mouth dropped open. Breea gave him a little nod. She waited for the cart to rumble up, then climbed up the ladder on its side. Tettle had seen her and was kneeling on the high seat floorboard with his forehead bowed to the icy wood.

"Drive on, captain," said Breea, and settled on a stained wool blanket draped over the long seat.

Tettle rose with a respectful and subdued, "Queen."

Breea slid over as Simarn and Neprawn came up the side and found a place on the bench. The cart rumbled forward, rocking gently until it lay to the left side of the road to allow the army to pass. A horn nearby howled and Kultash cavalry began streaming past at a fast trot. Breea looked at the plodding oxen and wondered how they could match such a pace. She rubbed her thigh where pain made its way through her weaving. When she looked back over the canvas roof of the cart, her breath caught. It was like looking down a long summer field full of multiplying fireflies. She stood to watch. In the forest to either side, sparks of lantern light flashed on and off between trees while others paused then flared and split into two or three or more. Altogether there was a movement inward toward the road, where the soldiers gathered speed to rush past Breea's perch. Close to her in the cart, she could sense the women and girls shifting with purposeful movement. Iron hinges squealed and the chimney rattled. A wisp of eloquent flute melody rose and she breathed deeply as though to bring it into herself like a tendril of sweet-scented smoke on the night air.

A woman beneath the canvas began to hum, and motion caught Breea's eye to her right. It was Tettle—his hand touched his forehead then raised the palm to the sky. His expression amazed her, and she stared to be sure of her assessment. The man looked content—in the midst of a march to war with giant Dauthaz wolves close to, and sitting beside a woman who could—by his own witness—kill men with her eyes.

Neprawn began humming, and she turned the other way. The seated warrior's head was level with her own though she was standing. His gaze looked into the dawn forest, scanning in slow arcs. Breea marveled as his humming played light counterpart to the flute song. Beside him Simarn's shoulders relaxed under cloak, armor, and woolens. The cart rocked and Breea gripped the backboard, noting that Simarn's body had stayed in a fixed lean toward Neprawn.

Remembrance touched Breea like a friend's hand and she was looking into Ambard's eyes by candlelight on the night of their last meeting. All that had happened since swept through her in a rush, breaking the harmony of the music. Trembling lightly from the clash of emotions within her, Breea looked about for the source of this evocative music, but someone called her name and she looked ahead.

Rust and Beelt were dimly visible fifty paces away sitting on their oxen mounts, but no one else. Kultash streamed past the cart in a never-ending clatter of hooves on iced snow. Who had called to her?

On the road ahead, the flow of the army deflected around a ring of lantern light in its center. It was the place of Balor's death. She could sense the flow of essence from the spot streaming up into the sky. What had she wrought? Ajalay's warning about Alach who could not control their power was manifest in this place. One of them had been remembered for two thousand years in the Ballad of Jiwan City-Slayer. Bay-ope's favorite song. The music brought her memories of dear friends.

Astride the first ox, Rust raised his lantern and looked back. Tettle made a signal and Rust slipped off his mount to the left, vanishing behind the bulk of his ox. Only the outline of the giant ox against the dirty yellow of lantern on the snow could be seen. The lead oxen angled that way, taking the following teams closer to the edge of the road. Tettle slid to the very end of the bench and peered down.

Around the warm place in the road a ring of Kultash stood with lantern poles. Beside them Arin and a Kultash priest argued. Breea reached out with her senses.

The Kultash sond-hean said, "Here flows the breath of Blessed Het who burned the defiled Dauthaz—"

Arin broke in. "Here the *Chosen*—"

Their talk ran together in angry streams.

"Arin!" called Breea.

He looked up in surprise, then dodged to the ox teams through a gap in the stream of horses trotting past.

When his head came up over the cart side, Breea said, "Let them have their sacred ground."

"Master, they do not see—"

"Arin," said Breea. "Carsythe awaits us."

"Your word is law, Chosen."

"Who began that?"

"Master?"

"Where began the notion that my word is law?"

Guilt suffused his bearded face, and his eyes dropped.

Breea heaved a tight, irritated sigh.

In defense, Arin said, "Master, it is written."

Scornful, Breea said, "By who?"

His head came up, and he said with guileless conviction, "Lutna, Master. First Chosen of the One."

A shiver gripped Breea's skin, and she sat on the bench beside Simarn. After a bit she looked over at the priest. He clung to the ladder and swung with the motion of the cart. He had saved her life in the Batusha Guild Hall, and then at every wild leap after, this man had been there, preparing men's minds for wherever she landed. He was also learned—a scholar in his realm of belief, and perhaps in others. In truth she owed him more than she could tally.

"Arin," said Breea, and gestured for him to come. "Tell me, what else is written?"

His eagerness was boyish as he came up over the side. After passing awkwardly in front of everyone along the footboard, he could not decide whether to stand or kneel. She patted the bench beside her. He stared at the spot, then gathered his cloak about him and sat with nervous dignity.

Breea leaned against the backboard and put her soot-blackened boots on the footrest. Arin set his boots wide to brace himself against the cart sway, removed his fur-lined gloves, and put his hands palms up upon his thighs.

"In the time of our ancestors…"

All sound and movement under the canvas behind them stopped as the women paused to listen. At the end of the bench Tettle was still watching how the cart ran at the edge of the road, but he had turned his head to hear Arin's tale.

Half a bell later, the canvas behind Tettle shifted back. A young girl wearing a headscarf rose behind the priest. She stared at Breea, then Arin, then touched the company captain's arm. When Tettle turned, she looked down demurely and lifted up a tankard of steaming liquid. Breea caught the scent of apple cider and spices she did not recognize. The company captain glanced at it, then pushed it toward Arin. The girl looked both excited and scared. She sidled over using one hand, and lifted the mug. Arin didn't notice. Breea nudged his shoulder and indicated the girl. He turned and took the tankard, then offered it to Breea.

"For you," she said.

He frowned, but took a sip. A little moan escaped his lips. He turned to thank the girl, but she was gone, tarp closed. Breea heard breathless whispering as the girl gave report to the others below. An older voice spoke and the stove door creaked open. Iron clanked as more wood was tossed in. Breea looked back and saw sparks streaming out of the pipe top. They must be heating more cider. Behind the cart Breea's guard walked mostly out of sight from her vantage. After them trudged a double row of Broken Barrel soldiers lit only by the occasional lantern of the mounted soldiers riding past them. They carried spears slanted back over their shoulders.

Arin continued, and Breea settled back to listen. His tale was surprisingly close to the histories within the Tetr emerald, and while she enjoyed his resonant recitation, he had yet to tell her anything new. Folding her arms, she closed her eyes.

Dozing, she rubbed the tip of her right index finger were it had begun to itch. She froze, and her eyes snapped open.

Simarn felt the queen tense. Without thought, Simarn yanked back the string of her bow and slapped a black bolt into the groove. Heat and light seared out from the queen, and Simarn flinched away, pressing against Neprawn. She felt him lift his left arm to shield his face. His other hand reached between himself and Simarn and drew his long saber.

At the same time the queen seemed to float upward to stand on the bench—piercing arcs of burning emerald in her hands. She stepped across the priest and Captain Tettle and strode off into the air. The Batusha priest caught his breath and swung around to the rear.

He cupped hands to his mouth, and roared, "*Batusha!*"

Simarn surged after the queen, shoving past the priest, but stopped in shock at the sight of the queen striding into the pines, a fire of white and green   the snow steaming in her wake. Simarn looked down the cart side and lifted her boot over the edge. A howl of cold hatred slammed her back and ice stabbed her through the heart.

Gasping for breath, she forced herself up, checked her bow, then crawled over the shivering captain, trying to get to the cart edge to follow Breea.

A boy's voice screamed, "Wall!"

She looked and saw the boy who had been riding the first

ox pointing to the right across the road. The captain beneath her rose with sudden violence, nearly throwing her from the cart seat.

He looked at the boy, then at the woods beyond.

"Ho right!" Captain Tettle bellowed.

A voice called back from behind the cart, "Right ho! Wall!"

"*Wall!*" roared a hundred men.

Ignoring all, Simarn looked toward Breea. In the distance the forest flashed and flickered as thought a lightning storm had come to ground.

Neprawn voiced a battle cry that made Simarn flinch. She twisted in time to see the giant warrior swing his saber two handed to meet a thing flying up at him. The blade deflected the creature aside even as it soared over, knocking him back. Its open jaws closed on the Batusha priest, somehow missing as the man dodged back over the seat with fluid grace. The wolf-thing landed on the footrest, shattering wood. It slid sideways and began to fall, scrabbling for purchase. It couldn't hold on, Simarn realized, because Neprawn had cut off its front left paw. She extended her bow and shot the giant wolf in one white eye the instant before it fell.

The cart shuddered. Women screamed and Simarn spun, rearming her bow. A wolf had leapt the sidewall of the cart and landed within, collapsing the canvas roof. She shot it in the neck.

Tettle leapt down, spear in hand, and stabbed the creature through the ribs. It turned and bit the haft to splinters. Tettle tumbled forward and the wolf leapt for him, only to find a shattered spear haft rammed up its throat. The beast whipped its head as it reared away. Tettle went flying into the side of the cart. The beast staggered, gagging on the spear shaft, and Simarn put a bolt into its exposed throat. Another wolf hit the cart and took the top rim in its jaws. It jerked backward as though trying to tear the wall down. Wood splintered and cracked. Simarn reloaded and released, but the thrashing cart threw off her aim. Neprawn leapt down past her, saber arcing down. The wolf saw him coming and let go, then jumped back up, sailing up over the edge. Neprawn's sword flashed across its neck and white blood sprayed. The wolf landed on the cart rim, hung up, hind legs thrashing. Neprawn stepped forward, only to falter at a woman's cry of agony at his feet. The wolf scrambled, trying to get its hind legs over the wall. Simarn took careful aim and put a bolt into its eye. The beast shook its head as though to dislodge what had stung it, then began to spasm and twitch. At a the bellow of an ox, she whirled away, pulling her bowstring back. Ahead, the boys had released four oxen. They stood with heads low, defending the rest of the teams. Rust released another ox and leapt through the air for the next.

Simarn took long aim and fired at the wolf charging the horns of the oxen, but she couldn't tell if she hit the beast. The wolf broke off, unwilling to face the hedge of massive ox horns. Simarn reloaded, but Neprawn was back beside her with a restraining hand on her forearm.

She turned to where Breea had been fighting. The woods were dark. Kultash wolf-horns howled and the thunder of hooves rose. The remaining wolves loped away into the dark.

Simarn and Neprawn had the same idea and leaned over to confirm that the first wolf was dead, limp across the tongue of the ox train where it met the cart. Neprawn's heavy gauntlet gave her shoulder a comradely slap. To hide the surge of pride his approval brought, she checked over her bow then scanned the area in a way that kept her face away from him.

From the front of the column, Kultash spear cavalry swept toward the cart with Sakuront at their head. He reined up beside the cart and swept his sword. The spearmen rode on. Before the First could ask, Simarn pointed at the woods. He charged into the dark forest. Simarn moved to follow.

"Simarn," said Neprawn.

She whirled on him.

"Keep watch," he said. "This is high ground. She is guarded." He nodded toward the forest.

A hundred Batusha warriors were streaming into the forest with lanterns. The light illuminated the queen struggling out through the snow. She carried something long and dark, dragging it behind her. Sakuront rode to one side, and Simarn twitched in anger. How dare he ride when the queen walked? Batusha warriors saluted with back-fist to palm. The queen fell to her knees in the snow. In front of her a black-bladed sword lay. Hilt to tip, it was as long as the queen herself. She was weeping over the thing. Sakuront dismounted. He sheathed his own blade and approached, going to one knee in the snow beside her. He pulled off his gauntlets and dropped them in the snow, then gathered both of her hands in his.

The queen's head came up, and she said, "Would you heal me, First?"

He didn't answer, but neither did he move. The queen laid a hand on his armored chest.

Simarn's heart contracted as she found herself on the edge of an abyss, dizzy with sorrow. Blind fury swept her back from the edge of memory of all that had been done to her, and she barred her teeth, grateful that her eyes were dry and no one was near to see her so affected. Men must not see her as a girl. In the snow, the queen lifted the handle of the long blade and set it into Sakuront's hands.

A woman's wail of despair tore into Simarn. The collapsed canvas cart roof had been pulled away and a woman in peasant woolens hung in limp despair in the arms of Arin and Tettle. Amid tumbled wreckage of supplies and weapons, Neprawn knelt beside a girl half Simarn's age, the one who had brought cider for the men. The girl's chest had been crushed. Neprawn covered the grisly result with a woolen shirt. The woman cried out again, her voice going ragged with bottomless suffering. Simarn felt wild rage flood her. She hungered for something to slay. A cry of pain brought her focus back to the cart. Neprawn had begun to set the broken arm of a woman, directing others to help him with the splint. He set his hand on the woman's shoulder and spoke. In fear, she nodded. Simarn felt a surge of sympathy for her, but Simarn knew the comfort of his hand, the latent power that could break bone, yet was never more than gently firm.

The cart swayed as Broken Barrel warriors took hold of the wolf-beast draped over the cart side and heaved it up and out. The rear door swung open and men stepped back as grain and swords fell to the snow. They grabbed the dead wolf that lay there and dragged it out, exclaiming at its smell. Quiet froze them in midmotion—then they knelt. The queen had come. Specks of blue light flickered about her like stars.

Simarn sat on the seat with a thump. She disarmed her bow and released the string with weary care, then watched in awe as the queen wove her miracles. Wolf-horns howled and the army began sorting itself once more. Across the snow at the edge of the forest Sakuront was still examining the massive blade the queen had left him. He gave it a swing and everyone near stepped back. His teeth flashed pale in the lantern light but Simarn could not tell whether in joy or hatred.

—⚬⚬—

The cart rumbled onward in winter sunlight that streamed through the trees. Simarn sat at the rear of the cart, her cloak-wrapped legs swinging with its motion. At the front of the cart bed below the high seat, the queen slept in a bed of furs. Dori was there, at the queen's feet, watchful and protective. All the supplies had been removed from the cart. Wounded men and Broken Barrel women lay under blankets shoulder to shoulder across its floor—those who remained unfit to ride even after the queen's touch. In the night, when the queen had collapsed after healing the last wounded soldier, Simarn had never seen grown men act with such despair. Only she and Dori had known what to do—put the queen to bed. Both of them had seen her sleep this way after battle. In the end it had been Simarn's declaration that she was the queen's guard that had swayed the warriors to listen and obey.

Shortly after, the First of the Kultash had come. He had dismounted onto the cart bed and gone to her. Solemn, he had stared at her face which was framed by her black hair upon the brindled fur of her bedding, then returned to his horse.

The warriors of the Broken Barrel seemed well pleased with his visit, talking among themselves in a low rumble as they awaited the order to march. They cast occasional glances at Simarn, but never let their looks linger. Their bearded faces were shadowed with exhaustion and grim in their watchfulness. Mounted Batusha warriors had come to encircle the cart. In the high seat beside Captain Tettle, four Batusha archers sat with bows in hand. Simarn thought all their precaution rather too late.

The dead had been buried and the wolves burned, sans heads, along with whatever else had been corrupted by their blood. There had been talk of burning the cart, but the Broken Barrel Company had drawn blades to prevent it, offering instead to carry the wounded. Simarn had watched the priests chant their worthless words over the gray stains. She knew that it was the queen's blessing that made the cart fit to ride.

The Broken Barrel men had also demanded the honor of carrying the wolf heads. Simarn was glad that they had chosen to do so at the far end of their column. Deep inside her a child's voice began screaming at the sight of them. That inner cry, which she knew to be her own the night her father had been slain, was her secret weakness. None knew, but it had nearly overwhelmed her on the Temple ramp facing the white horror.

The cart creaked as it passed down the road. Simarn watched the ranks of the Broken Barrel as they marched the white-packed road behind the cart. Many of their beards were parted here and there by random scars, and filth lined the cracks of their faces. Over their dark wool infantry uniforms they wore hides lashed to their legs and torsos over which was strapped a wild assortment of mismatched armor. The men of the Barrel looked like the worst of the foul— filthy dark-eyed rogues—the kind of men who fed on the souls of children. Simarn knew their kin from the city inn where she had been a slave. Yet about the Broken Barrel there was a sense of purpose and utter deference to the queen that gave them an odd nobility, like another kind of armor. Simarn knew it well, and felt a kinship with them that disturbed her.

The pine forest gave way all at once and sunlight filled the cart bed. Talk rose among the men. The city had come into sight. The cart halted.

She opened her cloak and hooked her bow to her belt, then stood and looked forward around the cart sidewall. The land flowed away in long, low hills, snow cloaked and open. She was glad to be free of the pines. Here you could see what was coming. The air was crisp, free of scent. In the forest the smoke had drifted among the trees and it seemed that the stench of pine smoke and foul flesh burning would never leave her.

At the end of a long slope of diminishing hills, Gimlek lay across the northern plains like a smoking gray ulcer. A High Path road could be seen leading north out of the city, and another westward, each flecked with black dots of travelers like fleas on linen. Scattered across the hills between the army and the city, small clusters of huts sent thin pillars of smoke into the sky. To the east the plain rose into forested hills. No roads went east. The furthest extent of farming and logging was clear a few leagues from the city. Pale on the horizon, white peaks glowed. There was no sign of people in that direction—not a single column of smoke. It was as people said: a land where men feared to walk. For a long while Simarn stared into its distance as a bewildering sensation rose within—a dream of life beyond surviving each day…in a land where men feared to tread.

Captain Tettle called, "Hup!"

The cart jerked forward and Dori began berating him in a severe whisper. Simarn didn't smile, but inside she glowed. Dori was caring for the queen, and Simarn would guard them both. Simarn made her way forward.

Dori, sitting at the queen's feet, looked up. There was no need to speak. Like sisters they knew the heart of the other, at least in relation to their lady and queen. Careful of the wounded woman beside the queen, Simarn sat with her back against the sidewall, put her bow in her lap, then laid a hand on the queen's furs.

CHAPTER 18

Soot

ANILA HELD HER HAND OUT PAST THE EDGE OF the canvas shelter. Big snowflakes landed on her fingers like clumps of cold down. The heat of her skin melted them, and the moisture steamed away in pale wisps that vanished against the shadowed snow of the narrow cleft which sheltered them from the wind. Spe and Ma were deep asleep behind her. The air was slicing cold, but Anila felt as though her body was buoyed by warm air. Two days past, to find the frozen waterfall and the escape tunnel behind its ice, she'd had to let her Breath free in every way. The feeling had been like the Limtir lord's approval—resonant with goodness and a sense of wellness so potent and rare that its experience illuminated all that she'd never known. It hurt to know what she had been denied in the Breath, but the hurt faded before the knowledge that she had accomplished the Limtir lord's request, for she had found the secret tunnel and led everyone away beneath the mountains. And ever since it had felt as if the world was whispering its secrets to her. She could feel the Limtir lady a hundred strides distant up at the entrance to the cleft. She knew where birds huddled in holes along the cliff wall, and that there was running water beneath the snow and ice nearby. Horses dozed under their blankets, breathing warm mist. The air was alive in its motion— drifting, whirling, pooling, and idling in an ever-blending dance.

Ma groaned in her sleep and Anila bent under the weight of the sound. To Anila's new senses Ma felt brittle and tight, bound up around some agony within. What remained of her life held tight to the Breath of the gem she clutched even in sleep. Lose that stone and Ma would be gone. The thought of life without stern, caring Ma ripped Anila like a sword through her chest. Sorrow melded with bright heat that flowed up from within, burning. She touched the center of her chest and came to a decision. She crawled back under the snow-laden shelter cloth.

Kneeling beside her mother, she whispered, "May all I say and all I think be in harmony with thee."

With brazen courage she touched her palm to Ma's cold cheek. Heat flowed and red light glimmered through Ma's blankets from the gem she held to her chest.

Ma's eyes opened and her head turned up to meet Anila's

gaze.

"Daughter." Blood was dark on her lips and a line of it drooled from the corner of her mouth down the side of her jaw.

Anila choked, "Ma."

The Breath roared within and glimmers of light began to whirl beneath Anila's skin. To her deep surprise, Ma's face eased at the sight, and she said, "Like your father."

Lines of long-suffered agony smoothed across Ma's face and she drifted back to sleep. Trembling, Anila sat back.

A glint of eyes to her right showed that Spe was awake and watching. What did Ma mean *like her father?* Surely not Da. Did it mean that she had a *true* father and that he had the Breath? The idea was so filled with dangerous hope that Anila dared not hold it fully, and shoved it away, calming her racing heart. One had only to look at Ma to see what crushed hope could inflict.

Changing her thought, she looked out at the trampled snow and wished they were all back in the ancient fort at the end of the tunnel. She remembered how the lady Valiena had sung and danced with her and Spe in the biggest room of the place after the endless dark passage. Anila had not wanted to leave the fortress, for it felt homey in a way the ruin on the other side had not. The fort was eerily intact even though the lady said it was more than two thousand years old. The place seemed to make the lady unhappy. They'd struck out into the waist-deep snow on what looked like a snow-covered High Path which led across wide meadows bordered by clumps of snow-laden trees. Misty cloud hid everything else from view, but the lady had said they were still in the mountains. At the end of the flats, the road had led through a pile of giant boulders and then down into this narrow defile, where the lady had made camp beneath an overhang of cliff. Anila knew Ma would be more comfortable back in the beautiful fortress than out here in the snow, but the Limtir lady was afraid Kultash might come. After preparing cold food for Anila and Spe, the lady had taken her bow and two quivers of arrows back up the way to watch for the lord Taumea. There seemed nothing to do but wait. Anila lay down beside Ma.

———*◦∾◦*———

Anila woke with a start. The canvas roof pressed down on her, chilling her shoulder with its weight of snow. Bright light shone in from a crack along the ground on the open side of the sailcloth shelter. The horses outside were awake and pawing with hungry frustration at the snow and ice. There was no sense of the lady. Anila pushed outside, getting covered with snow from the canvas. The sky above the cleft was brilliant blue. Two hands of fresh snow covered everything, but held no tracks. The lady had not returned.

Azsark walked up and nosed her. She pet him absently, thinking, then looked him in the eye. He dropped his head and she gripped him about the neck. When he rose she went up with him and hooked her leg over his neck, then slid down to his snowy withers. She pulled off the blanket that kept him warm at night and settled herself on his back.

Spe crawled out from beneath the canvas. She looked up at Anila on Azsark and her face grew worried.

"Stay with Ma," said Anila.

Spe ran forward and clutched one of Azsark's forelegs, shaking her head. The warhorse bent his neck to look down at her.

"Spe," said Anila. "You must be here for Ma. What if she wakes and we are both gone?"

"You Breathed to her," said Spe, looking up with tearful eyes, and Anila saw whole stories in them. Spe knew what was happening—with Ma, and that the lady was missing and Anila was going to go look for her.

"Be mighty," said Anila, knowing Spe would get the reference to the prayer for the tree.

Spe blinked, then Anila felt her sister's Breath flare. Spe stood away from Azsark, then lifted her hand in the sign for *protect*. Anila's heart cracked to see it, but she nodded and made the sign in return.

At a word Azsark started up the sloping road, following the trail broken the day prior, softened by new snow but still obvious. Anila forced herself not to look back.

Above, birds soared back and forth across the wide ribbon of blue, their cheerful calls a mockery of Anila's fear. The way leveled and made a gentle course through towering white boulders. Sun lit their tops with blazing warmth, and little birds flitted through the branches of snowy gnarled pines growing among them and caused little clouds of snow to puff downward, sparkling in the light. Anila could feel their little beating hearts.

The way opened and Azsark stepped into sunlight. She felt awe rush into her like a gust of Breath. Sunlight lit the valley with a brilliance that she could feel. To her left broad meadows of white led to steep forested slopes that rose up to sharp peaks. To her right the valley side rose more gently in a curved wall that made the valley an oval. At the far end of the valley the fortress lay in shadow, nestled against the mountainside. It seemed wrong to her that the world should be so beautiful and so terrible at the same time. She wiped her eyes and looked about for sign of the lady. There was none. Nothing at all. Fresh snow had wiped a smoothing hand over yesterday's tracks. Anila looked back over her shoulder, then ahead. For strength she put her hands to her breastbone and recited the Azsark Prayer. Hot Breath answered, and she basked in the courage it brought. Beneath her, Azsark shuddered.

She put a hand to his neck to comfort him. He flinched with a whinny and stumbled aside with a violence that almost unseated Anila. He shook his head and peered back at her with a bulging eye, head high. Had she hurt him with her Breath? His heart was thumping, but he did not seem fearful. He lifted his head back toward her like a barn cat that wanted more strokes. Anila reached for his neck, then thought better of it, and wrapped a handful of mane around her right hand. Gingerly she touched his neck with the fingers of her left hand.

Azsark gave a deep nicker and his teeth gnashed. Frightened, Anila was about to remove her fingers when he swung his head around and leapt forward. Anila held on with one hand and bounced painfully against his withers as he ran. With her other hand she managed to grab more mane and gripped him with her legs with all the strength she had, raising her rear from his back. Ice-cold wind in her face blurred her vison. Head down, she sang a lilting pattern and the air split before her. Vision cleared and she saw how fast they were racing down the valley. The snow beneath them rushed by like a white river. Breath flowed burning between them and Azsark did not seem to hear her call to stop. A few yanks on his mane had no effect. The fortress was nearing.

Anila reached for the air before them and called it with all her might. A cloud of snow exploded from the road ahead and Azsark dodged right. Anila was wrenched off his back and hit the snowy ground in a welter of white.

Her chest hurt and had no air. A gasp brought ice into her mouth and she cried out in fear. Snow exploded off her in a gust of wind. She took a painful breath, then struggled upright, bringing her head into the sun. She was in a bowl of snow almost as deep as she was tall. A worried sound from Azsark urged her to stand. He was floundering in deep snow beside the road, trying to make his way to her. He stopped at the sight of her head poking up over the snow.

Panting and covered in snow, she said, "Bad horse."

His ears, pointed at her, turned aside and he seemed to sag.

"Bad rider too," said Anila.

She looked around. There was no sign or sense of anyone about. The fort, close now, was silent and still.

Gathering her Breath, she blew a path for Azsark and herself back to the center of the road. Anila brushed and beat at the snow clinging to her, and dug it out of every opening in her clothing. Azsark shook himself and regarded her with a cautious eye. She stepped close and leaned her head against his flank, letting sun-warmth soak into her. Cold water trickled down inside her clothing, but between the sun and her Breath she was warm enough. Azsark's coat was wet, and chill. He was trembling.

She touched his shoulder and let her heat flow. His skin twitched under her hand and he tossed his head, but he stayed still. The trembling stopped. Anila reached out for his head. He stepped back and lowered his neck, then raised her up.

Mounted once more, Anila took a deep breath, and gritted her teeth at the pains doing so brought, then urged

Azsark ahead with a little rocking motion. He walked forward so stately and careful it made her grin.

The smooth pale outer wall of the fort reared above them, and Anila noticed for the first time that the windows of the inner towers were reflecting mountains and sky. Unlike the fort on the other side, there was glass in every one. There were even windows in the rock face above the towers and walls. Directly before her the massive wooden doors stood open as they had found them yestermorn, and by the light of day the wood looked new and sound. In the utter quiet, a sudden sense of caution drove Anila to guide Azsark aside. She hid him behind one of the doors on the sunny side of the door. She wished she'd thought to bring some apple for him.

She slid off his back into the snow, then laid her hands on his chest. "Stay here, Azsark. Stay here." She backed up, pushing snow behind her. His big head swung to look at her, and she held both hands up, palms out. "Wait," she whispered.

Wading chest deep through snow, she made her way around the end of the door and up to the entry itself. Before going in Anila checked the snow that had blown in over the night, hoping to see some sign that the lady had been here, but the night's storm had drifted it deep into the entry hall. She pushed through the drifts until she came to stand on the interior stones. She looked through the open doors to the great hall, then side to side. The cold air was still. Ahead the great hall was gently lit by sunlight from high windows.

Afraid to break the silence, Anila whispered her sandals silent, then walked up to the arch leading to the great hall. The mosaic floor was clean. Not even a single leaf marred its intricate grace. She leaned in to look about. To either side stairwells as wide as her whole house curved around the corners of the room to a balcony that circled the hall. The air smelled like...she frowned and thought of the Azsark larder. She sniffed again and found the barest hint of candle smoke, dried blood, and horses, but those scents could be from her own clothing. At the far end of the great hall lay the arches and rooms which led back to the tunnel entrance. It was dark back there. Feeling exposed, Anila dashed to the right, then halfway up the stair. She crouched on the smooth white steps and peered through the stone balusters. After a bit she settled down on a cold step and looked around. Where had the lady gone?

With a frustrated sigh, she wrapped her arms around herself and pulled up her knees. Probably she should go back to Spe and Ma, but despite the uncanny perfection of the ancient place, she wanted to stay. Intuition flashed and she sat straight. The people who had made this place had the Breath!

The air quivered in the hall and she froze. A whisper of motion she could feel but not hear told her that someone was coming down the tunnel at the back of the fortress. Anila stood. It had to be the lady coming back after looking for her lord. Perhaps he was with her. The lady would be angry that Anila had come, but it wouldn't last. The Limtirians were the most frightening and nicest people Anila could imagine, but they—Anila's thoughts froze, for the air had quieted.

Why would they stop? Because they could see her trail coming in, but the Limtir lord wouldn't stop. He was expecting them to be here. Someone else had come. Chill fear sank long fangs into Anila and she sagged back down to the steps. There was no sense of cold, which implied a person and not Dauthaz, thank the tree. Yet whoever this was, Anila was all there was between them and Spe and Ma.

Anila forced a full breath into her constricted chest. She held the air, making it her own, then blew it out through her lips with a hint of song that was more thought than sound. The listening tube shaped itself across the sunlit hall and into the rooms beyond.

It was a man. She could tell by the sound of his breathing. Cloth shifted and there was a muted click, then a faint knock of wood on wood. Cloth rustled again, and she felt the man walking forward, though she could not detect his footsteps. She leaned forward to see. He should be in sight. The man's breathing stopped. Anila strained for a sound to tell her what he was doing. Cloth might have rustled, but she couldn't tell.

A hard snap crashed in her ears. She flinched back and thrust her hands out to protect herself from…something struck hard into the air before her. Between two stone balusters a black crossbow bolt hung motionless less than a finger's width from her palm, stuck in solid air—aimed at her face. She whimpered and scrambled away up the stairs on all fours. Through the railings she saw a figure in black charging across the mosaic floor, right arm out, black crossbow tracking her through the railings. The bow snapped again and Anila twisted, shoving both hands out. She fell hard on her side as the crossbow bolt flickered between balusters and lodged in the air beyond her hands. Anila ran, her sandals silent as they scraped for purchase on the smooth stone.

Anila felt the man reach the base of the stairs and she dove for the landing. Rolling onto her back, she summoned the biggest gust she could muster from still air. With a sweep of her arms, she flung it down the stair. There was an airy thump and a grunt, followed by the soft clatter of a body tumbling down steps.

Anila got up and ran, lifting her skirts to free her legs. There was only one thing in the world that hunted with a black crossbow—Soot—a Temple assassin. Every terror her mother had burned into her heart screamed within her. Tears blinded her as she dashed down the long landing. She could feel the man swinging onto the balcony behind her, bow raised. Desperate, Anila turned and tumbled over the balcony railing, spinning air as she went, controlling her fall with a roar of wind that whipped her skirts up over her face.

Landing hurt, slamming her feet and calves. Gasping, she stumbled out of sight back under the balcony to the inside wall. Using the wall for support, she whispered the air silent about her and struggled away, limping hard for a dark doorway.

Once inside she made for the next arch, turned right and dashed into another, and another, deeper into the building. In a dark room, she stopped to catch her breath and felt him hard upon her trail as he stepped into the very next room. She heard him smelling the air—he was tracking her by scent. How could she defend against that? She needed to get him off her scent.

Anila shaped a whirl like the one she used to make leaves dance for Spe. She sent it down the wall and then left through the door. Silent in its motion, it sailed into a far chamber, where it ran into a wall. The whirl unraveled with a swishing sigh. The assassin's bow gave a snick, and a bolt cracked against the wall in the far room. He padded after.

Anila ran the opposite way, feeling for another opening in the dark. She kept going, pausing to listen for the assassin. Her sense of him grew faint. As she went, she came to realize that she had missed her chance to stop the man. Instead of leaping off the balcony, she should have knocked him off like Spe did to the Dauthaz on the ocean rocks. If she could.

She needed Spe's strength to fight this man.

Light ahead led her back to the great hall. Crouching by a door almost under the stair, she peered back the way she had come. There was little sense of the Soot.

Anila sprinted into the great hall, then skidded around the entry archway and into the first hall. Azsark was standing in the snow, dark against the brilliance of the sunlit day outside. When he saw her running, he charged forward, drifts exploding out of his way. His head came down and Anila slammed into it, arms clutching. Azsark all but flipped her onto this back. Anila gripped handfuls of mane and Azsark spun about. His muscles tensed and they went airborne, leaping the entryway drifts.

They raced down the snowy road and Anila looked back, fearful of what she would find, but no dark figure marred the sunlit white. The wind of their passage was cold, though the sun was warm. Ahead, beyond the end of the valley, Spe's Breath glowed to Anila's senses like an applewood bonfire.

A decision blazed through her, and she sat up.

"Stop, Azsark."

The warhorse slowed to a quick though careful halt. He gave his neck a toss then stood still, breathing hard, ready to fly in any direction.

For as long as Anila could remember, Ma had bound Anila with the knowledge that to reveal the Breath was to die. Ma had forced Anila to see herself tied to the blood-dark scaffold, the curved knife of Temple justice descending. And so, like a rabbit she had stayed hidden, and then helped Spe hide too, no matter the cost. For Ma it was the only path to life.

The lord and the lady of Limtir had shown Anila that there were many paths. Some led through mountains.

Anila touched Azsark's neck and he turned to face the fortress. She looked at the high wall and beautiful towers shining in the sun—made by her ancestors. Inside its halls lurked the deepest terror of her life. The lord and lady were gone. Ma could not face it and Spe was not ready.

"I am a maker," said Anila. "I will not run. By the tree, I will not run."

She reached for the Breath of the sky. It answered and her inner heat roared to meet it. Wind lifted the snow about her in a whirling curtain of sunlit sparkles.

"Forward, Azsark."

Anila sent a breeze ahead, questing for the Soot. He was there, a spot of warmth to the right side of the archway into the great hall.

When she was close, Anila stopped Azsark. She could feel the Soot's gaze upon her though she could not see him in the shadows. Raising her arm, she lifted her white whirling from the snow and over her head. Her chest burned with the effort. With a cry she called a wind from the cold sky and with it heaved the spinning whirl of ice into the entry hall. The whirling sailed through. She gave it all her strength, accelerating its spin. It passed into the great hall and she tore at its shape, pulling back her Breath. It wrenched apart with a violent hiss of snarling wind.

Caught by the wind, the Soot was flung from his position by the door and into the great hall. He slid across the floor into Anila's view. His crossbow was in one hand, a long black dagger in the other.

Anila slid down from Azsark's back. Her wind had

cleared the doorway of snow, coating the stones in the great hall and beyond. Her skin shimmered, and snow whipped and whirled about her like dancing spirits. The Soot came up to one knee and fired his bow. Anila raised her palms and the bolt was caught in midair two arm lengths away, then whipped aside. Though she was almost blind with pain, she could see the determination in the set of his head and body. He meant to kill her no matter what she was.

She yelled at him, "I will not run!"

His bow came up as his other hand drew the string and slapped a black bolt into the arming groove.

With the air she struck as hard as she could. Blown off his feet, he tumbled back. His blade went skittering but he kept the bow, though it was no longer armed. The Soot rolled to his feet and dashed for the dark doorway on the far side of the hall. There was fear in the run—a touch of desperation.

Flames of Breath burned Anila from within and she fell to her knees, gasping.

Like Spe! she thought.

The Soot was getting away. Anila channeled everything she had into a lance of air aimed at his fleeing back. The air slammed into him and he went flying, landing hard on his face and sliding across the polished floor. Then he was up again with a stumble and he sprinted through the far archway.

"Tell them," gasped Anila. "I will not run."

Breath coursed through her like a river of white-hot coals, and she screamed, falling forward onto her hands. The floor was warm under her fingers and accepted her Breath as rock absorbs sunlight. She sagged down to her elbows as the agony faded. Feeling vulnerable, she looked up, questing for the Soot. There was nothing. Azsark's hooves rang on the stones as he came up beside her. His warm breath blew through her tangled hair. She reached for him. He raised his head and she stood with his help, hugging him.

"Oh, Azsark. I couldn't. I wasn't strong enough."

A voice said, "Anila?"

She shrieked and whirled.

Lady Valiena was standing in a doorway leading from the side of the hall, armed bow in hand. The lady ran cautiously across the floor, looking about for a target.

Too stunned to react, Anila simply stared.

The lady came up, taking in the wild patterns of blown snow that surrounded Anila. In a quiet voice the lady said, "What are you doing here? I heard a scream. We felt wind."

Anila gasped. We? A dam broke inside and she leapt to embrace the lady. Anila felt the lady's warm hand on her head.

Anila said into the folds of the lady's coat, "There's a Soot in the tunnel."

The lady stiffened. The hand left Anila's head and she heard the lady draw her bow halfway.

"Come," whispered the lady.

Anila closed her eyes and felt for the assassin. There was still nothing. The lady stepped back and Anila let go.

"I didn't run," said Anila.

The lady's eyes, hard with fear and fury, widened with understanding. She nodded, and motioned for Anila to follow.

CHAPTER 19

Het's Own Vengence

RUST TURNED HIS BACK ON THE APPROACHING city and walked up the cart tongue between ox teams, ducking under each yoke. Halfway to the cart, the bull Broketail dropped his head, dipping the yoke to catch Rust, but Rust knew the bull's tricks and rolled on hand and hip over the yoke instead. Broketail bellowed like he'd been stabbed by a brand and Rust gave the bull's rump a swat as he passed. Batusha mules made a racket in response to the bull's cry. Rust looked back and saw Broketail craning his neck in the yoke to look at Rust with one bulging eye. Broketail's yoke partner started turning in response and Broketail yanked the yoke back, jerking the other ox's head straight. Broketail was too smart for an ox. The animal was either demanding extra feed, plotting escape, or actually escaping. Tettle said he was a horse reborn in a bull's body as penance for the offenses of a former life. Rust figured Broketail would be a pig in the next life as penance for this one, and never admitted to anyone that the troublesome animal was his favorite.

The cart loomed and Rust climbed up to the seat, careful of the splintered wood that one of the Dauthaz wolves had shattered. Despite the queen's blessing, the smell of decay lingered, and he avoided touching any part stained by Dauthaz blood. He had not seen that part of the battle. His only thought had been to release Slayer and the others, and to protect Beelt. The boy was already sitting at Tettle's feet, kicking his feet happily.

Two company warriors were now leading the cart as they entered Gimlek behind the Kultash. Captain Tettle had decreed that it would not do have the company led into the city by boys. Rust didn't mind leaving the duty to others. The view from the cart was the best.

Tettle made room for Rust on the bench and he slid in beside his captain and a Batusha warrior who ignored him. There was a murmur of talk behind, and Rust looked down into the cart to see the queen awake and going from man to man, talking to those who were awake and touching them with care. Even in torn, soot stained, and bloody clothing she commanded a presence that enveloped him. All the world vanished.

Tettle elbowed him. Rust jerked and faced ahead. An

oxboy was not fit to stare at the queen, but he had her in his mind's eye, and he had felt the weight of her hand. How many could claim as much?

The Batusha archer beside him looked back and made a little grunt. Rust felt his face burning. The warrior leaned his bow against his chest and pulled off an armored, fur-lined gauntlet. He held his hand toward Rust, palm up, then flipped it over. There was a line of pink scar on both sides, showing that the man's hand had been cut nearly in half.

"The Master healed that," said the warrior. He flexed the hand, and Rust felt the man's pride.

"She touched my shoulder once," said Rust.

The warrior nodded as he pulled his glove back on. "We are all touched by the Master."

A feeling of kinship bloomed in Rust. The Batusha way seemed so different from the infantry.

A man in the cart woke with a gasp then wailed, "The cold!"

Rust turned an ear to listen.

"I am here," said the queen.

The man said, "I f-followed you. What was…"

"An Oregule. Life Bane. My enemy."

Rust swallowed at the snarl in her voice. What was an Oregule?

"You knew his n-name."

"And he mine," said the queen.

A chill gripped Rust.

A Kultash warrior came riding down the column leading one of the First's immense horses. The horseman passed the cart and reined around the rear. Rust couldn't resist looking. Neither could Tettle.

The queen was kneeling among the wounded. She laid a

hand on the forehead of a man and said, "Sleep."

She stood and looked beyond the cart. Rust followed her gaze. She was looking past the army, back up the forest road. Had the queen killed her enemy? Her manner hinted that she had not. Another shiver ran over Rust. The howl at the start of the battle had been the most terrible thing he had ever heard. The queen squared her shoulders, then made her way back through the wounded, caught the tossed the reins of the horse, and drew it close so that its barding touched the back of the cart. After she whispered a few words into the horse's hear, it turned its head aside and she leaned out, caught the saddle horn, and levered herself into place by the strength of her arms. For a moment Rust thought her face looked pained. An impressed murmur rose among the Broken Barrel soldiers behind her. The queen urged the horse into a trot back up the column. The Kultash warrior followed on. In a flailing rush, the mounted Batusha warriors who surrounded the cart followed after.

Out of respect for the Batusha man beside him, Rust held back a grin at the Batusha's inept handling of their mules. Rust had never ridden horse or mule himself, but he knew terrible horsemanship when he saw it. The queen moved as though she and her horse were one being as she sped up the long black ribbon of the Kultash army, leaving most of her guard to struggle after her as they could. Only two were able to keep pace with her. After he lost sight of them, Rust settled back in the seat. A frustrated sigh at his ear startled him. He twisted to find himself face to face with the girl who dressed like a Batusha aspirant—she who had killed three wolves the night before with poisoned darts from an assassin's crossbow. She stood on the shelf that the women and girls would stand upon to pass food up to whoever was driving. Her eyes were locked on the distance where the queen had gone. Curious, Rust leaned back to peer down at the black crossbow that hung at her waist. She covered the weapon with an irritated flick of her red cloak, and Rust looked away.

Horns howled down the Kultash line and the army came to a halt. The vanguard must be at the gate.

"Whoa," called Tettle and the cart stilled. Sitting in the winter sun, Rust remembered the feeling of the queen's hand on his shoulder. The sun warmed his neck and shoulders, and he dozed.

Tettle's "Hup!" woke him. By the sun less than a bell had passed. Word passed down the line that all but the Kultash would bed in the city barracks.

"Have they room?" asked a Batusha archer down the bench.

No one answered.

When the oxcart came near to the city, part of the answer became apparent. The snow-draped city wall was halfway to ruin, unmanned. Perhaps the city had no garrison, Rust thought. Icicles hung from the high arch of the gatehouse like sparkling fangs. As they passed under, Rust peered up at them, only to receive a cold wet drop in the eye. He cursed and wiped at the water.

The city closed about them and the air went colder without the sun. The streets were black with icy frozen filth. Crowds of cityfolk watched from the windows of three-story buildings that lined the way, or stood aside along the route. At a big square where six streets merged, a soldier in a pale surcoat met the men leading the oxen and led them away from the tail of the Kultash column. The cart rumbled along a wide avenue until a massive fortified building loomed over the houses. Rust looked behind to see the rest of the army following. The cart rolled through a tunnel with a roof low enough to make Rust and the others duck down. They emerged into a long cobbled yard within a barracks that rose four stories above the stalls of a stable that had once been home to over a thousand cavalry, but seemed now to hold less than a hundred horse. Soldiers in surcoats blazoned with a sheaf of barley were emerging to watch. The cart was led all the way to the back of the yard facing a corral. Rust shook his head. They should have turned the cart around. There was room here if you knew you how. Now he'd have to do it before they left. Tettle said nothing. He seemed lost in memory. Rust tapped Beelt and they climbed down to care for the oxen.

The men walking back from leading the cart directed Rust to put the oxen into the corral at the back. Rust nodded to the obvious order without comment. He and Beelt got to work. A few Gimlek soldiers stood around and watched, though most seemed more interested in the companies flowing in at the head of the yard. Tettle's voice rose above the growing din, ordering the Broken Barrel to retrieve their supplies and gear as it came in.

At the first ox team, Rust lifted Beelt to Slayer's back, then set a staff under the yoke, pulled the pin from Slayer's neck hoop, and caught it as it fell.

Rust said, "See if they have feed in there."

"Doon, Slayer," said Beelt, and Slayer lowered his head. "Sa, sa."

The ox sidestepped to the right out from under the yoke, and Beelt said, "Hup."

The Gimlek soldiers watched in astonishment as Beelt rode the immense beast into the corral. Beelt dashed back.

"Not but rat shit," he said.

Rust jogged to the back of the cart, where Batusha men were lifting their wounded comrades away. Rust waited then went in and hefted a sack of grain that had been used as a pillow. He leapt to the ground, bending his knees with a grunt, then trotted to the corral. He slashed the bag with a dagger and dumped out the sack into a trough.

To a young man sitting on the corral's top rail, Rust said, "We need hay."

The man looked over the army flowing into the yard and said, "We ain't got that much." But he swung down from the fence.

Rust jogged back to the cart. Beelt was mounted and ready. Rust propped up the other side of the yoke, and Beelt rode the ox away. Rust lowered the yoke to the ground one end at time and unhooked the chains to the cart tongue. A bigger crowd of soldiers had formed to watch Beelt ride into the corral. The men exclaimed and laughed, and Rust listened for the cruel edge that would spell trouble. It was largely absent. These were regular soldiers happy for the distraction. Rust levered one end of the free yoke up to his shoulder, then walked his shoulder to its center and hefted it up. This gathered a few impressed comments, and a few mildly insulting comparisons to the Lillhup, but he was used to that. He carried the yoke down the teams, gathering more comparisons to an ox from idle spectators. A few Batusha men and aspirants awaiting a cart for their wounded turned to watch him set the giant piece of wood on the ground, then shift it end and end beneath the cart. He jogged back up the line to where Beelt was mounted on the next ox, looking proud.

When Rust braced up Broketail's side of the yoke, the

ox bellowed, but it was halfhearted. He was exhausted. All the animals were. Still, the way the bull's fist-sized eyes swung to look about told Rust the beast was ready for any chance, especially if it involved fodder other than stale grain and old hay. Beelt climbed up Broketail's docile yoke partner, Slowmoon, and sat to watch with a slightly awed gaze. No one but Rust could handle Broketail. As Rust released the animal, the bull stepped out of his own accord and Rust stepped over in front of the beast. It lowered its horns at him. The horns stretched farther than Rust could reach and the bull's head was almost as long as Rust was tall. Rust stood his ground, then stepped close. He peered into one of Broketail's eyes and stroked the beast's forehead. Broketail blew out a gust of air and snot, splattering Rust's boots. Rust made a face, then slugged Broketail between the eyes. The massive animal stepped back as though it had taken a great blow. Without breaking eye contact with the bull, Rust stepped aside and pointed at the corral.

Broketail stepped forward and Rust lifted a horn over him as the bull stepped into a languid trot. Rust let a hand caress the bull's flank as it passed.

A murmur sounded from the onlookers. There were no more jokes.

By the time the oxen were in the corral, the stable yard was a solid throng of Yasharn soldiers, but still not all the stable stalls were full. Rust watched the shouting bustle for a moment. It looked like every other muster he'd seen. He went under the cart and got the block and tackle from its net, showed Beelt how to hook it up, then started hauling the sections of cart tongue beneath the cart. When done he coiled the rope and rehung the tackle, making sure Beelt saw him put everything away neatly. Blowing a gust of air through his lips, he looked around to be sure he'd not forgotten anything, then he sat on a cart tongue. Beelt plopped down beside him and blew out his own gust of air. They shared slightly fermented cider, cheese, and dried meat from their secret stash under the cart. Men and horses passed by on all sides. There was a good deal of shouting and loud talk of taverns and women. Most men seemed glad to have arrived at a true city. The company was gone from view and he wondered if they would be able to keep their vow.

"Can we go out?" asked Beelt.

"We'll stay with the cart."

Beelt pouted, and Rust felt guilty. The true reason he did not want to go roaming was that he feared running into men of the company in some dark street or stinking tavern. The queen had wrought a transformation upon the company, yet Rust knew them of old. The memories burned, and he reached up for the wooden practice swords tied to an underbeam. Tettle had shown him how to channel his emotion into the litanies of sword and shield. Beelt jumped up, thinking that the swords were for him as an alternative to exploring the city.

Rust relented and handed him a little wooden blade, then took up his own. Rust was too tall to stand under the cart now, so he took a low stance and let Beelt wale away at him.

A sneering laugh caught Beelt in midswing, and the boy lost his grip on the weapon. Rust turned to see a group of eight Batusha aspirants peering under the cart.

The largest of them was a boy of pale face and twisted lips. He said in a singsong voice, "Come out, come out, my stinking ladies. Come out to dance."

Rust stepped out the side of the cart. Beelt joined him, and Rust handed the little boy his practice sword. The

Batusha boys came round the end of the cart. They all wore fine leather boots, chainmail, thick brown cloaks, and red wool surcoats blazoned with a starburst of weapons that was the Batusha sigil. Swords in oiled-wood sheaths swung at their hips.

The big one said, "Ho hoi, oxboy. My horse shit." He waved a hand at the stable yard where the dirty ice was coated with a layer of fresh, trampled horse dung. "Clean it."

Rust stared at him without speaking.

The aspirant stepped closer so he could look down at Rust. "Clean it, oxboy, or I'll make mash of your balls and feed the dogs your cock."

Beelt reared up, but Rust put a hand on his chest. "Get a shovel, Beelt."

Beelt stared at Rust in horror and betrayal. Rust shoved him back. Beelt stumbled, then sprinted away.

Another Batusha aspirant walked over. He wasn't as tall as Rust or the bully, but his stride had the fluid lightness that Tettle had trained Rust to see—the walk of a true fighter. He wore a sword like the others but no armor and his cloak had a border of red.

The group of aspirants behind the big one looked all at once like a gaggle of children in armor rather than a unit of a weapon's guild. Rust got the odd impression that some of them had saluted the new boy, though they hadn't moved. Paleface ignored the new one and spit at Rust's boots, then spun and walked away, head high. The group followed him like a pack of nervous hounds.

Rust breathed deeply, calming himself. The new aspirant was gazing at him, eyes appraising. The aspirant walked away without comment, behind the cart.

Beelt came back with a wooden shovel. He was sniffing

and there were new tear streaks down his filthy face.

"Fight?" he asked in a weak but hopeful voice.

Rust clenched his jaw, then said, "We're the armored arse of the Blessed Host, Beelt. We fight for two reasons. 'Cause we're ordered, an' for the queen. Them boy's nobles. Lookit their gear, for hound's sake. Better'n Tettle's. Strike a noble and it's the flayer's scaffold for the likes of us, Beelt. 'Specially if you thrash 'em."

The unarmored Batusha aspirant stepped out from behind the cart. Rust stiffened.

The aspirant said, "Batusha's mostly common. Horben's as common as pigeon shit. Any soul can aspire to the guild, but rank is earned. That's as written by Lutna, first Chosen of the One. Anyone can challenge any of us."

The aspirant looked over his shoulder to where the others were still visible down the yard. Rust felt temped to call the boy back. It would be a deep satisfaction to shove the pale boy's face into the dung. If he could. Batusha were said to be the best in Yash. But law was law. Rust looked away.

Beelt's face was pinched in thought, then he piped, "Horben's gotta insult the queen!"

"The queen?" said the aspirant.

Rust said, "Your Master."

The aspirant looked disappointed. Apparently Horben wasn't that stupid. Did the Batusha boy think Rust could take Horben? Is that what the aspirant wanted?

"Thrash him yourself," said Rust.

"Already have," said the aspirant with a confidence that reminded Rust of the iron eyes of this boy's masters.

"I'm Tam," said the Batusha boy.

"Rust."

Tam blinked at the name, then said, "Spar?"

Rust glanced at the hilt of Tam's fine sword.

"That's for battle," said Tam. "I have wood ones, or we could wrestle, or fight foot and fist."

Rust said, "You wanna thrash me?"

"Maybe." Tam grinned. "Truth, I want to spar with someone I haven't fought a thousand-thousand times."

Rust did want to fight, but was still not convinced that this wasn't some noble boy pretending to be common so he could come down to see the blood of a stable boy. There was an implied compliment in the aspirant's words. The other aspirants came near to pissing themselves when this one came by, so why would he assume that Rust would be a worthy opponent?

Tam said, "Maybe then we could share weapon litany?"

Rust's eyes flashed with interest. No one knew the weapon litanies of the guilds.

Tam added, "You could show me what the armored arse knows."

Rust felt himself flush, and pushed Beelt roughly out of the way. The little boy didn't complain. The fight was on!

Tam indicated they move to a better spot. The boys walked around to the front of the cart to be out of the way of the men and horses still flowing through the yard. The stalls were filling up, but these at the back were blocked from view by the cart and were yet empty.

They unbuckled their weapons belts. Rust dropped his broken sword to the filthy brown ice, but Tam carefully hung his over a rail of a stall door. The moment Tam's hand left the weapon, Rust was in motion, elbows up, driving low.

Tam let on that he was surprised, then melted aside and gave the infantry boy a nice heave that sent Rust sliding headfirst into the bracken and manure at the back of the stall.

Confident, Tam skipped back into the light and Rust exploded from the stall at twice the speed of his first attack. Rust's shoulder took a shocked Tam in the midriff and they sailed backward through the air. The part of Tam's mind that cataloged and assessed opponents reflected that Rust's first charge had been Rust going easy on him, but now, covered in manure, that kind of mercy had been discarded. Tam had a real battle, and he rejoiced—then the icy cobbles slammed into his back.

The fight was silent, fast, and brutal. Beelt stood near, his mouth hanging open.

Shouts echoed across the busy courtyard, and an instant ring of hollering spectators formed. Tam noted them only as an element of the battlefield. Rust was a lot stronger than Tam had judged, and a good grappler, but knew less than a warrior's trisk of the techniques Tam did, yet Tam found hold after hold shattered by Rust's brute ferocity. There were no pauses in the fight, and after each had landed heavy blows it became clear that both could take punishment. Thus Tam did not expect it when Rust broke away and rolled to his knees, head bowed and back bent as he set his hands on the ground at his knees.

Was the infantry boy yielding? The crowd was quiet and all eyes were turned to something behind Tam. He rose, spinning to face their point of focus. The Master stood at the edge of the ring, men crowding away to give her space. She was still in the charred and torn clothing she'd worn on the road. Tam *chak'ood*, noting that more than half the crowd were Broken Barrel soldiers. They had been first into the yard, but it seemed they had yet to enter the city.

The Master said, "Rust. Rise."

She gathered both with her gaze and said, "When you are

done, report to me what you have learned of each of your fighting styles."

"Aye, Queen," said Rust.

Tam dared not answer, for his mouth was filling with blood from cuts in cheek and lip. Holding the *chak'ood* pose, he bowed crisp and deep, and hoped that would be respectful enough.

The Master's eyes seemed to twinkle. "I look forward to your insights."

Tam nearly choked on the blood pooling in his mouth. He had seen her fight in the streets of Yash. Everything he knew of combat was rat piss in comparison. Then she was gone, and the ring of men closed up behind her.

Tam spat a stream of blood to one side and looked at Rust. The infantry boy's bruised and dung-smeared face was a mask of despair enlivened by dawning fear. He looked precisely like Tam felt. Crazy laughter bubbled up and Tam choked, trying to hold it in.

Rust's face darkened, but Tam held up a placating hand as guffaws burst from him. He sobered as Master Scaukra Tafitamar shouldered his way through the throng with a pair of spear-wood practice blades in hand. Scaukra tossed one to Tam and the other to Rust. Both he and Rust caught the wooden swords by the hilts and they shared a brief look of fellowship at the action. In the weapons litany of the guild, a sword was a sword, and every blade sharp. Tam was surprised that an infantry company would have the same discipline. Yet perhaps he should not be, for it had been Rust's easy power of motion that had given Tam the sparring idea.

Master Tafitamar said, "Begin."

The men of the Broken Barrel Company roared, "*Wall!*"

Tam and Rust each flinched at the sound and Tam wondered briefly why Rust looked surprised by the war cry. Rust recovered fast, and attacked.

Tam moved and there was a crack of blades.   Rust grunted in pain and looked down at the tip of Tam's wooden sword jammed into his woolens between two ribs. A sigh went through the men watching. Tam's only move had been to parry as he stepped in, knees bent, arm extending in a stop thrust. There were slide marks on the ground where Rust's momentum had shoved Tam back. With true blades Rust would have simply impaled himself to the hilt. Both boys stepped back.

Tam thought, *If only the Master had seen that!*

His elation did not last long.

A rectangular shield came skittering across the gritty ice to Rust. With a boot, Rust stopped the shield and flipped it up and caught the massive shield with an ease that spoke to strength Tam would have doubted possible had he not already grappled with the oxboy. Rust caught the inner grip in the air and half a breath later his brown eyes glared at Tam over the rim. Tam had never faced such a big shield but the tactics against any shielded opponent remained the same. Open the shield if you could, strike for the head, weapon arm, and leg, and always remember that a man with his eyes behind his shield was blind.

Bells later, the evening sky above the barracks set the city aglow and still the crack of wood rang from the stable yard. Tam could smell heated ale and heard the bellows of the stable forge. Every window of the barracks and every merlon of the fortified roofs above were jammed with observers. Wagers flew faster than blades.

Tam breathed through his mouth and could feel that his

face was a mess of blood from a shield bash to the nose. Rust moved with a painful limp. The crowd watched, intent. The pair were even for "kills" inflicted upon each other. Master Tafitamar had rotated them through every practice weapon the guild had brought, returning to swords.

Rust was nearly invulnerable behind his shield, simply waiting for Tam to take a misstep. Tam had destroyed Rust at axes, but Rust had regained his honor in their spear duel. Tam knew that he was tiring faster than Rust. He needed to do something spectacular. The honor of Batusha was on the table.

With deliberate focus, he closed the distance between them, relying on his blade skill to keep Rust from touching him. Tam kicked the shield with one boot and Rust stiffened his stance. Tam dropped his sword and leapt. His hands gripped the top of the shield, but before Rust could smack his fingers, Tam wrenched back. Rust stiffened against the pull and Tam jumped onto the shield with both boots. Using his body like a fulcrum, he shoved the bottom of the shield into Rust's front leg and heaved back. Rust toppled forward then went with the motion, intending to crush Tam beneath the shield. As Tam fell, he set his boots to midshield and gripped the rim. The ground smashed into his back and Rust fell into the palm of his shield, suspended on Tam's legs and arms. With a mighty heave upward, Tam shoved Rust, on his shield, into the air.

Tam rolled out from under as Rust crashed back down. Before Rust could react, Tam rose to his knees, pulled a wooden dagger from his belt, leaned in, and drew it across Rust's throat before the boy could react.

The crowd exploded with a bellow that sent pigeons flying from their perches. Tam stood, put away his dagger with care, then offered his hand. Rust unhooked his arm from the shield and accepted the hand.

The Broken Barrel's captain strode up to Rust. There were tears of pride in his eyes. He laid his hands on Rust's shoulders and looked like he was unable to speak. Tam found Master Tafitamar watching him. The master touched the back of his fist to palm in a silent salute. Then a small crowd of women descended on the boys, clucking and cooing with disapproval at their wounds. Gentle hands took Tam's wooden weapon and soft bodies swept him away with Rust.

———⟨∅∅⟩———

Harsh smoke burned Breea's nose as she rode deep into the city with a strong Batusha escort in the wake of six local Kultash who had come to guide her to their barracks. Despite an invitation to call upon the Lord Governor and the Gimlek Temple Pontiff, she had gone first to check on the wounded in the city barracks to see that her healing weaves had not torn. She did not even know where she was to stay this night. Her leg throbbed and she let power flow into the weaves that held it intact. Her rest in the cart had helped, but her weaves were more woven splint than the deep healing Yavay'adil could fashion. If he had ridden with her…she thrust aside the thought and studied her guides. These Kultash wore no cloaks, instead showing an armor of polished squares sewn to thigh-length coats of leather and wool, split for riding. She remembered seeing such cavalry on her journey to the capital south of here. Likely they had been hunting her at the time. The streets were thronged with locals who flattened themselves to walls to make way for the Kultash. Here and there groups of her own soldiers strode with eager purpose toward farther reaches of the city. She wondered how she would collect them all when it was time to march.

Neprawn was near, and she slowed her mount to come abreast with him. "I will change before meeting the Lord Governor."

"Yes, Master. Dori has gone to the guild house to prepare for your arrival."

"We have a guild hall here?"

"Another guild, Master. The Surreda Weapons Guild." Neprawn frowned, which made his face very solemn.

Breea guessed at his thoughts and said, "You think they will call for a test?"

"Master, they might. They follow Lutna, yet..."

"It will be well, Neprawn. I like fighting."

He looked at her sidelong and his beard moved in a small, approving grin.

"Though I have not always accepted it, yet something sings within me with a blade in my hand."

"Het's will," said Neprawn with calm conviction.

Breea didn't answer. Certainly her father had believed in the god, and after her mother had vanished he had once claimed to have been in Het's own presence after Breea had balked at joining him in prayer by asking what made Het different from all the gods of all the peoples of the world. The subject had thrown him into a well of sorrow so deep that Ajalay had needed to take the role of Tetr-Sanis. After the argument Breea had vanished into the mountains for the entire summer. Upon her return Ajalay had taught her how to listen to the essence. There were powers in the world in truth, but gods? Breea was yet unsure.

The Kultash ahead had slowed to better hear her

conversation with Neprawn. Something about their intrusion on their conversation prompted her to jab at their imperious backs and she said, "How goes my guard's training?"

Neprawn glanced back. Breea knew Simarn was out of earshot among the fifty warriors following.

"Master, aspirant Simarn has a will of forged steel. Her arms are weak for the sword, but that will advance. She's fearless but bruises easily. With a crossbow she gives the boys something bitter to chew. I've started her on long basillard, as it's a lighter blade. Doubtful she'll ever make a saber sing, but dagger and thin blade she'll master."

The Kultash were listening hard.

Breea asked, "What about a Sacha blade?"

"Meric?" said Neprawn. "I reckon that might be ideal, but I don't know it. None do outside of Mericsland. Sure no men know its litany."

She looked at him.

His eyebrows went up as he got her meaning. "Master, I will seek her a teacher when we get there."

The Surreda Guild Hall was in an old section of the city. Two-story buildings crowded the road shoulder to shoulder in a variety of ornate and pleasing styles. Many had shops on their first levels. Those that were open showed merchants waiting in candlelight, watching people pass on the streets, or chatting with customers. All conversation halted as Breea's party passed. Hard, focused looks followed her. With his left hand, Neprawn subtly checked the pull of his sword. Batusha closed ranks.

Wishing to be away, out of the city, Breea looked skyward. It was a smoke-muddied evening-blue. What would this sky look like through the branches of Gamanthea-Dur? The thought of home settled her, for Lupazg was no longer there. He was here with the black blade he had stolen from Ajalay's weapons cache. Why had he left Limtir after winning it from Breea's people? The battle among the pines was her second victory against him. In their first he had sought to draw out her death to savor the hunt, and had been unprepared for her capability in the mountains of her home range. There had been no such restraint in him this time. Yet, weave for weave, and strike for strike, she had bested him and taken back the blade that had killed her friends. Was he less, or she greater? What did Sakuront think of that ancient weapon? The essence of the air had gone quiet when he swung the thing. Had he felt it? Did he know that the sword symbolized the death of her home—a wounding that bled without pause within her. When his callused hands had taken up hers in the snowy forest, she had trembled to feel those hands. It was a feeling that betrayed the one love she'd held in her life—and then walked away from—though Ambard had gone first. Her heart shied from these thoughts and returned to what knowledge she was missing about the Oregule. Why was Lupazg here? Why did the wolves attack the oxcart? And worse, would the spider soon return through its medallion as well? What would she do if it did?

Ahead, Batusha pack mules filled half the street in front of a stone building that felt older than its brethren. The stone edges and ornament were blurred by the slow hammer of time and stained black by what was likely many centuries of city smoke. Batusha warriors unloading gear came to attention where they stood. Local guild warriors peered curiously at the party.

The Kultash rode aside and stopped across the street. Breea dismounted carefully.

"*Anule*," she said, and the Batusha men relaxed.

A big man with sharp eyes and a broad belly that pushed out his brocaded waistcoat came out of the guild house door. Local guild warriors saluted him with right-hand fists snapped vertically beside their shoulder.

The man glanced at Breea's tattered dress with a frown of distaste, then looked up, and up.

"Neprawn!" he bellowed.

The tall warrior stepped forward and the men slapped right hands to each other's shoulders, though Breea noted that the round man could not reach Neprawn's. The fact seemed to irritate him somewhat, as though he did not enjoy being so much shorter than Neprawn. Breea thought that amusing—everyone was shorter than Neprawn.

"Master Piad," said Neprawn. "My Service to you."

"Service indeed, ya tree trunk. Come!" Piad turned away.

"Master Piad," said Neprawn. "Greet Batusha Master Banea."

Piad turned back, his gaze not on Breea but on the Kultash across the street.

That was curious, Breea thought. Was he reluctant to meet a woman warrior with Kultash near? That felt wrong based on what Sakuront had said. She stepped forward.

"Breea Banea, my Service to you, Master Piad."

Master Piad's nostrils flared, his eyes glittering as they stayed locked on the Kultash. Breea *listened* and could feel the man's heart pounding. His cheek twitched in a flash of snarl. It was impossible to tell where the anger was directed, at Breea herself or the Kultash, but Piad's eyes flitted to Simarn's waist where her crossbow was hidden beneath her cloak. Could it be these were not Kultash? What then? Breea's breath stopped, and she held herself still, binding her power tight as it roiled.

"Come," said Piad without looking at her. "All of you. Everyone. Come." He turned and walked back through the door.

Breea touched Neprawn's arm to still his indignation at the slight, then followed the Surreda Master. When a Surreda guildsman near the door moved as though to enter before her, Neprawn took a long stride to block the man. The Surreda warrior looked up at Neprawn in consternation, but upon seeing Neprawn's face, stepped back without objection. Breea passed within, listening to ensure that Simarn was following.

The entry hall was unadorned stone lit by candelabras hanging by chains from a flat roof. The candelabras were adorned with wicked-looking spikes facing downward. Ornament to the ignorant, death to an invader when dropped from above. The building was fortified like Batusha. Breea reached out to touch a wall, sensing men beyond its thick stone. It was a relief to be within a fortress.

The hall curved tightly, and Master Piad led them past an open iron-bound door and into a room festooned with the trophies of a thousand campaigns. Banners, weapons, shields, hides, locks of hair, and tapestries hung from the walls one upon another so thickly that the stone could not be seen through them. Heavy wood furniture blackened by the grease of countless hands was piled with Batusha gear. Batusha warriors faced Breea and *chak'ood*.

"*Anule*," she said, watching Piad.

Warriors of his guild moved closer for a better look at the woman Batusha called Master. She could feel her own men pouring into the room behind her, fanning out on either side. In the time it took to take five slow breaths, the room had sorted to Batusha facing Surreda across mounds of gear.

Before anyone could call for a test, Breea said, "I will dress to greet the Pontiff and Lord Governor." She glanced about as though searching for a place to do so.

Piad's shoulders relaxed, and he bowed expansively. "Lady Banea. Of course. A room is prepared."

He strode toward a side door, his men melting out of his way. Breea followed.

Master Piad clapped and a pair of girls came running.

"Lady Banea," he said with a nobleman's condescension, "you are not overtaxed from your journey?"

There was a path in his words, but Breea was unsure where it led, and her ire rose.

Keeping her voice light, she said, "I am well, Master Piad, though I fear that the Dauthaz wolves have ruined my dress."

Piad choked on his reply.

Breea gave him a pleasant smile, then nodded for the stunned girls to show her the way.

In a set of rooms on the second floor, Dori looked so relieved to see Breea that she suspected the girl would have rushed into Breea's arms if Breea had offered embrace. There was a fine split skirt laid out upon the bed. On a table clearly brought to the room for Breea, twin candelabras dripped wax on either side of a warped polished-metal mirror. A round copper tub steamed to one side.

"Bless you, Dori," said Breea and walked straight for the bath.

Dori began to usher out the serving girls and Neprawn, but Breea called to him. After the door closed, Breea *listened* through the walls for anyone within earshot, then said in a low voice, "Neprawn, spread the word to Batusha that Soot may be riding as Kultash in the city."

The big warrior's hands settled on the hilts of his weapons.

"We do not know," said Breea. "You must ignore them. Give no sign, but get our gear under cover. This is not the time for tests and I care not at all what Surreda calls me. We require rest and supply."

"Your word is law, Master."

"Where is the Oregule medallion?"

"Locked in my chest, Master."

"I do not sense it. Is your gear here?"

"I will find it, Master."

Breea nodded. "No one is to move in a group of less than ten. Myself included. Ten masters will accompany me to the Temple. Our best."

"By your word," said Neprawn, and *chak'ood*.

Dori opened the door and he strode out, ducking under the door lintel.

The bath was not overly warm, but after so many days of travel it felt like the embrace of a dear friend. Simarn walked the rooms, then took station beside the door. She was taking to her training quickly. It brought to mind what Breea was about to walk into at the Temple. Between Soot playing at being Kultash and the severe looks of the townspeople, Breea knew it was not to be a pleasant welcome. She was Dauthaz to these people—the armed woman. And now she had walked into their city. Did Sakuront know? How would he react?

It did not matter, for she would destroy any who opposed her. Dori had paired the skirt with a blouse the color of a clear sky an hour after sunset. Finally she added a hooded cloak of shimmering white fur that looked like ermine.

Amazed at Dori's resourcefulness, Breea played with the idea of wearing her bear-fur cloak, but that would be provocative beyond reconciliation. A "woman in a bear-fur cloak" had driven the Yasharn of this area to a frenzy during her first passage. Already she had ridden into the city wearing blades. The Temple edict against a woman touching a blade would be enforced in Gimlek. Only the presence of her army and a couple hundred guildsmen had stayed the hand of this city's rulers. Perhaps she should have remained outside the walls. Her army needed a rest and supply, and she did not want to destroy this city, yet if she must, she would. The sound of tumbling skulls echoed within and set her heart pounding. Essence-fire burgeoned, straining the fabric of her boundaries. When the surge had passed, the Tetr emerald weighed heavy on her chest.

Deeply sobered, she stepped out of the bath. Dori rushed over with what looked like some bed linen. Breea dried herself and began to dress. Dori was silent as she helped. Simarn looked worried, and Breea guessed they were both picking up on her mood. Last on the bed lay her daggers. All three of them stared at the weapons.

"What do you think?" asked Breea.

Simarn nodded once—*take them.* Dori's hands were clasped at her waist as though to hide their trembling. She shook her head—no.

Breea swept up the white ermine cloak, set it about her shoulders, then gestured for Simarn to lead the way. The girl raised her bow, then rehung it at her belt. Breea nodded that she had made the correct choice. Simarn paused, then *chak'ood.*

Dori opened the door.

Sabar, Ootha, and two other Batusha masters saluted.

Walking into their midst she surveyed the warriors. All wore silver chainmail beneath plates of gleaming steel etched in gold. Over their articulated chest and torso armor they wore surcoats of fine red wool that had the Batusha starburst picked out in gold thread. Red wool cloaks lined in black fur hung from their shoulders. Their helms were etched in gold but practical in design with a slight peak at the crown and glittering camails that flowed over their necks. Each wore a saber and a long fighting dagger.

Ootha looked at her waist and blinked.

Breea said, "You are my blades tonight."

The men grew in her sight, backs going rigid with pride of duty. Without another word she walked to the stone stair that spiraled down. At the bottom there was an antechamber that opened to a smoky hall lit by hearth fires and iron chandeliers with half their candles burning. The urgent lilt of young warriors telling stories halted and dozens of heads of both guilds turned. Batusha came to attention. Surreda men eyed them and Breea.

"*Anule*, Batusha," said Breea, then called, "Master Piad."

He'd risen when she entered the room, but a frown creased his shiny brow when he realized that she expected him to come to her. There was calculation in his eyes and Breea knew he was judging the line between being Master and ruler of his hall against being a gracious host to a woman of dubious and somewhat dire reputation. Breea held her gaze flat and unmoving, and waited.

That seemed to decide him, and he strode for her with a call of welcome that yet held enough condescension to make clear his superiority. "Lady Breea!"

Eyes lowered, she let her boundaries unravel. Without

the daggers there was no sign of her essence unveiling—an unexpected benefit to leaving them. Piad closed with her and reached out a hand for hers as though to offer a kiss. She swung her unbound gaze up to his eyes. Piad's body quivered as though he'd been struck.

"I will test you now, Master Piad," said Breea, and set a hand upon his chest.

He stood in shocked immobility while she *listened* to the patterns of his body. His heart raced and Breea wondered if he'd heard the tale of her defeat of Sakuront—of what her hand upon a man could do. There were no weaves within him. He might be a corrupt man, but if so, it was not of the essence.

"Care for my guildsmen until I return, Master Piad. They have earned much."

When he did not reply, Ootha growled, "The word of the Chosen of the One is law."

Piad's eyes flicked to Ootha in sharp astonishment. The Surreda Master looked to each of the four Batusha masters around Breea, then seemed to shrink where he stood. He shook his head in denial. Breea noted that he dared not meet her gaze again.

Aside to Sabar, she said, "My escort?"

"Upon the street, Master."

"The Kultash?"

"They wait, Master."

"Arin?"

"Last word, at the Temple with the Dauthaz wolf heads."

"The First?"

"No word, Master."

"Neprawn?"

"Gone to the barracks, Master, with nine guildsmen."

She turned and walked out. From a shadowed corner of the next room Scaukra stepped out. He looked gaunt, eyes rimmed in red. Even with her healing, the road had been hard upon him.

Breea stepped close and put a comforting hand on the shoulder opposite his wounding.

He voiced a cry of relief, head bowed. Breea bound the flow of essence and Scaukra stood straight. For a brief second his gaze met hers and his eyes cleared, showing once more that odd mixture of emotion she'd seen in him from the moment they first met. Deep emotion and knowledge whirled behind the gaze, but he looked away.

What did he know? Later she would have hard questions for him. Breea walked on.

Scaukra said behind her, "You are the Will."

Frustrated, Breea turned back.

Scaukra added, "He is the Sword."

"Blood and puss," muttered Ootha.

When Ootha said nothing more, Breea turned in question to Sabar.

Sabar glared at his brother, then said, "The Will and the Sword, Master, are Het's own vengeance. Het's wrath—" He turned to Ootha. "What's Arin's word?"

"Manifest," said Ootha.

Breea consulted the Tetr emerald to see what it knew of this, then heaved a sigh. It felt like Alach history twisted to suit a religious reading. That did not make it less dire, or less true. Sakuront had to be the sword here, and what had she given him? An Alach blade brought from Limtir by an Oregule. If there was a god named Het, perhaps he had a sense of irony. Or destiny.

"So be it," she said.

Sabar and Ootha looked at each other, then at the other masters.

"So be it," said the twins. The other masters echoed the words.

"I knew a Meric lord," said Breea, "whose philosophy we shall adopt. Let us crush these Temple mice."

The men chuckled and followed her out. She glanced back at Scaukra as she rounded the corner into the entry hall. His face was haunted. The look sobered her, but she hid the feeling.

The outer door was opened by Surreda guards. An open aisle across the cobbles was formed by two rows of eight horses facing inward that led to her noble horse Fahri, resplendent in Kultash armor and a barding of red cloth, her reins held by a nervous-looking Batusha aspirant. Embroidered on the front of Fahri's barding was a starburst of weapons in gold. Every animal was covered with a similar barding, though they lacked the gold sigil. At the head of each horse a Batusha aspirant stood holding the animal by the reins beneath the chin with their right hand and a lantern in the left. Mounted on the first pair of horses, two armored Batusha warriors each held a spear from which draped red cloth. The spears leaned in and the flags draped open to show the Batusha sigil. It was an impressive sight as gold thread in the flags caught the lamplight. Had Batusha brought their horse barding and flags all the way from Yash? It felt like something that Arin would have insisted be done. That there were almost twice the warriors she had requested for escort felt like something Neprawn would have insisted be done.

Up the street a short distance, the six false Kultash sat their horses, watching with patient disdain.

Breea walked beneath the flags and went down the aisle

toward Fahri. All the men were dressed and armored like Sabar and Ootha. She mounted, then found that she did not know where to ride among her men. While she waited to see how they would sort themselves, she stroked Fahri's neck and wove a binding of earth and air to be used at need.

The two flag-wielding warriors took point, followed by Sabar and Ootha. The brothers' horsemanship showed the effect of days of riding, guiding their mounts with almost practiced ease. Sabar looked back at her. Without direction Fahri stepped into position behind the brothers with an assured stride. Breea grinned and murmured Breowic praise to her. Nine pairs of masters took position behind Breea.

From the guild house a line of Batusha warriors strode. Each held a steel-bowed crossbow which they offered to the sixteen warriors behind Breea. The false Kultash froze at the sight of the crossbows, then wheeled their horses to take a leading position ten horse lengths ahead of the Lank brothers, Ootha and Sabar. The crossbows were sophisticated weapons and reminded her of the crossbows of Limtir—weapons made with Legend Time metallurgy and knowledge. With swift dignity and poorly concealed grins, the Batusha men hung the bows from their saddle horns and flipped aside cloaks to show open bolt bags at their hips. Breea felt like singing out.

The crossbows were a master stroke. What would assassins loathe more than death itself? Being forced to ride with armor-piercing bows at their backs wielded by guild warriors. Ootha peered over his shoulder and caught her pleased expression. He turned back and seemed to puff with pride.

Sabar cupped his hands and called, "Hup!"

The Batusha column snuffled at the joke. A false Kultash

glared back and Sabar waved a negligent hand for him to proceed. Breea considered the stiff backs of the assassins as they kicked their mounts into action. This was a ril of Soot, she was sure. By Taumea's assessment such a group could outmatch him and Breea together. Sending a ril in the guise of Kultash showed a kind of cunning blunted by its clumsiness. It revealed alliances that needed secrecy for true effect. The rulers here had revealed an overweening conceit—a belief in an unassailable position and a childish desire to show off their sharpest blade. This would not be a night of words and maneuver as she had foolishly hoped. Regret at leaving her blades behind tugged on her spirit until she remembered her own words to her men. With her were twenty of the finest blades in Yash, and if Scaukra's cryptic proclamation was to believed, then a god supported her. Breea shook her head in denial. *I am my own will.* She looked at the sky, half daring a god she was unsure existed to contradict her. Looking up reminded her of the endless vantages the roofs provided for an assassin.

Breea closed her eyes and *listened* to the city about her. There were no ambushes on the way.

Near the heart of the city, the horses walked up a long icy slope until a gatehouse blocked the way with tall doors bound in iron. The gatehouse and walls to either side were heavily manned. Bobbing, whispering heads filled the merlon gaps between the wall's crenels. The warriors of her escort looked up at the wall with steady, assessing eyes. Breea thought back to the fortified bridge where her pony had been slain. On the back of hot essence, her senses rode the chill night breeze and flowed through arrow slits into the interior, feeling for the disposition of men within. Men crowded at the slits, peering down at her, but no bows were aimed her way. She let the molten power within her subside, though she knew that the crowds of men were likely here to keep her from escaping.

After the doors were opened, the procession passed into a city of completely different design. It was a Legend Time city, or rather a small remnant of one. The streets were of fitted stone swept free of snow and well lit. Buildings like palace fronts sat shoulder to shoulder along a gently sloped avenue lined with lamps hanging from the limbs of ancient leafless oaks. Warm light flickered in the windows of the buildings to either side, and nobles appeared there to gaze at Breea's passage. The gatehouse doors boomed closed behind her. No one walked the well-lit streets. The houses, while grand, had been repaired many times over the centuries, but never with the skill of the original builders. The place was like the memory of a once great city.

Breea's party followed the false Kultash up the broad avenue toward the crest of the hill. A thousand strides away, the road and palace houses ended at a broad dark square. By the light of the lamps Breea could make out the face of a Temple shaped in pale stone at the apex of the hill.

It was beautiful, and she wondered what it would look like in the sun on a summer day with the oaks in full leaf. As they drew closer to it, her senses caught the echoes of ancient weaves, but when she reached for them her awareness passed through without effect. If felt more like a reflection of loss in the air where once there had been power.

Across the dark plaza, shallow steps ran the width of the temple face to a landing as high as Breea's head atop Fahri. A double line of lantern poles led up the dark steps to a peaked double door that stood wide open. Temple servants in long pale tunics rushed down the stair to take the reins of the false Kultash. They dismounted. Breea let her senses flow upward and into the Temple. The warmth and beating hearts of two hundred men filled rooms to either side of the door. The strategy was bluntly plain. To these leaders a few hundred soldiers would appear to be an overwhelming force even for guild warriors and a Dauthaz woman. If she surrendered, it would be the scaffold; if she fought, death. To this mind, they couldn't lose.

Yet why not take her in the street? The gatehouse and that wall surrounding this enclave seemed trap enough. The servants led the escort's horses away. Through the tall Temple doors she saw a long colonnaded nave. Near the door candlelight flickered on stone columns. No one was visible. The false Kultash were one step from the top. They were leading her in. Someone wanted her inside the Temple. Why? She knew. They had Arin.

The six assassins collapsed onto the threshold, lungs and hearts crushed within by the weaves she had laced into their bodies on the ride. Blades whispered from Batusha sheaths and crossbows armed.

Breea leapt from her horse and dashed up the stairs. A thunder of boots followed. Breea could feel their desire for battle, hear it in their breathing, felt it in their hearts.

She swept her hands forward, and commanded, "Kill."

Her warriors streamed past in a flow of bright steel and claimed the area of the door with a sickle-moon formation. Breea walked through the Temple doorway after them. At the far end of the long nave, the three Dauthaz wolf skulls had been arranged with their snouts leaning together like a tripod at the focus of the chancel. On a broad raised altar behind the heads stood a small phalanx of priests, twenty at least, facing the door. The one at their center stood behind a cracked white altar and wore a shawl of woven gold. The Gimlek high priest. To his right a high scaffold had been built. Between wood posts rising from its platform a naked, blood-streaked man was suspended. He was laughing. Arin.

The Pontiff shouted a command and men Breea sensed to either side came pouring out of arches beyond the columns. Batusha bows fired and the first few men fell. Bows were set aside and their wielders drew blades with relaxed calm. When the first wave of Temple soldiers hit the Batusha line, the attackers were cut down as though by a scythe. The next and the next fell in similar fashion. The Batusha line hadn't moved, and as far as Breea could tell not a single Temple soldier had landed a strike. The Temple charge faltered, and those nearest the implacable Batusha line backed away.

A dark pleasure rushed through Breea. These foes were not Dauthaz, and in skill were nearly children to a line of guild masters. More Temple soldiers came pouring in through the arches beyond, making thick crowds among the columns. Breea could feel their courage returning.

Making a spear of her will, she sent it plunging into the earth. The stones groaned as her rage flowed into them. Batusha held their ground around her as the stones trembled beneath their boots.

The Temple soldiers scuttled back in fear and confusion.

A man wailed, "Dauthaz!"

Sabar said, "No, lad. Het's own vengeance."

Breea stepped toward the priests. A boom quivered the air and Breea spun to look out the door.

Down the avenue at the gatehouse, faint cries were drowned by another boom. The essence of it hummed against her like a thrust of wind. That kind of power could come only from an Oregule. Fearful, Breea rubbed the scars on her fingers. There was nothing from them. Gathering herself, she tapped the deep essence of the ground and swept power into herself. Her skin flashed alight, and riding the essence-heat, her senses quested. She found only air. The next booming strike ended with a shattering crack and she sensed that the doors of the gatehouse had been broken.

Weaving heat and death, Breea strode back out the Temple door only to halt in disbelief.

"Tomes," she said as the unmistakable form of Sakuront strode from the gatehouse tunnel—shiny black sword in hand.

Kultash warriors with drawn blades and wearing the chainmail of his Ulshan poured out the gate after him. They remained at respectful distance and ran lightly to keep pace with the First's long stride.

When he drew close, Breea could see that he wore only a pale shirt, cloth pants, and sandals. All were splattered with blood. He came up the Temple stairs in three long strides. His eyes burned with such rage that Breea stepped out of his way, then matched his pace on his left side. Together they went into the smoky Temple. Batusha came up in a defensive arc behind the pair. Temple soldiers milling uncertainly to either side went still at the sight of the First. A sword clanged to the stone floor in mute surrender, and others followed like iron rain.

From the far end of the nave, Arin sang out, "Witness!"

Breea felt Kultash sweeping into the Temple behind her. Screams and battle noise filled the Temple as the Kultash cut into the Temple guard.

On the altar, the priests broke and fled for a door at the back of the chancel.

With her power upon her, Breea wove, and the men slammed into the unyielding air with cries of shock and pain, then of dismay.

Breea drew the priests toward herself. Some cried out in terrified prayer. Others clawed at the walls of air, their shoes sliding across the floor.

Sakuront stepped forward. His blade made no sound as it blurred and dipped, lopping heads and cleaving bodies. All she could hear was the whack of bone cleaved and the thud of bodies and splash of viscera hitting the floor. The echo of the last priest's scream left the hall quiet like the forest after the thunder of a nearby lightning strike had died.

Twenty men had been slain in the space of half a breath. She stared at the black blade. Not a drop of blood remained upon it. The weapon had displayed none of these qualities in the hands of Lupazg. Sakuront strode forward, his feet splattering blood and fluids.

Too late, Breea shook herself to release her weaving and Sakuront rebounded from her walls of air. The sword flashed a silent arc and Breea gasped as she felt it part her weave like cloth.

The First looked back at her with a frown.

"My weave," she acknowledged, wondering what exactly she had given him in that blade.

His frown deepened.

"I weave the essence of things."

The First looked at her for a moment more, and his eyes flicked to the smoking bodies near the doors, then he turned away and walked out of the gore, leaving red footprints. Breea ran around the slaughter and up the scaffold stairs to Arin. Shivering and bloody, his whole body was discolored and swollen, yet he grinned at her with puffy lips that leaked blood. With care, she untied him. Holding him upright, she took her ermine cloak and wrapped it about him.

A dying cry echoed through the building as Kultash caught some hiding Temple soldier. Sakuront remained in the middle of the floor glaring about with deadly calm, but there was nothing else to slay. Nearby his officers gathered their courage and stepped forward to make report.

Breea wrinkled her nose at the stench of violent death. Beside her Arin sighed like a happy man. Breea eyed him with doubting regard. His face was barely recognizable.

"I'm blessed," he said serenely.

Feeling her heart warm, Breea summoned all she knew of healing—sparkles of blue exploded into the air about them. Arin tried to kneel, but she caught and held him up. His heart was strong, but he had been beaten savagely. It amazed her that he was standing at all, and she poured her strength into him.

When she was done, his back was straight and most of the swelling gone. At the last she'd felt as though someone had tried to help her healing. It might have come from the altar on the stone dais in the center of the chancel. Was there an orb here? The Temple was quiet, smoke drifting about its high rafters. Batusha had surrounded the scaffold and positioned themselves at strategic locations through the hall. Kultash guarded the doors, but most of them seemed to have vanished with Sakuront. Bodies lay in pools of dark blood throughout.

"Arin, where are the men who went with you to bring the Dauthaz skulls here?"

"Master, we had twenty guildsmen and two masters. The Temple guard had not been raised then, and the priests were seeming pleasant, so I sent the men to town and stayed to await your arrival."

"I am sorry I did not come sooner," said Breea.

"Master, all is as it should be."

It surprised Breea to realize how much it meant to her, his forgiveness and lack of blame. Impulsively she hugged him. When she released him, his face was flushed but his expression calm.

Breea went to the scaffold steps, and Arin followed, waving off her hand. She descended, then followed instinct toward the wide, waist-high stone platform that supported a worn, dirty white altar lined with dark cracks. The platform had narrow steps on all sides, and Breea ascended. A presence grew in her mind and she looked back at Arin in excitement. He came up beside her.

"The Elder faith," he said. "The People of White Stone. Lutna wrote of them as older even than the memory of his people. Few of their works remain."

Breea touched her fingertips to the stone. It felt warm. An image of the Temple as it had been originally built grew in her mind. The altar was like the Yash High Temple orb, yet of a different nature. It felt not so much woven as forged, and it was wounded—cracked almost to shattering. There was a sense of otherness in its nature, different from anything she had ever felt. When she reached for that sense, the building shuddered. Breea yanked back her essence, then sneezed at the dust and stone grit that drifted down from the high ceiling. A sense of longing remained, linked in some way to the Temple as it had once been. Her breath caught as she understood.

"Master?" said Arin, flinching as a piece of ceiling stone bounced from a rafter and shattered on the floor nearby.

"I'm not going to destroy the Temple, Arin."

Breea set both palms on the stone.

"I am going to rebuild it."

Arin whispered, "Thus the Chosen made bright the blade, the path, and the hall." He looked at her with wide eyes.

"Perhaps," replied Breea with a grin. "My friend, you may wish to step out. Take everyone with you."

Arin's stared at her in surprise, the mask of his position momentarily gone, face open. Breea realized that she had touched him by naming him friend. It was true, but before she could say more, he spun away and called, "Batusha! We depart. Holy warriors of the Ulshan, she asks that you go with us. The Chosen has spoken."

Arin walked down the platform steps and away. Breea's fur cloak rippled and shimmered as he led red- and black-clad warriors down the nave and outside into the dark. For a moment she worried for him. It was bitter cold outside, and he had no boots.

Calling to her inner flame, Breea let the molten heat of her essence flow into it. The stone absorbed all she could give and more—so much that her hands began to ache with chill as the stone drew upon her.

Baring her teeth, she summoned all that she was. The altar began to glow beneath her hands and she could feel it healing, drawing mote together with mote, sealing ancient wounds. Yet it was too little.

Breea sent her will into the earth beneath the Temple, sensing there flows of essence of a kind hotter and more massive than anything she had yet known. The altar's draw upon her power grew savage and sent a spike of pain through her chest. With a cry she forged a path through deep rock to the essence below, and a plume of heat bloomed upward.

Fear followed pain. What came was the kind of essence-power that destroyed cities and burned forests to ash. Before such essence her own was less than a spark. Breea knew no binding for this. Pouring her will into the ground, she sought a way to halt the rising. Its forefront touched her awareness and she recoiled and jerked her hands from the stone, feeling as though her soul had been singed.

The Temple swayed and cracked and creaked. Stained-glass windows came apart and the pieces shattered on the floor. The altar was a blaze of white too intense to look upon. About to break and run, Breea found herself brought up by a presence that spoke without words. The intent was clear—she was not to flee.

"What am I to do?" she said.

There was no answer. There was no weaving against what was coming. The city would die in flame.

You are the Will. Scaukra's words.

Was this what he knew? Had he seen her here? Closing her eyes on fear, she leaned down and touched the altar. The stone was hot. She opened her eyes to a vision of the Temple as it had once been.

The raw essence of the deep world struck the Temple—and was absorbed, channeled, and transformed by the altar. Shimmering essence flowed past Breea like a mountain gale. It was essence she could shape. Breea began to weave. It was not knowledge that guided her, but simply a sense of what felt true. With weft of intent and warp of power she built the Temple, reforging in stone what it had once been.

When it was done, she sagged down beside the glowing altar, leaning against its warmth. The stone looked new, its ornate bas-relief carvings crisp. With a hand she traced the design beside her face, then sat back to look at it. The scene depicted was of her, leaning upon the altar, streams of power rushing up and about her into the Temple ceiling, which was a dome. Breea looked up and gasped. Where roof beams had once supported a pointed, vaulted roof, there was the open interior of a vast glowing dome. Using the altar to lever herself up, she stared at the Temple remade.

"Tomes," she said.

Yet again, her sense of what it meant to be Alach was remade. She felt a pang for all that was lost to the world and that she had no one with whom to share her discoveries. Giving the altar a caress, she went down the platform steps on weak legs and headed for the front doors, where the first light of dawn was visible over the mountains of the Haunted Lands.

CHAPTER 20

We Made it Fly

WRAPPED IN FLEECY SHEEPSKIN, ANILA LISTENED to the sound of steel sliding across stone. It was dark yet, but the lady had the cook fire crackling. Anila was curled around the warmth of Spe, who slept with such profound peace that Anila was almost drawn back into slumber, but the next gliding stroke held her awake. It was almost musical, shifting in tone with the speed of the stroke, ending with a delicate bell-like ring so faint it was almost impossible to hear. That was her favorite part. Without looking she knew just what the Limtir lord looked like as he bent over the whetstone in the firelight with his armor scales glinting gold with his movement. The sword hilt he held in his right hand, and with the fingers of his left he guided the patterned steel across the stone with patient care.

As soon as it was light enough, the lord would scout, bow in hand. While he was out, Anila, Spe, and Ma would work to pack the camp while the lady cooked. Sometimes the lord returned with a white rabbit or a fat bird he called a grouse, a name that made Anila feel like giggling. Then he would eat, and when he was done, the lady would feed Anila and Spe and Ma. The lord and lady would raise packs and saddle the horses, and see everyone mounted. Each midday the lady made a small fire to heat food while the lord did his sword dances somewhere near. Then they would ride on to the next place for the night. After the evening meal, the lord would sharpen his blade.

Anila loved all of it. Only with Spe at the Azsark tree had she known such serenity. Out here in the snow among the changing forests, the Temple and the Kultash were a fading memory. Ma seemed a little better with the help of Anila's Breath, and only thoughts of the Soot kept Anila awake in the night, but when the lord began to sharpen his blade, sleep found her.

The blade sound stopped midstroke and the lord gave a quiet, frustrated moan. As he straightened from his task, the bones of his back popped in a little cascade. Both Anila and Spe had Breathed to him, but his fights had hurt him, and she never saw him rest. Everyone said rest and meat were what healed a body, but Anila had yet to see the Limtir lord sleep. Anila knew he hurt most of the time—she could sense it in him, and her hearing was better than it had ever been—but he never made any sign except when he thought no one could hear.

Feeling guilty for lying abed, she pushed back the sheepskin. Cold air made her shiver and Spe whined softly, pushing back into Anila for warmth. Anila laid a hand on Spe's shoulder and Breathed a gentle warmth to her sister. Spe sighed like a content cat. Anila tugged on her winter sandals, covered Spe with the fleece, then crawled outside. Standing, she made an inner call to the Breath. Warmth spread through her and a whirl of cold breeze caressed her cheek. The flames of the fire leaned toward her as though to warm themselves. The lady was used to this morning pattern and only smiled in greeting.

Anila glanced shyly at the lord. He wiped his blade, sheathed it, and looked toward the east where mountain peaks reared above the trees, stark against the first brush of dawn light. If the lord wished her Breath, he would ask, but today he said nothing. Disappointed, Anila went to the first of her tasks for the day. The lady slept outside the shelter on nights when there was no snow. Kneeling at the end of the sleeping furs, Anila began to roll them.

The Limtir lord brought his unstrung bow to the fire, squatted down, and dipped two fingers into a cup of warm oil the lady had ready, then began rubbing it in with heat from the fire. The scent of sap rose from the bough bed beneath the furs where Anila worked, reminding her of the scent of pine. A quiver of Breath touched her and without thinking she stood and walked to the lord, then knelt beside him. The wood of the elegantly shaped bow was a deep red-brown, lustrous in the firelight. After a bit she saw that he had stopped work and that both he and the lady were watching her. Embarrassed, she jumped up and rubbed her nose as if to clean away the scent of pine. Neither Limtirian made comment and the lord returned to oiling his bow.

After he left, Anila faced his trail and listened to the crunch of snow beneath his boots for as long as she could. She should be with him. In her heart it was the most certain thing she knew. They all knew that without her the Soot would have found him wounded in the fortress and probably killed him and the lady both. He had not even been able to move until Anila Breathed to him. But how to help? Breath alone was not enough. The fight with the Soot made that plain. If only the lady of the pines had told her more. What if the lord died because he was wounded and Anila wasn't there? A tremor shook her—fear and Breath and so many feelings it was like a storm within. Gusts of wind shook the branches of the trees nearby.

The Limtir lady came up beside her, gazed after the lord for a moment, then touched her shoulder to say that Anila should return to packing.

Angry and sad and fearful, Anila said, "I can help him!"

The lady drew Anila in for a hug, but Anila broke away.

"He knows," said the lady. "And he fears."

"Me?" said Anila.

The lady looked at the shelter as though to check that Ma was sleeping.

"What you must become," said the lady.

Anila frowned. What could that be?

"There is a war, Anila. To us it has already come. Some it has not yet touched, but it will cover the world. Our hope lies in the Lr'icuna—she who illuminates the path. The Lr'icuna is a warrior. Like Taumea, and more, for she has the Breath, and someday she will wield it as Taumea wields a blade. That is what he will not ask of you, to learn to wield the Breath as a weapon."

"Why?" asked Anila, meaning why would he not ask this of her. Had she not already proved that she would stand and not run?

The lady understood, for she said, "Because of his care for you. He cannot bring himself to lead you upon the warrior's path. He fears the price is too great for you to bear."

Anila clenched her jaw. Her Breath rode emotion up from within. Orange sparks lifted from the fire in the breeze she brought.

"I will teach you what I know," said the lady. "But of the essence and the Breath, that you must learn on your own."

Spe stood out from the shelter and said, "With me!"

The lady did not look at Spe. Instead, her pale brown eyes held on Anila with grave intensity. The responsibility was hers.

Anila said, "The pines told me things."

"Then you must use them," said the lady.

Anila touched the center of her chest and swallowed.

The lady's face softened with a calm smile. "Come, the tea is hot."

Tea before the lord had his? Anila glanced at his tracks in the snow.

"We are women, Anila, and we have much to talk about. Tea must be had for such talk."

"Is that a eatit?" asked Spe.

"Edict?" said the lady with a smile. "It is what we do, though no one tells us so."

Spe accepted this and skipped over to the fire heedless of the packed snow under her bare feet. The lady looked like she was about to speak on that, but said nothing.

Anila joined the lady at the fire and at the her direction set more wood upon the coals.

The lady said, "This is the story of how I became friend to the girl who is known to the Yasharn as a woman warrior-born, and to my people as the Lr'icuna, she who illuminates the path. You will meet her someday."

Spe clapped her hands, then carefully accepted a bowl of steaming tea.

The lady handed a bowl to Anila and began. "In the old Temple of Petrall upon the Timaret Plains, there once was a kitchen girl…"

—◆◆◆—

It was nearing midday and Anila was ready to eat. She'd skipped first meal out of excitement because of what the lady had told them. Azsark led, pushing his way down the snowy valley. Where the wind had piled the snow in graceful dunes among the oaks, Spe blew it clear with great spirit. Low gray clouds, immense dark trees, and a rushing river of clear water flowing over dark rocks made the day feel colorless. When it began to snow, the lord took the lead and led them up the valley side to a flat bench of land. He stopped them beside a fallen tree, lopped off branches for firewood, then walked out into the snowfall, bow in hand. Anila stared after him. The lady was clearing snow for her cook fire, not looking Anila's way. Ma sat hunched on her horse with her eyes closed.

"I am a maker," Anila whispered.

She sang her winter sandals silent and set out after the Limtir lord. When Spe leapt up to follow, Anila heard the lady say, "Spe, have you heard the story of the moonbeam who lost her light?"

Anila pushed after the lord, cautiously following his trail around the bole of a tree whose spreading base looked to be as wide as Anila's old village home. On the other side, the lord was kneeling in shallow snow beneath the length of a branch that was as thick as a horse and at least twenty strides long. His cloak, armor coat, padded wool tunic, and shirt lay folded in a stack behind him on a knob of tree root. Anila ducked down behind a drift, then moved so she could look through the gap the lord had made in going through the drift. He sat on his heels, back straight, hands on his thighs. The snowfall grew thick but only a few flakes made their way to his hair and shoulders under the broad limb. Bandages dark with stains wrapped his arms in various places and one went round his neck. Where his skin was visible it looked like angry storm clouds reflected in muddy water. Under the mottled skin he was muscled unlike any man Anila had ever seen, and she had seen hundreds shirtless during the start of harvest.

In a motion too fast for her to understand, the Limtir lord went from kneeling to a straight lunge, right knee bent, thigh horizontal, left foot still placed where he had knelt. The Limtir blade he held straight out, his body leaning forward slightly. A little chill gripped the small of Anila's back then rippled out across her skin. Anila found that she was holding her breath, but when he began to move she almost cried out. Calm savagery roared in silent power upon the Breath of the air as his blade whirled about him like a bird in flight.

When he finished, Anila dropped her head and wept as she had the first time she and Spe had been able to fly. Boots crunched through the snow. She dared not look up, and he passed without pause or comment. Back at the fire, Spe made a happy exclamation. Feeling stunned, Anila raised her head and sat watching the snow fall until her eyes were dry.

There was a finger-width of snow covering her before she rose and walked over to the place where the lord had danced. His footprints had a pattern to them and she tried to remember how he had moved, but all she could see was the sword flashing like a bird's wing, and wisps of cloud.

Spe came bursting through the low drifts in a running cloud, then charged across under the tree limb to smack into Anila, almost knocking her over. Anila's flash of anger was smothered by Spe's hug.

"We're leaving," said Spe. "Did you see him dance?"

There wasn't a good answer to that question. Dance was an utterly inadequate word for what she'd witnessed. For Spe's benefit, she nodded.

Spe took Anila's hand and led her back to the horses along the trail.

—⁓⁓—

Spe's giggle woke Anila in the dark. She was alone in the furs and blankets, though where Spe had been was yet warm. Anila threw off the covers and scrambled out of the canvas shelter and stood. Snow kissed her face like chill moth wings. By starlight filtering through the clouds she could see that the dark coals of the fire were covered by a dusting of snow. The black trunks of oaks ringed the camp on a bench of land near the top of the northern ridge over the valley. There was a sense of otherness upon the air. Spe was a beacon of warmth up the slope to Anila's left, but the *other* was all around, moving in. It did not feel like the Soot, but they were not people either. Breathing in, she sensed that

Spe was surrounded as well up on the ridge.

Anila crossed her hands over the center of her chest and with a piercing cry, summoned everything she had. The night seemed to pause, snowflakes held still in the motionless air, then they all went into motion at once riding wind inward at Anila. A whirl spun around about her, doubling and binding and accelerating until it was keening with a high whistle. Anila raised her voice in harmony with the keening wind, turned left, and leapt up the slope, wind at her back.

Spe stood on bare ground on the ridgetop within a circle of low walls. Dim shapes stood about her, but as Anila arrived they vanished. Anila wrapped her whirling about the both of them.

With an angry stamp, Spe let out a burst of heat that blew Anila off her feet and wiped her whirling from the air. Anila struck the ground on her back among rocks and gravel.

Into the sudden quiet, Spe cried, "You scared them!"

Enraged and hurting from landing on frozen rocks and gravel, Anila nearly hit Spe back with a focused gust, but held the blow.

The sisters glared at each other in the near darkness until Spe said, "You're on fire."

Wisps of pale light twined about Anila's hands like dancing water-grass in the clear flowing water of an irrigation canal. Before she could comment, the Limtir lord's voice made her jump.

"Explain, Spe. Scared who?"

Anila twisted to look at the voice. The shadow of him stood against the tallest section of wall. How had he come upon them without noise or her sensing him? Even as she thought it, she knew. He had been here first. About him was a pool of calm that hid him from her Breath unless she knew where to look. Anila stood with a painful gasp as she found a new place that ached from hitting the ground.

"Anila scared them," said Spe in a belligerent tone that made it clear that she was the injured one.

The Limtir lord didn't reply, but Anila heard him slide his sword back into its scabbard.

In a weaker voice Spe said, "They liked me."

The Limtir lord walked past Anila and said, "You did right, Anila."

Anila felt warm at his words, but could see Spe staring up at the Limtir lord in forlorn betrayal.

The lord went to a knee before Spe and said, "Spe, why do you think they were friendly?"

"They said so."

"What did they say?"

Spe shrugged.

The lord looked over his shoulder at Anila. She was examining the phenomenon of her hands, but the lord Taumea needed her, so she ran over and gathered Spe into a hug. Her little sister burst into sobs, mumble-weeping into Anila's skirt. The Limtir lord was looking at Anila, clearly waiting for her to translate.

"She's sorry for hitting me," said Anila. "The...what?" She bent over and Spe talked into her ear. "The not-people wanted to know where she was from and if she could help them."

The lord looked about.

Anila added, "They're gone."

"You can sense them?"

"Yes, m'lord."

"Good. Let me know if they return."

He gathered both girls, one in each arm, and carried them back to camp. The lady emerged from behind a tree and Anila heard her sheathe a dagger. Lord Taumea put them down in front of the shelter and touched their backs. Anila ducked under, held the cloth open for Spe, and noticed that her hands were no longer aglow. The lord and lady walked away to the far edge of the shelf. Anila followed them with a listening tube.

The Limtir lord said quietly, "We have reached the Haunted Lands."

"Opalah," said the lady. "I felt a presence, but…"

"Many," said the lord. "They spoke to Spe. Asked for her help. I saw them about her. Shadows. They seemed fine with Spe, and she with them, but I do not think they appreciated my presence in the ruin. If they are spirits, I am not sure they are the spirits of people. The shapes were…Anila's weaving seems to have scared them off."

The lady asked, "What did they want with Spe?"

"She didn't say. Anila interrupted. With force."

There was the sound of cloth sliding on cloth and the lord's armor creaked faintly. They had embraced. The lady sighed. "I think I aged fifty moons when she voiced that cry. The air roared like a storm had descended from the sky."

The lord chuckled. "Coming into her strength."

"Taumea, she wants to know how to fight."

"Let her come to it on her own," he replied, and his voice sounded sad.

The lady asked, "Will you come to bed?"

He didn't reply, but they started walking back, stopping by the horses to check them. Anila looked over at Ma who slept on, then pulled the sheepskin over herself and Spe. With one arm she pulled on Spe and her sister wriggled close.

Spe turned her head up toward Anila's and said, "More are coming."

"Spirits?" asked Anila.

Spe shrugged. "People."

Anila thought it over, then asked, "Did they say from where?"

Sleepily, Spe said, "From where we came."

Cold fear spread through Anila. When the lady and the lord crawled under the shelter, she sat up and said, "There are people coming from the mountains."

She shivered in the wash of cool calm that flowed from the lord.

"How far?" he asked.

"I don't think she knows," said Anila.

The lord began to move back outside, but the lady caught him. Anila could hear the lady's fingers moving against his hands in their sign talk. The lord turned to Anila. When he reached his hand toward her, she was ready, and rested her fingers on his callused palm. With care she let her Breath flow into his hand. There was a burst of heat from Spe and before Anila could react, little burning hands gripped both hers and the lord's. The lord jerked up and away as though stung, tearing the shelter canvas.

On his knees with the torn canvas about his head, he took a shaky breath, then let it out slowly. "Blood and martyrs."

"Forgive me," begged Anila.

"Forgiven," said the Limtir lord with a smile.

The kindness of his voice was cool ease for the wave of fear that burned her heart.

Extracting himself from the damaged shelter cloth, he added, "It is...uncomfortable...to a body to be gifted with that strength of Breath."

Anila barely heard him, distracted by the lord's blade. It was humming. She watched him duck out and stand— waiting for him to comment. The humming pulsed at the pace of his heart, slowing as he recovered.

Throwing back his cloak, he set off at a run going back up the ridge. He was going out to fight for them, again. Some part of her could not understand why, but the rest of her basked in what it said of her worth to the lord Taumea. The lady sat whispering prayers until the sound of his footfalls through the snow were gone.

In a worried voice Spe asked, "Is he coming back?"

"Yes," said Anila.

"I didn't mean to," said Spe.

"He knows," said Anila, finding herself echoing the lady's words.

Letting her Breath ride the snowstorm, Anila followed the lord as he worked his way up the forested ridge. Soon she had a hard time sensing his powerful calm.

None of them slept. The lady turned, then turned again. Anila lay quietly beside Spe and could tell by Spe's breathing that she was awake as well. Should she have gone with the lord? It was certain that he would not have allowed it. Thus her task was to think of ways to make the Breath a weapon. A weapon was something used to kill, like a bow or sword. The Breath was neither. Was everything that killed a weapon? What about a rabbit snare? Did the rabbit see it as a weapon? Anila felt not. It did not even see the snare. There was something in that.

Anila settled closer to Spe, humming to herself as she considered. In the dark winter night with Temple hunters and other-spirits beyond the trees, the idea of being able to fight seemed like a blessing. The truth of fighting made her tremble and think of the Soot. Anila raised her hand, weaving invisible strands of air about her fingers. She thought back to the dance the lord had done in the hearth room after his first fight with the Kultash, and then what she had witnessed beneath the oak. There was something terribly beautiful and important in the way the lord moved. It was impossible to imagine what he looked like in battle. She needed to see him fight. A shudder racked her body as premonition flowed over her like ice water. See him she would. And there would be blood upon the air. With a gasp she sat up, panting.

The lady rose on one arm. "What do you see?"

How did the lady know?

"Blood," said Anila. "Blood in the air."

"Breea would dream like that," said the lady. "Hers is a river."

"This is why I must learn to fight?" said Anila.

It wasn't really a question, and the lady didn't reply. Spe sat up beside Anila and warmth blazed from her. It was Spe's way of offering comfort, and Anila took her sister's hand, needing the warmth and care.

The lady said, "You're like a campfire, Spe. I can feel that from here."

Spe hugged herself happily, and Anila realized that Spe was visible as the first touch of dawn was graying the snow outside. The lady crawled forward, shook a little fresh snow from the edge of the shelter cloth, then took up her unstrung bow and a quiver of arrows and crawled out. Anila followed and watched the lady string her bow in the dim light. The snow had stopped and the morning was chill and silent. Anila sent her Breath to roam the air, but there were only trees and ice and little spots of animal warmth beneath the snow and here and there in hollows of the oaks.

"No fire," said the lady. "We'll eat on the move. Feed the horses."

The lady handed her dagger to Anila to cut the last apple. Anila held the blade and looked at it for the first time as more than a tool. The blade was long and thin, silver like a fish, with a handle of pale wood protected by a guard shaped like a sickle moon. It was warm from being under the lady's cloak. She had slept with it beside her. A hundred times Anila had seen the lady use it, but not until now had Anila realized that it was likely made not for cooking, but for killing. A fighting blade.

"Swift, Anila."

She ran to the mound of snow where the saddles and supplies were piled beneath a blanket. With a gust she cleared most of the snow away and threw open the blanket. The apple, when she found it, smelled so like home it brought water to her eyes—not home in the village, but home with the Azsark. The lady's blade sliced through it with ease and soon Anila had the horses fed. They were looking gaunt and had scraped through the snow to find what browse they could. She stroked Azsark as he nuzzled her and wondered what they would do when they ran out of fodder for the horses. The regular provisions were growing low as well. Anila untied her horse and led him to where the lady was folding the shelter with Spe's help. Ma had still not arisen. Anila went to her among the blankets and furs. Her face looked gray, like the dawn.

"Ma?"

Anila touched Ma's face. It was cool. Anila Breathed to her until she could see the red glow of the gem streaming out from under the blankets. Ma did not wake. Spe came over, wading through the churned up snow. Anila couldn't breathe. If Ma died…

The lady knelt and felt Ma's forehead. After looking under the blankets at the shining gem, she stood.

"We'll need Taumea's sword to make a pole cart. We need to get her into the saddle. I can tie her in so she won't fall. Anila, Azsark would be best. Can she ride him?"

Anila nodded.

The lady stood. "It will be hard to lift her. See if you can get Azsark to kneel down."

"I can lift her," said Spe.

The lady looked at Anila.

Anila nodded. They could do it, easily.

"The packs too?" asked the lady.

"Yes," said Anila, wondering why she had never thought to do this before.

"Packs first," said the lady. "Leave Tiyha warm in the blankets until all else is ready. Help me pack."

When all was ready, Anila and Spe stood before a double pack bag and considered how to lift the thing.

"You call and I'll shape," said Anila.

Spe was ready, grinning. Cheered by Spe's confidence, Anila began to sing. Spe spread her arms and gave a piercing cry. Warmth blasted out and the horses flinched, rearing their heads. The lady went to calm them.

Anila swept Spe's Breath beneath the pack, folding and weaving the air beneath it. The pack rose. Thinking of the lord's swordplay, Anila swept one arm down and lifted it up before her in a smooth sweep. The pack went soaring into the air on a column of wind.

Spe screamed in joy and the pack launched into the low

clouds above. Spe slapped both hands over her mouth, eyes gone huge at what she had done.

"Sing!" shouted Anila as she struggled to keep her Breath connected with the pack.

Spe sang out, but gentler, watching Anila for guidance. The blanket pack came down as Anila shaped a pillow to catch the tumbling thing. Cloth had ripped and pieces of clothing came soaring down in the misty air. Anila lowered the pack to the ground. A spare boot thudded into the snow nearby.

Spe said, "We made it fly."

Anila sat with a thump. What if that had been Ma? Feeling drained, she looked to see what the lady thought. The lady indicated they try with another bag. Anila stood.

"Gentle," she said.

Spe nodded.

With care, they lifted the packs, and then the saddles to the horses. It occurred to Anila that this could be used as a weapon. She did not like the idea. There was beauty in the Breath. To use it to destroy felt like a betrayal. Yet this was not bad. They were helping now.

Humming a song Ma once used to put the girls to sleep, Anila wrapped Ma in layers of air, then shaped the air into a bed like a cupped hand. Holding her own hand in the shape she made, she sent a little puff of Breath at Spe, who hummed in harmony. Anila raised her hand and Ma rose into the air, cloak and skirt flapping gently. They set her gently upon Azsark's back. The lady was beside him on her own horse and reached out to steady Ma, lifting her back so that she sat astride Azsark. He flicked his ears and ducked his head away from the gusts of wind that ruffled his mane.

"Steady, Azsark," said the lady.

Anila relaxed her grip on the air.

Using blankets and furs for padding and support, the lady tied Ma into the saddle.

Doubtful, Anila looked at Ma roped into place, head lolling.

Anila went to Azsark, and said, "Don't let her fall, Azsark. Understand? Take care of her."

"It is a Windrider way," said the lady. "She will not fall. Windriders use it to bring home wounded who cannot ride on their own."

Somehow Anila knew that this would also be how those warriors who had died would be returned home.

The lady led them up to the ridgetop and Anila saw that the whole area was covered with circular ruins like overlapping beehives. The sense of *other* was here, but faint. Behind Anila, Azsark carried Ma, rocking back and forth. Through the entire lifting and tying in, Ma had gripped the stone. Anila held to that. Ma lived.

They left the ruins and continued along the ridge, lady in the lead. It felt strange to Anila to be riding another horse, but the big mare did what Anila asked. The pace was slow, and Anila began to play with the air. She took hold of branches and shook the snow from them. Once she caught a crow in flight. It flew away, screaming caws. Spe watched for a while, then settled back against Anila and dozed. Always, Anila kept her awareness taut at the farthest extent she could, hoping to sense the lord on their trail. The lady looked back at every opportunity, but she led them on as fast as the horses could go, feeling their way through snow that was at their knees.

At midday the lady checked Ma and tried to wake her, but failed. Anila gifted Ma with warm Breath while the lady made a small fire and heated tea. Sipping from cups, they sat where they could watch the trail back along the ridge.

"Why did we leave him behind?" asked Anila.

The lady sipped her tea. "The horses are slow in this snow. We must keep moving to stay ahead of pursuit. Our path will be easy to track, and easy to follow as we have broken the trail."

That did not answer for Anila, but she asked no more. The lady did not like to talk of what Taumea did when he went out.

The lady collected their tea bowls and said, "Tonight you will select our place of camp."

They rode into hazy afternoon sun. Near evening Anila began searching for a good camp. It took three tries and was getting dark before the lady accepted Anila's choice, explaining what made a camp defensible. There was a lot more to consider than ease to water, firewood, and protection from the wind. The way the lady spoke, the camp itself was almost a weapon.

"You and I shall share the watch tonight," said the lady after they had placed Ma among the furs beneath the shelter cloth.

"Can I sit first?" asked Anila. She wanted to sit with Ma for a while.

"And me," said Spe.

The lady nodded. "When Opalah's light shines from the south, wake me. What way is south?"

Anila flushed, then pointed off the ridge, hoping that was correct.

"Opalah bless," said the lady and crawled into her blankets.

Anila moved closer to Ma. Spe came over and laid her

head on Anila's lap. Ma's breathing was irregular, like her body was only sometimes remembering to breathe.

Spe asked, "What's wrong with Ma?"

"Hush. We're on watch."

Spe pressed her lips together in her sign of quiet and secrecy. Anila stroked her sister's head for a while. Who knew what ailed Ma, but it was getting bad. When Spe was asleep, Anila folded a fur to replace her leg under Spe's head, tucked blankets over her, then crawled out into the moonlit night. The sky was mostly clear and the air sharp against her skin. A horse shifted, a hoof squeaking on packed snow. A call to the Breath warmed her and she let her awareness soar. There was a surprising amount of life about, most of it beneath the snow. Cold air moved in the sky, deep in strength. Thinking of the problem the lady had stated regarding their trail, Anila sent her Breath into the white ice. It had layers, each made of ice, but with its own pattern of Breath and substance. A called breeze moved the freshest snow, but after some tries to fill the horses' steps she saw that it would take a tremendous amount of such movement to hide their trail. How could she shape this? A whiff of pine made her jerk back. Ideas rippled through her mind. Reaching back under the shelter, she pulled out a blanket and set it on the hard trampled snow before the shelter. She sat and considered the challenge.

—◦◊◦—

Taumea ran the ridge, keeping as much as he could to shallower areas of snow beneath the oaks. Tireless, he ran through the dawn and through the day, breaking new trail all the while. There was a tower of rock on this ridge he'd seen from the valley floor the day prior. From its peak he would be able to survey everything back to the ancient road they'd followed out of the high valley. He needed to make the climb before night so that he could look for the fires of any host on their tail. Spe had said people, not person. People made a mark upon the land, and men would be loath to travel the Haunted Lands without fire at night.

He looked over at the bearish cat-like apparition that had been pacing him for two bells. It had done nothing but run with him so far, making no sound and no mark upon the snow. Its long fur danced with its motion and gave its bounds a wild, almost exuberant feel. Taumea fancied that it merely wanted someone to run with. Deep down, however, its otherworldly silence strummed a wary fear that Taumea could not dismiss, and he wondered what the apparition would do when he stopped.

The rock pillar he was aiming for reared through the trees, and Taumea pushed onward. Panting, he stopped at the base of a slope of snowy boulders which formed the base of the stone promontory. The creature stopped with him, gave itself a shake as if to clean snow from its fur, then sat on top of the snow. It did not look at him, and Taumea raised his gaze to consider an ascent. Broken and sheer, the stone rose as an uneven column. Tiers of snow ringed the stone bastion at intervals up its length, reminding Taumea of a fortified tower. Dark striated rock showed through where it was too sheer for snow to collect.

From the corner of his eye he studied the apparition. Winter sun through the leafless oaks cast no shadow about it, yet the light was as clear upon the thing as were the shadows of branches that crossed its fur. It was decidedly wrong and a chill flashed over Taumea. He returned to his study of the snow-blanketed rocks. Such a traverse and climb would be hazardous, but there looked to be a way. If he could get to the top of the rocks, there was a narrow crack which led to the summit.

His cloak he folded and set atop a stone he brushed free of snow. The warmth of the girls' Breath would keep him warm and the cloak would hinder the climb. Plowing forward into the boulders, he paused as the apparition leapt ahead, bounding up from snowy crest to snowy crest until it stood beside the sheer side of the tower proper. Taumea was about to continue when the creature's head turned to look directly at him. Chills ran over Taumea's body like ten thousand cold-footed mice. He knew that look. It was exactly the look the hounds of his youth would give when they expected him to follow—half invitation and half summons—that look said *this is the way*. The apparition bounded away around the base of the tower.

Following its route was not workable, so Taumea went around the tower instead, following the edge of the trees where the boulder-fall stopped. The eastern side was in the lee of the tower and the snow depth reduced. The apparition was gone, but there was an easy walk to the base of the tower up a ramp of snow. Without hesitation Taumea strode up to the tower and found the apparition sitting above him in the upper end of a very steep angle of snow. With a boot Taumea cleared the base and found a worn step. Grinning, he set to work.

Dark evening sky crept up behind the mountains, but was held back by sunset light that clung to their peaks. Taumea achieved the top of the tower as the gloaming faded and night swept up from the valley floor.

Breathing hard from the work of clearing the way, he

brushed himself clean of snow, then cleared a spot to sit among the broken spires of dark stone that formed the towered peak. The apparition appeared at his side sitting atop the snow, facing east. It was so close that had it been a living animal Taumea would have been able smell its scent, and it was big—sitting at his feet its head was a good six hands higher than his.

On the mountain, the trail down from the high valley was too far to see in the dim light. Letting calm settle him, Taumea leaned forward and carefully observed the valley to the south, cataloging the landmarks he had noted in their passage, and was thus able to draw the trail of their route along the valley floor in his mind. No sign of motion, firelight, or sound rose from their back trail below.

After dark shrouded the valley, he leaned back against a pillar and watched the moon rise over the toothed peaks. A cold breeze sighed past, lifting the apparition's fur, which reflected the moonlight with a faint glimmering like sunlight on water seen through a fog. Taumea suppressed an urge to touch the thing.

Its ears perked and Taumea's gaze shifted past the beast. He stood. A line of pricks of light descended the mountain all the way into the high forest slopes. He watched long enough to know what was coming. Taumea turned to thank the beast for its help and found it looking at him. In the moonlight its dark eyes held such a depth of sorrow that Taumea instinctively reached out to comfort the apparition. It vanished.

Deep among the stone pillars the snow was glowing from within with a light the color of early sunset. Taumea made his way through the pillars and over broken stone, then knelt in the snow and brushed it away over the light. A broad, massively fanged animal skull lay revealed in warm light that sprang from a gem embedded in its forehead.

"Is this you?" asked Taumea in wonder.

Silence was the only reply. The light began to fade. Taumea pulled off a glove and touched the gem. It was loose in the bone socket. With thumb and finger he picked it up. It was cold. The yellow glow flared then went dark. Thinking of the grief in the creature's look, Taumea clenched his fist around the gem. How long had this ancient beast waited for someone to come? Had it died at the top of this tower waiting for a master who would never return?

Taumea stood and placed the gem in a secure pouch, then headed down the precarious stair and considered his strategy. If he attacked the Kultash—for he was certain that it was they who came—he could be sure to slow their advance, but he would not be able to stop them. He no longer had the help of the pines and there were too many for any one man to slay, even with the Breath full upon him. The Kultash were too fine a warriorhood. They knew now what manner of foe they faced, and still they came. The path to survival was by way of the Alach gifts of Anila and Spe. If he could keep the girls a sufficient distance from the pursuit, then Spe might be able to call another storm to cover their tracks. They would need to be moving by first light.

After retrieving and donning his cloak, he pushed it back from his shoulders, lifted his sword in his right hand to keep if from swinging about, and ran into the moonlit forest.

CHAPTER 21

Temple Dawn

BREEA WALKED OUT THROUGH THE TALL FRONT portal of the Temple and found her Batusha escort kneeling among a hundred Kultash out on the flagstones of the courtyard. Their heads bowed at her appearance on the landing. A soft susurration was on the air. Breea turned her head, listening. It sounded like prayers. From her vantage atop the Temple steps she saw that the streets of the high city were covered with bodies. It reminded her of the carnage in the streets of Yash, but these folk were alive—and praying.

What had these folk seen while she wove the Temple whole? Its light cast her shadow across the square. Breea turned to see what she had shaped and stepped away from the edifice with a little stumble.

The entire building had changed. Columns as tall as the walls of Limtir framed a soaring doorway. To either side statues of men and beasts and things that were like both glowed in niches three times Breea's height, two to each side and three high. At first she thought the creatures were like Lupazg, but the figures were more animal than a man with animal features. All wore clothing and a few were in armor. Sheltering all was a sweeping eave that curved to a fine peak, its design reminding her of the graceful roof peaks of Limtir. Above this roof towered a tall, straight-sided dome. Breea ran down the steps and out onto the courtyard to see better. From the apex of the dome a spear of bright stone pierced the dark morning sky. The building glowed with the intensity of a full moon. There was a balance and splendor to the structure that even Limtir could not match.

Dawn's first sunlight struck the dome and the white stone flashed into warm brilliance. Breea sang out in surprise and pleasure, then she wiped her eyes for the beauty of the place. She turned to see what her warriors were feeling and found that Arin stood near in the ermine cloak. A borrowed leather belt cinched the cloak closed at his waist. His head and shoulders were bowed toward her in humble obeisance.

That was not good. She needed Arin to see past the glamour of her Alach nature. He was her chief adviser. Adviser? She clenched her jaw. How did it come to pass that she had an adviser? Despite being a prophecy manifest and able to weave essence as the Alach of old, she still felt like Breea, a girl who wanted little more than to be a scholar and run the forests with her man. And what made her queen? Right of parentage? Was her mother truly a queen? If her mother was Alach, why had she vanished?

Shaking free of that dark thought line, Breea said to Arin, "Be not blind."

The priest's head snapped up and he blinked as he sorted her meaning. The words were advice from the Wisdom of the One and advised that Het's will could only be seen by a man with his eyes open.

In acknowledgment, Arin bowed deeper yet. Anger flashed through Breea until he straightened and she saw the mischief in his eyes. He was teasing, showing that he could jest with her. Grateful, she shook her head at him.

Their pact reaffirmed, she asked, "Was the Temple Pontiff among those Sakuront cut down?"

"Yes, Chosen."

"The lord of the city?"

"The word is that the Lord Governor retired to his residence before your arrival. It is thought that he did not agree with the Pontiff's choice to oppose you. He is there." Arin indicated an ornate gate behind which rose one of the grandest houses in the high city.

"I should like to call upon him," said Breea.

"Shall I announce your imminent arrival, Chosen?"

Breea's eyes narrowed. "No. Have him come to the Temple. Bring two chairs to the altar."

"Master," affirmed Arin with a cunning grin that lifted the corners of his mouth. He stepped away to speak with the Batusha masters.

Breea liked that he had reverted to calling her Master. Was it because she was acting tactically to overawe the Lord Governor and thus gain easy provision and passage out of the city? How much had changed that the title of Master felt more comfortable than being called Chosen? Sadness pressed at her chest, and she longed to talk with friends of all that had happened. If Valiena were here, she would have some plainswoman wisdom that would set all in its place. Taumea would grin and tell her what she truly was, and how others saw her, and then shake his head in good humor at her thin denials. Tomes, she missed her friends.

Arin returned and she drew in a deep breath, pushing back against the weight of place and duty, then asked in a firm voice, "How soon to secure supply for wilderness travel?"

"Provisioning has begun, Master," said Arin. "What would you have done with the cart of the Broken Barrel?"

"Let them do as they will. They have Lillhup oxen. The host will pass another night in the city. We will leave at tomorrow's dawn."

Arin pushed his hands out the front of the cloak and chak'ood.

At the sound of his back-fist to palm, Batusha chak'ood in turn. A few masters left at a run toward the Lord Governor's house while another pair set out for the gatehouse that led to the rest of the city. Others set out for the nearest palace-house. The remaining six arrayed themselves about her in a discreet, defensive ring.

"Are your feet not cold?" asked Breea.

Arin looked like he was about to utter a grand statement, then rethought and said, "No, Master."

She took him at his word. Voices called out in greeting and Breea turned to see Neprawn's tall figure coming up the avenue, stepping over the still prone. As he neared, she saw that his gaze was fixed on the shining Temple. His face was grave and he did not look at Breea. Before he spoke, Breea knew what he would say of the spider Oregule's medallion.

After a salute that echoed back off the Temple, he said, "Master, it is lost."

Despite foreknowledge of this, Breea felt his statement cut a chill into her heart.

"In the forest," she said.

"Yes, Master."

Shame darkened his face in the light of the Temple dawn.

Breea felt ill. Now there were two Oregule. The histories were clear that Oregule became vastly more powerful if they wove in concert. Could she face two? A vision of Sakuront with his silent blade flashed in her mind's eye. A hand drifted to the Tetr medallion and her eyes narrowed. Perhaps.

Neprawn looked miserable, and Breea said, "You did not fail, Master Neprawn. It was why the wolf attacked. He came for the spider's medallion. We could not have known."

Neprawn's demeanor did not change.

Breea stepped up to the big warrior and punched his chest armor. He swayed back slightly and looked down at her in confusion.

Breea said, "If I say that you have not failed me, you may not wear so mournful a face."

"I...by your word, Master."

Breea forced a grin through her worries. He made an effort to return it, but merely looked sad. In Breea the thought of Lupazg outwitting her sparked deep rage. Why had he abandoned Limtir? And how did he know she'd had the spider Oregule's medallion?

Her anger wasn't for Neprawn, but the wrath in her eyes

seemed to wipe the failure from the big warrior's face. He stood to attention, gaze straight out over Breea's head. Her rage settled as she studied him. His face was illuminated on one side by the Temple and on the other by dawn sunlight. Breea found herself admiring his magnificence. Simarn could find no better suitor if only the girl would allow herself to return his attention.

Boots pounded on the stone and grinning Batusha masters jogged past carrying a pair of ornate, high-backed chairs. An awed murmur rose from people in the streets. Sakuront stood in the Temple doorway. His shirt and pants were pure white. Breea hissed and took a step back, bumping into Neprawn.

The First strode across the landing to the top of the stair. The dark metal of his sword seemed to cut against the Temple glow, blindingly dark in its contrast. The First's black hair and dark skin looked pale in comparison. The Batusha masters went up the steps and slowed to a halt before him. The First asked a question. The masters put down their chairs. Sabar stepped forward and spoke. After listening, Sakuront's head snapped to look at Breea and he interrupted Sabar with a question. Sabar raised his arms to the Temple facade and his voice rose in tone and his arms swept out to emphasize his narration, lifting and sweeping, lifting and sweeping.

There was movement within the Temple and white-clad Kultash came up behind the First with their heads craned forward to hear what Sabar was saying.

Breea gathered herself and walked forward. Neprawn's long bootfalls and Arin's bare feet padded after her, followed by her Batusha guard.

The First of the Kultash watched her climb the Temple

steps, his eyes both burning and awed. At the edge of the top landing, Breea stopped. Warmth came off the Temple stones as though they contained the sun's heat. She had not noticed that before. Sakuront stared. Was he speechless?

"Master," said Arin.

He was looking over at the Lord Governor's palace. The gate was open and a procession was emerging.

"Masters," said Breea to the Batusha men who had brought the chairs. "Will you set those by the altar?"

They saluted her. White-clad Kultash made a path for them to carry the seats into the nave.

"First," said Breea, "will you join me to meet with the Lord Governor?"

"Chosen," said Sakuront. "I will."

He gestured to the Kultash in the courtyard to guard the entry. The men came running, and Breea walked in with the First at her side. Arin remained at the door and stood in the center of its span to await the governor.

At the altar platform, Breea had the chairs placed facing one another across the bright white stone. Sakuront placed himself directly behind the altar, sword point at his feet, haft held in both hands at his belly. Without direction, white-clad Kultash formed a half circle enclosing the altar platform. Sabar and Ootha placed themselves on Sakuront's flanks and more masters flowed into place to make solid wings of red, silver, and gold.

At the doorway Arin was greeting the governor's procession and declaring in a ringing voice who awaited within. Breea went to Sakuront's side and pushed at his hip with her fingers until he sidled sideways with a discomfited expression. Suppressing a grin, she took position beside him, and her Batusha masters adjusted their stances to symmetry out and behind. Neprawn took a position behind the chair to her left. Breea looked about. It was an impressive martial display. Around the sides of the platform the white Kultash made an eerie cordon that seemed to fade into the pale stone of the Temple. Beside her, Sakuront's white shirt and pants seemed to highlight his massive musculature in a way coat and armor could not. Threat and power radiated from him like a…Breea bit her lip. He looked like a warrior-king from an Alach history story. She looked away before her heart could complete its backflip, and felt her face flush.

Arin came down the nave at a stately pace. One regally dressed, portly old man followed him. Apparently Arin had forbade entry to the Lord Governor's attendants, advisers, or guards. That would have been easy with Kultash and Batusha guildsmen at hand to insist.

At the base of the altar steps, Arin stood aside and said in a ringing voice, "The Lord Governor of Gimlek!"

The old man was shaking, jowls quivering. Instead of advancing up the steps, he fell to his knees, stifling a cry at the pain that brought him. Tears cut bright lines down his face in the light of the Temple altar. He bent forward and prostrated himself, fingers clutching at the first step.

Arin regarded him without sympathy. "Rise, Lord Governor. The Will and the Sword will speak."

The old man's breath rushed from him in a long wheeze as though he were being trodden flat by the weight of the titles. Breea wondered how much of his fear was born of Yasharn religious belief and how much out of guilt and fear for his part in the attack against her.

When he made no other motion, Arin ordered, "Rise! Take your place at the white altar."

The man gathered himself from the floor and stood,

using the platform steps to aid himself. Arin offered no assistance.

"My lord," said Breea in a cool voice, and indicated the chair to her right.

Haunted eyes glanced up only enough to judge her meaning. He shuffled up the steps. Breea sat without ceremony. The Lord Governor sagged into the chair opposite her, his body tilted away from the presence of Sakuront.

Breea touched the Tetr emerald. Was there no iron in the man? How had he defied the Temple Pontiff? The emerald spoke to her of his lineage, a ruling family that dated to the building of the first city wall. None of it gave her insight into the man, and she felt impatient.

"Why did you oppose the Pontiff in the plot against me?"

"Chosen?" He glanced at Arin, and Breea guessed that Arin had provided direction for addressing her, but he said no more.

Raising her right hand, she placed it upon the altar. Its glow brightened and the old noble flinched back. Breea sighed inwardly. He was broken, and expected death as his reward.

"Place your hand upon the altar," said Breea.

When he failed to move, Breea turned her head toward Ootha at her right, but the Lord Governor seemed to think she was looking at Sakuront, for he thrust out his right hand with such speed that it slapped against the stone. Breea bound it there before he could react to its warmth. When he realized he could not move, a guttural moan of terror sighed out of him. Though she would never forgive him for allowing Arin to be captured and savagely beaten in preparation to be flayed before her, a surge of empathy for the man drove her to lend him strength. At her will, essence flowed into him. The noble screamed, then fainted.

Breea cried out in frustration.

"What do you want of this man?" Sakuront asked.

"Provisions," she said, "Tents. Horses. Safety for our men in the city. Warriors if there are any of worth. Support! More, he will need to make this city whole—rebuild the walls and gather supply. Not all the blight that is Yash was made by the Oregule, and all of that may be healed by a strong hand. This realm was magnificent in the Legend Time."

She put both hands on the altar and basked in its essence-heat. Her emotions rose with the warmth. "The Yasharn realm needs men who will stand at the right hand of truth and fight what comes. I hoped he might be one and with a touch of awe I could spur him to act."

Sabar gave a derisive snort.

Breea looked at him and he stood to attention.

"I thought he would be more," she admitted, then half grinned. "I guess I awed him nearly to death. How did he defy the Temple? He opposed the Pontiff, who had Soot and Temple guardsmen."

"And Kultash," said Sakuront. "The Ulshan was corrupt."

The First said it with such finality that she suspected that he had already dealt with them. What, then, was the source of this man's power? She caressed the medallion and listened. No one moved while she stared into the distance. When it was done, Breea silently blessed Ajalay for the gift of the Tetr medallion.

"Arin!"

He came running up the steps of the platform.

"Return to Surreda Guild Hall. Bring Master Piad. Scaukra as well."

"Your word, Master."

He chak'ood, then jumped to the floor and ran into the sunlight streaming into the hall from the tall portal at the end. For the first time Breea could see the path ahead and how to shift the pieces. Her spirit soared as though to join with the essence whirling beneath the bright dome above.

Feeling hopeful and brave, and with a bone-deep need to move, Breea stood and swung to Sakuront.

"Will you join me in morning prayer?"

With an open hand, she indicated the floor.

The First pulled in a breath and smothered a grin—the first she had ever seen from him. He strode around the insensible Lord Governor and down to the floor. A gesture brought his Kultash running. Breea took off the Tetr emerald and coiled its woven-gold chain around it on the altar, then joined them.

"Chosen," said Sakuront. He swept his blade in a low arc, giving her the floor.

Breea bowed to him and skipped out to give herself room. The First and his Kultash sat on their heels, blades drawn and laid across their thighs. It was almost like Limtir Tomeguard practice.

Breea stilled herself, then slid into the low stance that began her favorite form series, Cat Hunts Butterfly. Striking, she launched into motions so familiar that performing them was like coming home. Her clothing snapped and whip-cracked with the force of her blows. Her body felt light. She added Wind and Rain to the form, blending them into Cat Hunts Butterfly in Storm. Essence seared her flesh with joyous heat as she performed the whirling patterns of attack and defense. The air sparkled in her passing, and the shock of what she was making nearly stunned her to stop. Cat Hunts Butterfly was an Alach combat form. Every move built upon the next, weaving air and inner fire until wind began to howl about her as she moved, crackling with bright essence, seeking to lash out in hot savagery. Too much! Spinning, she wove a boundary at the source of her power and slowed, bending her knees until she spun down to the floor, pivoting on one heel, dragging her fingers across the stone in a circle, bleeding off the power of the deadly weave she had shaped. Head bent to her knees, she settled to a halt.

Unfolding, she stood amid the smell of scorched stone. Sunlight upon her face was like her mother's caress.

Wondering what Sakuront thought, she met his eyes and heat flashed through her as though she had been hit by a wave of essence.

On the altar platform, Ootha whooped a battle cry. Grateful for the distraction, Breea turned to the grinning Batusha masters and gave them a short bow. Her heart was roaring, or was it her ears? She felt exultant and confused, and tears tried to start in her eyes—that must not be. Training her entire childhood with the Tomeguard had taught her that warriors do not weep on the practice floor. It had been a sharp lesson—for herself in the derision it had brought, and for the boys who had learned that the sharp end of her temper was not dulled by watery eyes. Swallowing emotion, Breea bowed to Sakuront and his men, then walked back up the platform steps.

In the chair beside the altar, she watched Sakuront lead his Kultash in their fluid, deadly prayer, and felt a fluttering deep down that had nothing to do with weaving essence or her fate as an Alach. It was the nervous excitement of a girl who has found that she is admired by a man. It was foolish. She had simply been too long without Ambard. By force of will she pushed away the reaction and donned the Tetr emerald.

On the floor the Kultash faced into the sun, their pale blades refracting light almost like glass. What had happened to them? Breea wondered. Their white clothing and armor was disturbing. About them was an aura of the Temple's ancient essence, and there was nothing of the twisted essence of Oregule or Dauthaz, but the color made her shudder. Was that absurd? The altar was white. The Temple as well. Perhaps the Oregule were of the age before the Alach, the time of the People of White Stone. How old were Lupazg and his kind? Did the builders of this ancient Temple have the knowledge of how to kill Oregule permanently?

Sakuront's voice called out a fast chant in time to his strikes. The Kultash answered in counterpoint, faster and faster. The First was pushing them hard and their unison suffered, but it remained an incredible display. Breea looked to her Batusha masters to share the moment with them. There was no appreciation in their narrowed gazes. They stood rock still, only their eyes moving, tracking the Kultash blades. They were memorizing the Kultash movements! Sobered, Breea looked back at the Kultash weapon litany with new eyes.

The Lord Governor stirred and gripped the arms of the fine chair, then pushed himself upright. Breea watched the man with cool regard.

"Lord Governor Erissohn," she said, using his family name. "You have my gratitude."

He glanced around as though seeking something familiar, finding nothing.

"You chose well," she continued. "Not to oppose me. Choose well again."

Looking confused, he bobbed his head.

"Gimlek needs you, Lord Erissohn. Beasts of legend walk again, and Het has chosen his champions."

Erissohn swallowed, or tried to. He seemed to have a difficult time of it.

Breea said, "The Pontiff has passed. So too the ril that sought me, and all the Temple guard. The Temple is remade. Your decision shall be whether to stand within it or without."

On the nave floor, the Kultash finished with a cry that boomed through the hall. The tone lingered in the air as though their voices had plucked the dome above like a bell. Breea sensed horses galloping toward the front of the Temple. Erissohn sat straighter as he considered her words. Life had returned to his eyes, and at long last she glimpsed in them a man who wielded sufficient power to oppose the Temple. Inside, she rejoiced. Perhaps all the man needed was hope. The city's fate lay in his hands, as well as those of his chief ally, the Master of the Surreda Weapons Guild who followed in Arin's wake with uncertain steps.

These men would swear upon their souls to care for this city or their blood would stain this ancient floor. A flicker of brilliance shimmered through the altar stone. She stood. The Lord Governor did as well, though slowly as he stared down the nave in surprise and consternation. Fear flickered across his countenance and he turned to find Breea watching him. She held her gaze steady on him, and he looked down, then hid his hands in his sleeves as they began to quiver.

Arin led Master Piad up to the altar. Scaukra followed them slowly as he stared about the building. White-clad Kultash swept around behind the three to encircle the platform. Breea motioned for Scaukra to stand with Neprawn, and for Batusha to remove the chairs. Sakuront took the place at Breea's right hand. Arin, dressed once more in Batusha priest robes, stood at her left, though back a little. Breea gestured to Guild Master Piad that he should stand opposite her. Stunned and defiant, he obeyed. Neither he nor Erissohn looked at each other. Light from the altar illuminated their clothing and faces with soft, clear light.

Breea put her hand on the altar, then indicated that they were to do the same. The men followed her example, and she could see the courage it took for them to do so.

"Remove your hands at your peril, rulers of Gimlek," she said and summoned the altar's power.

The stone grew hot. Sweat beaded the faces of both men and they finally looked at each other. Their fellowship was clear. She had been right.

"Upon this altar I bind your souls to the fate of this city. As the city, so too your souls. Rebuild. Resupply. Be the heart of the realm. Make steel of the golden grain, and anchor Yash with your strength. Swear it. Upon your souls. In Het's sight. Upon this altar."

Master Piad was staring at her in wondering fear, his mouth open.

Lord Erissohn dropped his other hand to the altar and cried, "I swear!" His face shone with sweat and fervent belief.

Master Piad's eyes fixed upon his hand, fingers splayed on the bright stone. His shoulders fell.

"I will," he whispered, as though surprised by himself. "By Lutna. By Het, and upon your word, Chosen One. By my soul."

"Be it so," said Breea.

She straightened. As their fingers left the stone, she struck the dome above with her will. It responded with a booming tone that resonated in her chest and vibrated in the stone beneath their feet. Both men flinched and clutched at their hands as though in pain.

When the echoes had faded, Breea said, "The host marches at dawn. There is much we need of you this day. Priest of the guild, Arin, will tell you what the host requires."

Master Piad and Lord Governor Erissohn bowed to her, then followed Arin down the platform steps.

With a look at Sakuront and her Batusha masters, Breea stepped down and followed Arin and the city rulers down the nave and out into the open to the sun.

Breea stepped to the edge of the landing where Piad and Erissohn had halted. The Lord Governor's retinue stood in a nervous group at the north end of the landing. Breea surveyed the crowd that had formed. They seemed to rock back at the sight of her and Sakuront, and a murmur rose like the breath of a sleeping giant. A few hundred Kultash in bright chainmail and her Batusha masters had formed a cordon at the base of the stair, with Batusha holding the center. The townsfolk kept their distance from the warriors. The entire courtyard was filled with townsfolk staring in quiet awe. More were walking up through the high city streets.

Impulsively, Breea walked down the steps and whispered into the ear of a Batusha master. "Let them pass."

The warrior chak'ood then led the other masters aside, which left a wide gap in the center of the line. Breea beckoned to the throng of townsfolk. No one moved. They did not seem to know what to make of her. She walked toward them, and those nearest tried to back out of her way but made little progress for the people behind were trying to see. A few touched foreheads and others began to prostrate themselves, but Breea stepped close and made two rise—a nobleman in brocade and pantaloons and a lank-haired woman in layers of dirty clothing. The rest paused their obeisance.

"This is your Temple," she said, and walked backward, pulling the pair forward.

Her words were passed back person to person through the crowd. Their faces reminded Breea of children unsure whether to be afraid or joyfully awed. She led the pair up the steps, then stepped aside and gestured for them to enter the Temple. She turned to find the crowd following through the gap left by Batusha. Smiling, Breea stepped out of the way. Sakuront made sign and the Kultash cordon backed up the stairs to the landing, then swung back to make a funnel for the crowd to follow. At another sign Sakuront's white-clad Kultash formed a wedge and stepped down the south end of the landing. People below made swift way for the warriors, though they stared at their white garments in wonder. Breea and Sakuront walked after the wedge, and Arin gestured for the city rulers to join them.

While passing she caught comments about her and Sakuront. Some repeated her words from earlier like a chant, and many were amazed to see the First of the Kultash in pure white. There were tears on more than one face, and Breea fought the urge to turn around and look again at what she had made. Something told her that this dawn illuminated the finest act of her life.

Looking out over the heads of the crowd, Sakuront guided the wedge to where Breea's horse was guarded by Batusha and more Kultash within the garden walls of a palace along the main road.

"Chosen," said the Lord Governor. He bowed deeply to her and Breea gave him a regal nod as Ajalay might have. He bowed again and backed away with a third bow. She hoped his resolve was enough, for there was little else she could do to bind him to his...with a shiver, she realized that she could bind him to his word, but the idea repulsed her. She had seen men bound by weaving in the city and the memory made her want to think of gladder things. The journey ahead needed preparation, and the first step of that was sustenance.

To Piad she said, "I am famished, Master Piad. Where can we find a good meal?"

For a long breath he could not seem to muster a reply.

Sakuront stepped up and raised a hand to the Temple. "Chosen, here will be the Ulshan of White Stone."

Breea's breath caught. It fit her desire for the city like sword to scabbard. With Kultash dedicated to defend the white Temple, she could leave the city. She had only to enable its survival until the Kultash could shape their Ulshan.

She eyed Sakuront's sword. She smiled, feeling a savage pleasure.

Sakuront frowned.

Breea said to him, "I long for the day when you wield that against Oregule."

"By your will, Chosen."

His reply gave her a little thrill. In it was respect and possibly a touch of warmth. She wanted to ask what had happened to him—how he had been captured and his escape and what came to pass when he was in the Temple when she remade it, but she merely nodded. On the road, perhaps, if she could get him to talk.

Breea looked up into his eyes and said, "I am going Oregule hunting."

The massive blade came over his head then down in front of him, horizontal and held out as though in offer. Breea touched the blade with her fingertips. Quiet bloomed from the weapon. They stared at each other in surprise, then with effortless grace, he lifted the blade and set it back on his shoulder. The sounds of people and horse and wind returned. Ootha swore under his breath.

Breea beckoned and led Sakuront through a massive wooden door into the house. A servant in yellow and green livery fled. Breea chose a room. It was splendid inside with walls of pale stone marbled with yellow.

After listening to ensure that no one was near, she said, "The wolf Oregule that we fought among the pines is the one that took my home, but I do not believe that I was the quarry."

"Were they not hunting you?" asked Sakuront.

"I sprang their trap early. I rode ahead. They could not have seen that I would."

Sakuront put the tip of his blade on the floor and rested his hands upon its guard. His eyes narrowed.

"Their target was the oxcart," he said.

"In part," said Breea. "When I rode ahead, I think the Oregule's Dauthaz wolves mistook me for their quarry. When they attacked later, the Oregule lured me into the forest, and most of the remaining wolves seemed intent upon tearing the cart to pieces. Their second goal was the spider Oregule's medallion. It was among Batusha's supply and was taken, but that is not what I fear. I fear that they succeeded in their aims."

Sakuront looked away south where the forest of the battle lay. "The girl who died."

Not trusting her voice, Breea nodded.

Letting essence-heat wash away her sorrow and fear, Breea said, "The Oregule sought three things: my death, the spider's medallion, and young Alach."

"Alach," said Sakuront slowly.

"Children who are destined to oppose and destroy the Oregule."

"Why children? You outmatch the Oregule."

"Perhaps. Singly. Yet the histories tell of Oregule weaving in concert. Terrible weaves, beyond sense to believe. Beyond what I can shape alone."

"What is a spider medallion?"

"The Oregules that I have faced each wore a medallion. Upon their defeat they turn to mist and all that remains is the white disk. I believe that it is the source of their essence. From it they can return. It is how the wolf took Limtir. I defeated the wolf, but on my journey to Yash it took Li—"

Trembling, Breea touched her chest where Lupazg's medallion had scarred her.

"The source of their essence," said Sakuront as he sought to understand. "Has the spider…returned? Are they two?"

"Likely."

"Will they hunt you?" asked Sakuront.

"They may yet try, but if so why have they hesitated? Beyond you and I there is nothing in this city that could oppose them. They are hunting the children, Sakuront. When the army marches, I will hunt them down and crush them. Will you join me?"

For the first time since she had met the First of the Kultash, his white teeth flashed in a smile.

CHAPTER 22

A Sword for Gold

THE SOUND OF A BELL WOKE TAM. HE SAT UP IN
the bed, dislodging a girl from his chest. The sound had been
like a Temple bell, but deep, as though Het himself had
struck a bell the size of the world. Floorboards creaked
beyond a curtained partition. Tam rolled out of bed and
tugged on this pants. By the light of a guttering candle he
saw the curtain move. Rust looked out, eyes wild and
questioning.

A young woman's voice implored beyond the curtain,

"Rusty, come back. It's cold."

Rust looked ready to fight, but not sure where the enemy lay. He'd heard the bell as well. Something had happened. They got dressed fast. At almost the same time they stepped out from the curtains, each holding a candle saucer. Together they took the dark stairs two at a time down to the common room. At the bottom they paused to survey the sleeping men sprawled about. They were a mix of city guard, Yasharn infantry, and a scattering of Batusha warriors.

In a tight voice Tam said, "I need my sword."

"Tettle has mine," said Rust.

Tam looked at him in surprise.

Rust shrugged. "Saw him pick it up."

Tam felt his face flush. He hadn't thought of his sword after winning and then there had been girls all around him. Master Tafitamar was going to flay him if the sword was gone.

Rust said, "Let's see if he got yours too."

Tam nodded, willing to hope.

They left their candles by the door and went out into the cold air of the street. The sky above was strange, almost as if there were two dawns. The boys looked at each other, then Tam led the way down the street and into the courtyard of the city barracks. They jogged past sleepy guards and piles of gear to the far end of the yard, where Tam saw the Broken Barrel captain pulling a tongue beam out from under the cart. Rust didn't greet his captain, just ran up and grabbed a loop of chain and set to helping. Tam joined in and soon they had the tongue section out in the open.

The company captain started arranging the chains, looking at their joins to the wood, checking turnbuckles. Rust helped, and asked as they worked, "Captain, my sword?"

The man glanced up at the high cart seat. Rust went to climb the cart, but the captain's voice brought him up short.

"Only 'cause they was women," said the captain. "No man of the Barrel walks away from his blade."

"Sir," said Rust with lowered eyes.

"How was she?" asked the captain.

Rust's eyebrows went up and his face relaxed in blissful memory. "They…" He didn't finish.

The captain chuckled. "Find me a smith. If there are none who'll come, we'll stoke it ourselves."

"Captain?" said Rust.

The man straightened and eyed the boys. Tam realized he'd known all along that they were here for more than helping him.

Tam spoke first. "Captain Tettle, have you seen a guild sword? My sword?"

"Wish I had. Looked a bit after picking up this one's. Ask Beelt. Got a welt the size of a bull's nut on his skull. Won't tell me how it came to him. Mayhap he challenged one of them guild lads."

The implied accusation made Tam flush. If it had been an aspirant who had struck the little boy, then Batusha honor had been pissed on by its own.

Rust bent to look under the cart, but the captain said, "He's in the pen."

"The pen?" said Rust, appalled.

Tettle simply grinned and returned to his work.

Tam followed Rust to the stable pen, leaping to the top rail after him. The ground inside looked like a mountain range made of sleeping oxen. Their heads curled around toward their bellies, one horn reaching almost to their hind leg. Nestled in the curve of a bull's neck sat a tiny boy. Tam marveled, for the kid was less than half the size of the animal's head. Even in deep shadow Tam could see that one side of the boy's face was swollen with a lump pushing out his hair above his left ear. He looked haggard, like he hadn't slept all night. The ox's eyes opened and the head swung around to look at Tam and Rust. The bull shifted his weight to stand, and the boy leapt up and caught the base of one horn. As the bull stood, the boy swung up his legs and with one foot on the bull's head flipped himself on top of the horn with a gasp of pain.

The head rose. Rust reached out and put a hand on the bull's snout. An immense tongue reached up to touch Rust's forearm. Nostrils big enough to fit Tam's fist flared as it sniffed. Beelt ran down the animal's snout and into Tam's arms.

They sat on the top rail of the fence and listened as Beelt explained through hiccups of misery how he'd seen a Batusha aspirant take Tam's sword and belt and followed him until he came to the group of aspirants from the day before. They'd seen him then, and caught him and forced him not to tell by threatening to slit the throats of the Lillhup if he spoke, but when they left, he got up and followed them again. He saw the biggest sell the sword for gold to a blade merchant in the market. When he was seen and caught again, he stabbed one with his eating dagger then fled all the way back to the Lillhup. The aspirants weren't dumb enough to attack him among the oxen, but they promised to flay him and the oxen as soon as they found him again.

Rust comforted the boy, but Tam was impatient to find the merchant. At Tam's silent urging, Rust retrieved his broken sword from under the cart seat. Rust pulled his dagger from the belt and held it in offer.

Honored, Tam accepted the blade and thrust it into his belt, then asked, "What were you going to do with the shovel? Yesterday."

Rust knew exactly what Tam was asking, but felt shy about speaking his true intent.

Tam misunderstood and took the silence to say that Rust would have shoveled the yard at the aspirant's command. Tam looked down to adjust his belt.

"Beat him bloody," said Rust.

"With a shovel?"

Rust shrugged.

Tam laughed and said, "I should have let you."

They both grinned, then noticed Captain Tettle watching them. The man gave a short nod. They set out at a run for the marketplace Beelt had described. The market was setting up, but a merchant was there, a scarred graybeard in a booth surrounded by cheaply made weapons.

When Tam and Rust stopped beneath his awning, he smiled with a predatory eye and said from his rug-draped chair, "Batusha and Broken Barrel. Looking for some steel to continue your duel?"

It set Tam back that the man knew who they were. He must have seen them fight, or maybe the story of their battle had been told.

Rust said, "You bought a sword yesterday."

"Bought a few. You looking to improve on that?" He glanced at Rust's broken blade in its rough scabbard.

Tam, "You bought one from Batusha aspirants."

The man rose from his chair and glanced at Tam's empty waist. His eyes narrowed to lazy slits.

"Could be."

Tam stepped forward aggressively and the graybeard went cold, but held his ground.

"You will return the blade," said Tam. "I will retrieve your payment. Fair trade."

Cloth parted and a burly man emerged from the back.

"A trade made is a trade done," said the merchant.

Tam felt battle calm settle over him.

Rust stepped up. "Tam, let's bring the captain."

Tam shook his head. "These shits will vanish like piss in a stream."

The burly man stepped forward, fists curling. Tam was ready, but Rust was faster. There was a crack of bone and the burly man fell in a quiet heap, jaw disfigured and hanging loosely from his face. Shocked, the merchant stared, then flinched at the bite of Tam's dagger pricking his belly through his clothing. Tam forced him back through the curtain. Rust came in rubbing his knuckles.

The blade merchant's eyes were savage, but wary.

"Where?" said Tam, pushing on the dagger.

The man hissed, baring his teeth. "Chest."

Rust looked about, then went through another curtain.

"It's locked!" he called.

When the merchant said nothing, Tam didn't ask where the key was, he simply pushed the dagger a finger's width deeper. The merchant groaned and there was murder in his eyes. He tried to grab Tam's wrist and knee him in the groin. In pure reflex Tam twisted aside from the knee and slid his dagger's blade in to the hilt, angling it up under the ribs as short-blade litany taught. The graybeard's eyes went wide. He shook his head in denial and died.

In that moment Rust emerged from the back chamber and two city guardsmen entered from the front, swords in hand. The merchant hit the cobbles with a thud. Instead of attacking, the guards looked from Tam to Rust to the blood dripping from Tam's dagger then down at the dead man at his feet. Despair washed over Tam. Not only had he lost his sword, he'd murdered a man to retrieve his mistake.

The moment held—no one daring to move. A sliver of hope let Tam breathe. The guards appeared to recognize him and Rust. Doubtless the guardsmen had watched his fight with Rust and knew that if they attacked, they were not likely to win. What then of their duty? Tam could not explain why he had killed the merchant—his body had acted before thought.

Rust cleared his throat. "They stole the guildsman's sword at the challenge. The blade is in this chest here which is also like to have the blade seller's gold."

The first guard took a step back and sheathed his sword. His fellow looked confused, but put his blade away as well.

"You better show us that chest," said the first man.

"Yeah," said the second, catching on.

"This way, sir," said Rust, and held open the curtain.

Tam shivered and collected himself. He was a warrior of Batusha. This was not his first kill.

A search found a set of keys in an inside pocket of the merchant's coat. The curtain to the back parted and Tam tossed the keys at the city guard who stood there. The man flinched but managed to catch the jangling metals. They were nervous, these guards. That could be useful.

With deliberate care, Tam cleaned the dagger on the merchant's clothing, and thought about his next moves. A lock clicked in the other room. Tam sheathed the dagger and strode into the small space. A long chest against the back wall was open. Within lay a dozen fine weapons nestled among bolts of cloth, a few leather sacks that looked to be full of coin, and a few bottles of dark amber liquid. Tam brushed past the guards and lifted out his sword and dagger. Both weapons were wrapped in the leather belt he had tooled himself. He put them on, then straightened his cloak and faced the guards.

"The guild owes you a service for your assistance in retrieving our stolen property."

The taller guard gave Tam a short bow, his experienced eyes backed with relief. Tam saluted the man with back-fist to palm, then whirled and strode out. Rust, caught off-balance by the sudden reversal of their fortune, didn't move.

Outside, Tam stepped over the body of the burly man without looking at him. He paused as though to survey the curious crowd that had formed, but he was listening for Rust. Rust came running, and Tam set out. People stepped out of his way as Rust's bootfalls followed him across the square. When they left the square down an empty street, Rust stepped up beside Tam.

After a look over his shoulder, Rust said, "Hounds, that was…"

The Broken Barrel oxboy looked so relieved it nearly made Tam laugh. It lacked all truth that Rust was afraid of anything or anyone beyond the men who had trained him. Tam knew his skill, but Rust seemed unaware of how much power he held. He was easily the strongest and fiercest young warrior Tam had ever fought. Tam slapped his shoulder and Rust flinched under the blow.

Ignoring the reaction, Tam said, "My belly is afraid my throat's been cut. Let's find some food."

Rust looked unsure. "I should go back. Tettle…Captain will—"

"He won't," said Tam. "We'll go back to the tavern."

"Can't," said Rust, scuffing the filth-crusted ice of the street with his heels as he walked.

Tam got serious. "Rust, you are my blade brother, and we have work to do for the Chosen. Stand to."

They stopped. Tam backstepped two paces then saluted Rust with a cracking back-fist to palm. With a fluid motion Tam drew his sword and offered its tip to Rust, who stared like the world was spinning.

Tam spoke in a clear, practiced voice, for he had recited these words a hundred times in the guild hall, but never to another warrior. "I am Tam Karin Beddig, first aspirant of the Batusha Weapons Guild. My Service to you."

Rust looked at the blade with dawning understanding, then flushed with emotion. He stood straight and bowed.

Tam said, "Touch my blade with yours."

The heavy-infantry oxboy drew his broken half-sword and clinked Tam's blade. For a moment Tam froze with disbelief. Rust's weapon was like a bar of pitted rust that was vaguely sword shaped, though its edges gleamed.

Fortunately Rust didn't seem to notice the reaction. With a flourish, Tam sheathed his sword and set out up the road. He heard Rust put his blade away then jog to catch up. They walked in high spirits until they found the tavern. Unarmored Aska-Wuthos were piling out the front doors looking up at windows where flush-faced women leaned out, touching their chests over their hearts and extending their hands to the men who waved and called what sounded like bits of poetry, though they spoke it in a language Tam had never heard. One woman cupped her breast and offered that, and a soldier started back inside. His fellows caught him, swung him round, and pushed him down the street.

The soldiers nodded to Tam and Rust as they passed. Before going in, Tam stopped to look down the street at the Aska-Wuthos.

"You know who that was?"

Rust looked. "Aska-Wuthos?"

"Her champions. Blessed them so they could fight Dauthaz. They fight like she does."

"You saw the Chosen fight?"

Tam suppressed a grin at Rust's worshipful face, for in truth Tam felt the same, and he said, "I saw her slay a hundred Temple guard with blades of green fire." Tam punctuated his statement by slapping a hand on the tavern door handle but didn't move when he saw raw emotions running across Rust's face like waves of infantry.

Tam made a questing sound and thrust his jaw at Rust for him to speak up.

"I saw her change from black nothing to a girl and then into red fire," said Rust. "She can kill a man without touching him."

Impressed, Tam nodded. They went inside into a roar of voices and a miasma of smells. The common room was so packed that men were standing by their fellows at some tables. Tam and Rust could see no chance for a place. More men were coming down the stairs near the back. A serving man in a filthy canvas apron took one look at Tam's uniform and waved them toward a set of doors at the back. Proud of being a guildsman, Tam led Rust through the throng. Both boys eyed the plates of meat and potato hash being dropped before men already seated. Neither of them had eaten since their battle. Girls and boys of a variety of ages wielding mugs and plates seemed to swim like fish through the room—their faces serious with focus. Tam noticed Rust watching the young servers. No one interfered with them, even to moving their feet or squeezing against their fellows to let the kids scoot past.

Rust saw Tam watching him and Rust shouted, "Like Beelt!"

Tam nodded and wondered why Rust was concerned with the kids. In the guild you didn't exist until you tested to aspirant.

The tavern doors swung open with a crash and Kultash in the thick mail of the First's Ulshan strode into the room. Men took notice, but the din continued unabated until a Kultash officer brought up a wolf-horn and let loose a piercing howl.

Into the grumbling quiet he called, "First's word! Gimlek Ulshan have been summoned."

A voice replied, "No Kultash here."

The officer ignored the response and gestured for his men to enter. Dark looks followed the Kultash as they made their way across the room.

"We're the Army of the Chosen," said the voice, as though that explained why there were no local Kultash.

The warrior in the lead sneered through his beard and turned to spy out the speaker without stopping. A boy in his path with two full mugs in each hand backed away, then pressed against seated men and desperately lifted his mugs out of the way. Men at the table reached to help him, but the Kultash did not see, and ran him down. Beer splashed and soldiers rose with bellows of outrage. The Kultash kicked the boy so hard that he slid across the floor and into the legs of the next set of chairs.

Rust's hand was on his blade hilt before thought, but he found himself unable to draw. A hand had closed about his bicep like a band of iron gripped a cart wheel. The room went loud with a rumble of moving chairs as every man stood.

While Kultash and soldiery glared at one another, a voice whispered beside Rust's ear, "Do not kill them. Beat them until they piss blood. Shame them to the fifth son. But never kill a Kultash."

The iron hand tightened until Rust nodded through his rage. The grip released and he turned to see a tall, broad man with clear blue eyes and a clean-shaven face straighten up beside him. The man's shirt was woven of cloth that looked almost like water. Aska-Wuthos. Tam nudged him from the other side and Rust saw Tam staring at the man with a touch of awe. A champion of the Chosen! Had her champion just urged him to beat a Kultash near to death? Did the champion think he could? The man looked down at him and gave a slight nod. Inside, a barrier Rust hadn't known was there bent then snapped like an axle breaking under load.

Rust stepped past Tam. Heads turned and soldiers gave way after a glance at his face. Rust felt a livid awareness of everything in the room including Tam's soft bootfalls as the Batusha boy guarded his back.

The Kultash who had kicked the boy saw Rust coming and his right hand few to his sword hilt. Rust leapt and with his left hand caught the man's wrist before the blade was half drawn. The Kultash was taller and broader than Rust. Unconcerned by the boy's move, the big warrior heaved against Rust's grip with the intention of drawing through the impertinent boy, likely hoping to gut Rust in the process. The blade showed another hand's breadth of metal, then stopped. The Kultash's free hand flashed for Rust's face but Rust had seen the intention and deflected the blow inward across his body and caught the arm at the wrist. The Kultash warrior tried to wrench his hand back, but Rust held it firm.

Looking into the Kultash's eyes, Rust began to pull the warrior's arm back across their bodies. The Kultash bared his teeth and strove to twist out of Rust's grip. Nothing happened. The arm kept moving and the man grunted as he tried to draw his blade once more. Rust tightened his grip yet further and fear flashed across the Kultash's face. Rust twisted the man's sword arm until the warrior was forced to let go of the handle. The blade hilt tilted down and the weapon slid out to the floor. The Kultash heaved against Rust with wild effort, face gone purple. Rust's boots slid on the planking, but he held.

Kultash warriors who tried to draw their swords found themselves grabbed by a dozen hands each, then held in place to watch. There was a commotion by the door and calls of threats and outrage. Rust ignored everything but the enemy in his grip and straightened his wrists to force the Kultash warrior down. When the man's knees thumped against the floor, Rust bellowed all the rage built within him for every year of his life under the power of men who would kick a boy. The man's wristbones gave with muffled cracks and the Kultash whined in agony. Rust let him go and the man wilted to the floor.

Trembling, Rust turned to see a Yasharn officer kneeling by the unmoving form of the child. The officer's face was grim. Rust's hands curled into fists and he swiveled back.

A Kultash watching cried, "Dauthaz! Your death is ordained. Het's wrath upon you and your kin!"

The room stilled to deathly unease at the declaration until laughter spilled over them. The tall Aska-Wuthos who had advised Rust strode up to the immobilized Kultash.

"Nay, Sa Kultash. Fairly met, and fairly won. You have no claim."

"Death upon you, Wuthos!" cried the man.

The Aska-Wuthos smiled as though he had been waiting for that. "I accept. Name your weapon."

The Kultash bared his teeth and his nostrils flared. But he said nothing.

The Aska-Wuthos seemed to reflect on the Kultash's rage, then said to himself, "Yes, that bears truth. By the Chosen whose blessing I bear, that is the path. Brothers, release the good servants of Het's will. We shall take the Dauthaz claim to the First and to the Chosen, and seek their judgment."

Hands let go the Kultash, who looked sick. He didn't move. In a grating voice he said, "Fairly won."

"Well said," replied the Aska-Wuthos. "All that remains is the honor debt between us."

From the door a line of Kultash strode brusquely into the center of the room. The foremost wore an officer's sash. The man's face was sour and angry, then disgusted as he looked down at his man. The broken warrior was hunkered over his blade making futile efforts to pick up the weapon, whimpering in pain. His cohorts raised him and sheathed the weapon in his scabbard. The officer whirled and led the Kultash out.

When they were gone, the soldiers filling the tavern roared with glee, and what felt like a hundred hands clubbed Rust's back with such approving fury that he stumbled forward under the blows. They put a chair on a stout table and lifted him into it with cries of "There's a man! A bear! Breaker of wolves!" At the urging of dozens, the prettiest serving girl climbed up and sat herself in his lap. A path formed across the room and the roar calmed as the little boy who had been kicked limped down the aisle with a mug of beer in hand. The shock on Rust's face made men laugh.

A city soldier ruffled the little boy's hair as he passed and said, "Takes more than a kick from Het's hounds to break little Bootstrap."

A man lifted the boy to the tabletop and Rust reached out with a shaking hand and accepted the mug from the boy's own trembling hand. Rust took a long drink and the men called their approval, though most seemed also to be calling for more beer.

Rust shouted to the boy over the din. "You do a good beetle!"

The boy looked like he didn't know if that was a good thing. Rust stuck his arms akimbo and made a face like he was dead. The boy grinned and blushed. In response, the tavern girl spoke into Rust's ear then relaxed against him. He enjoyed her warmth, emptying the mug.

After a few mugs more he looked about for Tam and found the aspirant near the stair to the upper floors speaking with a gaunt Batusha warrior in a master's cloak who stood on the last step. The master warrior was looking at Rust as Tam spoke. Under the master's gaze, Rust sobered a measure. He sat up and gave an apologetic smile to the girl to ask her to rise. She did and straightened her skirts, watching him with lidded, appreciative eyes. Unsteady, Rust almost fell off the table, then made his way to Tam.

The master warrior's gaze was like Tam's first appraisal, but far darker. Rust stood straight, or as straight as he could with the beer sloshing in his empty gut. The Batusha master led them to the door at the back of the hall, and Rust marveled how a path seemed to make itself magically before him. Once inside the back room, thick doors were closed and the tavern noise went soft and distant. Here the talk was relaxed. Some senior Yasharn officers of the Chosen's army raised mugs to Rust. The food smelled good and Rust's stomach gave a rumble that would have done Slayer honor. A beautiful raven-haired woman was suddenly in front of him smelling of olibanum and sex. She laid a warm hand on his cheek and kissed his forehead, her loose hair tickling his face.

Lost in a heart-thundering daze, he had to be led to a table by Tam.

A local officer in an embroidered uniform said, "Bootstrap's her nephew. You earned with the Night Hawk, boy. Her word's better than coin in this city."

Rust sat with Tam at a small round table. He looked about, but the woman was gone. The Batusha master was there, sitting at his own table, but thankfully not looking Rust's way. Food was brought and Rust ate until his head cleared and his belly ached. He kept seeing the Kultash in front of him, face twisted in helpless pain. Rust flexed his hands and wondered what he would do the next time a Broken Barrel soldier tried to cuff him. Rage flashed through him. Tam looked at him sharply, and Rust leaned back in the chair with a deep breath to calm himself. He had his answer. A young Batusha aspirant he hadn't noticed brought a few sheaves of parchment and a small, narrow wood box and dropped them on the table. What was that for?

Tam emptied his mug of cider. "Can you draw?"

Rust shrugged. He'd never even touched a piece of parchment.

"Master Tafitamar said we should draw our litanies to compare for the Master," said Tam. "We'll need to show too, of course, all strikes that struck true which litany did not illuminate, and counters if we can make them."

Rust nodded, but the thought of failing the Chosen made him queasy.

"What did she say to you?" asked Tam. "On your lap?"

Rust's fear faded for a moment, and he grinned. "She's done in the hall at nine bells."

"She got a friend?" asked Tam, and they snickered, thinking of the night just past.

Tam pushed his plate away and opened the wood box which was full of lengths of charcoal. He pulled the parchment to him. While Tam chose what he wanted, Rust looked across the room at the Batusha master. The warrior was lean and wore his beard in a goatee, though he had not shaved in recent days. The aura of coiled threat that most of the Batusha men had was there, but something about him seemed far away.

"Master Scaukra Tafitamar," said Tam in a whisper. "Trains us aspirants. He brought the Chosen to Batusha before even she knew that Het had chosen her. He has sight."

Rust looked away from the warrior with the feeling that the man knew that Rust was staring at him. Tam had drawn a series of figures with amazing speed—as graceful and precise as his sword work.

"Spear litany," said Rust, recognizing the feint and strike he'd used on Tam.

Tam's mouth tightened with remembered pain. Rust's spear strike to Tam's thigh had nearly won Rust the bout.

"I should na hit so hard," said Rust.

With a disturbed frown, Tam said, "The blow was fairly won."

Rust felt himself blush. A warrior did not apologize for

a landed strike. He simply didn't want to lose the first friend he'd ever had.

Tam shook his head like Rust was a strange one and returned to sketching.

Rust studied it and asked, "What's that?"

"Counter."

"You can't. Not like that."

Across the room Scaukra shifted his eyes to the arguing boys. They stood up, cast about for something to use as weapons, then gave up and used their arms like spears, testing redirection and leading feints. The sight brought a touch of peace to Scaukra, for in the hearts of such young men lay the future. If they lived.

The muted roar of the outer room settled like ash, and Scaukra stood. The boys hadn't noticed the sound, but both, he was pleased to see, caught his motion and their right hands swung to blade hilts. Other men in the room were already in motion toward the door. Lancer Grent, who led the army's rear guard, was quickest to the doors, but he checked with Scaukra before he pushed them open.

At the front of the tavern, a thick knot of men stood around the door—immobile, listening. The rest of the room was rising, but quietly so as to hear what others were passing back. Scaukra and the officers strode into the room.

Men near turned to look at them and one said in a low tone, "The First has declared the Gimlek Ulshan corrupt. Kultash hunt Kultash and the Ulshan is filled with blood."

A man closer to the door listened to a fellow then called to the room, "The Pontiff is dead!"

Men and officers moved up to listen, but Scaukra knew what was being said. Het's will had come. Corruption was being cleansed. And none of it mattered. He shuddered in the echo of his visions. Tam and Rust came up as the tavern hall began to empty into the street where townsfolk were moving past in the same direction.

Scaukra cried, "Hold!"

The whole group stopped and looked at him.

"Pa-hoc Hean, look to your men. The Chosen will act."

Lancer Grent replied, "I return to the barracks. We will saddle."

There was a rumble of agreement from Breea's men.

Scaukra gave them a nod, and turned away and walked back to his seat in the far room.

Tam and Rust followed him, then sat over at their table. Scaukra picked up his drink and downed it in a burning gulp. It didn't help. He clapped his chalice to the table to demand a refill anyway. With her healing, Breea Banea had burned a foreign sensation into his heart…he closed his eyes and saw her walk into the Crystal Chalice in Yash, nervous and beautiful, her black hair catching light from the lanterns—innocent and unknowing of her power. With her arrival his plots and plans lost their purpose, for in her presence the pain faded, and he felt—implausibly—as though he were home once more. The cry of gulls over the walls of his home city were like the calls of children dying…

A girl's gasp snapped him back to the room. Had he said something? The serving girl held a reed-woven bottle. He leaned forward and took it from her and she scurried away. The boys at their table went quickly back to work. He poured himself another measure, then ignored the drink. He rose and walked out.

Tam and Rust leaned over to watch him stride through the outer room. The tavern was all but empty, and eerily quiet. Master Tafitamar stopped in the open doors, framed against the light, his cloak billowing slowly in a breeze from the street. Tam and Rust exchanged a look then Tam swiftly rolled the parchment and gathered the charcoal into its case.

"He sees something. I must go."

Rust's jaw clenched. He did not know how to say that he wanted to go with Tam without sounding foolish. He knew but one word that represented unity of purpose.

Rust said, "Wall."

Tam understood, and gripped Rust's shoulder. Together they crossed the hall to join Scaukra in the doorway.

The master's eyes looked through the people passing.

He turned on the boys. "Find her."

CHAPTER 23

Spe's Storm

TAUMEA SLOWED TO A HALT IN THE SUNLIT SNOW.
Twenty strides away the knee-deep tracks from his night run
up the ridge vanished into a smooth and unbroken expanse
beneath the leafless oaks. Feeling uneasy, he checked his
back trail. The camp of the night before was close, though
the girls should have moved at first light. The winter midday
sun was faintly warm against his face and he squinted
against its brilliance. The only sound was an occasional drip
of water from the tree branches. A faint, cold breeze too light

to move the branches carried no scent.

Cautious, he walked up to the edge of the perfect snow. Left and right he could make out the edge of the affected area stretching away in either direction. Where he stood the snow was covered with a hoarfrost of sparkling facets, but what lay ahead looked fresh and soft. He went to a knee and found the snow fluffy as though freshly fallen. There was no new snow on the branches of the trees. Haunted Lands, indeed. Was this the correct path?

To his right a massive head stretched forward past his shoulder. His sword whipped out as he leapt away to land in the snow five strides from the trail. The apparition of the night before sniffed the edge of the fresh snow. Taumea's shoulders fell and his blade tip scored the snow as he lowered the weapon. With a sigh he sheathed his blade and waded back to the trail. The beast continued to sniff along the edge.

"Strange, is it not?" said Taumea. "By the girls or some other power?"

One tufted ear flicked his way, then the apparition walked out onto the fresh snow—casting no shadow as it went and leaving no sign of its passing. Taumea took a careful look in all directions, then followed it, his passage making a trench in the powdery snow. The creature loped away. Taumea hitched his sword and set out after it at a run. Snow exploded forward with each stride, and in spite of what was to come and why he was running, Taumea found himself smiling.

They came to the place on the ledge where the night's camp had been. The apparition circled the clearing, sniffing the snow, then sat and looked at Taumea.

"Blood and martyrs," he muttered as he looked about the

untrodden snow.

He went to look off down the slope. Far down, near the valley bottom, he caught sight of their trail up the ridge. He looked back the way he'd come, then nodded. The snow had been smoothed in a big ring around the campsite. The girls.

He plowed his way up to the top of the ridge and surveyed the ruins in sunlight. The apparition wove in and out among the remnant walls as though looking for something or someone. It seemed forlorn.

Taumea touched the gem at his waist and the apparition came trotting out of the ruin toward him, then shook its fur like a bear. It looked at him with an expectant gaze, head up and ready. The thing was so big that its face was on a level with Taumea's. It was a magnificent beast, powerful and lithe with eyes that were easy to look into though they seemed to absorb the sunlight like dark amber water.

Without warning it leapt away, heading down the broad ridgetop, dodging tree trunks with wild grace. Taumea sprinted after in a welter of snow.

—◈◈◈—

Anila hummed in the saddle and stared in concentration up into the cloudless sky. One hand held Azsark's reins and the other was wrapped around Spe, who was standing on the saddle seat facing backward to watch the snow whirl like water in their wake. They were last in the line of horses. Spe hummed too, her hands gripping Anila's coat to brace against Azsark's movement. Bitter-cold Breath flowed down out of the sky and into the snow at the horses' feet. The ice roiled and billowed with Breath all the way down to the rocks and grasses beneath. Azsark walked carefully as though he were fording a stream. The whirl settled in their wake like wind-smoothed sand.

The Breath was strong within Anila, linking her to Spe's sun-like power. Any time Spe started singing louder, Anila gave her a squeeze and Spe quieted her voice and Anila wrapped Spe's power with her own, over and over until Spe's flame seemed to settle. The shape of the air and the land came to Anila in a picture she couldn't see, but somehow knew—every tree and animal and every layer of air and the sun's Breath beaming through them.

Spe gasped, heat flaring. Anila squeezed her and struggled against her sister's Breath as it burned through the layers she'd wrapped around that molten ember.

At the edge of Anila's awareness a presence came running. It felt like neither man nor animal, and it was strong.

In the same moment, Spe said, "Ani, look!"

Anila twisted in the saddle and cried out, summoning her wind for a strike. Without being asked, Azsark whirled in the snow to face the thing rushing toward them. Spe turned in Anila's grip to keep it in sight.

From the head of the horse line, Anila felt the lady Valiena come charging down the line. She passed Anila, standing low in the stirrups, bow bent to her ear. The creature slowed its lope and looked back over its shoulder. The Limtir lord came running lightly through the snow. He raised an arm in greeting.

Spe clapped her hands and bounced.

Valiena held her bow drawn at the long-furred beast but did not release, frowning down the shaft of her arrow. Anila looked from lady to lord to beast. The lady lowered and eased her bow, then slid off her horse. Anila released the wind back into the sky. The beast looked up as though following it into the air, and Anila got a chill. The lady met the Limtir lord and they embraced. Anila relaxed, though she kept her gaze on the cat-like creature.

"Taumea, what is that?" asked the lady in a wary tone.

The beast was staring quizzically at Spe, who was staring back with a similar expression. The Limtir lord dug into a belt pouch and raised a golden gem to the sunlight. The creature vanished and Spe gasped. After kissing the lady, the lord came up to Azsark, patted the horse's neck, then raised the yellow gem.

"What make you of this?"

Spe reached for it, but Anila caught her hand. The Breath coming off the gem was the strangest thing Anila had ever sensed. Spe sat down, her eyes fixed upon the stone, though she did not reach for it again. Anila did not feel afraid of the gem, but a deep sense warned her to treat it with deference and care.

Anila said, "My lord, it is dangerous."

He grunted and grinned and she got the sense that he had stopped himself from saying the same of her and Spe.

He tucked the gem away, and said, "Your smoothing of the snow is song-worthy. Can you heal what my passage has done?"

Anila nodded, happy with his approval. Filling her lungs with cold air, she reached up into the deep sky and began to sing. The lord watched for a moment then led the lady and her horse back up the line.

When Taumea reached the horse saddled for him, he said to Valiena, "The Kultash have come through the Haltir tunnel."

Valiena closed her eyes for a moment. "How many?"

"The entire Ulshan. Ten pa-hoc."

"A thousand?" said Valiena. "They did not heed your warning."

"Val, have you any sign more of Breea?"

Valiena shook her head. "Opalah's light has guided us, but I have recognized no signs beyond what I saw in the canyon, but Taumea, I know our path is illuminated."

Song swelled and Taumea turned. The snow shifted like thick fog around Azsark's legs.

"They are learning."

"That and more," said Valiena.

Taumea rested his left hand on the hilt of his sword and raised his eyes to the mountains. "That is well."

"Taumea, what is it that you brought?"

"An ally, I hope," he said. "Helped me sight the Kultash."

With a sigh Valiena leaned against him, her hair soft under his chin. "What are we to do?" Her voice was tired.

"We wait for a sign."

Leaning back in his arms, she looked up at him in surprise.

He looked about—his usual watchfulness, but also to make a point. "We seem alone in these Haunted Lands. Yet allies abound. Ancient pine and Alach children. This shadowless cat. I think we are meant to stay, Valiena. The cities west of here—Gimlek and Potre—are Yash. No succor there. East is Iplock which we have already fled. If Breea is to come as you believe, then we stay. We fight. And we survive until that day."

Face soft and proud at the same time, Valiena said, "I did not know you believed so truly in my sight."

Taumea touched the gem at his waist. "I looked into the

eyes of a spirit and it named me friend. Doubt withers in the face of such."

Valiena kissed him so intensely that his heart leapt. She broke off, leaving him breathless. From a saddlebag she retrieved a water jug and a leg of rabbit. He devoured the rabbit and emptied the jug, thinking fondly of things to do with her. Valiena saw his look and returned it, promising with her eyes. Before he could respond with action, she took the leg bone and wrapped it in a cloth among others.

The girls' song eased and the snow settled.

Taumea let his desire settle, and said, "We need a storm."

"From this?" Valiena squinted into the bright sky.

"Val, do you recall the Alach history Breea read to us as we crossed the Timaret?"

Valiena's gaze went to the girls. Then she looked up at him as though to ask if they were truly capable of what had been written.

Taumea looked away and peered down the spine of the ridge. Though the oaks were leafless, their numerous limbs were thick enough to obscure the view. "There is an outcrop ahead. I saw it from higher on the ridge. It will afford a good view. We must be there before nightfall. How is our food?"

"Bones for broth."

"Have you eaten today?"

Valiena gave a tiny shake of her head, and Taumea understood. She had fed the girls and kept the last leg for him.

"How fares their mother?"

Valiena met his eyes with a bleak expression. "We need to build a pole cart." In a whisper so soft he had to bend to hear, she said, "All that sustains her is that gem, but I fear she will never wake. Lashed to the saddle will end her. She needs warmth and shelter."

Taumea said, "I will hunt a place we can defend."

Valiena stroked the horse beside them. "It cannot be far. We have no more apple."

"How much farther?"

"I thank Opalah that they have lasted this far without good fodder. The Azsark apples carried them beyond any horse I know. I fear that without more their end will be swift. They need grass."

Without reply, Taumea walked to the girls. He examined the smooth expanse where his track had been.

"Well made."

Both looked pleased.

"I need a storm, Spe. Can you bring wind and snow?"

"I will pray!"

"Anila," said Taumea. "Can you gift the Breath to our mounts? They are weary, and today we need each one to share in your strength."

Anila nodded, back straight. The way her eyes flashed with pride of purpose gave him a pang of remembrance of Breea. Anila's eyes carried more than simple feeling. True power backed the little girl's gaze, more than he had seen yet. It was precisely like looking into Breea's eyes.

He took Azsark by the reins and led him up the line. With Valiena holding the reins of each horse, Anila leaned over from Azsark's saddle and put her hands upon the shoulder of each animal.

By evening the ridgetop had narrowed as they approached the outcrop, falling away to either side in steep rocky slopes. Taumea squinted ahead against the setting sun that flashed through the branches of the oaks until he rode into the cold blue shadow of the rocks. The forest ended at the face of an immense boulder. He reined up and the line of horses behind halted. At the far end, Anila's song ended in a cough. A gust of wind blew snow from the trees, and Taumea turned his horse and rode back. Spe turned around in Anila's arm and slid down in front of her with a thump. Spe leaned her head back on Anila's chest and was asleep in a breath. Taumea gave Anila a deep nod of thanks. The girl closed her eyes and laid her cheek on Spe's head, shoulders sagging. The snow leading to where they stood looked as fresh as a new-fallen blanket. Too fresh, for it lacked the bits of bark and lichen that lay scattered over the rest, but that was not something the Kultash would know.

Taumea rode back up toward the boulder. Valiena was checking on Tiyha. The rock face was sheer and a good thirty feet high. His hand jerked toward his sword when the cat apparition appeared at the top looking down at him. Shaking his head, he dismounted and made his way around the boulder on its north side. On the far side he found a snowy tumble of rocks and began to climb.

At the top a cold wind clawed at him, tearing away the residual warmth from the girls. He found the apparition sitting near on a bare pillar facing north, its fur catching the light of the setting sun and ruffling silently in the breeze. A series of snowy ridges ranged far away north to where a bar of black cloud seemed to be rising from the horizon. Sunlight caught at its ragged leading edge.

They were going to need shelter. The apparition turned west, into the sun, and Taumea followed its gaze.

The ridge they were on wound its way west, where at the edge of sight, similar ridges running down from the mountains softened into forested hills. In the evening haze only their peaks caught the light.

To the sunset, Taumea said, "Where are you, Breea?"

He turned a full circle searching the landscape below for a secure camp. There was nothing worth the name, but two valleys to the north and a league west a hill rose over the valley rim. The light of the sun lined patterns of straight snow, like walls. It was a massive castle ruin or possibly a small city. If they could get the horses there and out of sight, it would be an ideal place to shelter. The cloud northward was visibly larger, rolling south.

"Gods above," whispered Taumea, then spent a minute studying what he could see of the lands between him and the ruin on high hill. They would need to traverse it at night. Not difficult in moonlight, but in a storm…

Urgent, he slid down the rocks. The apparition jumped lightly down after.

At the horses he said to Valiena, "A storm comes. There is a ruin that may shelter us to the north."

Taumea led them back up the ridge until its north slope had gentled enough to enable a traverse down to the valley floor. The wind had risen, but was not so fierce that Taumea did not hear the Kultash wolf-horns howling far up the valley. Their nearness twisted worry into his heart. He looked back and saw Valiena checking her bowstring. Anila looked tired, and fearful of the sound. Spe slept on.

Taumea caught Anila's eye and made a smoothing motion with one hand. She closed her eyes and began to sing. The wind died around them, and for a moment he thought she had misunderstood his request. Snow began to shift in their wake. Anila was using the essence of the wind.

The horses moved well, and soon Taumea was looking across the small river that gurgled down this valley. He found a wide place to ford and led them across.

Near the top of the next ridge, Taumea could hear the wind whistling through the branches of the oaks above. The sun had set and all color with it. With a light kick, he urged his horse upward into the wind. The air felt bitter and full of teeth. Taumea shivered and pulled his cloak tighter.

The view was obscured by trees, so he urged his mount under an oak branch, lifted himself into the tree, and climbed swiftly into its upper branches. The wind whistled, swinging the limbs and making his eyes water. The valley beyond was wider than the others and clothed in forest and snow-covered meadows. Opalah had risen over the mountains, sending her pale light down valley to where the castle hill reared above the valley floor. Examining the wider view, he grinned at himself. He was truly starting to see the world through Valiena's eyes to think of the moon as Opalah. Downvalley at the edge of sight, there seemed to be another kind of forest rearing dark and thick as though in full leaf and with no snow. Stars above were coming out, only to be obliterated by the rolling mass of cloud that dominated the sky. Below him Anila topped the ridge and the wind died. The girl's voice was ragged. Taumea checked the slope ahead of them then started down. At the lowest branch, he walked the limb over his horse, swung over and settled onto the saddle, anxious to reach the bottom of the next valley before cloud curtained the moon from view.

They didn't make it. Dark rushed across the valley, and Taumea tensed as though to take a blow. Before it hit he marked the edge of a river terrace through the forest below.

"Hold," he called back and dismounted.

Anila's voice broke and wind rushed at him. He said comforting words to his horse and stroked its neck, then worked his way back in the dark. Next to Valiena, he put a hand on her leg.

Over the wind he said, "Water bag."

Valiena handed it to him by feel and he felt the crackle of ice within.

Anila coughed hoarsely. Taumea hung the water bag from Azsark's saddle, untied Azsark's lead rope, then took a sleeping Spe from Anila's arms. He delivered Spe to Valiena, returned, and mounted Azsark behind Anila.

He wrapped his cloak around her and lifted the water sack and said, "Drink."

Anila did, then coughed. Taumea urged Azsark ahead and around the other horses. He took the reins of his horse and led them down, able to distinguish snow from tree but little else. The way leveled and he sighed with relief. They were on the flat of the river terrace. Putting the wind on his right, he followed it down valley, letting Azsark set the pace. Anila was a bundle of warmth for which he was grateful. They had used most of the blankets to wrap Tiyha. The wind gusted and Taumea turned his face from its claws. The dark deepened and Azsark slowed to a halt. Here they would camp. He felt Anila shift and she opened his cloak to look out.

"Not much to see," he said over the wind. "We must camp here."

"I think he knows the way," said Anila.

"Azsark?"

Anila didn't answer. A chill nothing to do with cold slid up Taumea's back.

"The cat?" he asked.

"Yes, my lord."

"You see him?"

She rocked and he guessed she was nodding.

"Take the reins, lass. Go on. I'll tie my horse to Azsark."

Anila gasped, though it sounded like surprise rather than fear.

Taumea knew the feeling when it came to the apparition. "What's he doing now?"

"He's in a tree. My lord. My Breath is back. I could sing again."

"Not yet. Hold here."

Taumea felt his way to Valiena. "Anila can see the spirit. How fares Spe?"

"Like a brazier of coals," said Valiena. "But she doesn't wake. Are we to camp?"

"I'm going to follow it, Val. Anila thinks the spirit wants to lead us."

"Opalah guide us."

"She has," said Taumea and knew precisely the look of surprised affection Valiena would show at his statement. "I'm going to link the horses. Stay with Spe."

"Taumea, the gem."

Pale gold light was streaming out the top of the leather pouch. He tugged off a gauntlet. The gem was warm as he raised it in his hand. Snowflakes streamed past in its light. Using the gem's faint glow, he made quick work of linking the horses.

After remounting Azsark he lifted the windward side of his cloak to shelter Anila and said, "Will you hold this?" He offered her the gem.

Eye's sparkling, Anila cupped her hands and Taumea set the gem in her palm. Its light flared and she gasped.

Taumea wrapped her with his cloak up to the neck and said, "Can you see him?"

"Yes."

"Take the reins." Into the dark where he imagined the apparition waited, he said, "Lead on."

It took a few tries before the apparition learned what a horse could traverse, then they were off the terraces and crossing the valley through meadow and copse. By the wind tearing at them Taumea judged their path as west-northwest. When the wind eased, Taumea heard river sounds. This would be the lee of the hill. Snow was falling heavily.

"M'lord? It wants us to cross."

"Not in this dark. We shall camp here in the shelter of the hill. You have done well, Anila. Do you see a grove that might give us shelter?"

Anila looked about and started to raise the gem, but Taumea covered the light.

"Care, lass. Make no beacon out here for enemy eyes. I took a chance on the slope, but we're in the center of the valley now."

Anila sat quiet for a while and Taumea was about to prompt her when the wind went silent about them. Over the river he heard a faint cry and drew back his hood. Hounds, braying. A roar he felt rather than heard quivered the air and the gem flared under the cloak. There was a faint savage scream of a dog in pain. Anila was breathing fast. When she looked up at Taumea for instruction, her eyes flickered with inner fire and shone with fear.

Taumea flung open his cloak and said, "Cross. Now."

He drew his sword and was shocked to find the haft humming in his hand.

With the gem in one fist, Anila put her other hand on Azsark's neck. The horse surged ahead and slid down the bank and into the water with a loud splash. The lead rope went taught, then the horse behind was following. Ice water seeped into Taumea's boots as Azsark forded the chest-deep channel, then the horse staggered up the rocks onto a snowy shore. Taumea leaned right, touching the warhorse's flank on that side with his heel. The horse turned, and by the returning light of the moon Taumea slashed through the lead rope. He held Anila to him with one hand and urged Azsark back toward the water. The air trembled as darkness thrashed in the trees of the far shore. Valiena was last to reach the shore, twisted in her saddle to face back, bow drawn to her ear. Taumea felt a surge of relief and pride. Light glowed through the clouds. Her bow loosed and a hound yelped. The sound of a snarling battle drew close.

Anila's breathing became panicked, and Taumea whispered in her ear, "Breathe easy. Our friend is fighting for us."

Keeping an eye on the far bank, he urged Azsark to the water's edge near Valiena. The sounds faded. When nothing more happened, Valiena unwrapped the pale scarf she had used to hold Spe to her torso.

To Taumea's questioning look Valiena said, "Peace itself."

The apparition appeared between their horses. Valiena stifled a shriek, then held Spe as though to comfort herself as much as the sleeping child.

The apparition was sitting facing the water. The head swiveled, and its wide, noble eyes looked to Taumea's face, then it nosed toward Anila with a gentle motion. When it was close enough, she reached out and pet the side of its massive jaw, her fingers rubbing through the fur. Taumea started. Snowflakes were landing on the broad head like a layer of down. Taumea tugged off a gauntlet and reached out. The massive head rose and cold soft fur ran through his fingers. Then it was gone.

Valiena sniffed. In cloud-filtered moonlight her face glistened with tears, though of wonder or fright or relief Taumea could not tell. Probably all. Her hood was back and her pale hair spilled out, seeming to glow in the faint light. She had one hand on Spe's head and the other held her bow with nocked arrow. He gazed at her, letting the vision calm him.

Anila raised her hand and offered the dark gem to Taumea.

"You keep it," he said.

Anila said, "It's yours."

He sheathed his sword carefully around Anila, then took the proffered jewel and tucked it back into its pouch. Before speaking, he held his hand there in thanks.

"Where now, Anila? Where is the path?"

"He's up there." She pointed in the dark.

"Is there a road?"

"Yes, lord."

Taumea retrieved the cut rope from his old mount and tied it to the end leading from Azsark's saddle. He considered checking on the girl's mother, but there was little they could do for Tiyha here.

"Lead on."

Valiena whispered a prayer to Opalah. Anila leaned forward and put both hands on Azsark's neck. Anila blew the way clear with soft cries that were almost birdlike, revealing an ancient road. The road was largely intact, though covered with rock in many places. Sound of the river faded below, replaced by a roar of wind above. Clouds of snow began to hiss down upon them. Taumea raised his hood.

Wind howl grew until it was close. The way leveled. Anila sang a few notes, then coughed. Azsark stopped, unable to continue. Ahead of them Taumea could make out deep drifts of snow.

Anila raised her arms. Breathing out in a gust, she swept her hands down and a weight of air dropped on them. Azsark took a nervous step back, but held his ground.

When Taumea got his breath back, he said, "Blood and martyrs, lass."

"Forgive me. Spe's storm answers…fast."

"Spe's storm?"

Taumea chuckled and Anila's luminous eyes looked up at him but he was looking into a tall darkness ahead of them that the moonglow could not penetrate. Within, the apparition's eyes reflected the gray light.

Anila asked, "Do I go ahead?"

"Yes. Go ahead."

Azsark's hooves clopped on bare stone, echoing as they entered.

CHAPTER 24

Knowledge Guide Your Blades

TAM WATCHED SCAUKRA UNTIL THE MASTER warrior vanished into the back room of the Spear and Porridge, then asked Rust, "Can you ride?"

Rust didn't want to reveal that he'd never ridden a horse, nor did he want to explain that he could ride the company oxen, so he said, "Not in the city."

Tam took that in with a frown, then said, "Hoi! You ride

the Lillhup?"

Pleased that Tam seemed impressed, Rust nodded then said of the townsfolk who walked past them in a steady stream, "Are they going to the Temple?"

"Stables," said Tam, looking the other way. "We need mounts." He dashed away and Rust followed.

Near the barracks a line of supply wagons was waiting to enter the inner yard, some of which looked to be abandoned by their drivers. The boys ran through the entry tunnel into the yard, where the officers from the tavern were calling in the guards. Men ran over and others began to trickle out the barracks doors. Tam led Rust into the section of the stable that housed the Batusha mounts.

Out in the yard, a piercing whistle echoed.

"Hounds," said Rust and went back outside.

Back by the ox pen, the entire Broken Barrel Company pivoted with lowered spears. The whistle trilled and the ends of the line bent back into a half-moon. The whistle piped and every other man stepped back and the formation tried to close into a bristling fist formation. There was some cursing and spears waved as they sought how to arrange themselves.

Tam came out and watched for a moment. "They are a little slow."

Rust chuffed. Fast or slow was not the matter. The Broken Barrel was not a company that drilled at dawn. Other than their single-minded chase across Yash to join the Army of the Chosen, he'd never seen the company awake at this hour. In truth he had expected them to fall back into the barrel at Gimlek. Secretly he wished them shamed before the Chosen. He knew their hearts—no different from the Kultash he'd crushed.

Tam said, "Go if you need to."

Rust's reply was edged. "I am not of the line."

Tam said no more. They walked back inside and Rust felt ashamed for his harsh tone.

"Captain Tettle is my arms master. In secret until the march. He wasn't always captain. Where's your horse?"

"Mule," said Tam with disdain, and pointed to stable hands saddling a long-legged mule mare.

Rust grinned.

Tam said, "You mind riding double?"

Rust shrugged. "We could get a cart."

Tam made a face.

They walked up and the mare mule's big head swung round. Tam reached into his coat and unfolded a cloth, holding its contents out with both hands. Her lips scooped up potato hash from the tavern. Tam moved the cloth so the mule found all the food. Rust decided not to call Tam out for what was clearly a deep fondness for his disparaged mule.

"Where do we look for the Chosen?" said Rust.

"We start at the guild hall."

Tam mounted and held a hand for Rust.

Rust shook his head. "I'll run."

"Your death," said Tam. He clicked his tongue and tapped the mule's flanks.

The barracks yard was already thick with men. Carts were being brought in through the tunnel and unloaded by gray-clad supplymen. Officers called direction and order was forged from the mass, but the mood was subdued. Rust had heard talk from the girls in the tavern. The city hummed with the news that the armed woman and the First were to take their army through the Haunted Lands. Rust wasn't sure he believed in the Haunted Lands, but sure it was that the city and most of the army did. The Broken Barrel whistle piped, but Rust looked the other way as he jogged beside Tam's trotting mule.

They left the yard and Rust settled into a solid pace beside the mule. He found himself aware of the morning light on the buildings, and the different way people dressed. The air was cold and smelled like a forest had been dipped in shit and then burned with cooking lard, but it felt good to run. Tam jounced along on his mule, studying the buildings and streets as they went.

"You know the path?" asked Rust.

"We learn every guild hall in every city," said Tam, and turned his mule at the next street.

On the new way, Rust slid to a halt, and Tam leaned back on the reins. From the top of the hill the light of the Temple dome shone down the long street, making the smoky air glow, illuminating the people walking toward its light.

Tam said, "We must be swift."

Rust asked, "Was that there when we came to Gimlek?"

"It was not. The Master has acted."

"You think she...?"

Tam nodded, then urged his mount ahead.

In the face of such power a sense of unworthiness swept over Rust—he was nothing—an oxboy worth less than his animals.

Tam looked back and called, "Ride or run?"

Swallowing his self-doubt, Rust sprinted. They turned down a side avenue and entered an older quarter of the city.

The guild hall surprised Rust with its simplicity. Its weathered stone facade was more like a modest village Temple than home to a weapons guild. A young aspirant came running from what looked like a sally port to take the mule though Rust could see no obvious stable. The guards at the door allowed them entry without challenge. Inside, the air held a faintly spicy scent of centuries of wood smoke. Tam walked first and Rust watched his friend's back straighten and his pace slow. Heart pounding, Rust did the same.

The chamber they came to was stacked chest high with pack boxes and gear. Guild warriors and priests were reviewing lists and counting materials. Rust was more interested in the walls, for they were festooned with campaign trophies—thousands of trophies.

Tam strode up to the first group, saluted with back-fist to hand, and said, "Word for the Master."

"At the Temple."

A head popped up over the gear and Rust's breath stopped. It was the girl aspirant. Her eyes blazed with an intensity he'd never seen in a girl—a fire of determination blended with the slashed-soul haunting of one who had known suffering. She hurried around the gear stacks to stand before Tam then gave him the Batusha salute. She wasn't wearing gloves and gave a small flinch when the back of her right fist slapped into the cup of her other hand.

Tam eyed her with wary appreciation then gave her a grin.

"I'm not a master, Simarn. We are aspirants."

She dropped her hands and said, "I will go with you to the Master."

Tam glanced at the warriors and priests, but they offered no guidance.

Rust glanced at Simarn's hands. They were blistered with patterns he knew well. Weapons training. The black crossbow hung from her belt. The bow that had killed more Dauthaz than anyone but the queen.

Tam turned to a young aspirant standing nearby. "My mule and a mount for Simarn."

The boy dashed away and Simarn called after him, "Greedy-guts!"

Men chuckled and Simarn blushed intensely. Rust had never seen anyone color so impressively, and he stared.

Tam said, "Should have named mine that." To the warriors and priests he said, "Where do we mount?"

"The street."

Tam struck back-fist to palm. Simarn spun to them and saluted as well. Rust bowed to the priests and warriors, but no one was looking at him. He followed Tam and Simarn back outside. The guards at the door were discussing the people heading for the Temple. Tam's mule and Simarn's horse emerged from an alley Rust had not noticed. Simarn greeted her horse, then mounted with ease. It was odd to see a girl in pants so mounted, especially armored with a blade at one hip and Soot crossbow on the other. He noted that she took care to cover both weapons with her cloak. Even then she looked like a story. Someone should make a song of her. Tam was mounted and urged his mule into a trot. Simarn didn't even glance at Rust as she followed. Feeling ignored but pleased to be in their company, Rust matched pace with Tam's mount.

When they left that section of town and emerged onto a main avenue, Simarn jolted in the saddle at the sight of the Temple, but she did not slow her mount. One hand fell to her crossbow beneath her cloak, and Rust wondered what she'd seen at the queen's side to think first of killing at such a sight.

When the avenue began to climb the hill to the high city, the crowd grew thicker and Tam yelled, "Way!"

People parted, but not fast enough.

Rust surged ahead, cupped his hands to his mouth and roared as the men of the company did: "Way!"

People scattered.

Proud, Rust ran ahead of the others. The crowd kept parting until two hundred strides up the long slope a red-barded horse appeared, its rider holding a red flag. More horses followed, one nearly twice the size of the others and its rider was the queen. Behind her were more Batusha men and what looked like mounted Surreda Guild warriors.

Tam spoke to Simarn and they maneuvered their mounts to one side, facing up the street at an angle. Rust ran back to them and stood near the head of Tam's mule, embarrassed now not to be mounted. He tugged on his coat to straighten it and sighed at his clothing, the same he'd worn on the road. The horses were almost upon them and he stood to attention.

Tam and Simarn cracked their back-fists to palm. The banner-wielding Batusha master glanced at them without moving his head. The next two masters looked identical. They eyed the trio of young warriors, and one looked back at the queen. She angled her mount and approached. The priest that was always near the queen followed her. The masters called and the troop began to form a half-moon in the street. Crossbows clicked and spears lowered. People who had stopped to watch kept their distance.

The queen's gaze fell to Rust and she gave him a small smile. He felt a thousand feet tall.

To Tam and Simarn the queen said, "Anule."

Both dropped their salutes.

"Master," said Tam. "Scaukra seeks your word."

Her face fell slightly. "Where?"

"The Spear and Porridge, Master. A tavern near the

barracks."

She gestured that they show her the way.

The banner bearer jerked his head and Tam and Simarn took positions behind him. Rust didn't know where to go and decided to follow the column after they had passed. When the queen gestured to the cobbles at her side, he didn't understand.

Her mount walked after the twin masters who had ridden after Tam and Simarn. A Batusha master behind her whistled and Rust looked. The man pointed at the street beside the queen with a sharp gesture. Feet skidding on the ice, Rust leapt to obey.

"I saw you running," she said.

He couldn't think of anything to say to that.

"I ran the forest near my home," she said. "The Gamanthea-Dur Su. Have you ever run a forest?"

"No, my queen."

"If you like to run, you must try it. Fast is the finest way. Let your heart choose the route and your focus make a path."

"Yes, my queen," said Rust, though he had not understood.

A furtive glance showed that the queen had her face tilted to the light. It was a young face, smooth though not soft, and not much older than he. Sunlight off her black hair shone with a hazel glow. Rust stumbled and went nearly to the cobbles before he recovered. Footing regained, he tensed, waiting for the laughter from those behind. There was nothing. Mercifully, the queen did not look at him.

At the tavern the identical masters dismounted and led the way inside. The queen walked after them. Tam and Simarn followed her. Rust stepped into place behind them. No one objected. In the dark of the tavern, the queen glowed with pale radiance. Master Tafitamar emerged from the back room.

"Scaukra," called the queen across the tables, then wended her way to him with long strides.

He saluted her.

"You will tell me what you have seen," she said.

Rust sensed the tone of a continuing discussion. The tallest Batusha master came up behind Rust and directed him to take a guard position with Tam and Simarn at the stair leading to the upstairs rooms. With focused diligence, Rust checked over the room with his eyes then peered up the stairs. Disappointed that there was nothing to fight for the honor of the queen, he imitated Tam's guard stance. The queen and Scaukra stepped into the officer's eating room. She reached for the doors, her face serious and somehow reminding Rust of a thunderstorm before the wind and rain hit.

Breea gathered the doors to the main hall and swung them closed. She had questions for Scaukra that did not brook an audience. The yellow lantern light inside gave Scaukra's face a dismal cast. He looked ill. Possibly he had yet to recover from Simarn's bolt through the lung. Breea was unable to decide how she felt about him. She owed him her life, and sensed his loyalty to her, yet there were too many mysteries about the man. She took a chair and he sat opposite, very straight. The master warrior was nervous. The contrast with the utterly confident man he'd been when they first met was striking. The Tetr emerald whispered to her that now was the time to press for answers.

"Scaukra, why did you plot with the High Temple against Batusha?"

His eyes fixed upon hers. He looked caught, but did not

answer.

"Your mistress Pareetha," said Breea, "was bound to the Oregule within the High Temple."

Scaukra closed his eyes and frowned as though her words had hurt him.

"I tracked her," Breea went on. "Pareetha told the Oregule's Dauthaz word of Batusha that only you could have uttered."

"My life is yours." His voice was low.

"I want truth, Scaukra. Did you know she was in thrall to the Oregule?"

"No, Master. Pareetha began as my servant. I trained her to enter the Temple's service."

"Why?"

"I sought the destruction of Yash priesthoods."

"Sought," repeated Breea.

"No longer."

"Why?"

A tide of pain rose in Scaukra's eyes. Before she could prompt him, he said, "On the coast of Kalatris there was an independent city, Tallghiv. Tallghiv was not of Yash. A Yash High Temple delegation came to negotiate trade with the king. The delegation were not priests, but Soot. They slew the court then flayed the king, his wives, and children. Their skins they stretched on racks and set them to dry in the sun like fish. The Army of the Blessed came after, and with every pa-hoc, a priest."

Scaukra's face was bleak, but his voice had grown so strong with hatred that Breea's inner flame roared in kind.

"They flayed every royal child but one. In the street and from the walls the priests called for that one. Return, little prince Kalatris. Return, or a thousand will die by day and a thousand by night until your return. The first thousand were gutted on the wharf and dumped into the bay. The water bled. I tried to return, but those who hid me tied me to a log of driftwood and four men swam me out of the bay with the tide. When they released me upon the headland at dawn, they gave me a basillard sword. Avenge us, they said, and walked back into the water."

Breea sat back as the Tetr emerald spoke. Scaukra's character opened before her—complicated, haunted, loyal, and compromised.

"You joined Batusha and became a master to set the guild against the Temple. Priesthood against priesthood. Your given name is not Scaukra?"

He shook his head, but was hesitant.

"Why do you no longer seek the destruction of the priesthoods?"

"Scaukra I am, and will remain, Master. Of you, I began to dream. I saw the High Temple fall before you made it so. I dreamed of the death of Guild Master Htaas. I dream of your works."

"My works. Tell me what you see, Scaukra."

"Oregule, Master. Slaying children."

Essence crackled in the air about Breea, and she stood and went to the doors. She needed sunlight and fresh air.

When she touched the wood, the portals shattered outward. Batusha masters in the tavern hall whirled and drew their weapons. Simarn swung up her crossbow, cocking it in the same motion. Tam had his blade out, and Rust was half crouched, fists balled—eyes wild.

The shattering had not been her intent, but Breea did not feel like apologizing. She strode straight across the room using warps of wind to shove chairs and tables from her path.

Outside, Fahri stood apart from the other horses. No one dared hold her bridle.

Like me, thought Breea with a grim smile and turned her face to the sunlight.

Scaukra emerged into the light beside her.

"I am going to hunt them, Scaukra. The Oregule. I will need your sight." To the warriors about her she said, "And your blades."

Like branches cracking in a gust of wind, Batusha chak'ood in a ring about her. Master Piad raised his fist in the Surreda salute, and his guild priests and warriors followed his example.

"Anule," said Breea in pleased voice.

With a swift binding knot, she bound the flame within and looked up at the sign of the tavern. It was a carved relief if the likeness of an armored man stirring a pot with a spear. She strode back inside and sat at the largest table. Batusha and Surreda came after, but did not sit. Batusha set up a guard perimeter. Before the wolf attack, such precaution for her would have amused her. Neprawn ducked into the kitchen. His voice rumbled. A face peered out and then vanished.

"Sit with me," said Breea to the assembled warriors. "Clear that side. Make a space for our aspirants."

Men rushed to do her bidding. Sabar and Ootha were the first to sit at the table with her. Master Piad made sure he was the third to sit, and others followed until three sides were full. Simarn stood at Breea's left shoulder.

Breea looked at Tam and Rust. "What have you learned?"

Tam came forward like the champion he was. Rust followed after with a worried look. Both moved with the youthful grace of young men who had already ten years of training behind them. Likely, Breea mused, they both had killed men. They stopped before the cleared edge of the table and honored her with chak'ood and bow. They were exactly like the boys Breea had trained with for her entire girlhood. Tam pulled parchment from his coat and passed it across the table to her. Sabar took the coil, unrolled it, and held it open for Breea's perusal. After glancing at the drawings, she nodded to the boys. Tam took the lead and began to explain a feint and thrust with spear that had passed his guard twice. The aspirant moved like a cat, reminding Breea of Ambard, the first man she had ever loved. She struck down the thought and focused on what the boys were showing her. Rust more resembled an oak tree than any animal, yet his action brought to mind Sakuront—movement so easy it made massive limbs appear to weigh nothing. Did Tam know that Rust might outmatch him someday? It was guild training that had enabled Tam's victory.

Food came on platters and Breea tore into it without paying attention to what she ate. Weaving made for tremendous hunger.

Scaukra prompted the boys when they ran out of ready words, reminding them of key strikes in their battle. When they tried to come up with better counters, Master Piad made a statement. Others responded and Breea relaxed into enjoying her food as more men launched into the debate. Scaukra disagreed with Piad, and the guild master stood up, then looked at Breea with a frozen expression. She gestured toward the other side of the table with an eating dagger. The boys scooted back and Piad and Scaukra drew blades. Breea found herself leaning forward. Steel crashed and sang. The result was inconclusive, with neither landing a blow.

Argument raged around the table. Grinning, Breea shouted her own opinion.

Quiet flashed through the room. Feeling her face flush, she sat back and motioned for them to continue. No one moved. She forced a smile and waved them on despite the disappointment that bit hard at not being among these men as a compatriot. Her hand touched the Tetr emerald where it hung over the burning core of herself. She would need to have care. A word from her turned the haft of a weapon that could raze cites and rewrite the path of realms.

The boys were staring at her still. She nodded them toward the masters. They obeyed and began to imitate what was being shown. Scaukra's face was flushed and sweat was on his brow, but his eyes were clear as he wove his sword-like basillard around Piad's long blade. The Batusha master called the boys over and began to show what had been decided. Piad helped.

Breea was full of food and wine among men as fine as the best of Limtir. She did not want this to end, but an Alach queen had duties. What these men thought necessary to cross mountains in winter was not likely to be correct.

When she stood the room rose with her.

"Thank you, aspirants. You have gifted us with much to consider. We march against an unknown enemy. Who among us has faced the Kaul Kaul?"

Neprawn raised a palm, surprising most, including Breea. Yet he was the only one.

"We will learn from one another, and we will learn from our enemy," said Breea, though she was thinking of the Oregule. To the boys she said, "Knowledge guide your blades."

Tam chak'ood and Rust bowed low.

To the room Breea said, "I will return to the guild hall. Then I wish you to show me what has been made ready for the march. There is a fleet at Iplock to carry us to the Meric shore. I intend for this army to be in those boats a fortnight from this day."

The warriors of both guilds chak'ood, then said as one, "I Serve!"

Breea touched the Tetr emerald in reply, then caught Master Piad's eye. "Master Piad, will you ride with me to your guild hall?"

"I Serve, Master Banea."

They rode through the morning city, its stenches and smells rising with the warmth of the winter sun.

"This city and Yash are the heart of your realm," said Breea.

"Ushau is mighty," said Piad, naming the realm's greatest north coast city.

Breea nodded, then said. "Isswarn has invaded Yash."

He looked at her sharply, but said nothing.

"Master Piad, you must build an army out of Gimlek. After Isswarn has invested the capital, it will fall to Gimlek to break that siege. You must wait until next winter or the following."

The guild master looked at her again, searchingly this time.

"For the Issil," he said.

Breea nodded. The master was learned. "They cannot take the cold. As it was with Lord Farnad. Yash cannot fall, Master Piad. With the capital, so too the realm."

"Yes, Chosen," said Piad.

"Some may ask," said Breea, "why I have taken the Kultash to Mericsland."

"Carsythe," said Piad. "As with Carsythe, so too the Meric kingdom."

Impressed, Breea smiled at him and he colored a little in pleasure.

"I will return if I can," said Breea.

Piad raised his chin and looked all the way down the lane. "We may need you, Chosen."

CHAPTER 25

Knowledge of the Pines

"AT DAWN, TAKE THEM WEST," SAID TAUMEA. He and Valiena lay beneath furs near the back of the tunnel that had once been a gatehouse carved though the rock of the castle massif. Valiena's head was on his shoulder and his Limtir sword lay across his legs, both weights that comforted. Spe, Anila, and Tiyha slept against the rubble at the back. The cave was deep and still in darkness, but the entrance was a tall square of palest moonglow that howled with the storm passing outside. The apparition was a shadow that sat in the very center of the entrance, facing out. The spirit looked small in the opening, giving true scale to the entrance.

Under the furs Taumea found Valiena's hands and signed, *He watches for us.*

Valiena looked then settled into the furs as though to sleep as they had intended, but spoke instead. "How did they come upon us so fast?"

"A Kultash hunting ril," said Taumea. "Fast trackers. Het's Hounds they are called."

By feel Taumea took the amber gem from its pouch and placed it in Valiena's hand under the furs.

Valiena forced the gem back into his. Her fingers were trembling. He tried to return the gem but she balled her hand into a fist.

"Val…"

"Bright ways," she said with forced cheer.

Taumea knew the truth of what she felt, for what he would attempt now seemed beyond hope. He bent to kiss her, but stopped.

"Do you smell that?"

Valiena said, "Blessed light…"

They tossed off the blankets and stood.

Both of them twitched when Anila's voice said from the dark beside them, "My lord?"

Before Taumea could answer, Spe's footfalls padded up and she said, "Pine!"

Her eyes were lit with a glow like dawn.

Heat flared in Taumea's fist. He opened his hand, and in the light of the spirit gem was not surprised to find the apparition sitting beside him, looking down upon them all.

The tree scent grew strong.

Anila's eyes were wide and glazed. Memory flooded her, and a vision of the Limtir lord's sword appeared before her. Sparks of light traced twisty patterns along the metal as light flowed into the blade.

"Maker," she heard herself say, and felt the fire in her chest.

The air trembled, and Spe pushed on the center of her chest with a frown.

The adults were silent, waiting. Anila knew what she must do, what she could do. She reached a hand toward the handle of the Limtir lord's blade. He glanced at the lady, then turned his body until the iron pommel touched her fingers. Before she lost her daring, Anila wrapped her fingers around the cold metal, then pulled. The top of the blade came free of the scabbard, then stuck.

The Limtir lord handed the spirit gem to Valiena then gripped the haft of his sword and drew the weapon with slow care. He held it lengthwise before Anila.

Anila ran her fingers along its gleaming length. A melody arose from within and she sang soft and low. Spe came up beside her and rocked back and forth to the rhythm of her voice. In song, the metal spoke to Anila. She felt the intent of its maker, and the will of its wielder that bound man and blade in oaths that were released in violence. In blade and heart, she felt his will resonate the Breath about him and found that she could not tell what was blade and what was man. The scent of pine grew spicy, and she knew she'd made an important discovery. Here was the key to shape her song.

"Breathe," she sang, and Spe knew it was meant for her.

Like the sun emerging from behind a cloud, Spe's Breath was revealed—hot on Anila's skin. The Limtir lord sucked in a breath, but the blade never moved. Anila felt pleased that he could feel the song, and raised her voice, calling on Spe's power, shaping harmony, wrapping it into the weapons before her, both man and sword.

The blade began to vibrate under Anila's fingers. Dire songs within the metal rose to meet hers. Fear of what she was doing writhed its way up and she panicked, faltering. Cold fur brushed her face as the apparition nuzzled her. Its Breath rumbled in the air, vibrating through her, smothering fear with its thunder. Anila sang out, catching the unraveling threads with her will. When it felt right, she called upon Spe's power and the song slammed into the weapon. The Limtir lord staggered, then sagged to his knees.

Anila found that she was done and gave a little sob. The lord settled back on his heels, dropping the blade to his lap.

Spe screamed, beating at her chest. Anila caught her as her back arched, then lowered her to the floor. With all her power, Anila tried to stop Spe's Breath, but the flow of its heat shoved aside all her efforts. The heat grew intense and Spe's skin shone like the heart of a forge. Her clothing began to smoke. Anila leaned into the storm of searing Breath, laying her hands on Spe's chest. Ma appeared and stumbled to collapse beside them. Spe's hands scrabbled blindly for the shimmering gem in Ma's hand. Ma opened her fist and Spe's fingers came down over the gem.

Ruby light lit the tunnel, and Spe's body went rigid. Anila felt her sister's heat pouring into the gem. Spe fainted and the river of heat snapped off as though cut by an ax.

Ma sobbed hoarsely over Spe, her hand clutching Spe's, red light piercing out through every gap in their fingers. Beneath all there was a harmonic hum. The lady Valiena stood from where she had fallen back and approached the lord, her terrified gaze shifting from Spe to the Limtir sword.

The lord raised the blade from his legs and song filled the air.

The lord's eyes went round. He turned to his lady and said something in a strange language.

The air about him stilled at the words and the lady covered her mouth with a hand.

For Anila, he said in Yasharn, "Your words upon my blade do sing."

When the kneeling lord stood, the motion held such smooth power that the air seemed to pause to watch. Currents blended around him, both in the air and that which lay beneath the air in Breath itself.

"How fares Spe?" he asked.

Spe and Ma lay together, clutching the gem. Ma had fainted. There was a strange heat about Spe that Anila had never felt. Perhaps the pines would know. Anila raised her head, breathing in, but the scent of the trees had vanished. A hand settled on her shoulder, but she dared not look up and let him see how completely lost she felt.

The Limtir lord's sword sang into her sight.

"This is Blade Song," he said. "Have you heard of it?"

She gave her head the barest shake. She knew nothing, not even how she'd sung such a thing to be.

The lord said, "In the stories of my people, song blades were gifts of the gods bestowed to the blessed. Fear not, lass, for you are the hope of all."

Taumea sheathed the blade and took the spirit gem back from the lady. After kissing her forehead and both eyes and then lightly on the lips, he turned and walked away. In the red light of Ma's gem, Anila saw the apparition appear in front of him and pad out the entrance atop the snow. Taumea followed, plowing a path through the fresh drift into the night storm.

Anila turned back. Tears sparkled on the lady's cheeks. Spe and Ma slept together.

Taking a deep Breath, Anila said, "Azsark protect us."

Spinning, she ran toward the storm, whispering her feet silent as she went.

By wind and will, Anila managed to follow the lord's rapid passage back across the valley floor. She lifted herself over the river on a pillow of air, and by constant song used the wind to push herself after him. The apparition visited her twice, looking almost as if it were making sure she was keeping up. The bravery she'd wielded to chase after the Limtir lord faded in the dark storm-lashed forest until the giant cat trotted up alongside her and kept her company until some of her sureness of will returned. Branches cracked as a gust of wind roared through the trees. Anila stole a wisp of its strength and used it to push herself faster, closer to the Limtir lord. It was not the wind she feared in the night, but Temple men and what they would do if they found her alone.

Though she could not see the lord ahead, she felt him slow, and Anila was able to get within sight of him in the dark blowing. He was crouched in the snow on the windward side of a great oak and seemed to be waiting. The apparition appeared beyond, herding a figure wielding a long curved sword with both hands. The cat apparition charged the man and he staggered back with raised sword. The Limtir lord came around the tree. There was a flash of movement, then the lord was standing alone. He stalked forward and Anila kept pace. Soon she felt a group of men and animals ahead.

Among the trees stood a round shelter that was half buried in accumulated snow. Taumea pushed aside a heavy cloth door on the downwind side. Firelight spilled out into the storm and men cried out in dismay.

Another! Away! In Het's name!

Anila rushed ahead on a gust of icy air and landed beside the shelter entrance in a drift of snow. The shelter was larger than she had thought and the wind whipped its skin covering as though angry with its presence in the forest.

Within, the lord Taumea was speaking. "Nay. I invoke the Blessing of Judgment."

"What you may be," said an angry voice, "spirit or Dauthaz, neither can call for the Wisdom of Judgment."

"Nay spirit. Nay Dauthaz. Het's word. I will see the Ulshan's first warrior."

"You are a spirit. You do not live, but we will see you die!"

Anila stiffened, but the Limtir lord replied, "Will you break edict for fear? My life is for Het to choose."

With a tiny curl of wind, Anila pushed aside the bottom edge of the cloth. The Limtir lord faced inward, his back to her. In front of him a fire crackled. His cloak was thrown back and Anila could hear the humming of his blade in its scabbard. Crowded away from him in the other half of the shelter were twelve men and four big dogs. The animals ducked and shook their heads as though in pain. More than Taumea's presence, the reaction of their dogs seemed to unsettle the bearded Kultash. Looking at their faces and tasting their smell upon the air, Anila lost hope. Savagery of the soul radiated from them as it had from the Temple priest that she'd been forced to watch as he flayed a woman upon the scaffold. That lesson had sunk fangs of fear all the way to Anila's marrow. Could the lord not see? Speech to men like these was like asking Da to stop. Memories of pain tumbled over her. She shuddered and dropped her head.

Through her teeth she whispered, "I will not run."

The silence she'd woven about her caught the sound of her voice, but the Breath within billowed hot and rageful. Snow melted in her heat, and icy water ran down her neck.

Her head rose up and touched fur. The apparition's head pushed open the thick curtain and a curled forepaw stepped carefully over her. Cries of fear from the Kultash turned to battle cries that were overwhelmed by a shimmering harmonic as the lord drew his blade. Half the Kultash stumbled in the act of attacking, eyes locked to the weapon, but the others came on through the fire.

Feet planted, the lord set his blade to dancing. Bodies fell at his feet like sacks. The remaining Kultash turned and slashed through the wall of their shelter and fled into the storm. The apparition leapt after them, but the gaps cut into the wall were too narrow for it to pass and it took the entire shelter with its passage in a ripping flash.

The lord rose from where he'd ducked.

Crouched in the snow directly behind him, Anila reached into the drifts and Breathed a blanket of snow over herself before he turned to gaze about. From the forest, screams of agony and horror cut through the wind and the lord's blade gave resonant response. The lord raised the weapon and chuckled, and Anila felt a pang of fear. Was he laughing at their pain? Was that the warrior's path?

"Bring me another," he said.

Who was he speaking to? Anila held her breath, afraid to move. The lord raised his cloak hood and turned a slow circle, examining the forest in all directions, then he knelt and cleaned his sword before sheathing the blade. Using the yellow light of the spirit's gem he searched the packs and gear of the Kultash. Every few seconds, he looked up and checked his surroundings. Many times he sniffed what he found in the packs and placed an object in a separate pile.

The strange Breath of the apparition drew close and the lord stood to face the creature. In its mouth hung a man. It dropped the limp body at the lord's feet.

"Living," said the lord.

The apparition sniffed the body, nuzzled it, then looked at the lord.

"I can speak only to the living. They must be able to reply."

The apparition's head rose up until its eyes were level with the lord's. A massive furry paw lifted and came down on the body. The man screamed.

"Oh," said the lord. He held the spirit's gem to his chest and gave the apparition a short bow.

The apparition shook its fur and vanished.

After a look around, the lord knelt by the man. "Sa Kultash, make you ready."

"Death upon you, Dauthaz."

"Would Het allow the wise to fall to Dauthaz? Is your faith so impure?"

The Kultash did not answer.

"You have been guided ill," said the Limtir lord. "Speak true and I will send you after your brothers clean. Sa Kultash, this is truth."

The Limtir lord tugged off a gauntlet with his teeth, then put his bare hand upon the man's brow. With his other hand, he brought the glowing gem into the man's sight.

"Het's gaze, brother. You are judged. Answer true."

The man stared with fearful wonder into the gem light, then sobbed. "I Serve!"

"Who is hean of the Ulshan?"

"Abledd Shurans."

"Good. Where camps the Ulshan?"

"East and south. A valley over, may. We left sign."

"Know you what you hunt?"

"Aye. A Dauthaz with whore and git."

"Where?"

"Downvalley. There is a castle. But the dogs were butchered in the storm."

"You sent word after this?"

"Aye."

"Why did Hean Shurans fail to heed my warning? I left one alive. Hunt me not."

The man began, then checked his reply. He said with a snarl, "You? Dauth—!"

Anila flinched as the lord's dagger rammed down through the Kultash's face. The lord drew the blade from the man's eye socket and Anila hid her face.

When she looked back, the lord was stuffing a basket pack with bundles, holding the gem in one hand to light the work. He paused to take a bite of dark bread, then continued as he chewed.

When he began filling a small pack, just her size, Anila frowned, then blushed hard. She rose from the snow. The lord merely tossed the remaining loaf her way. She tumbled the catch, then fished it from the snow. Ravenous, she bit off a piece of her own.

The lord Taumea hefted his pack and slung it to his shoulders. He bent and lifted the second by its wood frame. He turned it so the straps faced her, and she jumped over, turned, and slipped the woven ropes over her shoulders.

"Can you make pantaloons of your skirt?" asked the lord. When she didn't answer, he said, "Breea always did this with her dresses so she could climb and run. Stand wide and hike your skirts a bit." She did and he took a piece of rope and made her a belt of it, then guided her hands to grip the back edge of her skirt and brought it forward, lifted and tucked it into the rope belt.

"Pantaloons," he said with a wink.

The wind was cold on her stocking-clad legs, but a call to her inner Breath fixed that.

Out in the forest, a hound howled mournfully in the wind. The Limtir lord froze and stared into the woods, then set a hand on her shoulder for a comforting moment. His hands went under her arms and he lifted her in the air. He settled her on his shoulders and gripped her ankles. Without a word, he began to run back toward the castle.

CHAPTER 26

Song Weaver

IN THE TENT BATUSHA HAD BROUGHT FOR THE queen, Dori arranged the sleeping furs, but it seemed pointless—her ladyship slept very little. Dori stood straight and stretched her back. She felt weak with exhaustion. After days of riding dawn to dusk, the army was deep into the Haunted Lands. In the clear cold days after leaving Gimlek, the sharp peaks of the haunted range had shimmered white on the eastern horizon, heavy with snow, but it was the night view that the men craved. Every night hundreds of men flocked to any high ground they could find to gaze back at the glowing Temple on the city hill. The talk of this evening had been of the storm rolling down out of the mountains. Most said this evening would be their last view of the Temple. The men looked worried, even the priests.

Unexplainable things were happening. Small things went missing, including a Batusha master's fine red cloak—taken right off his back if the tale were true. Some claimed sightings of strange figures watching from the forest, and ruins were avoided with almost religious fervor. Traveling here felt like walking uninvited through someone else's garden.

Batusha were silent about the route, but supplymen and some of the Yasharn talked, continuing to question how even the Chosen could cross this trackless winter forest that had been guarded by spirits against the living since the time of the ancients. Dori had no such doubts. Her ladyship was a woman Yash could not break. She had broken Yash.

Dori stared at the layers of brindled furs, considering whether to arrange them once more simply to feel the depth of their softness and warmth. She turned away—her own sheepskins were warm enough, and in truth the night was the only time she was ever warm on this journey. Dori stood on a chest and checked the oil in the lantern which hung from the center pole, then almost fell as she stepped down, gasping as the sudden motion poked at her tender inner thighs. Dori's back felt broken by the relentless pace, and she worried that endless days sitting on mules like a man would make her legs bow like those of the lancers.

A breath of cold air made her turn to the tent entrance. Tam stood within with her ladyship's evening meal on a wood platter. Dori hadn't heard him enter, but he had waited for her to notice him before coming in further. She smiled at him. They had formed a silent accord; she would forgive his silent way of moving as long as he did not startle her. Some nights when she grew frightened, he would stand guard near the little tent she shared with Simarn.

She took the platter and set it on a pack box beside the furs. Where had they put her ladyship's chair? She stifled a yawn. Tam stepped outside and came back in with the folding chair. He put it together and then gestured to Dori to have a seat. She shook her head.

It was a nightly play between them that Dori looked forward to all day long. Every night he found something to do for her, and every night she would curtsy to him and he would bow to her. A circle of Batusha warriors ringed the tent at a discreet distance outside, but neither Tam nor Dori ever said a word aloud.

They exchanged silent acknowledgments and he left. Dori stacked her ladyship's books beside the food and relived Tam's visit, noting little things like how his eyes seemed drawn to her no matter what direction he was facing, and how his bow was deeper tonight than last. He moved with such ease that he looked to be made of feather, but she knew from rare touches that he was more like warm iron. With a sigh she sat on a chest to await her ladyship.

The noises of the host eating their evening meal quieted as the music-spirit which had taken up with the army began its nightly flute dance. Dori leaned back against the tent pole. The song reminded her of the rhythm of the mule she rode, but tonight it had a questing feel as though unsure of what was to come.

Every company now put out offerings to the spirit, and if a company's offering was gone in the morning it was considered a great honor. Every night the spirit had different melodies. She'd heard the men talking, wondering if it was the lady herself playing to ease men's fears, but Dori knew it wasn't. The lady herself didn't know what it was.

The crack of gloved fists striking palms jerked Dori alert. She stood and gave her coat a tug, then tucked stray hairs behind her ears. Voices exchanged greetings and the flap was drawn aside by Simarn. Her ladyship strode into the tent, face cheerful.

"Thank you, Simarn," said her ladyship. Simarn let the flap close.

Dori felt her heart sink, for in the amber light of the lamps outside a snowfall had begun. Her ladyship looked as bright and warm as fire itself.

"Snow!" she said.

"Yes, milady."

"No mournful agreement," said Breea. "Snow is a league better than cold rain, and the heart of the storm passes to the east. Music and snowfall remind me of home."

"Yes, milady," said Dori in a tone meant to express cheerful agreement, but her voice sounded crushed through a fine mesh of duty.

The lady looked at Dori with care, then tossed her bear cloak onto the sleeping furs. Behind the pleasure at new snow, Dori could see a weariness in her ladyship, not of the body, for her ladyship seemed never to tire, but from a concern which ate at her daily. Her ladyship sat in the chair and grabbed a piece of bread with one hand and the big red leather book with the other. Dori took her place beside the tent flap, and eyed the book. The lady had been reading that one every night since Gimlek. Dori preferred it when the lady read the others. Her ladyship would begin to glow with a fierce light if she studied the red book for too long.

"Go to sleep, Dori," said her ladyship without looking up.

"My lady, this is my place, if it please you."

Her ladyship's good humor vanished and Dori felt a pang. Nothing was worse than her ladyship's anger, but she was looking past Dori, to the east.

"We'll leave the hills and enter the valley lands tomorrow, then begin our climb to the pass," said her ladyship. "The men are frightened. I'll need you to show them what bravery is, Dori. You can do that best when you are rested. Go."

Dori curtsied low and turned to leave. The music-spirit shifted tunes and the melody pulled at her heart.

Her ladyship gasped, and Dori stepped away in bare time as her ladyship rushed through the tent flap. Curious, Dori followed. Simarn looked at Dori in question, but she had no answers. Her ladyship stopped between the ring of Batusha warriors and the tent. In the lamplit snowfall, her daggers sparkled green. One hand lifted, fingers moving as though tracing something on the air. She turned until she was facing right. The hand made a fist and the air around her ladyship grew smoky, darkening into shadow until she vanished from view.

A squeak of shock escaped Dori's lips and two Batusha warriors turned to look at her. Blushing, she gave them a little curtsy and they returned to their outward-facing stance. Dori looked to where her ladyship had stood. All that marked the spot was a darkness where the snow had ceased to fall.

Her ladyship's voice said softly out of the air, "Go to bed, Dori."

The shadow moved away with only a slight whirl of snowflakes to mark its passage. Dori stared out into the night, trying to mark her ladyship's path among the rings of camped warriors, but there was nothing to see. With an awed sigh, she went back to the tent flap. She stopped beside Simarn and put a hand on the girl's arm and felt chainmail beneath her cloak. Simarn nodded to Dori as a soldier might, but there was a softness to her face that showed her appreciation of Dori's gesture. Dori entered the tent and sat on the chest to await the lady's return and protect her food from vermin and Batusha boys, which were the same in Dori's view—except for Tam and his lieutenants.

The lamplight dimmed and Dori looked up to find a shadow reaching out for her. Warm, irresistible hands made her rise and walk to her ladyship's furs, then guided her down until she lay upon the cot.

Dori tried to sit up, but a hand pressed her forehead and her ladyship's voice commanded, "Sleep."

Dori obeyed.

Breea lifted Dori's feet onto the furs, and with gentle affection arranged her bear-fur cloak over the young woman, tucking it in so no breath of cold air would reach her. Breea touched Dori's cold cheek and let a trickle of essence-heat flow into her. Dori sighed in her sleep and settled deeper into the furs.

Smiling, Breea left the tent and strode out through the cordon of Batusha warriors who, with Simarn, now guarded Dori. Among the low tents of Yasharn infantry she paused, listening for the threads of essence which wove the flute song. The source was near, and now that she knew its source was no spirit, tonight would see the elusive weaver found who had become a legend in their march to the mountains.

The song led her among the Aska-Wuthos to a ring of officers sitting cross-legged on the backs of their turtleshell shields. In their midst a cook fire crackled and glowed. The men were silent, gazing into the flames or above it where snowflakes vanished into its heat. Breea studied the weaving which enwrapped them and flowed out on lilting waves of song to the entire army. The song was pleasant, but within its melody was a weft of distraction. If a person focused upon the player, the weave led them astray. A voice would seem to call their name, or they would hear the song from a different direction. Using techniques learned in her tome of battle weaving, Breea carefully parted the strands of the warp which hid the musician.

Close to the fire on a thick piece of fur sat the flute-playing boy Breea had encountered on her entrance to the city of Yash. His back was straight, eyes closed as he played a flute of polished wood. He wore a Batusha master's fur-lined cloak across his shoulders and over his crossed legs. Visible at his waist was the hilt of a jeweled dagger on a tooled-leather belt. He gave no sign of knowing what Breea had done to his hiding weave, nor did the Aska-Wuthos warriors react. The weaving's effect continued to hold them. Their tired faces were peaceful.

Breea considered what to do with her discovery. It seemed he was also an accomplished thief. She wanted to thank him for all that he did in aid of the march, but there was no question which Batusha master was missing his cloak. Impulsively Breea unraveled her own hiding weave and walked in among the men. They looked up at her, then bowed their heads in respect. It was all the greeting she allowed from the men on her night walks among them. She squatted beside the fire and held her hands to its warmth.

Across the flames, the boy's eyes opened in surprise, but she held her gaze to the fire. A warrior poured a flagon for Breea. She accepted and sipped the warmed ale, letting the men get their fill of staring at her. The music took on a noble air and the warriors seemed to remember the drinks in their hands, and raised them to Breea before drinking.

In kind, she returned the gesture, took a sip, and pondered what this boy might be. The first time she could recall hearing flute music was—she stood, heart beating. Lupazg had come to kill this boy, and the boy had arrived with the Broken Barrel Company. It was his presence that had driven the wolves in their attacks upon the oxcart. The Oregule might try again any time.

The boy's music flowed on and she sent her will into the flames and through their heat into the ground below. Rings of warmth appeared in her mind's eye—the fires of the army in three layers of defensive circles. They would need to change that pattern as the valley narrowed. Essence warmed her skin as she pushed her awareness out, listening to rhythms in the cold ground. A few cold wisps of awareness fled before her heat. North and southwest the hoofbeats of quarter pa-hoc guard parties circling the camp came muffled through falling snow. The men of those scouts were among her favorites in the army—men of alloy steel, sharp and tough, recruited from all companies. They saw things out in the night forests and reported them to Breea only. So far her will and the playing of this Alach boy had kept the beings at bay. Most fled after touching the leading edge of her awareness. When encountered, she took care to avoid disturbing them beyond what her listening required. Her quarry were the Oregule.

Both Life Bane had paced the army since leaving

Gimlek, but no matter how far she scouted and listened, they seemed able to evade her, even when she found their deep tracks in the snow. That evasive skill she tied to the spider whose name she did not know. Lupazg was not a creature of stealth. The evasiveness also implied that the wolf deferred to the spider.

Afraid that the coming storm was the work of the Oregule to provide cover for an attack, Breea had this day moved air on a scale she could not have believed until she'd tried. Someday she would tell her friend Etrya Finwall what it felt like to shift the path of a storm.

Breea relaxed and the fire settled. The flute player was staring at her, his music ended. Should she leave him hidden? The depth of his hiding weaves were a wonder, yet were shaped to shift the minds of men. Did they work on Oregule? If he was revealed, would the Oregule attack? To fight the Life Bane now, before she attempted the mountain passes, seemed tactically wise. The help of this young Alach would enable much. He was cautious, skilled, and strong. How had he grown such skill so young? Other than his support of the morale of her army, and a love of other people's things, she knew nothing of him. He had followed her but never revealed himself. Was he afraid?

"I heard that song first," she said aloud, "on the day I walked into Yash."

The Aska-Wuthos were attentive. The men, she found, loved to hear her spin tales.

"It was a day colder than this. The road was mud frozen hard, yet it stank as only a city can. I was hungry and cold and friendless. Sighn had warned me not to come, and I wavered in purpose. Then a song came. It wove about us on the street like a warm breath of spring meadow air. It was like being back home. I had no finer moment in Yash."

Eyes shining with pride, the boy made as though to speak, but caught himself. He glanced around at the men and his back bowed. He reached into his coin bag and took out a piece of Limtir silver and turned it in the firelight. It was the coin Breea had dropped into his hat on the street that first day.

"When the spirit plays, I dream of the sea," said a warrior.

There were grunts of agreement around the fire.

When the boy's gaze rose at the praise, Breea met his eyes and gave him a wink.

Stunned, he clutched his flute and half raised it as though to play himself invisible once more.

Breea stood and said to the warriors, "My friend Valiena would wish you all moonlit dreams."

The men bowed their heads and said together, "Chosen."

She walked away, boots squeaking on the packed snow. Flecks of chill melted against her face. Warriors were crawling into tents to escape the growing snowfall. Breea held out her hand to feel the flakes on her fingers. The urge to smile came upon her once again. How was it that this storm made her so happy? Instinct turned her east, and she walked across the camp, nodding and smiling at the men who bowed and saluted her. The Kultash in the outer ring were already sleeping within their tents. Their guards bowed to her in silence as she passed. Wise and disciplined are the Kultash, she thought.

Beyond the camp at the edge of the eastern picket line, she stopped in the forest to listen to the essence of the snowfall. Among the trees with flakes of ice falling to her face, she felt at peace. Within every snowflake lay a hint of sparkling joy. No Oregule could have fashioned this. Then who? The flute player? He did not seem to have such strength, and why would he try?

Was her will being woven? She had read of mind-weaves and seen their effect on men as made by the spider Oregule. With fear sharp in her breast, she slashed about her with a whirling warp of violence woven to cut essence threads.

A cry of fear near her right elbow made her spin with green blades drawn, but it was only the flute player—revealed and stumbling back, hands raised in defense—his hiding wefts slashed apart by her essence battle stroke. A wooden flute case swung from his shoulder on a woven-leather strap.

"My queen?" called a sentry and came running.

Breea wrapped the flute player in cloaking darkness and sheathed her sparkling blades.

"A spirit," she said. "It surprised me, and meant no harm, but will not do that again."

"Yes, my queen. I reckon it won't." He bowed, returned to his post.

Breea walked into the dark forest, and when the boy failed to follow, a whirl of air around him gave him a push. She let her hiding weave unravel.

"How well can you see in the night?" she asked over her shoulder as she waded through the snow, breaking a trail for him.

The answer was both nervous and sullen. "Well enough."

When they came to the river that threaded the valley bottom, Breea brushed snow off a likely boulder and motioned for him to lay his stolen Batusha cloak over the seat. Reluctant, he did so, and Breea sat.

"Join me," she said.

After he half settled against the cloaked stone beside her, Breea said, "Can you hear the snow in the water?"

He appeared to ignore her statement, but then his head tilted forward to the hiss that blended with the water sound. His shoulders relaxed slightly. He brushed at his hair as though to rid it of the snow accumulating there. He bent over his flute case and brought out the instrument. Setting it to his lips he breathed a note so faint Breea had to strain to hear it over snow and water. The breathy tone found harmony in the hissing snow and with a trill the essence blended about him, making a flowing shell that caught the snow and directed it away from his head with gentle grace. He sat straight with a satisfied air.

Breea laughed softly. "Books of the world! You are skilled."

His head bobbed in acknowledgment as a busker did when someone dropped coin for their playing, then he carefully rubbed every snowflake off his instrument. Breea raise a hand to touch the weave, then reconsidered. It was too fragile by far for her to touch.

He saw her aborted motion, and said in a put-out tone, "I'm going to have to sing it all again."

Breea assumed he meant his hiding weaves, and said in a dark tone, "Don't stalk Alach."

His breath caught, and he started rocking back and forth to some internal rhythm. Had he not known that she was an Alach? His essence was unique, but essence it was, and she could sense its flame within him. What did he think of himself? He seemed a strange blend of confident weaver and little boy. There were many powerful men who could not sit with her and talk as he did now.

"Do you know the Ballad of Jiwan City-Slayer?"

"The Immolation of Fabet Goosedown," he said. "But not that one."

"My friend Bay-ope can move mountains with his voice," said Breea, and the boy looked up with bright eyes.

"Not move," said Breea, "though it feels like it when he sings. He has a voice like a war drum. You might have seen him in the city."

"I heard his battle cry!" said the boy.

"I think the world hears his battle cry," said Breea. "He would sing to us on nights like this." She lifted her head and sang, "In elder land, across the crimson sea, sailed Jiwan, lord of gem and gift of tree…"

After listening to a few verses, the boy raised his flute and Breea found herself accompanied. Surprised at how much of the song she remembered, she sang on. When she had no more words, the flute played on, and Breea listened to his weaving. It flowed across the landscape to encompass the army with subtle essence, and left no doubt as to the boy's nature.

Breea gasped. The entire army had heard her sing! He was embellishing the melody now, retelling the story without words. In the sound of such beauty, Breea found herself incapable of anger.

A tingle in her right forefinger rose to her awareness. Within, essence ignited like lamp oil tossed into a forge. The boy went tumbling off the boulder from the concussive shock of the weaves she'd set ready suddenly binding. Breea reached one hand to the sky and the other to the ground, and snarled.

A roar of sickening cold replied from the dark beyond

the river. Lupazg. Her summoned earth heat came surging from the ground around her and became warp to air weft. The air about her flashed alight. With a cry, she willed the weave at the trees of the far bank. A hurricane of bright wind leapt from her, crossed the river and into the forest beyond. The cloaking weaves around six charging wolves shredded like spider web before fire. Streaks of flame swept across their hides where their fur burned, yet they came on. Breea stepped forward and slammed a boot into the river gravel. Water leapt into the air—her wefts of war and warp of deep world power fused with a hiss and a broad arc of steaming water like a saber blade rushed away. The leading edge of the water blade stripped the bark from trees then slammed into the central four beasts, stopping their charge with a sound like trees breaking in half in a waterfall. The two wolves on either side made the opposite shore and leapt.

Breea swept her hands together and a wall of air shimmered alight—her last prepared battle weave. The wolf to her left flew into the woven trap, which wrapped around it like a living blanket of burning rage. The force of catching the soaring wolf translated through the weave and slammed Breea back over the boulder. She hit snow-covered rocks and heard the shimmering weave hit the water with an explosive hiss and wolf howl of agony. The other beast flew past, ears forward, mouth opening—but not for her. Breea thrust at it with all she could muster in the instant and caught its hindquarters with the edge of the essence-blast. The beast spun partway in the air, hit the ground in a welter of snow, flipped once, and came to its feet scrambling to the attack—facing her, not the boy.

Breea was up and charged in with both daggers even as vile cold bloomed at her back. She spun in the air to face the river where Lupazg's white form snarled on the far bank. His weave hit her in the air. Her blades parted the fabric of the attack such that its ice-rot essence slashed her flesh only at her shoulders. Falling, she wove a shield of air and let herself slam into the snow at the Dauthaz wolf's feet. Its jaws gaped and came down for her head, but her focus was across the river and deep in the ground.

Lupazg was out of sight from where she lay, but she felt his cold presence reel from the onslaught of deep earth heat that sprang from the ground about him. He jumped forward only to slam into the wall of air she'd woven about him. The Dauthaz wolf was struggling to get its mouth around the curved shield over her, and she spared a moment to slam a dagger up under its jaw into the skull. It toppled aside, and Breea stood. Lupazg slashed at the wall with dagger and claw, but she had studied well and her weaving withstood the attacks. Lupazg bellowed a defiant howl and vanished into white mist.

Breea choked on her victory cry as the mist rode the roaring heat up and out the high top of her woven walls.

Wild with fury, she sought his cold essence in the wind, but failed. Whirling she sought more foes, but there was no sign of the other Dauthaz.

Growling in frustration, she knelt and slapped her hands onto the hot rocks at her feet where her power had melted snow and steamed away the water. Through the ground she felt the limping footfalls of four Dauthaz wolves recede into the distance. Breea sat with a thump.

Snow-muffled Kultash wolf-horns howled To arms! To arms! The flute player was staring at her with huge eyes from a drift of snow a few strides away. His heart fluttered like a sparrow's wings in flight. With a moment of focus, she wove away light and built shadow about him.

For his ears she said, "Stay hidden."

As she stretched her bruised back and tested for broken bones, he answered her with a trembling wisp of flute song and vanished from sight.

Men's voices came through the heavy snowfall. Breea forced herself to stand, shelving her disappointment and anger at having failed to capture Lupazg's medallion. Lamplight flashed wild against the trees and lit the falling snow with crazy dances of light and shadow as men came running through the trees with glinting weapons. Breea questioned why it had taken them so long to come, then realized that the entire battle had lasted for mere breaths. Her army rushed up to form a wide ring about her. Some stared at the dead wolf at her feet while others looked past her for more threats. The edges of the circle built until there was a solid wall of men to the river's edge. Whispers from the men there spread through the army like a breeze through grain. The river boils.

One of the Kultash warriors in the first ranks shifted his feet, and she saw that he wore only knit stockings, no boots.

Touched, Breea said to him, "You think nothing of Dauthaz, warrior?"

The man looked confused. He seemed young, though fully bearded.

Breea looked at his feet. "Not even worth boots to battle."

Warriors chuckled. Mortified, the young man went to his knees in the snow with head bowed. He put his blade across his thighs. Breea walked up to him, but he did not look up.

"Few have done me such honor," said Breea. "To run to my aid in bare feet. Warriors with such will forge the fate of battles. I think our enemies will know your name."

She laid a hand on his shoulder and let essence-heat flow into him. The shock of it made him cry out and half rise. To honor him was good, but she also did not want his toes to freeze and cripple him for life.

A noble march sang on the air and Breea resolutely did not look at the snatch of shadow where the boy played. The music seemed to come out of the air itself, but she could not sense how he wove it so. All the men within earshot of her looked proud, and her words were passed to those who had not heard.

"May I know you name?" she asked the young Kultash.

"Leavar, Chosen one."

"My thanks, Leavar." Weaving her voice to carry, she said, "The wolf attacked here. Two of its servants are dead, and wounded, it ran. It will not return this night. I am going to bed. We rise before the dawn. Good night."

The men murmured sleep blessings to her in return as she walked through the throng. Batusha warriors moved with her. Before the edge of camp, Sakuront met her with his silent blade resting on his shoulder. Fresh snow made his shoulders and hair white. He did not ask questions, but fell into stride with her. Batusha warriors made a cordon about them all the way back to her tent. Solemn and noble airs followed them through the snowfall.

A fuming crowd of Batusha masters was waiting at her tent. They looked so mad and concerned that she had to work to keep down a smile. She guessed that a cordon of Batusha masters had rushed to her tent, ready to accompany her into battle, only to learn that she was not within. They might even have looked inside and seen Dori asleep in her place. They made a path for her to the tent, but she stopped before them.

To their eyes she had wandered off without cohort and had fought Dauthaz and worse alone, yet again. It was disrespectful of their devotion. She was not ready to tell them the truth entire, but a single layer of it might serve.

"There are ways of the essence that must be understood, sought, and learned. Not all may be done in the midst of the host. The wolf attacked as I expected. Two more of its Dauthaz are dead."

Mollified somewhat, they chak'ood. Quelling the ludicrous desire to embrace them for their concern, she strode past and into her tent. Sakuront followed her in without being asked. He wanted answers, that was clear. Now she had only to decide what to tell him.

Nestled among the furs of her cot, Dori seemed so young and full of peace that Breea forgot her purpose.

To both herself and Sakuront, Breea said, "I wonder if I will ever sleep like that again."

Apparently the First of the Kultash did not think it a question worthy of answer. Breea raised her head and listened for the flute player. He was outside the Batusha cordon at a campfire. She gave the wind about him a gentle tug. Breea sat in her chair and waited. A breeze ruffled the tent and the entry flaps waved. The boy stepped in and stood by the entrance, but without listening to the essence, Breea would not have been able to detect him.

"I found our music-spirit," she said to Sakuront.

Sakuront did not blink. Was he angry at her for going into battle without him? She certainly could have used his help. Lupazg's medallion would likely be theirs if he had been there.

Breea said, "The spirit, he is like me."

That got the First's attention. "He is Chosen?"

"He is Alach."

The First grunted, then the dark-wood color of his eyes seemed to intensify. "They came for him."

Breea marveled at his ability to connect events. This was why, beyond his physical prowess, Sakuront was First of the Kultash. He would have made a phenomenal scholar.

Breea said, "Reveal yourself."

Flute song parted the boy's hiding weave. He looked terrified.

"Sakuront Melayn, may I introduce the Song Weaver of the Army of the Chosen."

Sakuront bowed deeply. The boy's mouth dropped open. He looked to Breea afraid and begging with his eyes to be told what was happening. Was this truth? It could not be that he had been greeted as an equal by the First Warrior of the Kultash. Breea was impressed as well. Sakuront hadn't bowed to her like that when they first met.

"You are Alach," she said as though that explained everything, which in truth it did.

At the word Alach, the boy's breath stopped and he fell to his knees with his flute clutched to his chest. His head bowed to hide his face as he blinked the tears from his eyes.

Breea rose and walked to the boy. She remembered the day when she came to realize that she was an Alach weaver. Her entire life had tumbled together in one colossal moment of understanding, as if the avalanche of mysteries overwhelming her had transformed into a herd of horse and she was riding the foremost. When her hand touched his shoulder, both of them jolted as power met power.

To Sakuront, Breea said, "I have chosen that he remain hidden. His music will succor best in the guise of benevolent spirit. We shall weave together to keep him hidden from the

Oregule. But before the pass, we will strike." She gave the boy's shoulder a squeeze. "Will you give us your name?"

"Walaric." He raised his eyes, and there was essence-fire in them. "Walaric Song Weaver."

Sakuront's beard moved in a grin.

CHAPTER 27

Come the Wind

THE ROPE STRAPS OF THE PACK CUT INTO ANILA'S shoulders as lord Taumea ran. Despite the pain, she found the jouncing ride through the dark snow-dashed forest thrilling. She felt honored that the lord would carry her, and his kindness after finding that she had followed him was like cold water on the burns of fear that Da and others had carved into her heart. Though she knew it was wrong to feel so, she felt joyous.

A melody hummed against the lord's stride shaped a

pillow of air to lift her pack. He shifted his grip on her ankles when she got lighter, but he didn't slow his run. The snowy air was growing lighter with coming dawn, and in clear places between copses of trees she caught sight of the castle hill through the snowfall. The lord paused to catch his breath and check their back trail.

Wanting to please him, Anila used one of Ma's lullaby rhymes as the core of a song to soften the snow down the trail he had broken earlier. The Limtir lord stumbled when he started, then moved a boot through the airy snow. Anila felt him nod, and he started again, but tripped on something beneath. Before he could say anything, Anila reached for the storm. Wind blasted past them, scouring the softened snow from the path in a cloud that was torn away by the gale. The lord looked at the path cleared all the way down to the dark forest floor and she felt him chuckle. He squeezed her ankles then raced ahead, leaping logs as he ran down the snow-free way. In moments the lord had passed clear through to the end of what she had cleared, but he wasn't slowing down. Frantic, Anila called upon her deepest self for the strength to soften the snow ahead. At her piercing call, savage storm winds roared ahead to blast the snow away in a cloud of powder.

Eyes closed, she felt ahead, reaching through the Breath of snow to blend it with air and then tear away the mix with storm Breath. Fire seared her insides with the effort.

Lost in song she was not prepared when the Limtir lord stopped. Her belly rammed forward into his head and her song ended with a high-pitched oof! Getting her breath back with a cough, she saw that they were at the bank of the river. Across the water through the swirling snow the apparition came walking in its fluid way. It raised its head at the lord then vanished. Behind it the lady emerged from the storm riding Azsark. Spe's face peered out from the front of the lady's cloak. A little hand waved and a Breath of warmth touched Anila's face.

With a tired sigh, Anila rested her head on her arms on the top of lord Taumea's head. He lifted her down, and the weight of the food pack almost tumbled her backward as her pillow dissipated. Lord Taumea lifted the weight from her and set it in the snow beside his own.

Azsark was crossing the black water leading the other horses. He clambered up the snowy bank and dropped his head into the grip of Anila's arms. He lifted his head and she went up on his snout with a squeak. Grinning, she climbed over his head and down his neck. Spe stood up on the saddle in front of the lady and stuck her arms out. Anila scooted down Azsark's neck and pulled Spe into a ferocious hug. Relief to be back, and pride at what she had done, sparked Anila's Breath. Her warmth surged and the storm stopped around them. Snow fell straight down like a curtain and dawn light seemed to grow. She felt powerful, the Breath flowing without pain. Was it because Spe was here? It didn't feel like Spe's Breath. The other horses were jostling to get out of the water.

The lady touched Anila's cheek for a moment, then motioned for her to sit behind her. Anila let go of Spe, but her sister held on. Anila rubbed her back.

Suddenly Spe pushed away and said, "Ma's awake!"

A tremor shook the snowfall as Anila's deep fear of losing Ma surfaced. Before Anila embarrassed herself by weeping in relief, she reached with her Breath and asked Ma's horse to come near. The horse approached and the blanket-wrapped, hunched figure of Ma straightened. Dim eyes peered at Anila with concern. Without thought, Anila made a path of air between them, slipped off Azsark and walked to her mother. They embraced and Anila was appalled to feel how thin and light Ma had become. The fear burgeoned, but she quelled it to keep Ma from having to feel it as well. There was a sour scent on the blankets and the Breath of the red gem suffused Ma's body. Anila shuddered. Ma's own Breath was so faint it almost wasn't there.

Ma dropped her arms as though too weary to hold them around her daughter. Anila felt herself cracking inside.

In a voice like wind through dry grass, Ma said, "You are the Azsark."

Her hand opened between them, revealing the glowing red gem. Its facets looked stained, and Anila remembered vividly that the stone had been carved from the chest of the white-blooded Dauthaz who had come to kill them all. Ma pushed the gem at Anila.

"You will need this."

Anila recoiled from both the stone and the idea that if the gem left Ma's hand she would die in that moment. With gentle fingers, Anila folded Ma's hand around the gem, careful not to touch it herself, then Breathed to Ma. Ma sat straighter and Anila threw her leg over Ma's horse to sit in front. There was plenty of room for them both in the saddle. Anila took the reins and looked at the lord and lady, who were talking together. The Limtir lord had mounted. He saw Anila's readiness and urged his horse into the forest going downstream. The snow was so deep that it came to his horse's chest. Azsark took second spot after the lord's horse, and Anila urged hers after him. The packhorses followed.

Ma bent to Anila's ear. "Swear that you will take the Breath stone. Swear by the tree, Anila. When the white ones come. Take the stone."

Anila twisted to look up into Ma's face and found her eyes clear, and stern.

"Yes, Ma. By the tree."

Ma kissed her cheek, leaving a smear of wet that Anila knew to be blood. Only the power of Breath enabled Anila to sit without breaking from sorrow. They both knew what taking the stone meant.

"Go to Spedora, Anila," said Ma. "The lady told me what the two of you can do. We must run before the Kultash."

Reluctant to leave Ma, Anila said, "Who are the white ones?" Ma had not seen the smelly man, and Anila had never told her, so what enemy was this? Had the lady told her?

"Something worse than Soot and Kultash," said Ma. She coughed and spat to the side.

Anila thought she was finished talking, but there was more.

"Ani, your father is the Azsark."

The truth of it shattered Anila's soul like crockery exploding under a hammer. All the care she felt when beside the tree—the sense that she could do anything after touching its bark.

The agony of not knowing all this time tore through her and she bent forward with a cry, feeling as though she had been stabbed in the heart. And now she was forever leagues away, maybe never to return.

Another sob ripped out of her, and she almost didn't hear Ma whisper, "He made me swear the secret of his spirit."

Anila leaned and scrambled out of the saddle, landing hard in the deep snow. She buried her face in the drift and screamed. Breath ignited in the cauldron of her emotion and the snow flashed explosively to steam. The concussion flung her into the horse's side. The animal tried to bolt, but the snow was too deep to run far. On her back in the broken trail, Anila stared up into the storm as hot tears flowed.

Anger followed on the heels of sorrow, and she sat up. The lord and lady had come. The lord's song blade was out, humming with every snowflake that touched its blade. The lady had her bow half drawn and her blue eyes scanned the forest for a target. Spe's heat was there, ready.

Anila stood. She wasn't that mad at Ma. Mostly she was mad at the world that had made her life a living fear, even now. Priests and Kultash, Da and Soot. Anila turned east to face the enemies of her life.

"I will not run," she said, and for a heartbeat the snowflakes reversed their fall.

The scent of apple surrounded her. With it came knowledge. She knew what the Azsark Prayer meant. Her hands went up and at the top of her lungs she cried, "Breath within! Breath without! Come the wind!"

Lightning flashed through the sky and a mighty oak exploded to splinters. Shocked and proud, but determined not to show it, she faced the Limtirians and her mother. Ma looked strangely peaceful. Spe's eyes were enormous, but not afraid. The lord Taumea saluted her with his blade, sweeping the haft to his forehead, then lowering the blade toward her in offering.

He urged his horse up beside her, scanned the forest eastward, then said, "We will not run, but we must choose our ground."

He leaned over and reached down. She gripped his hand and he lifted her to the saddle in front of him. "Can you feel the land? The trees?"

She nodded, but was thinking of the Azsark.

The Limtir lord paused, then said, "Downvalley there are trees of a different kind."

Anila was shaking from the storm within her. The Azsark, her father, had sent her with the Limtirians. The good-bye had been clear—and, more, ordained. That was the word. The village priest had loved that word. Fate and purpose woven together. Laying her hands to her chest, she said, "Mighty of the trees, Father."

She shivered and raised her hands to let the wind pass through her fingers. With a pure note sung, she sent the Breath-feeling part of herself sweeping over the land westward. When she found the trees, she opened her eyes.

Anila didn't move for a few breaths. She could feel the lord frowning at her and sense his disciplined wait for her response, but the Breath of those trees made her nervous.

"I should ride with Spe," she said.

Lord Taumea patted her shoulder and she basked in his approval.

The lady Valiena shifted to another horse and Anila settled behind Spe on Azsark. Anila gave Spe a long hug.

The lord said to them, "Cover our track west. Leave the path you made last night."

Anila nodded though she did not understand why they should leave such an obvious trail to the castle.

To Spe she said, "You Breathe and I'll sing."

Spe settled against her and Anila felt like she'd stepped into the hearth of the village forge.

"Blessed Tree, Spe, not so much!"

Spe wriggled in irritation and bore down on her power. It dimmed, but not much.

Anila reached into the storm and brought it down, plaiting her intent into its flowing power and wrapping it with Spe's searing strength. A column of air spun down from the sky. Snow vanished at its touch, but so did tree branches. Anila released it and tried again, shaping the air more like the wedge of a plow but flowing—like the river beside them. It worked, and she touched Azsark's flanks. He strode down the cleared lane.

After a while she asked Azsark to stop. Turing back she used Spe's heat to Breathe the snow soft and sweep away the path they'd made behind, but it didn't look right after. The wind had sculpted the forest floor into frozen waves. Her remade snow was flat. After a few tries to shape it, Anila paused, panting from her effort.

Lord Taumea rode up to her, and said, "Leave it. Let them make what stories they wish when they find it. Forest spirits at work." He winked at Spe, but Anila saw that he had the apparition's gem in his hand—rolling it in his fingers. Behind his cheerful words there lay cool, savage song. Something was happening.

"Speed us to the grove."

———⌘———

The trees rose before them like a green cliff wall that danced in the wind. The snowfall had stopped and the view to their high, swinging tops was clear. From a stronger gust a few green leaves fluttered away against the sky. An expanse of gentle snowdrifts separated the grove from the surrounding forest.

Anila looked to lord Taumea for guidance, but his eyes were closed. His fist was wrapped around the amber gem and its light sparkled between his fingers. Its Breath waxed strong. The apparition was fighting!

Anila quickly urged Azsark across the meadow. The snow grew shallow before the edge of the grove, and the sound of leaves in the wind was a roar. Azsark stopped in the shallow snow. Under the trees was bare forest floor, dark with brown leaves. Deeper within there was green grass.

"Go, Azsark," said Anila.

The horse didn't move. He seemed to be staring at the grass, but refused to step ahead. The apparition's Breath grew strong and Anila turned to see it walking away. Its walk was half stalking crouch and its head was fixed on some spot in the distance. When it looked back at the lord, the message was clear. Danger. Come.

The lord and the lady exchanged signs and the lord galloped back the way they had come, following the apparition. The lady watched him go, then turned to Anila. The lady's eyes shone with such emotion that Anila had to look down before it evoked all that Anila had shelved away.

Anila laid a hand on Azsark's neck and Breathed to him. He walked ahead beneath the branches, his hooves going from crunching snow to silent tread on the moist leaves. The other horses would not follow and shied away from the edge no matter what the lady did.

The roar of the wind was quieter beneath the trees and she could hear water drops hitting the leaves. Anila slid down from Azsark and walked toward the trunk of the nearest tree. The spreading base could have filled the village square. There was a chirp behind as Spe summoned a puff of air to help her to the ground. She came running up and took Anila's hand. Together they walked to the trunk. The bark was like an oak but rougher and it was whorled with what looked like scars long healed over.

"Azsark Prayer," said Anila.

In harmony they sang, "May all I say and all I think be in harmony with thee, Breath within, Breath beyond, mighty of the trees."

Anila reached out to touch the bark, and Spe did as well. Deep and ponderous power flowed up through the heart of the tree and out its branches.

Spe said, "My da is a tree too."

Stunned, Anila gazed at her sister. Of course Spe would listen to what Ma said, though Anila hadn't known Spe could make listening tubes.

The sense of denial that guarded the grove faded and Anila breathed a deep sigh. She turned to the lady and waved. At the lady's urging the horses stepped under the trees. Needing no more encouragement, they trotted toward the meadow grass deeper within the grove. The lady let them have the lead, but reined in her own mount and hopped down. Azsark looked at his herd fellows with longing as their heads bent to the grass, then swung his head to the girls and held his ground.

Spe spoke as though in answer to a question. "I'll pray."

Anila asked, "For what?" When Spe prayed, the world changed.

Spe's small, dirty face turned up and up. "He's old."

Anila knelt and took Spe's hands in hers. "Pray for what? Did he speak to you?"

There had been no spirit in the tree that Anila had felt, but she trusted Spe.

Spe blinked at the limbs above, and said, "We should stop them."

"Who? Spe. Who?"

"They're old too."

"Who!" said Anila.

Spe's gaze dropped and her mouth moved like she was tasting a new word.

"O-ree-gue."

Anila shivered for no reason she knew.

The lady Valiena strode up to them. Her bow was armed and she wore three quivers full of arrows, but her eyes were haunted and sharp.

"What did you say?"

"Oreegule," said Spe.

Despair ravaged the lady's face. She dropped to a knee before Anila. There was desperation of a kind Anila had never seen in the lady's eyes.

"Go to him."

Breath bloomed within Anila and she raised her hand in the sign protect.

Spe raised her hand in kind.

Two bright tears fell from the lady's eyes.

At this, Spe jumped forward and hugged the lady, who cradled Spe's head to her with her free hand, but her eyes were on Anila. The import of what was to come sent a tremor through Anila. This was the fight that would decide everything. Without a word, Anila walked away to follow the lord Taumea's path.

At the edge of the grove, she made a path of air over the rough snow and began to run. The lord's horse tracks soon diverged from the trail they'd broken to the grove, going north. When she found his horse standing in the snow, Anila slid to a stop on her plank of air. Why would he leave his horse? To fight, that was why. Feeling alone in the cold forest, Anila whispered the Azsark Prayer and wrapped herself in wind to quell the quaking that rose from her belly. Fortified, she went forward toward the river.

The lord's tracks were clear and she followed them through a dense stand of trees. At the far edge, Anila froze. The Limtir lord was belly down, and half covered by a snowdrift with the apparition on its belly beside him poking its head into the drift. Not into the drift, into a cave dug through the drift. Were they hiding? Anila crouched in the snow.

The river rushed past beyond them though she couldn't see it. The apparition pulled its head out of the little snow cave and looked back at her. She rose up and shook her hands, begging for it not to tell the lord. It jerked back around and plunged its head back beside the lord. They were hiding! The fur down the apparition's back spiked and Anila cowered back among the trees, softly gathering a cloak of snow. The wind brought a foul smell as if something had died nearby, rotting. She wrinkled her nose, then stiffened. It was a scent she knew—Dauthaz, but far, far worse. Across the river something white came into view, and she clapped her hands over her mouth to stifle the cry that had nearly clawed its way to her voice.

A wolf, an impossible wolf, larger than a horse, had appeared on the bank knocking a drift into the water. It looked upriver, then sniffed the air, snout raised. The head swung to her. Where eyes should have been there was nothing, yet the Breath of its gaze sliced through Anila like a butcher's blade. A pale mist drifted up behind the beast, grew thick with gossamer threads that went opaque, and coalesced into a tall man dressed all in white.

White! Anila felt ice grip her heart. She hadn't thought to take the red gem.

The wolf crouched and leapt, clearing most of the river in a single arc. It landed out of sight with a splash that tinkled like the shattering of ice, then in another bound it rose into the air in front of the lord and apparition.

The lord erupted up through the drift, his blade clearing its sheath with a harmonic scream that expressed all that Anila felt.

———

Spe sat on a mossy wall that marked the edge of the meadow. Below her was a wide flat rock with a big steaming pool of hot water in the center. The water flowed over shining stone and into another pool, then another and another in a gentle slope to the river.

Azsark noisily cropped grass near her with the other horses nearby. Down on the flat stone Ma sat with her feet in the pool. The lady had walked away after carrying Ma to the water and Spe hadn't seen her since.

Ma sat hunched by the water without moving. Spe took a bite of dark bread the lady had given her then hummed a little gust of wind, lifting leaves. Anila was the best at leaf dancing, and always did it when Spe asked, but she wanted to be able to dance them herself. Maybe then the lord and lady would ask her first when they wanted to do something with the Breath. It seemed that Ma wasn't going to scold them anymore for using the Breath, so Spe scooted back from the edge, crossed her legs, set her chin in her hands, and got serious.

After she ran out of ideas, she gave up with a huff. She could blow leaves, lift leaves, crush leaves, but they never danced, never twirled like the wind spirits that sometimes danced in the old city around the Azsark. Missing the tree, she looked up. The trees here were nice. Harder to understand than Da Azsark, but he was her da, so that fit. People from other places were always harder to understand. The trees didn't talk to her though. Lonely, Spe stood up and walked over to Azsark. His big head rose a little and he regarded her while he chewed. The grass smelled nice, and Spe took in a giant breath through her nose. The air quivered, but not by her doing.

She ran back to the wall, but Ma hadn't moved. Not Ma. Spe did like the lord always did, and looked in every direction. They were deep in the grove and couldn't even see the snow outside from here. The lady was gone, and Anila was so far away Spe could barely feel her warmth.

Spe made the sign *protect* to comfort herself, but it did something else. The sun inside her came out. She needed to see what was happening, so she ran to the nearest tree and leapt into the air with a bird call that rushed her up onto the first big branch. Using calls for balance and help, she climbed up until she found a place where the bright snow outside the grove was visible. Dark horses were crossing the snow. Motion closer caught her attention. Men. Inside the grove!

Down below Ma sat by the water. Ma couldn't see them from there and if Spe called, Ma would just scold her and the bad men would hear. Climbing down seemed too hard. It was always harder to go down than up, and Anila was the one who made landing pillows. There was a whistle from the men and Azsark looked their way. Ma's head came up and hope surged in Spe, then Ma bent back to hunker by the pool. A horse whinnied in distress out at the edge of the grove. One of the bad men was trying to force his horse into the grove.

This time Ma drew back her cloak hood and listened. Spe

waved, then finally did her best rock-hopper-bird chirp. Ma looked up. Spe pointed at the men stalking in with bows bent and swords out. Azsark whinnied powerfully and held his ground before them. Unable to stand, Ma managed to crawl to the near wall and out of sight, but Spe knew there was no good place to hide there.

From away in Anila's direction, a scream like a song of war thrummed in the air—the Limtir lord's sword was fighting. The Kultash whirled to face the sound and called to one another in concerned voices. One directed others to check below the wall.

Desperate, Spe reached up into the storm like Anila did, then paused as Kultash began falling over and crying out in pain. They went down with a beat like a fast drum—crack-snick-crunch—men fell to the leaves or cried out and staggered. At first Spe was just as confused as they until one bellowed, "Archer!" and Spe knew it was the lady. It took a moment to feel the path of the arrows to find the Limtir lady up in a tree with a view of the meadow. Kultash charged around the spring while bow-wielding Kultash attacked the lady with their own arrows. That wasn't right. Spe made a scream like wind through the rock clefts on the seashore. Kultash twisted to look up at her, and more fell—shot by the lady. Some saw in the sky what was coming and tried to flee.

It crashed down—a fist of cloud that ripped through the branches and struck twenty Kultash. Men flew and tumbled like leaves.

Glowing so bright it felt like she was looking into the sun, Spe raised her hand to make another, but everyone was running and she didn't know where to hit.

In the distance, Anila sang three lilting notes—each filled with terror and desperation.

"Ani!" cried Spe and sent her Breath toward Anila—a long spear of howling wind and burning leaves that streaked away from her through the trees.

The world went white with pain and she tumbled from the branch.

Falling, there was music.

———*ຒ*———

The small part of Anila that was not pierced by fear sang in joy as the Limtir lord's screaming blade slashed down the wolf's chest. The white beast landed in an explosion of snow and tried to whirl, but the lord Taumea had followed its flying arc and the song blade sang savage victory as it sliced into the right hind leg of the wolf. The beast tried to leap away but only one hind leg worked. The lord floundered in the snow and the wolf managed enough distance to whirl with a bellowing roar. They faced each other—the lord holding his blade in both hands, legs bent and wide, and the wolf snarling, head low. A singing calm flowed from the lord. He began to swing his blade and raised his voice to sing in his strange language matching the rhythm of the humming blade. The wolf snarled and held its ground.

Across the river, Breath ripped like fabric as the cat apparition attacked the tall man on the far bank. Loops of icy Breath fell around and over the apparition and it vanished to come charging in from another direction. Anila had never felt such icy, Breathing strength. Even across the river its ripples hurt with cold, and she could tell the man was more than a match for Spe's heat. Gray fangs appeared in the air and stabbed down, piercing the apparition through the side. It vanished from Anila's sight, struck down. Horror erupted within Anila, sparking her fire. The ice holding her heart shattered, and she cried out in song.

"Help him!" said the lord and a hand dug into a belt pouch. He flung the amber gem to her.

The white wolf's blind gaze tracked the gem through the air and the lord leapt to the attack. They crashed together in a snarl and blade song, but Anila's world had become the spec of amber light soaring toward her. She summoned all her skill to cup it in the air and guide it to her fingers. It landed in her hands and burned them with cold. She bore the pain, filled her lungs, and sang three piercing notes in lilting song, each stronger than the last and each going deeper into her inner self. Snow puffed off the branches nearby and melted at her feet as she breathed from her own center into the gem.

Through the gem the mind of the vile man touched hers and she vomited onto the snow. When Spe's wind roared up to her, hope roared in Breath. Apple scent of her father filled her senses and she swept Spe's power into the gem. The cold mind vanished from the gem and a thunderous roar echoed across the water. The apparition rose from the ground and a massive paw slashed the man, ripping clothing and flesh, tossing him off the bank. Only he didn't fall, but floated down in a nest of white threads. Beneath his feet the river froze solid.

In front of Anila the lord and wolf fought, and the wolf was losing. When the beast attacked, lord Taumea was always out of reach. Furious, the wolf lunged and spun, but the lord was like water, moving sometimes right under the wolf's snout, and his blade bit every time the wolf came in range.

When the pale man rose from the river in a web of pale

thread, the air went so cold that it burned against Anila's skin. Where a man's eyes should be, there were eight dots. Spider's eyes.

The thing was looking at her. It recognized her. How? Lips peeled back from fangs. It knew and hated her. Indignant, Anila's back straightened. It had no cause to hate her. The scent of apple lingered and she gasped. This thing knew and hated her father, the Azsark. That made her mad and the air tasted of apple and pine. Behind the white thing the cat apparition stalked across the frozen river at the thing's back.

Lord Taumea's breathing was heavy, misting the air before him. His armor was ripped open across the shoulder, and blood shone wet in the wool shirt beneath. He edged toward her, but the limping, bleeding wolf interposed itself with a roar. Anila understood. It was keeping the lord busy so the spider thing could kill her. Fear whirled in the heat of her flowing Breath. A part of her was screaming the impossibility of fighting a creature so old and powerful no matter who her father had been. Lord Taumea looked over his shoulder and winked at Anila. He then stood easy and propped his humming blade on his shoulder. The wolf glared, then swung its head in question to the spider, immobile in the air. The lord stepped aside and his arm blurred as he flung his blade in complete silence, point first into the side of the wolf. The force of the throw buried the blade to the hilt behind the beast's left foreleg. A spasm shook the massive wolf—it took a step, coughed a spray of white blood, then dissolved into a cloud of thick fog.

Lord Taumea leapt toward the fog, but white loops of Breath rose from the snow and struck him down.

Anila attacked.

Lightning from high in Spe's storm came down and the crack of its passage sent Anila tumbling back into deep snow. Floundering to rise, she called upon the air and rose. The white man-thing was in the snow, rising also. A black streak smoked from its shoulder down its right leg.

Anila prepared another strike and called, "Come the—"

Cold leapt from the ground and stole her voice as it sank a thousand fangs of ice into her.

The pale man stood and drifted to her, settling to stand in the snow at the edge of the forest. Its smell was unbearable—a stench like crawling into a maggot-seething carcass and colder than the upper reaches of the sky. A gloved hand reached out and gripped her head. Nails of ice pierced her where its fingers touched. It pushed her head back until it could look into her eyes.

Anila screamed as her fire raged against the horrible chill gripping her.

The apparition attacked from behind, knocking the pale man forward and down. It lost its grip on Anila's head, but before the cat apparition could close its teeth on the spider-things head, it was smashed away by a crackling wave of cold. It landed in the snow and was buried by a cloud of hissing threads. The spirit gem went cold in Anila's hand.

The pale man stood and Anila backed way. Unblinking eyes looked into hers.

It hissed, "Kaass Alachk."

Its other hand raised and a twisted Breath whirled through its fingers. The sound of a galloping horse shook the air and the spider whirled, releasing Anila. Its Breath bloomed so strong that Anila's inner flame shuddered and flickered in its presence. She staggered back as a giant man on the biggest horse she'd ever seen came on at a full gallop along the edge of the trees. An impossibly long black sword was in his hand whirling silent in arcs that rippled the Breath of the air. Kultash! Yet all Anila cared was that he seemed to be attacking the spider beast.

Wild with fear, she closed her eyes and struck. The spider vanished in light as lighting blasted the world apart.

On her back, Anila looked up to see the spider thing on its knees. The black sword arced down, and the spider cried out in piercing dismay as the massive blade parted its Breath and cleaved through its shoulder. Ice mist exploded, whirled, then swept away into the sky. Anila struggled up and saw the rider come about to face the lord Taumea.

Blade song roared in harmony with the Limtir lord's battle cry as he charged the Kultash. The big man slid off his horse, and with a long forward stride, met the lord Taumea blade to blade. Silence met song and the Breath of the world seemed to bend. They both stepped back, and after a moment of reassessment, they began in earnest. Anila's jaw dropped.

Each fought with a brutal calm and a grace of motion she'd seen in the Limtir lord without realizing what it would mean in combat with another like him—and this Kultash was like him. They were terrible and beautiful to watch, then Anila snapped out of her shock and sang a snatch of song that whipped her Breath around the Kultash's legs. He stumbled and the Limtir lord's blade tip ripped through chainmail across his belly with a ferocious screech that scattered links of mail through the air.

The bearded Kultash looked shocked, not from the blow, but in noticing her for the first time. A swipe of his black blade cut the threads of Anila's Breath and he leapt back.

The lord Taumea gave him no space and the men came together once more in a flurry of sound and silence. Anila sang and caught the Kultash's sword arm, and the Limtir lord's blade opened the Kultash's thigh. The Kultash whipped his blade about and cut her Breath once more, but defended only as he stepped away, glancing at Anila as he moved.

With a mighty two-handed parry, he knelt in the snow, and said, "Amity."

His blade dropped to fall across his thighs. The Limtir lord's sword whistled harmony to his throat—and stopped—trembling with sound and the quavering of the Limtir lord's arm. He seemed to be shivering with cold. Taumea fell to his knees, thought the tip of his blade never left the giant warrior's throat.

"I am Sakuront Melayn, First of the Kultash. You are Taumea of the Tomeguard of Limtir." To Anila he said, "The Chosen One seeks you, Alach. As do I, in Het's name."

THANK YOU FOR READING!

If you enjoyed *Come the Wind*
and want to be among the very first notified when
Volume 3, *Fire Borne* is released, please visit,

http://www.alexanderedlund.com

..and sign up for New Book Notification.

As an independent author, you my reader are the best
source of getting the word out about my work. Please drop
a review on Amazon or iBooks and let others know how
much you enjoyed this story.

Thank you for reading!

ABOUT THE AUTHOR

ALEXANDER EDLUND is a native of the Arizona desert, but now chooses to live in wet climates, especially temperate rain forest.

Come the Wind is the second in a planned series of six books about Breea Banea. Look for more of Edlund's work arriving soon.